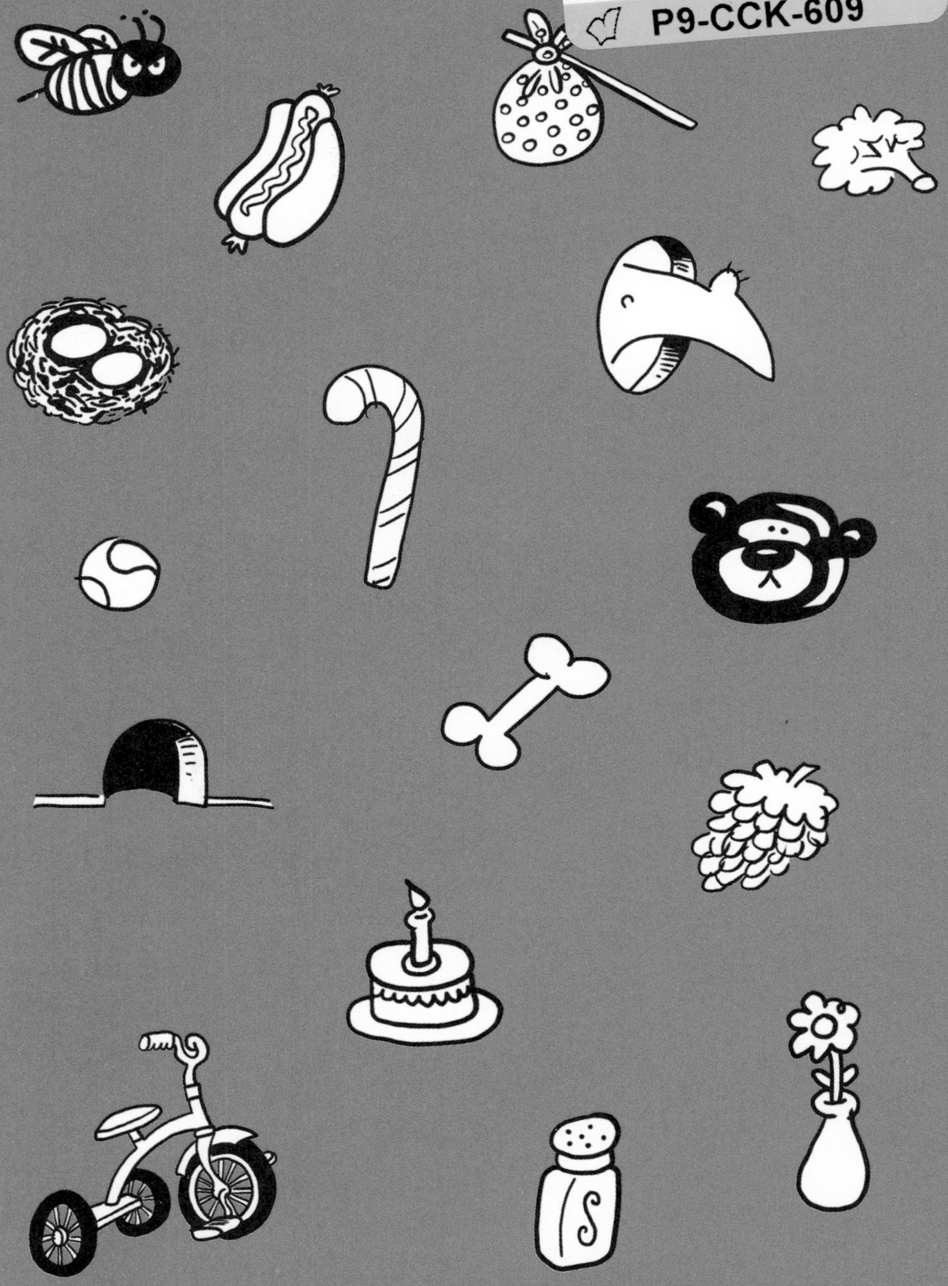

Schnozzer & Tatertoes

TAKE A HIKE!

Schnozzer & Tatertoes
TAKE A HIKE!

Rick Stromoski

union
square
kids

NEW YORK

union
square
kids

NEW YORK

UNION SQUARE KIDS and the distinctive Union Square Kids logo are trademarks of Union Square & Co., LLC.

Union Square & Co., LLC, is a subsidiary of Sterling Publishing Co., Inc.

ISBN 978-1-4549-4831-5 (hardcover)
ISBN 978-1-4549-4832-2 (paperback)
ISBN 978-1-4549-4833-9 (e-book)

Library of Congress Control Number: 2022043794

For information about custom editions, special sales, and premium purchases, please contact specialsales@unionsquareandco.com.

Printed in China

Lot #:
2 4 6 8 10 9 7 5 3 1

03/23

unionsquareandco.com

Cover design by Marcie Lawrence
Interior design by Rich Hazelton

For Lucy

CHAPTER ONE
The Adventure Begins

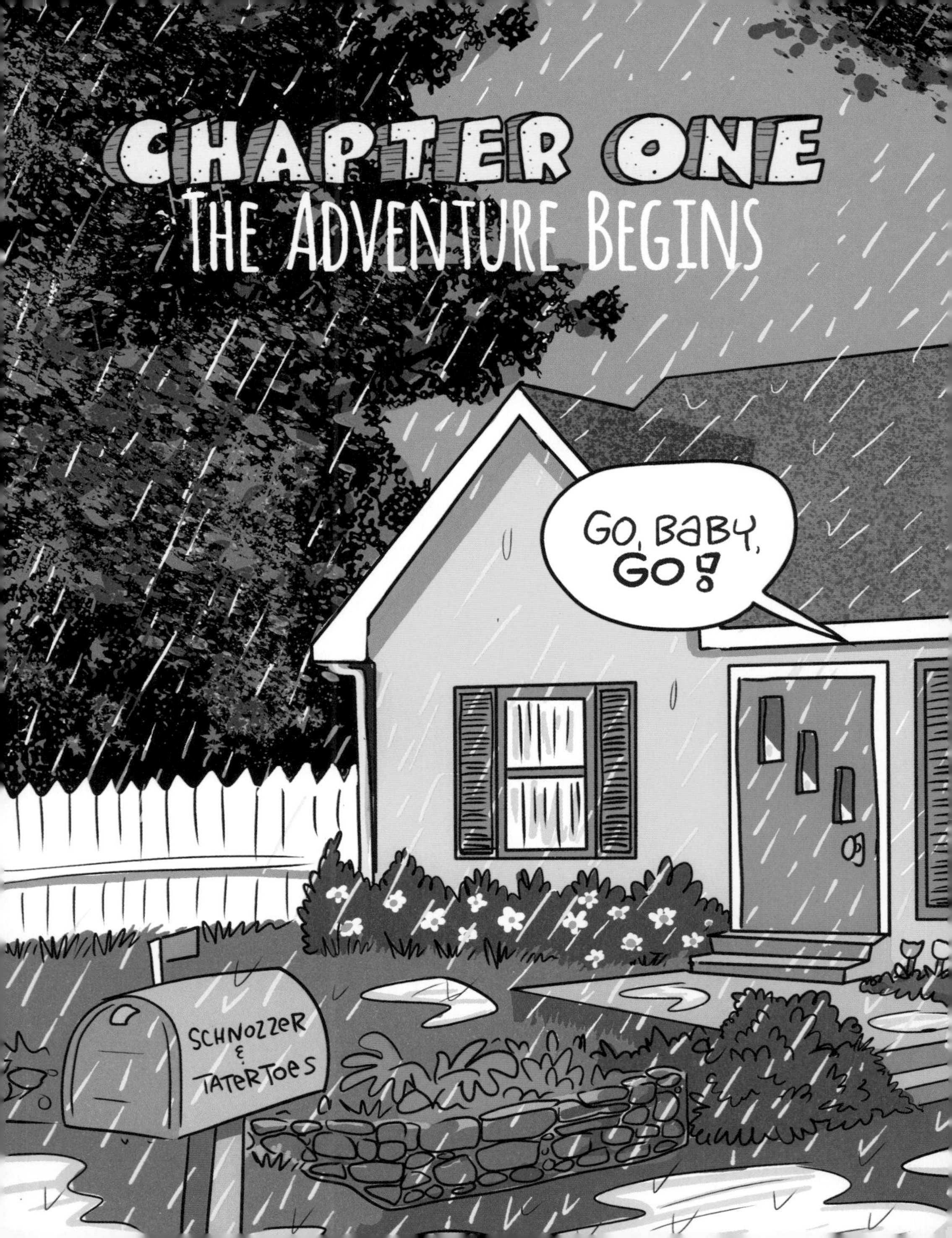
GO, BABY, GO!
SCHNOZZER & TATERTOES

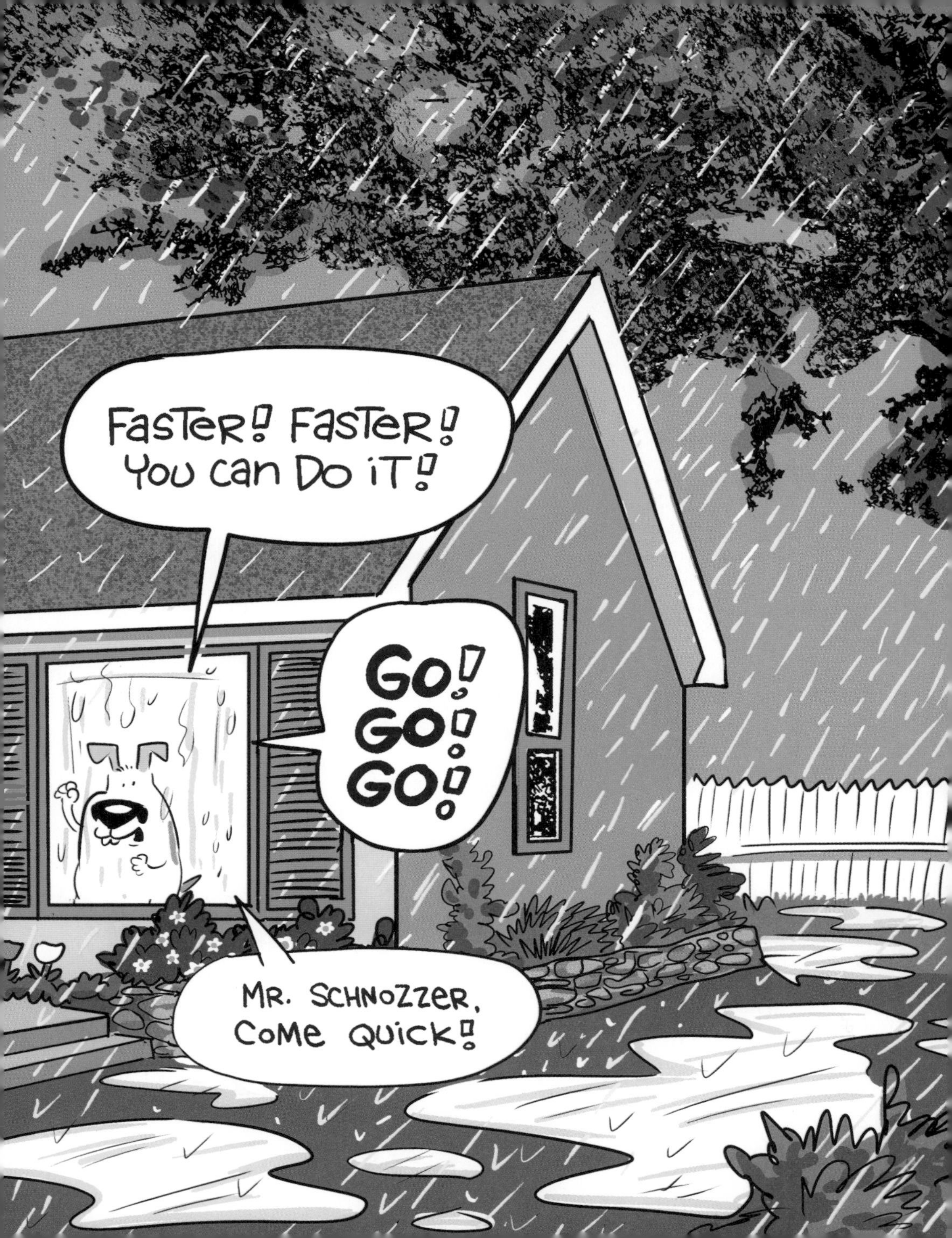
FASTER! FASTER! YOU CAN DO IT!
GO! GO! GO!
MR. SCHNOZZER, COME QUICK!

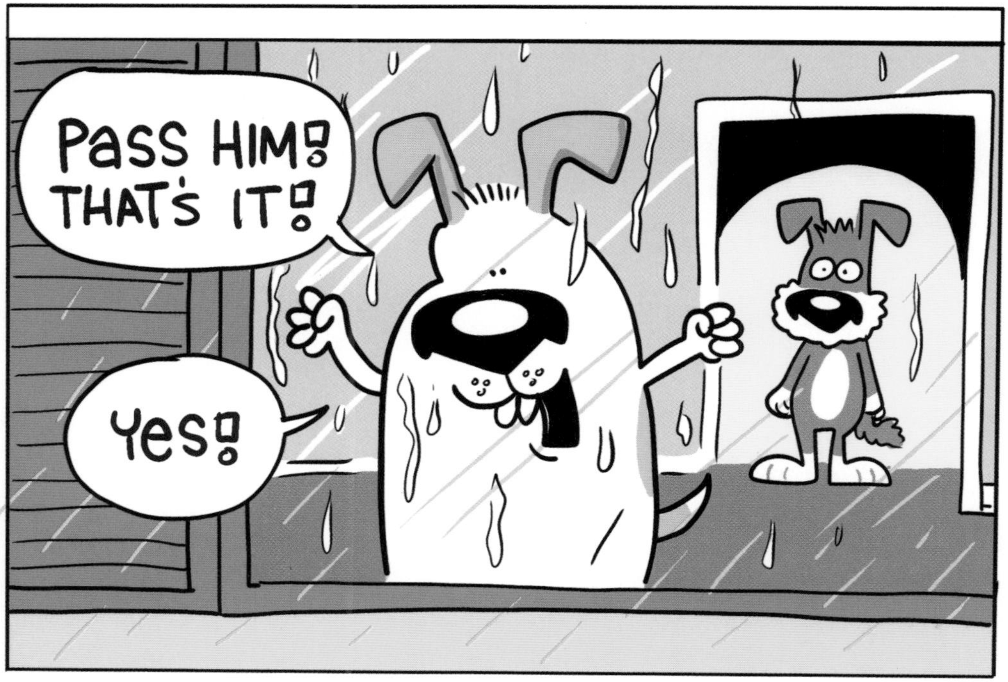
PASS HIM! THAT'S IT!
YES!

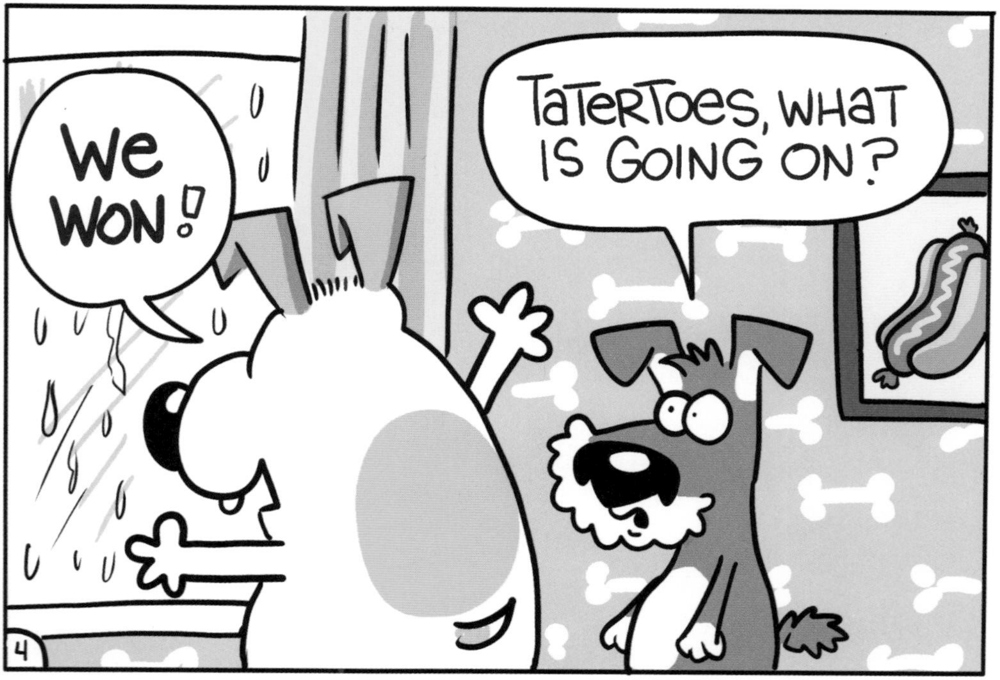
WE WON!
TATERTOES, WHAT IS GOING ON?

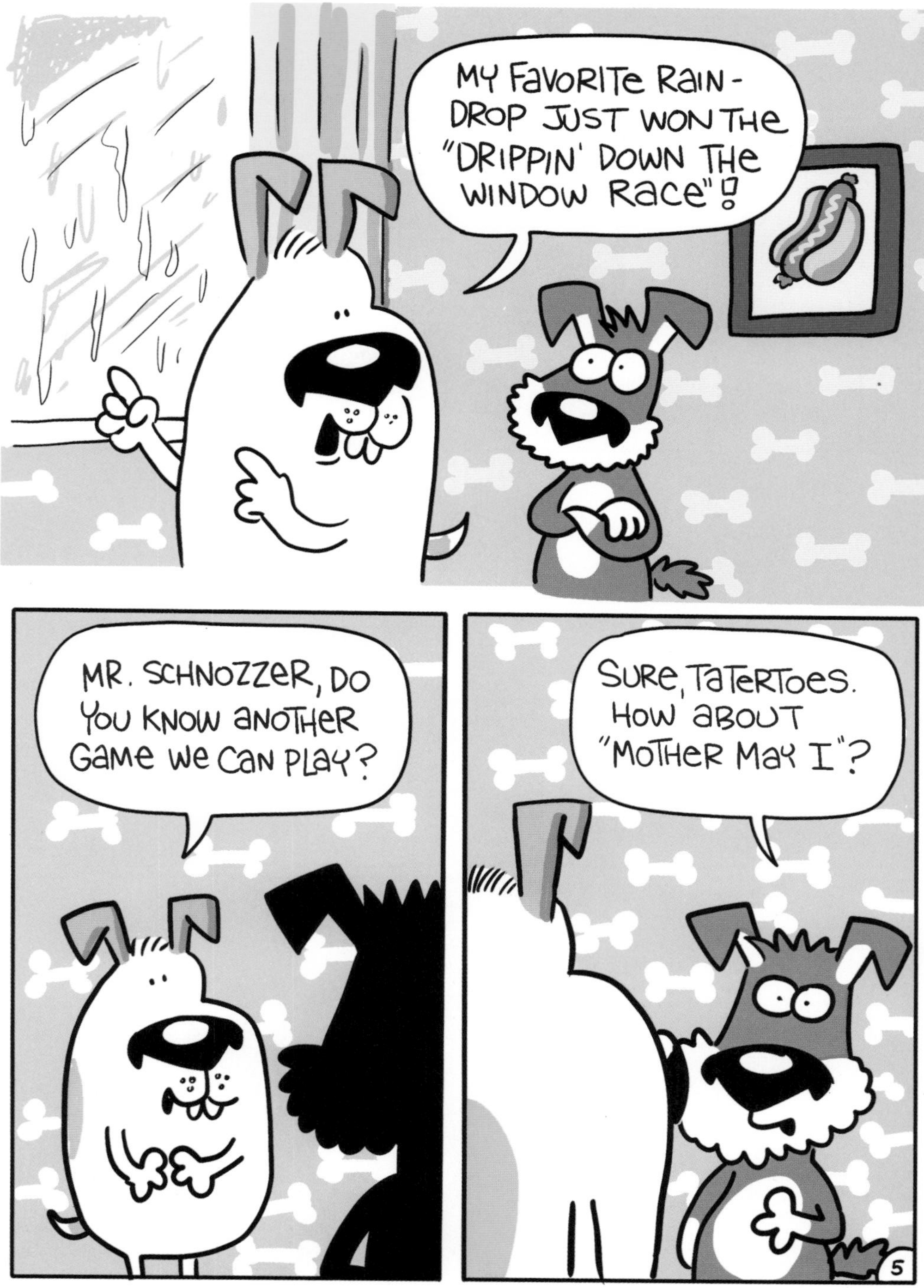
MY FAVORITE RAIN-DROP JUST WON THE "DRIPPIN' DOWN THE WINDOW RACE"!
MR. SCHNOZZER, DO YOU KNOW ANOTHER GAME WE CAN PLAY?
SURE, TATERTOES. HOW ABOUT "MOTHER MAY I"?

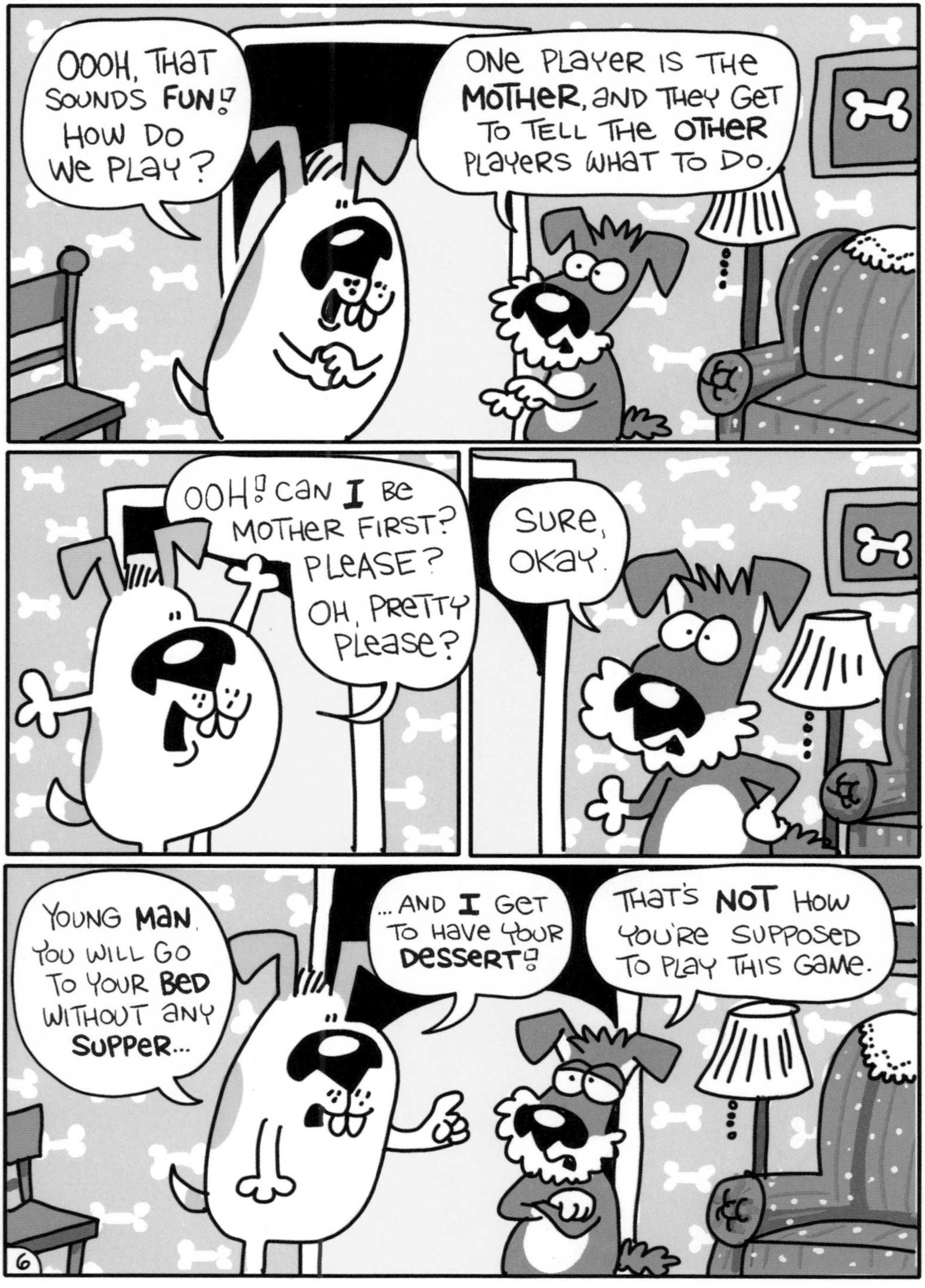
OOOH, THAT SOUNDS FUN!! HOW DO WE PLAY?
ONE PLAYER IS THE MOTHER, AND THEY GET TO TELL THE OTHER PLAYERS WHAT TO DO.
OOH!! CAN I BE MOTHER FIRST? PLEASE? OH, PRETTY PLEASE?
SURE, OKAY.
YOUNG MAN, YOU WILL GO TO YOUR BED WITHOUT ANY SUPPER...
...AND I GET TO HAVE YOUR DESSERT!!
THAT'S NOT HOW YOU'RE SUPPOSED TO PLAY THIS GAME.

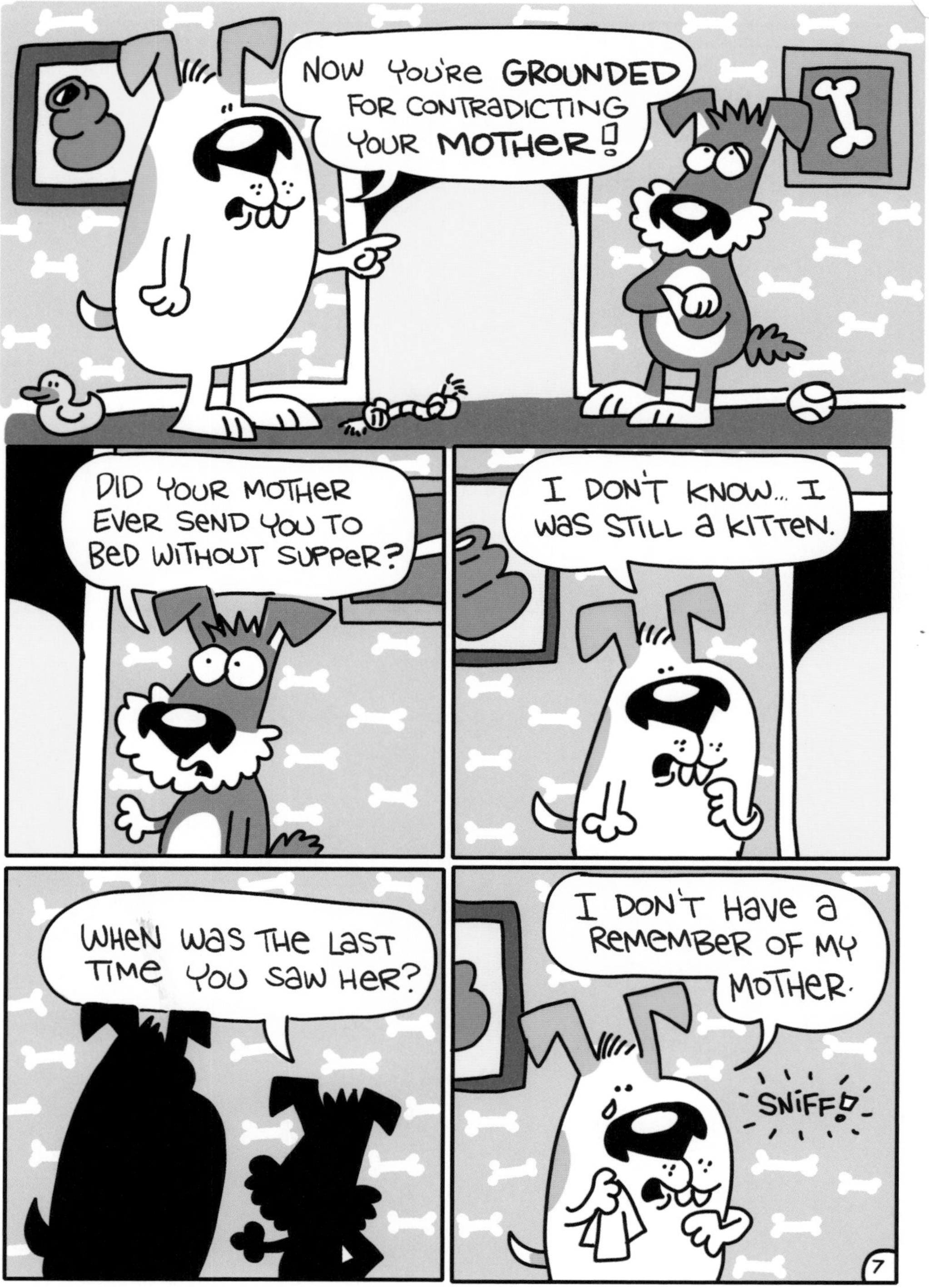
NOW YOU'RE GROUNDED FOR CONTRADICTING YOUR MOTHER!
DID YOUR MOTHER EVER SEND YOU TO BED WITHOUT SUPPER?
I DON'T KNOW... I WAS STILL A KITTEN.
WHEN WAS THE LAST TIME YOU SAW HER?
I DON'T HAVE A REMEMBER OF MY MOTHER.
SNIFF!

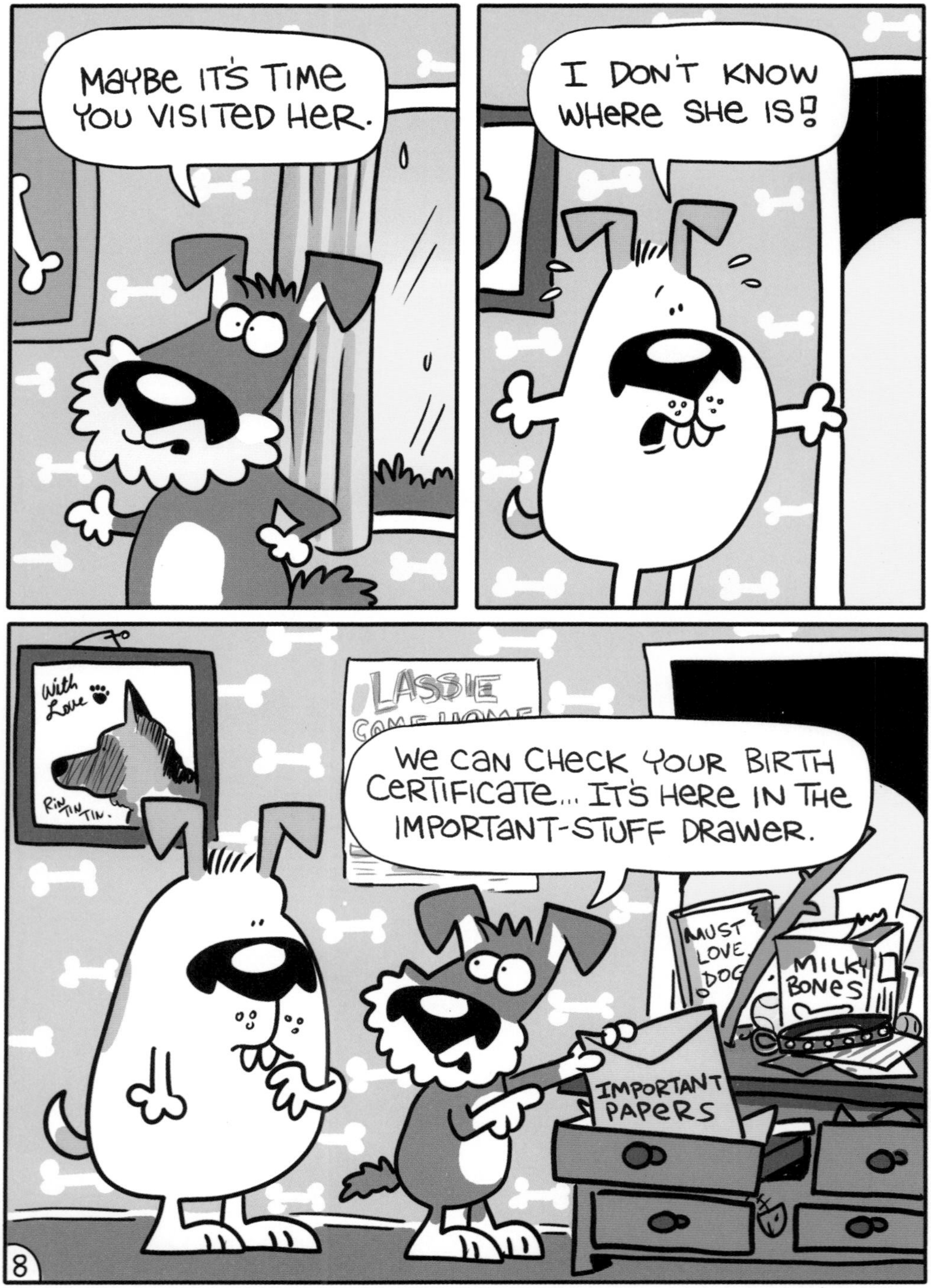
MAYBE IT'S TIME YOU VISITED HER.
I DON'T KNOW WHERE SHE IS!
With Love
RIN TIN TIN.
LASSIE
WE CAN CHECK YOUR BIRTH CERTIFICATE... IT'S HERE IN THE IMPORTANT-STUFF DRAWER.
MUST LOVE DOG
MILKY BONES
IMPORTANT PAPERS

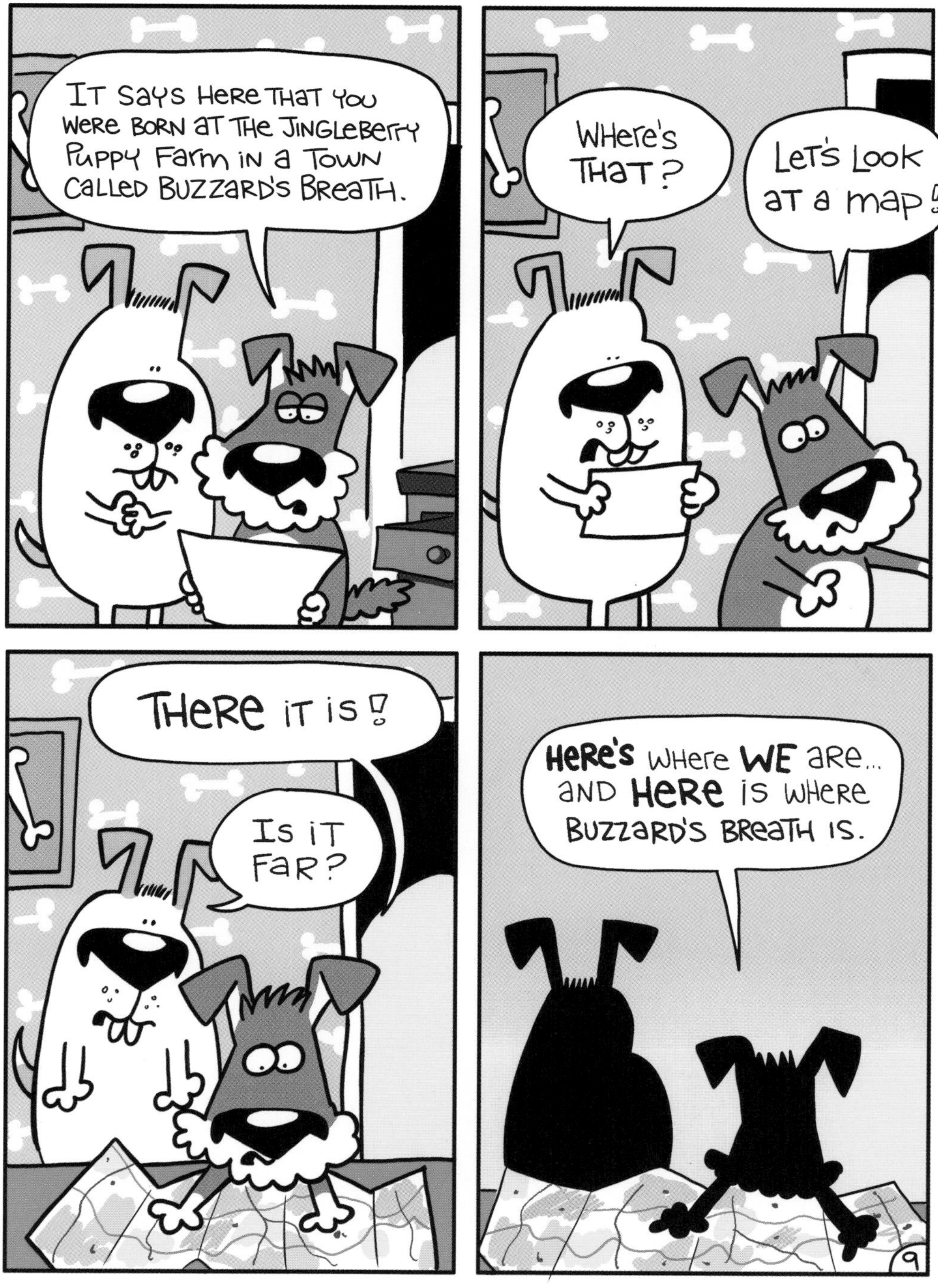
IT SAYS HERE THAT YOU WERE BORN AT THE JINGLEBERRY PUPPY FARM IN A TOWN CALLED BUZZARD'S BREATH.
WHERE'S THAT?
LET'S LOOK AT A MAP!
THERE IT IS!
IS IT FAR?
HERE'S WHERE WE ARE... AND HERE IS WHERE BUZZARD'S BREATH IS.

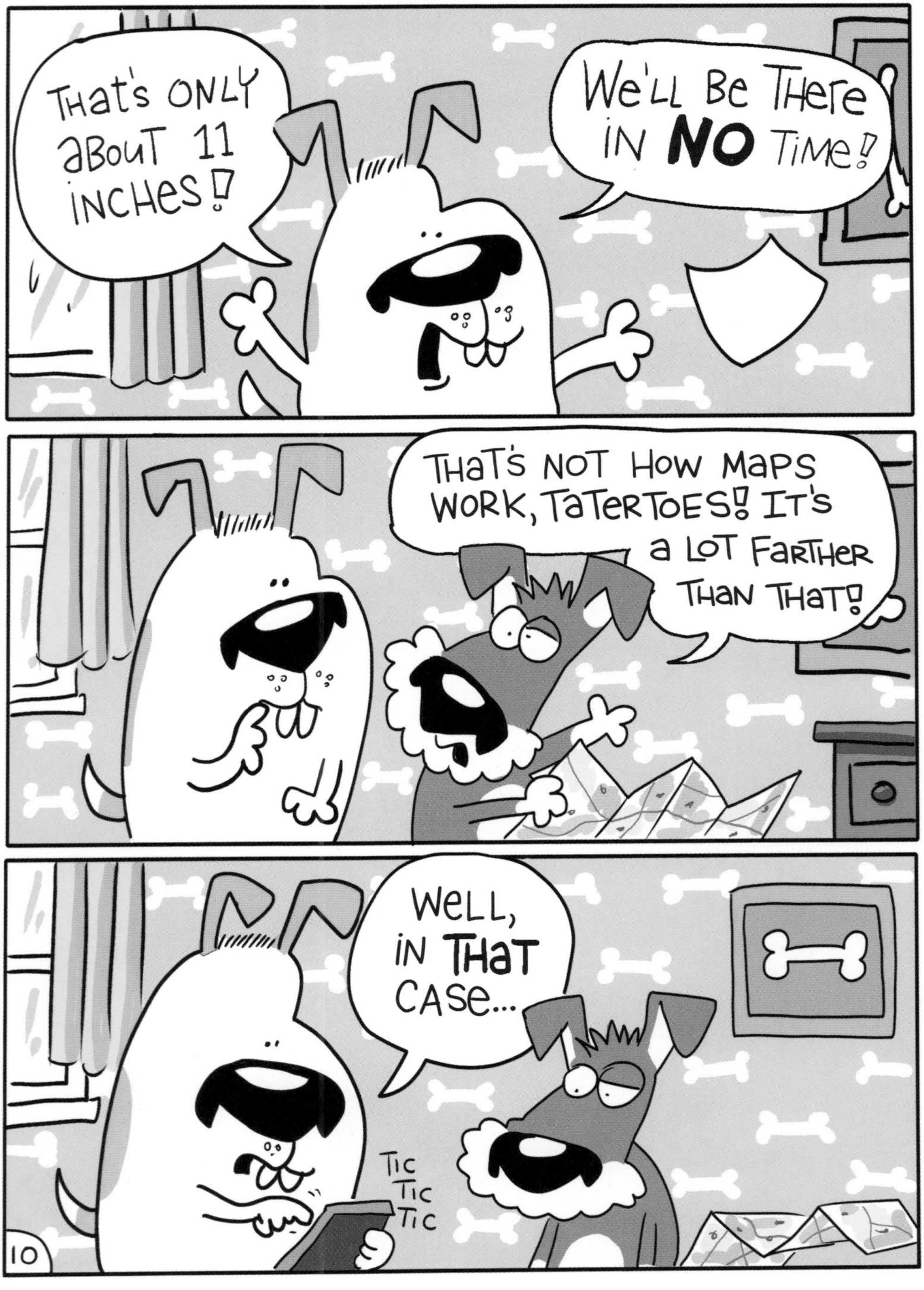
That's ONLY about 11 inches!
We'll Be There in NO Time!
That's NOT HOW Maps WORK, TaTerToes! IT's a LOT Farther Than That!
Well, in THAT case...
Tic Tic Tic

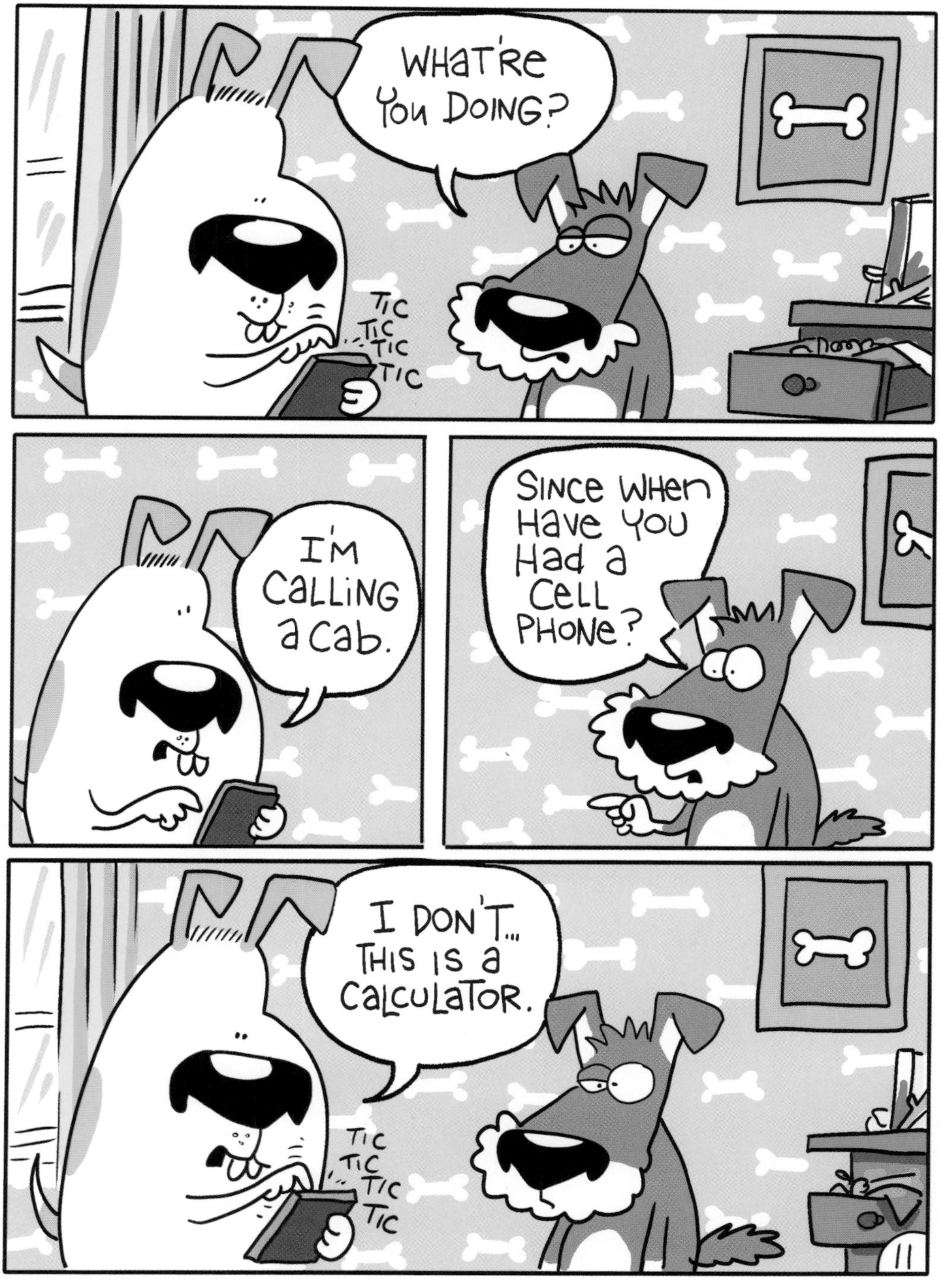
WHAT'RE YOU DOING?
TIC TIC TIC TIC
I'M CALLING A CAB.
SINCE WHEN HAVE YOU HAD A CELL PHONE?
I DON'T... THIS IS A CALCULATOR.
TIC TIC TIC TIC

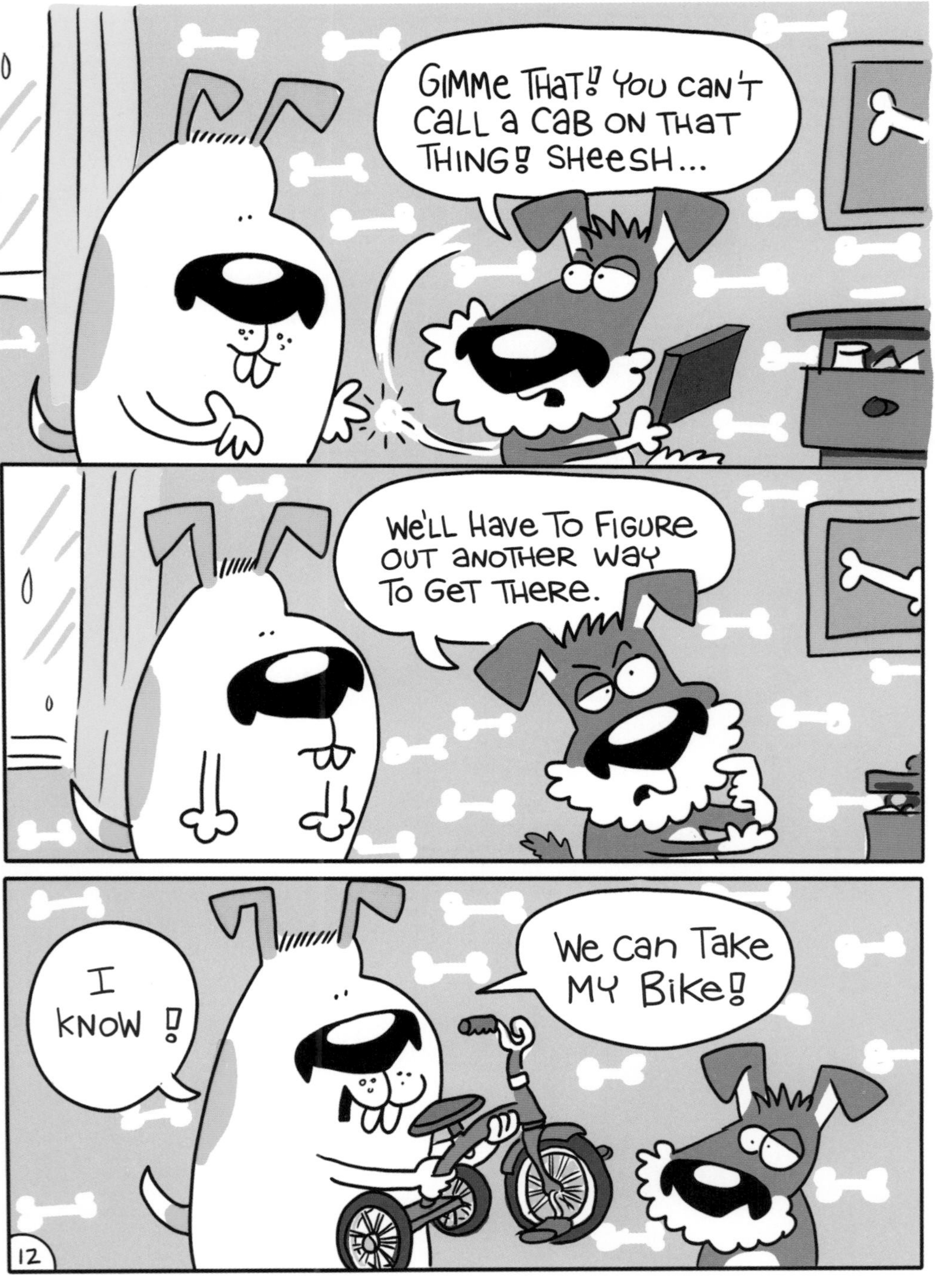
GIMME THAT! YOU CAN'T CALL A CAB ON THAT THING! SHEESH...
WE'LL HAVE TO FIGURE OUT ANOTHER WAY TO GET THERE.
I KNOW !
WE CAN TAKE MY BIKE!

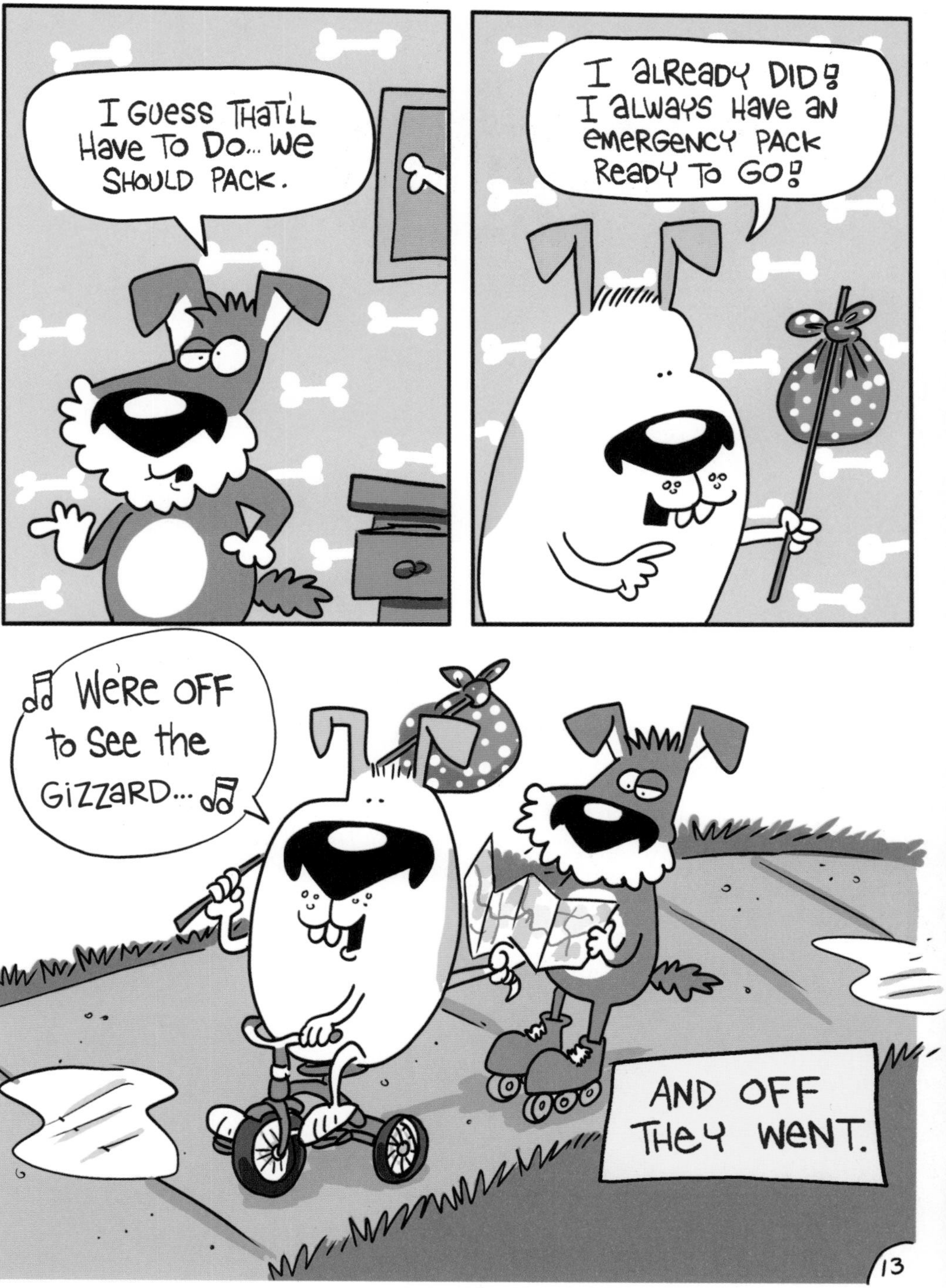
I GUESS THAT'LL HAVE TO DO... WE SHOULD PACK.
I ALREADY DID! I ALWAYS HAVE AN EMERGENCY PACK READY TO GO!
WE'RE OFF TO SEE THE GIZZARD...
AND OFF THEY WENT.

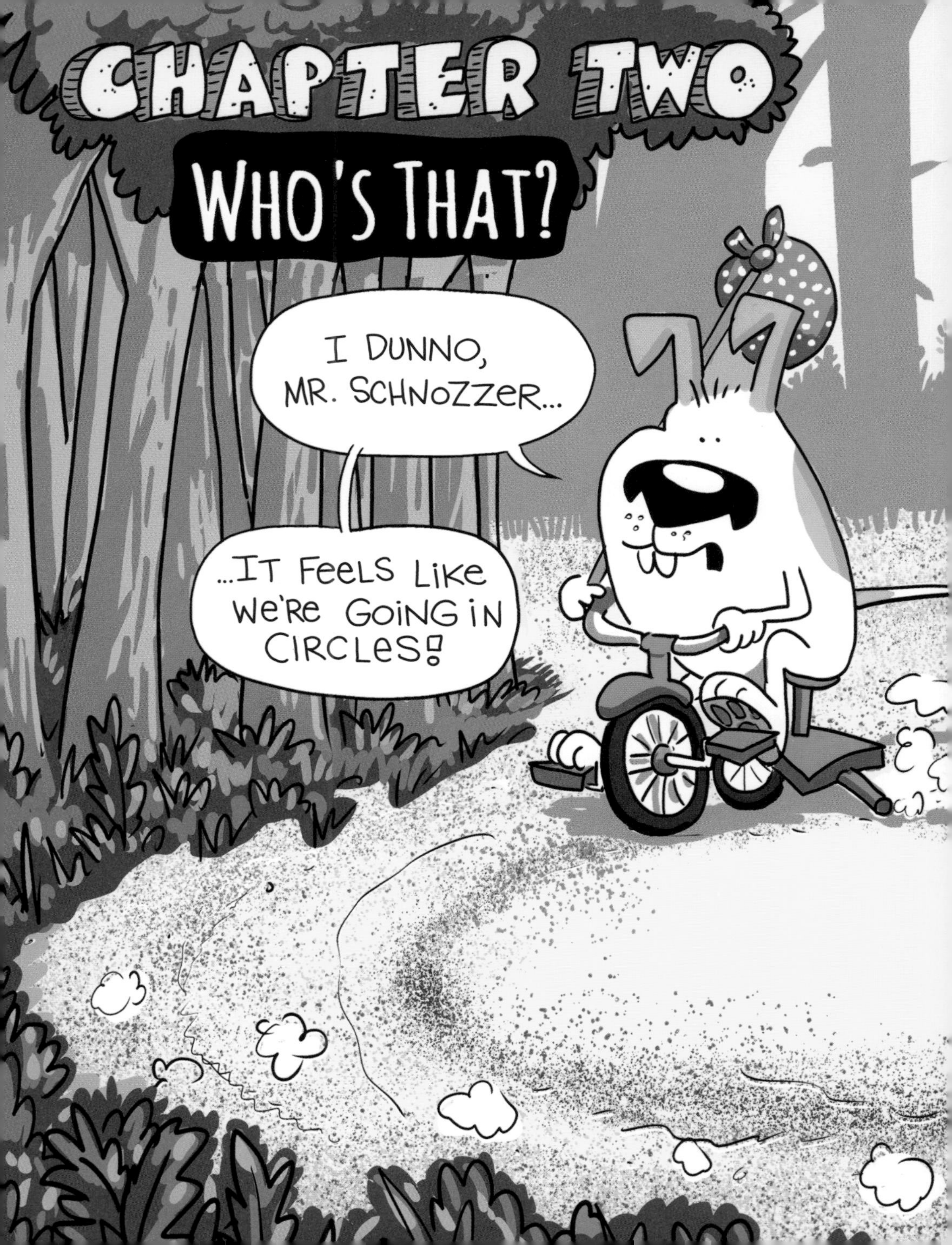
CHAPTER TWO
WHO'S THAT?
I DUNNO, MR. SCHNOZZER...
...IT FEELS LIKE WE'RE GOING IN CIRCLES!

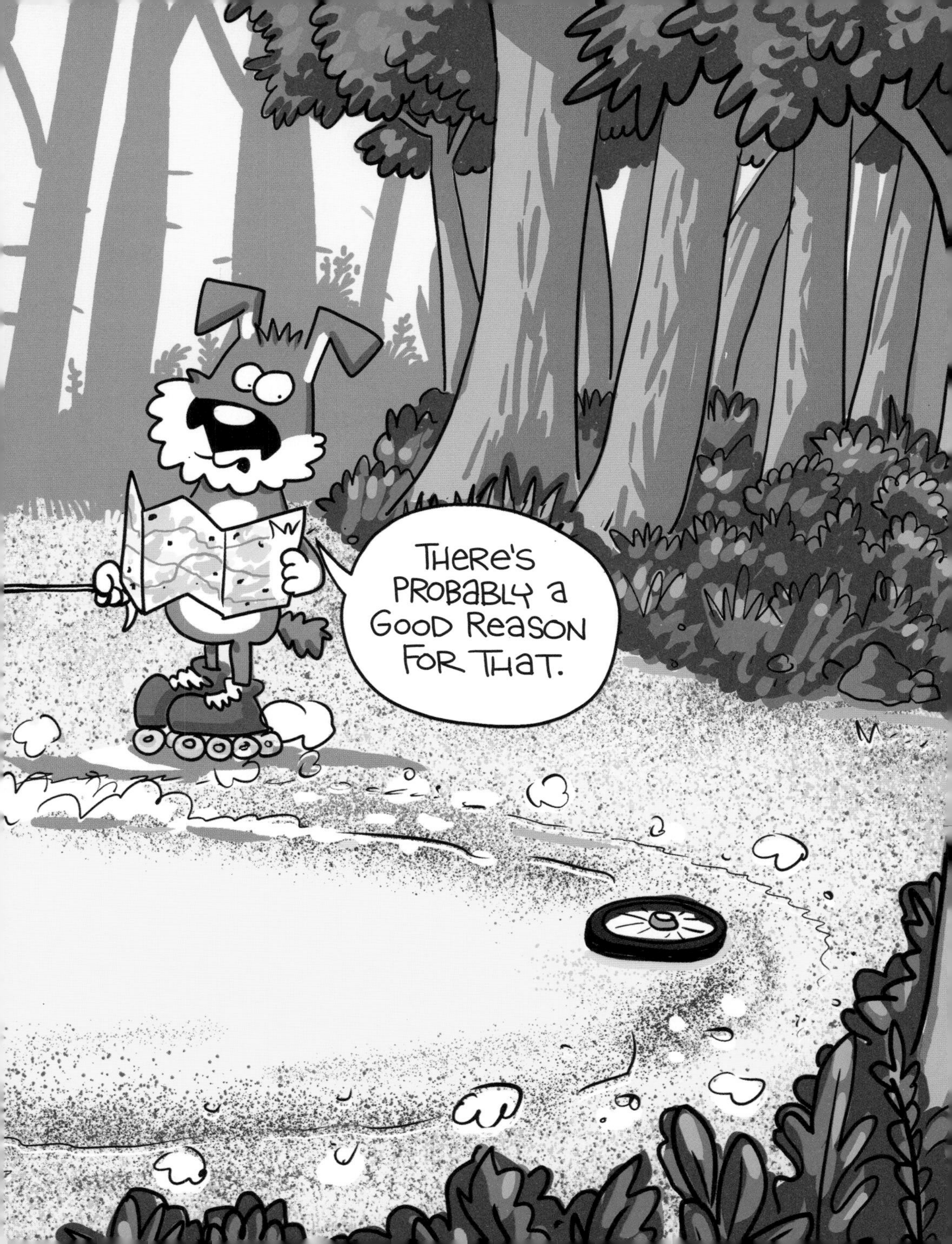
THERE'S PROBABLY A GOOD REASON FOR THAT.

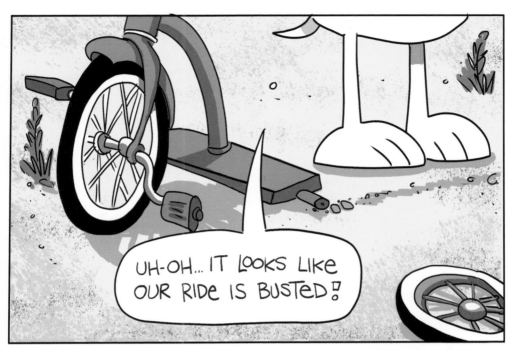

UH-OH... IT LOOKS LIKE OUR RIDE IS BUSTED!

WHAT DO WE DO **NOW**, MR. SCHNOZZER?

I GUESS WE WALK THE REST OF THE WAY.

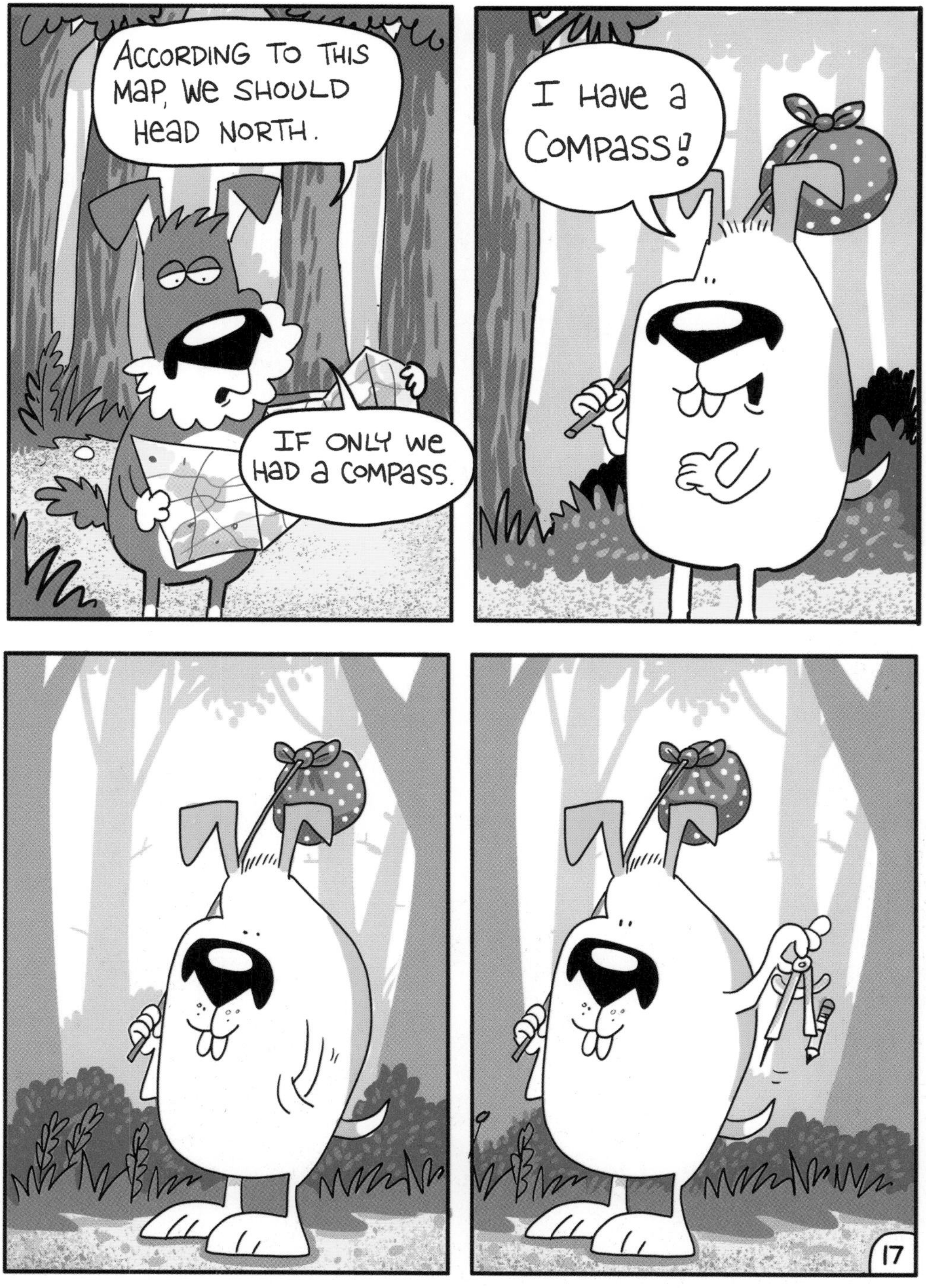
ACCORDING TO THIS MAP, WE SHOULD HEAD NORTH.
IF ONLY WE HAD A COMPASS.
I HAVE A COMPASS!

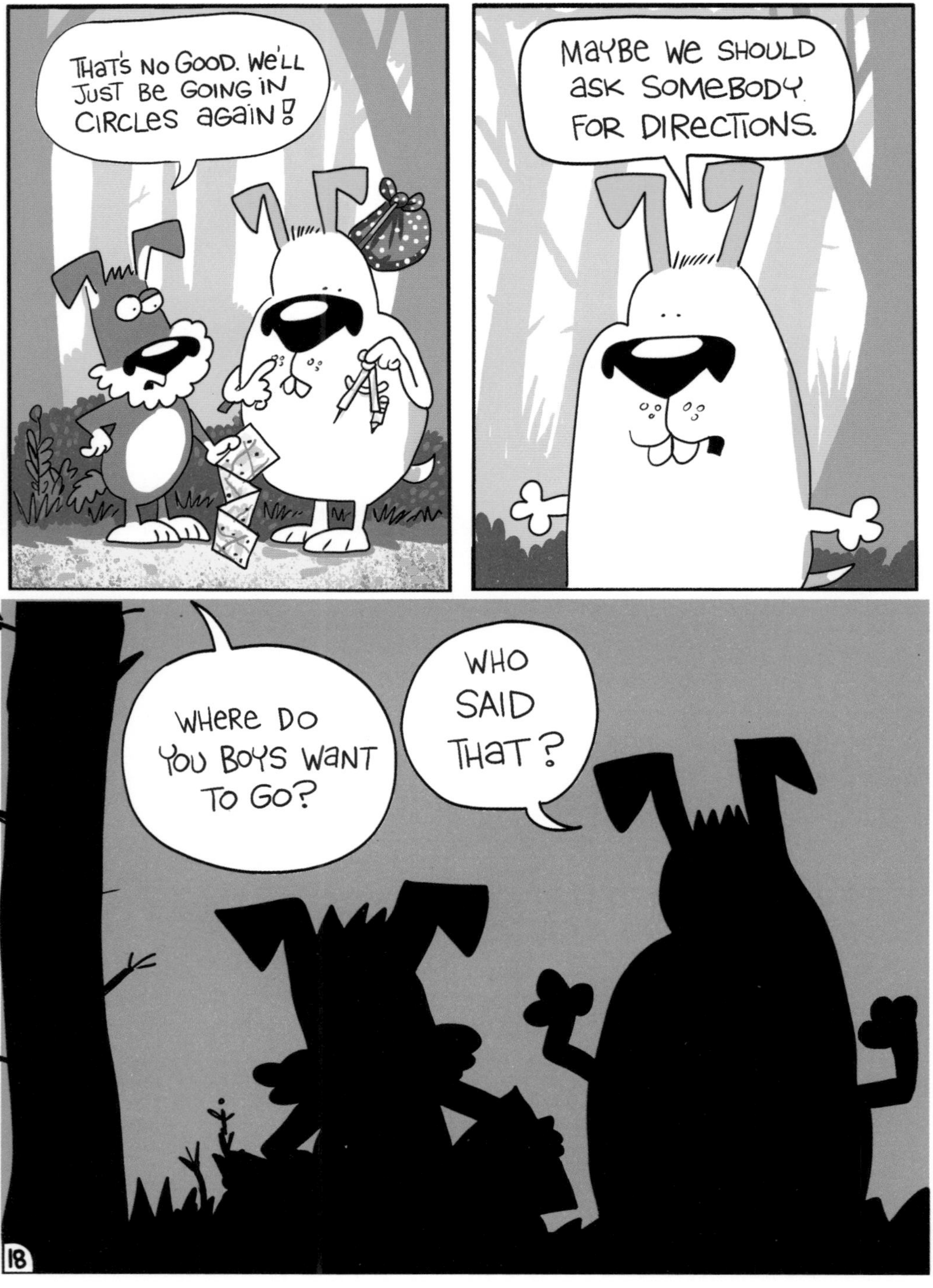
THAT'S NO GOOD. WE'LL JUST BE GOING IN CIRCLES AGAIN!
MAYBE WE SHOULD ASK SOMEBODY FOR DIRECTIONS.
WHERE DO YOU BOYS WANT TO GO?
WHO SAID THAT?

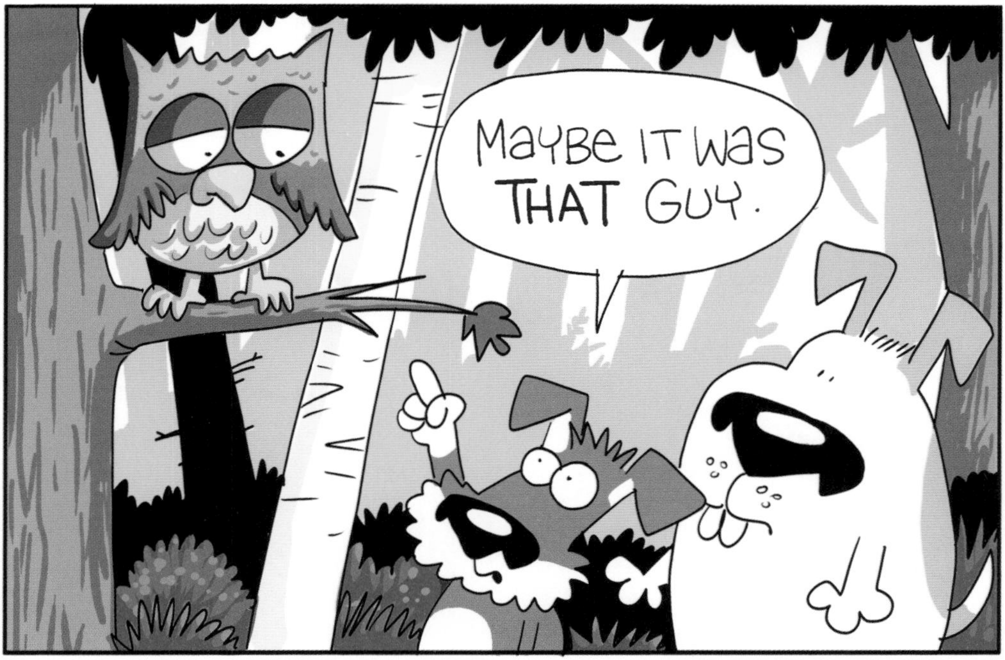
MAYBE IT WAS THAT GUY.

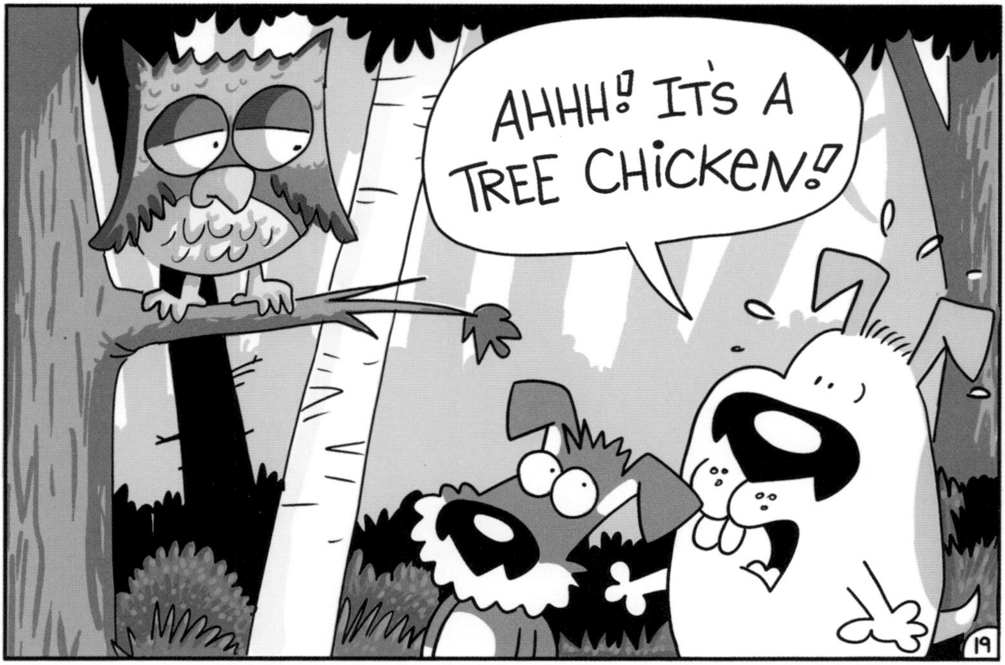
AHHH! IT'S A TREE CHICKEN!

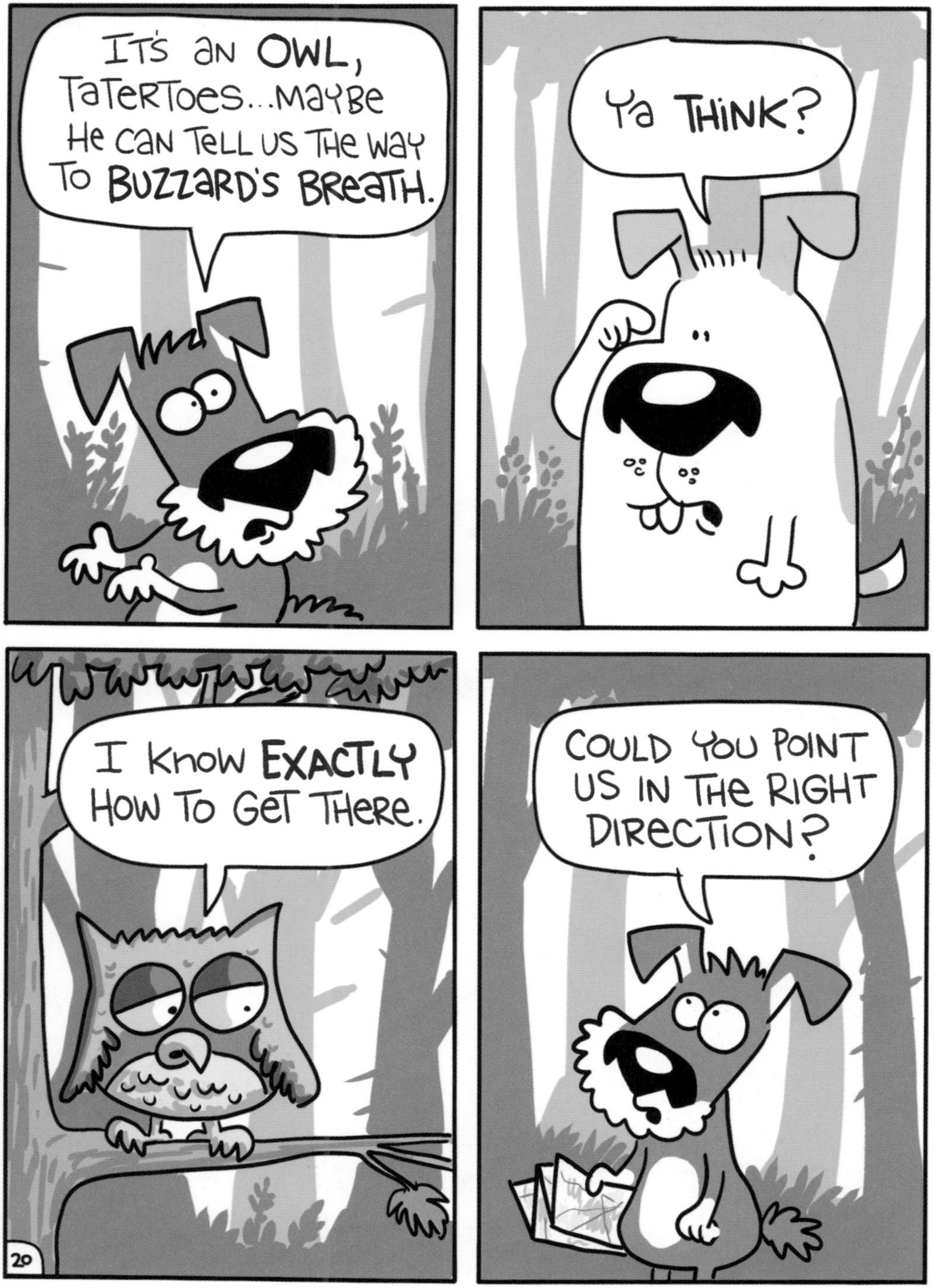
IT'S AN OWL, TATERTOES...MAYBE HE CAN TELL US THE WAY TO BUZZARD'S BREATH.
YA THINK?
I KNOW EXACTLY HOW TO GET THERE.
COULD YOU POINT US IN THE RIGHT DIRECTION?

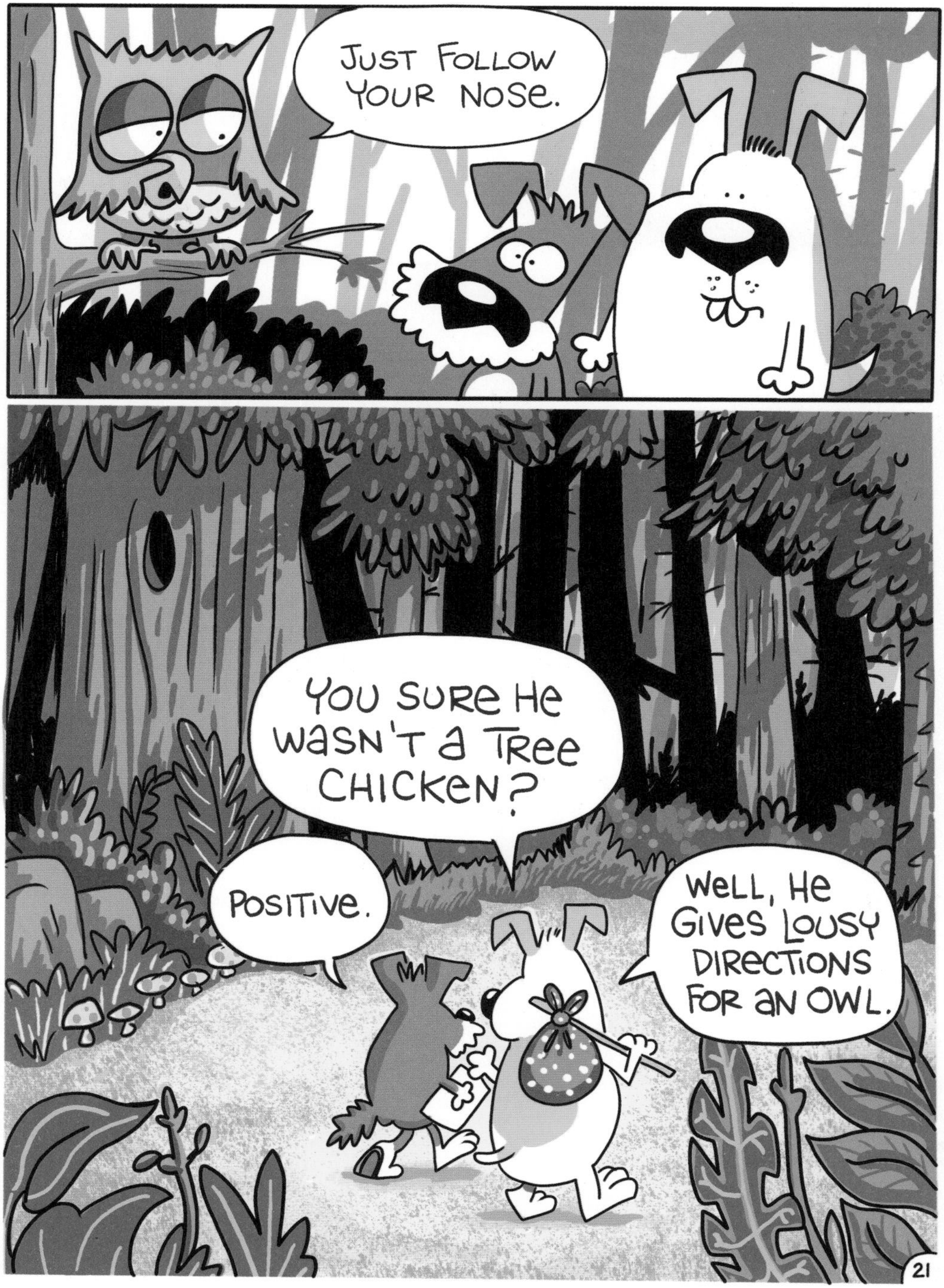
JUST FOLLOW YOUR NOSE.
YOU SURE HE WASN'T A TREE CHICKEN?
POSITIVE.
WELL, HE GIVES LOUSY DIRECTIONS FOR AN OWL.

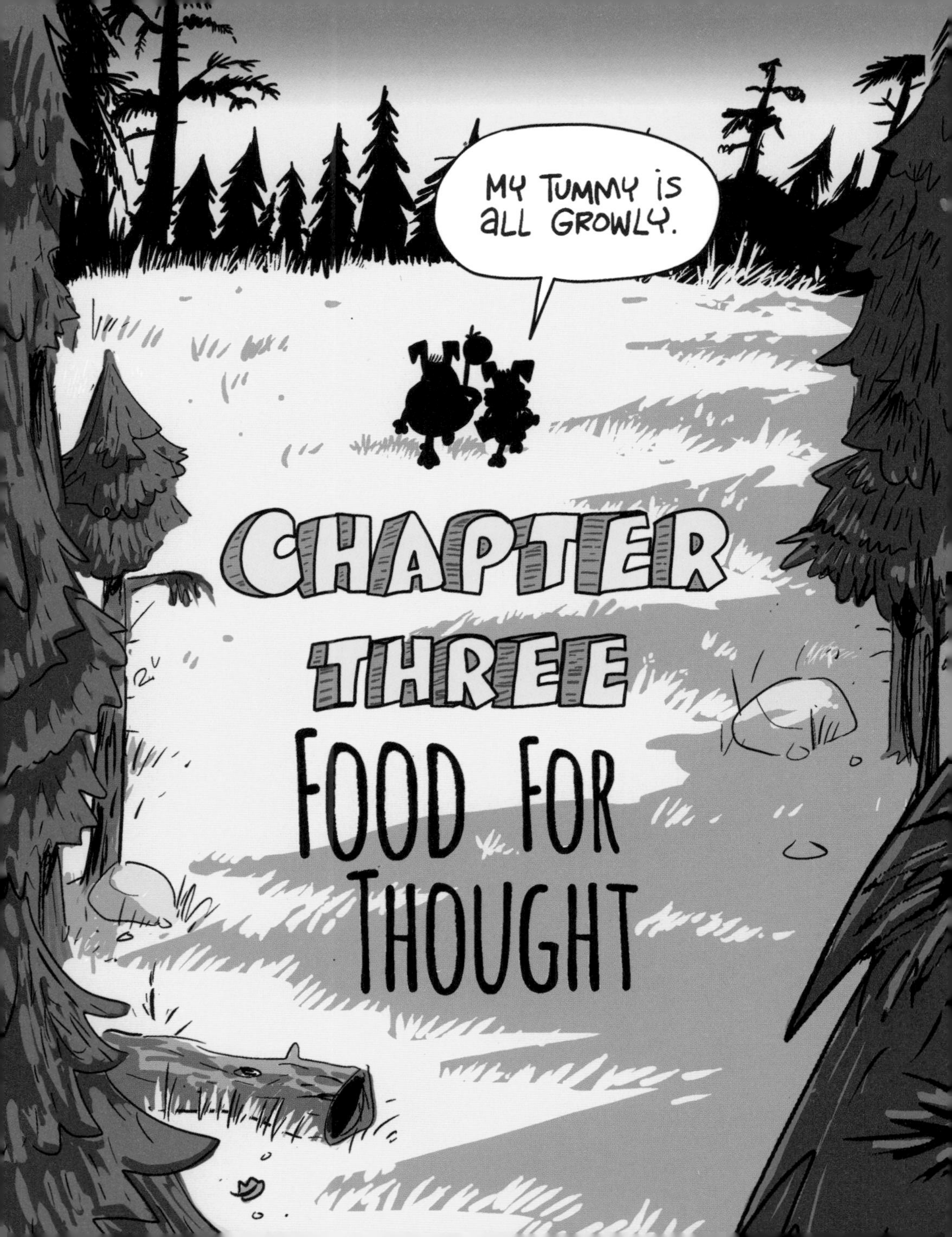
MY TUMMY IS ALL GROWLY.
CHAPTER THREE
FOOD FOR THOUGHT

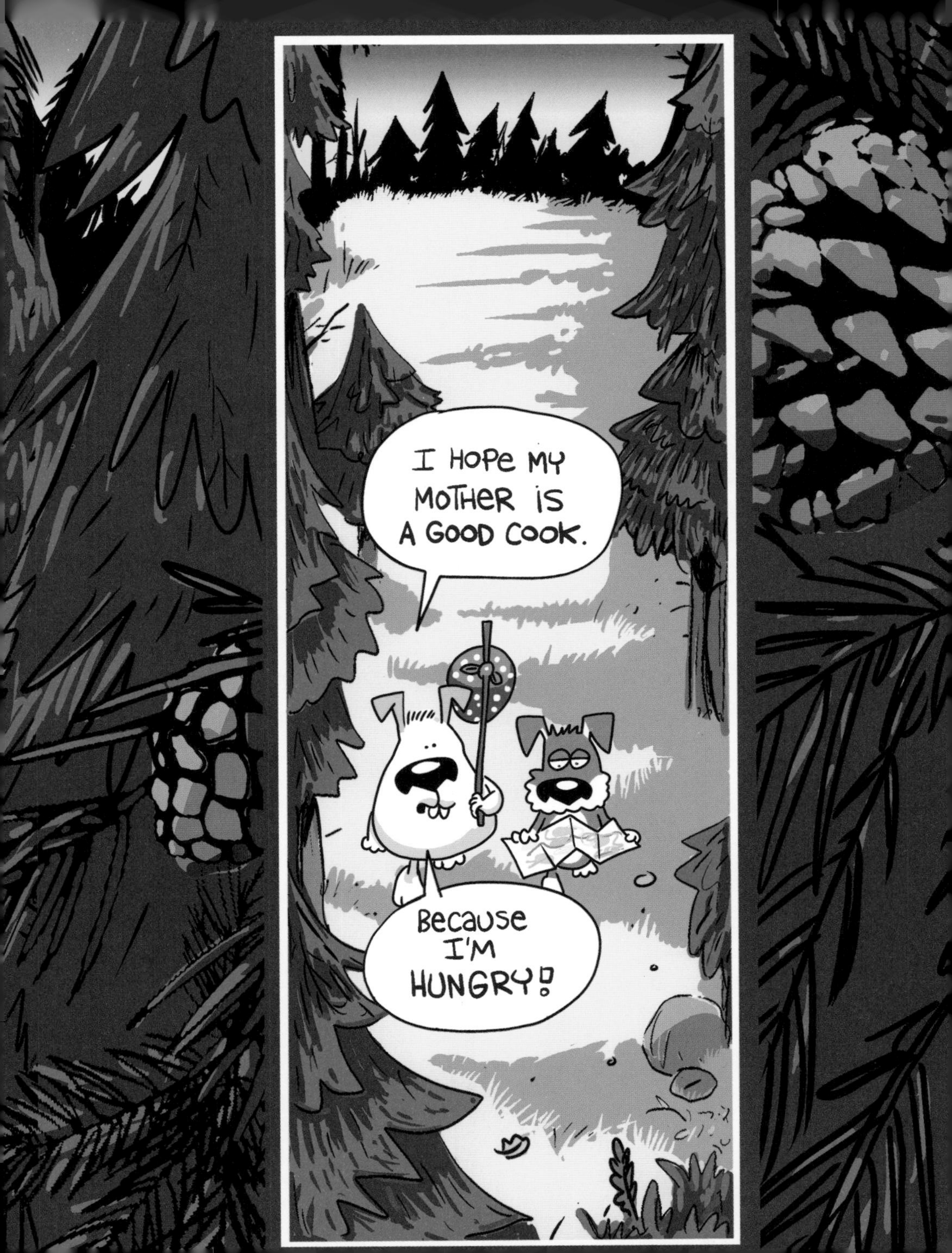
I HOPE MY MOTHER IS A GOOD COOK.
BECAUSE I'M HUNGRY!

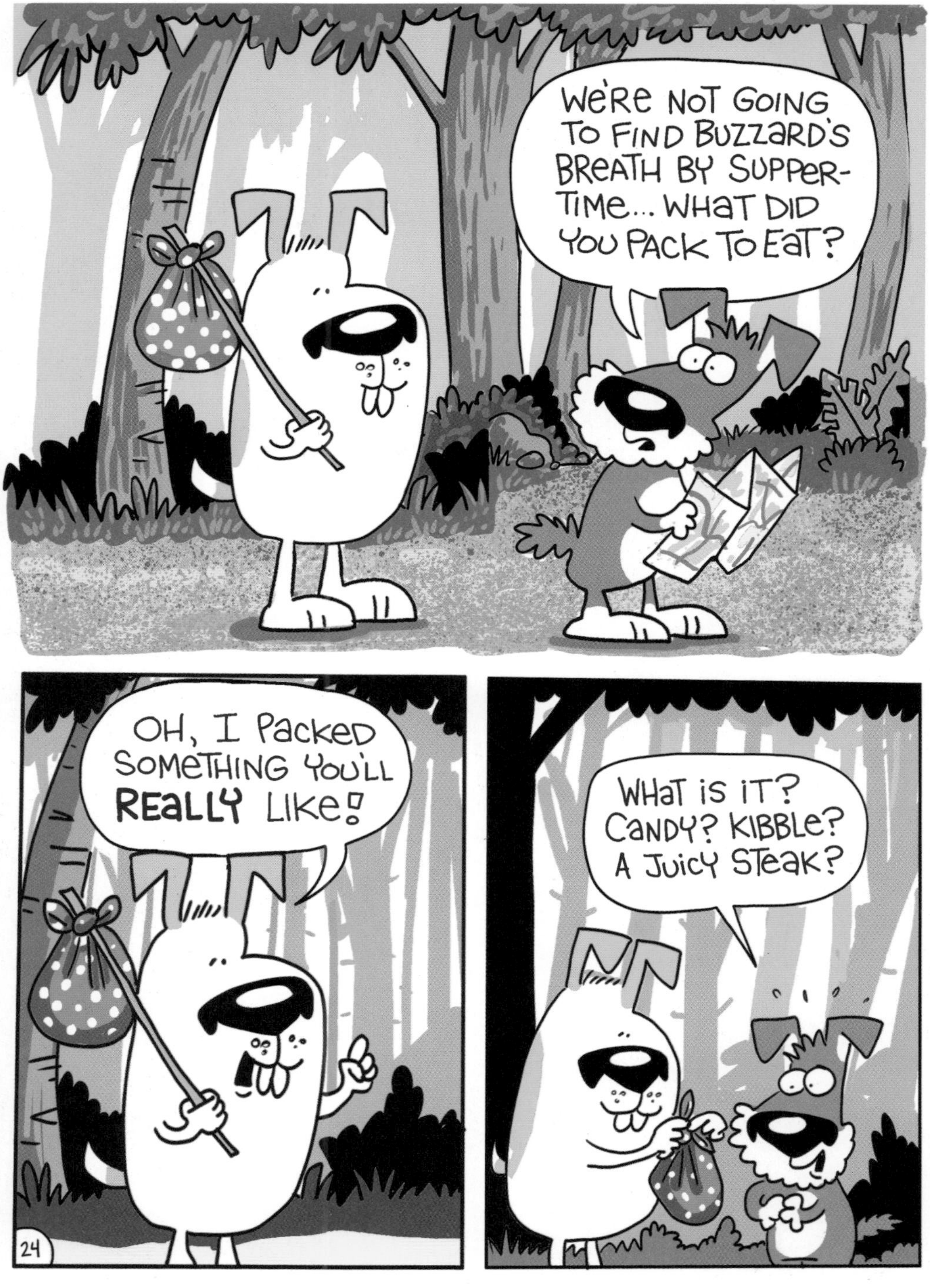
WE'RE NOT GOING TO FIND BUZZARD'S BREATH BY SUPPER-TIME... WHAT DID YOU PACK TO EAT?
OH, I PACKED SOMETHING YOU'LL **REALLY** LIKE!
WHAT IS IT? CANDY? KIBBLE? A JUICY STEAK?

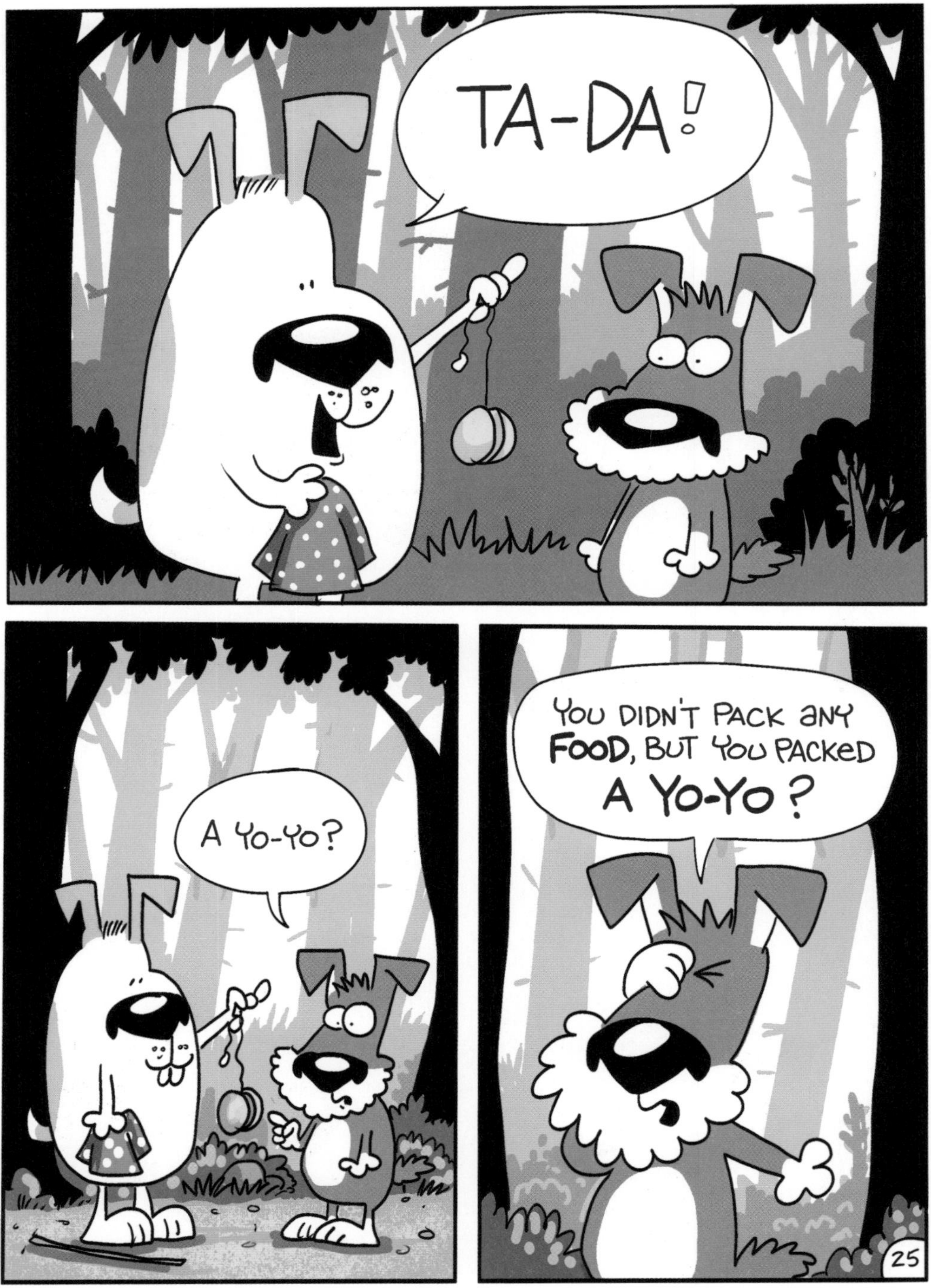
TA-DA!
A YO-YO?
YOU DIDN'T PACK ANY FOOD, BUT YOU PACKED A YO-YO?

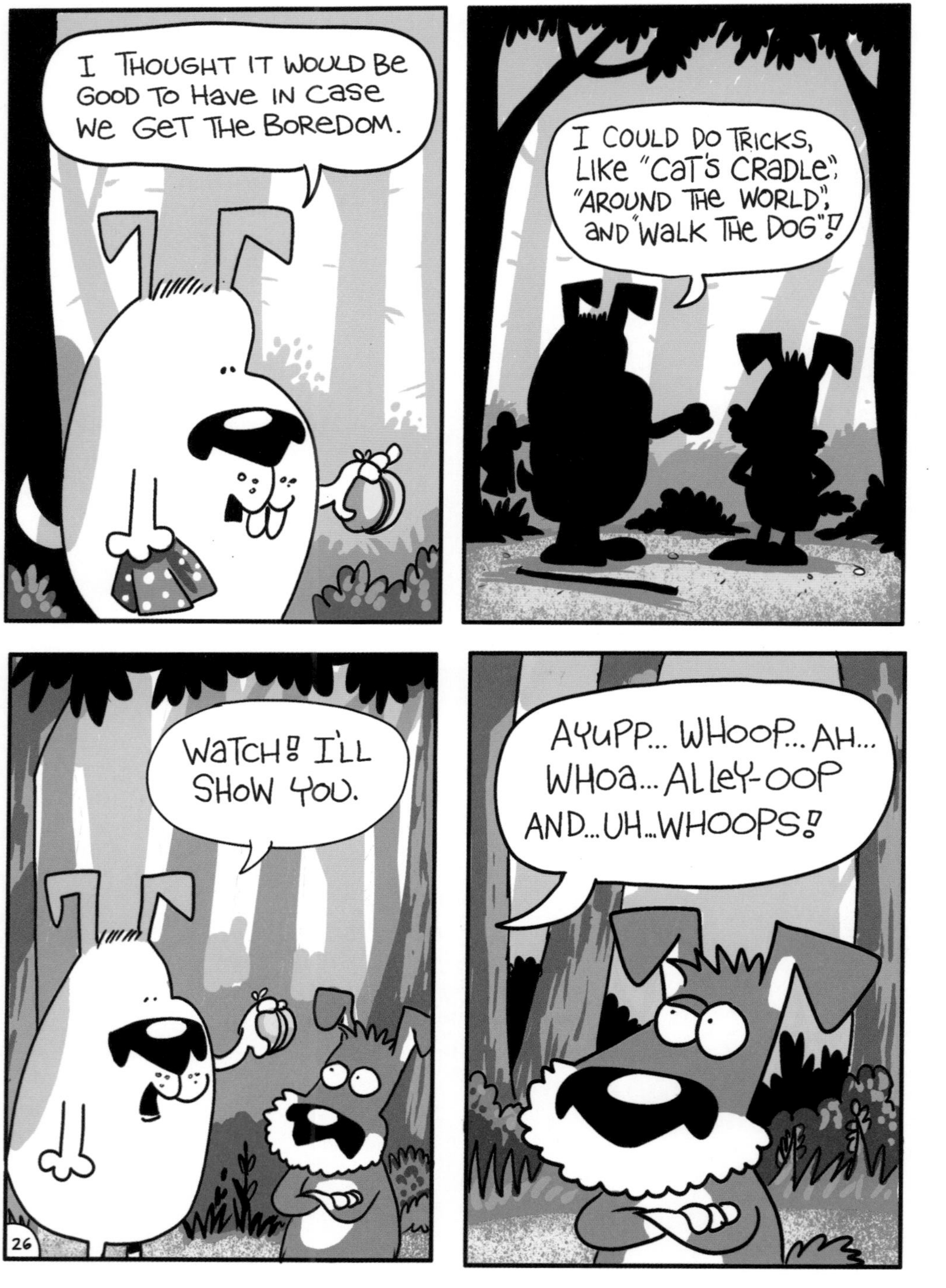
I THOUGHT IT WOULD BE GOOD TO HAVE IN CASE WE GET THE BOREDOM.
I COULD DO TRICKS, LIKE "CAT'S CRADLE", "AROUND THE WORLD", AND "WALK THE DOG"!
WATCH! I'LL SHOW YOU.
AYUPP... WHOOP... AH... WHOA... ALLEY-OOP AND...UH...WHOOPS!

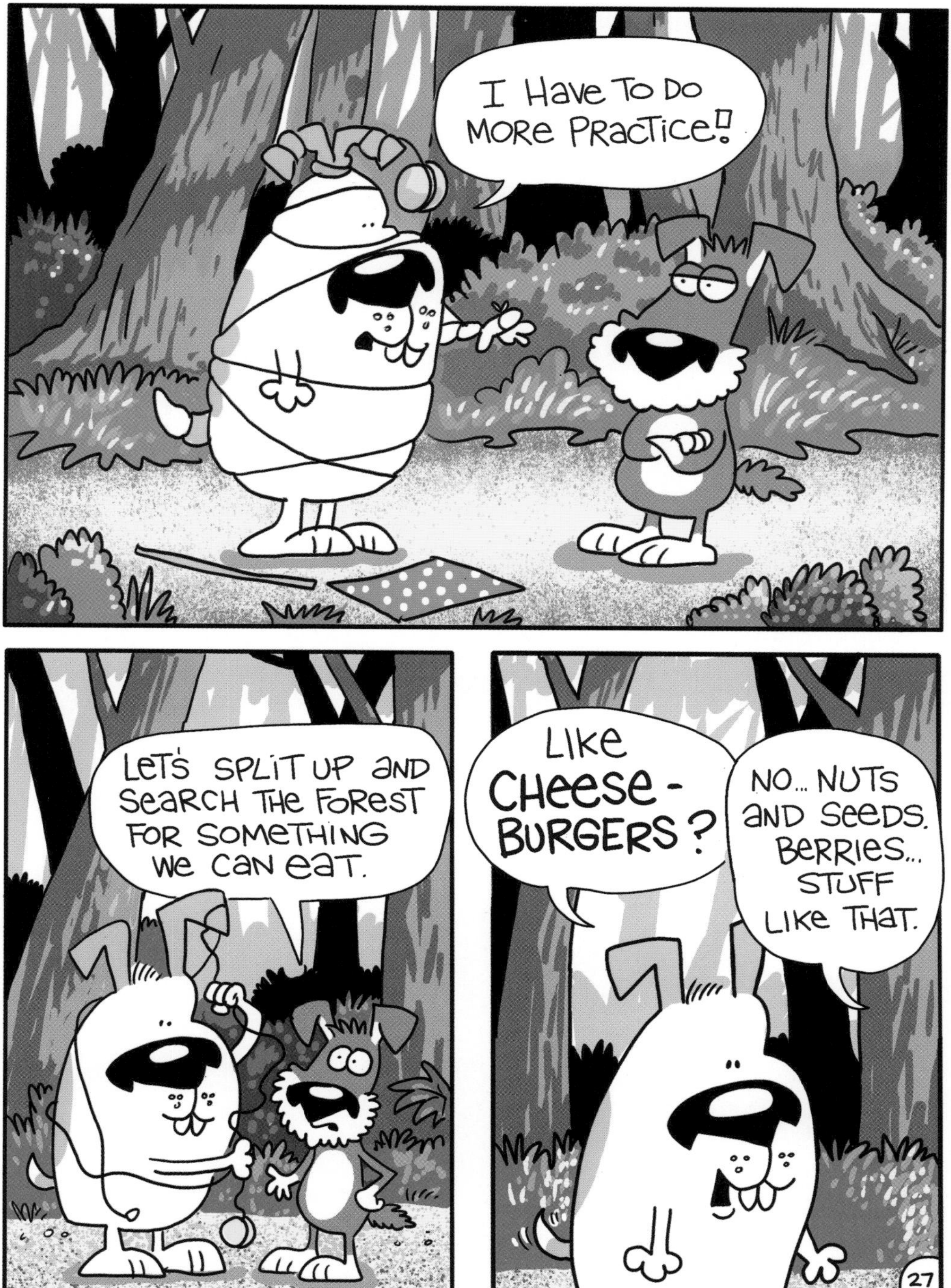
I HAVE TO DO MORE PRACTICE!!
LET'S SPLIT UP AND SEARCH THE FOREST FOR SOMETHING WE CAN EAT.
LIKE CHEESE-BURGERS?
NO... NUTS AND SEEDS. BERRIES... STUFF LIKE THAT.

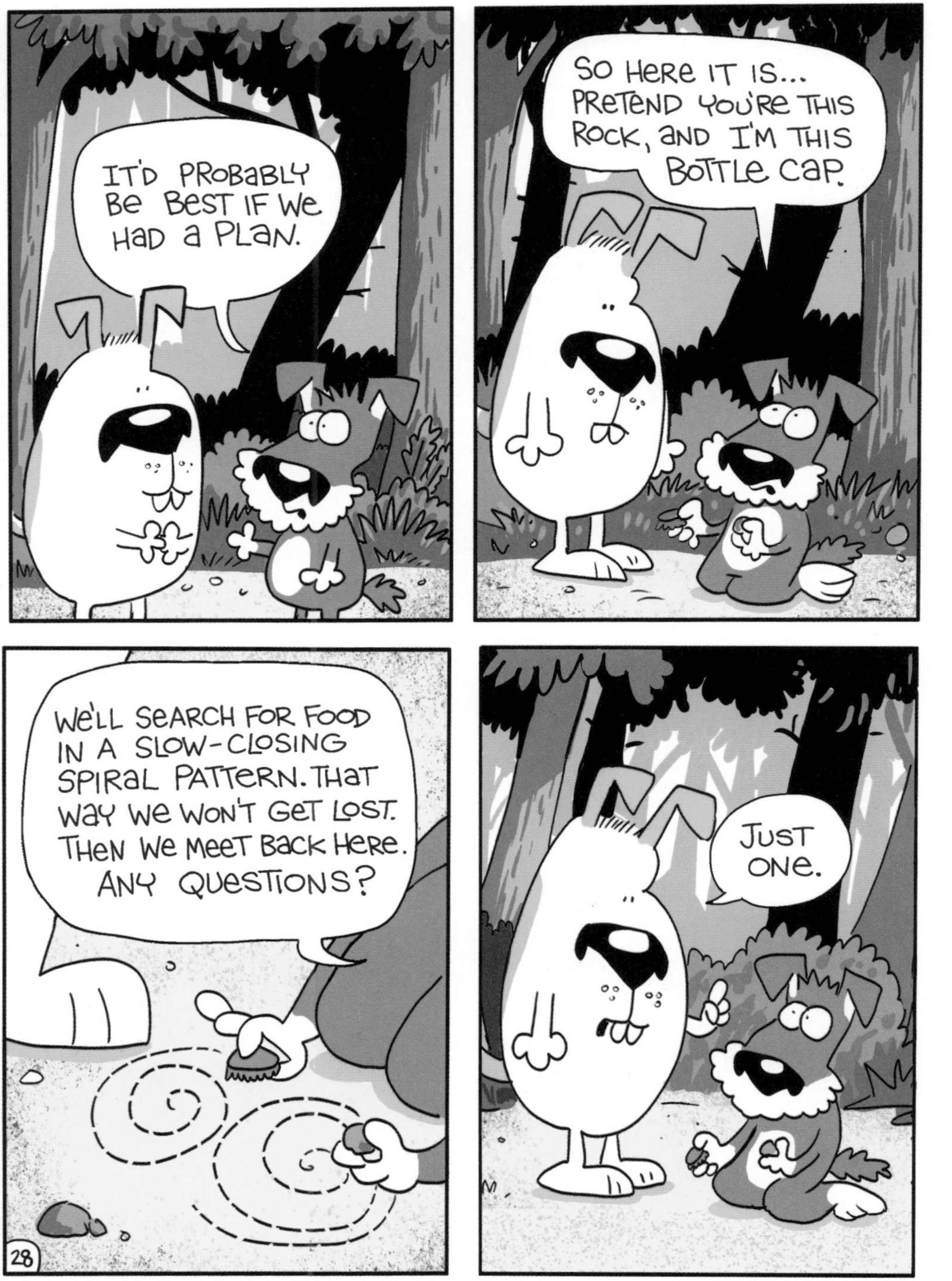
IT'D PROBABLY BE BEST IF WE HAD A PLAN.
SO HERE IT IS... PRETEND YOU'RE THIS ROCK, AND I'M THIS BOTTLE CAP.
WE'LL SEARCH FOR FOOD IN A SLOW-CLOSING SPIRAL PATTERN. THAT WAY WE WON'T GET LOST. THEN WE MEET BACK HERE. ANY QUESTIONS?
JUST ONE.

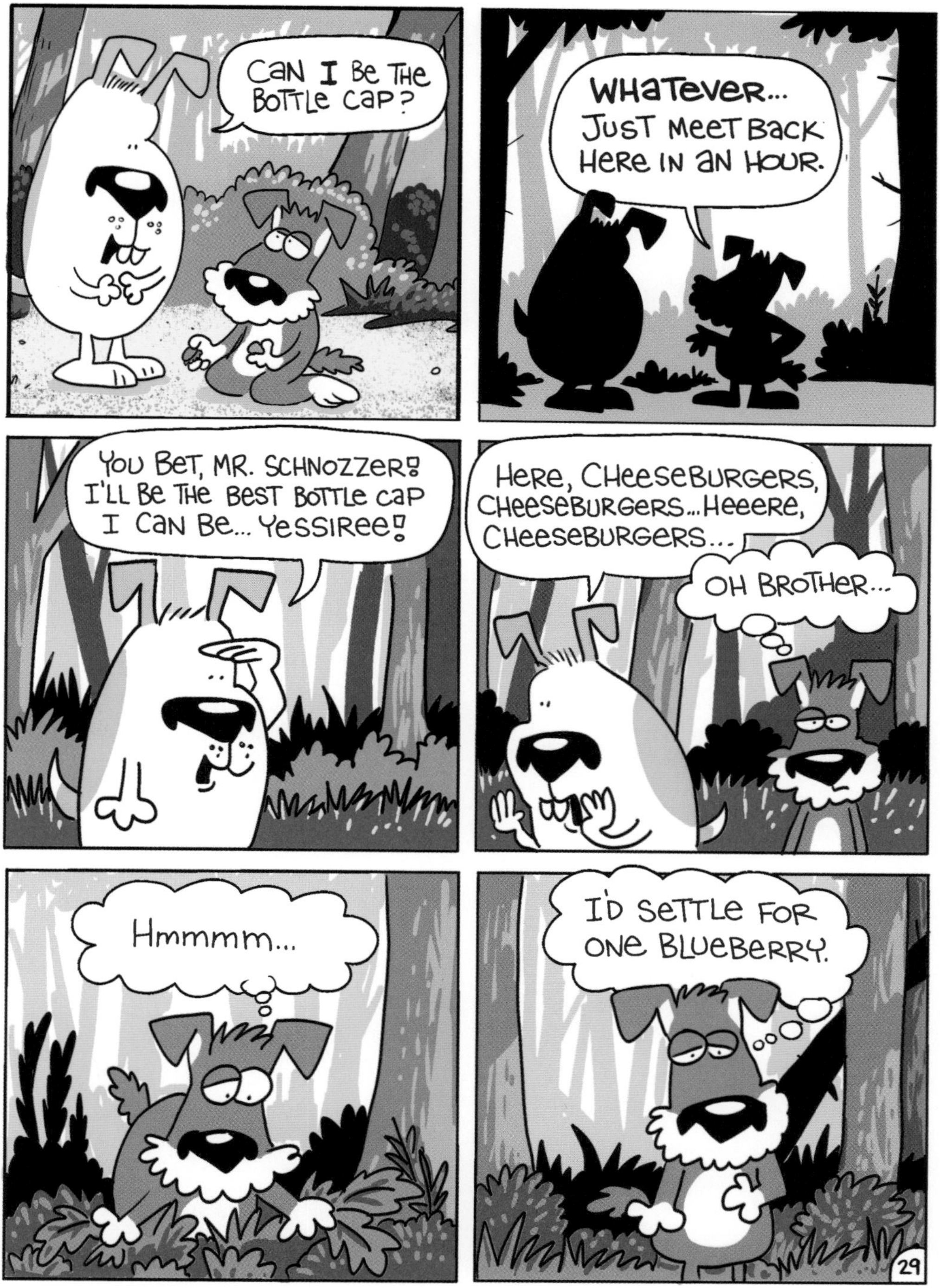
CAN I BE THE BOTTLE CAP?
WHATEVER... JUST MEET BACK HERE IN AN HOUR.
YOU BET, MR. SCHNOZZER! I'LL BE THE BEST BOTTLE CAP I CAN BE... YESSIREE!
HERE, CHEESEBURGERS, CHEESEBURGERS... HEEERE, CHEESEBURGERS...
OH BROTHER...
Hmmmm...
I'D SETTLE FOR ONE BLUEBERRY.

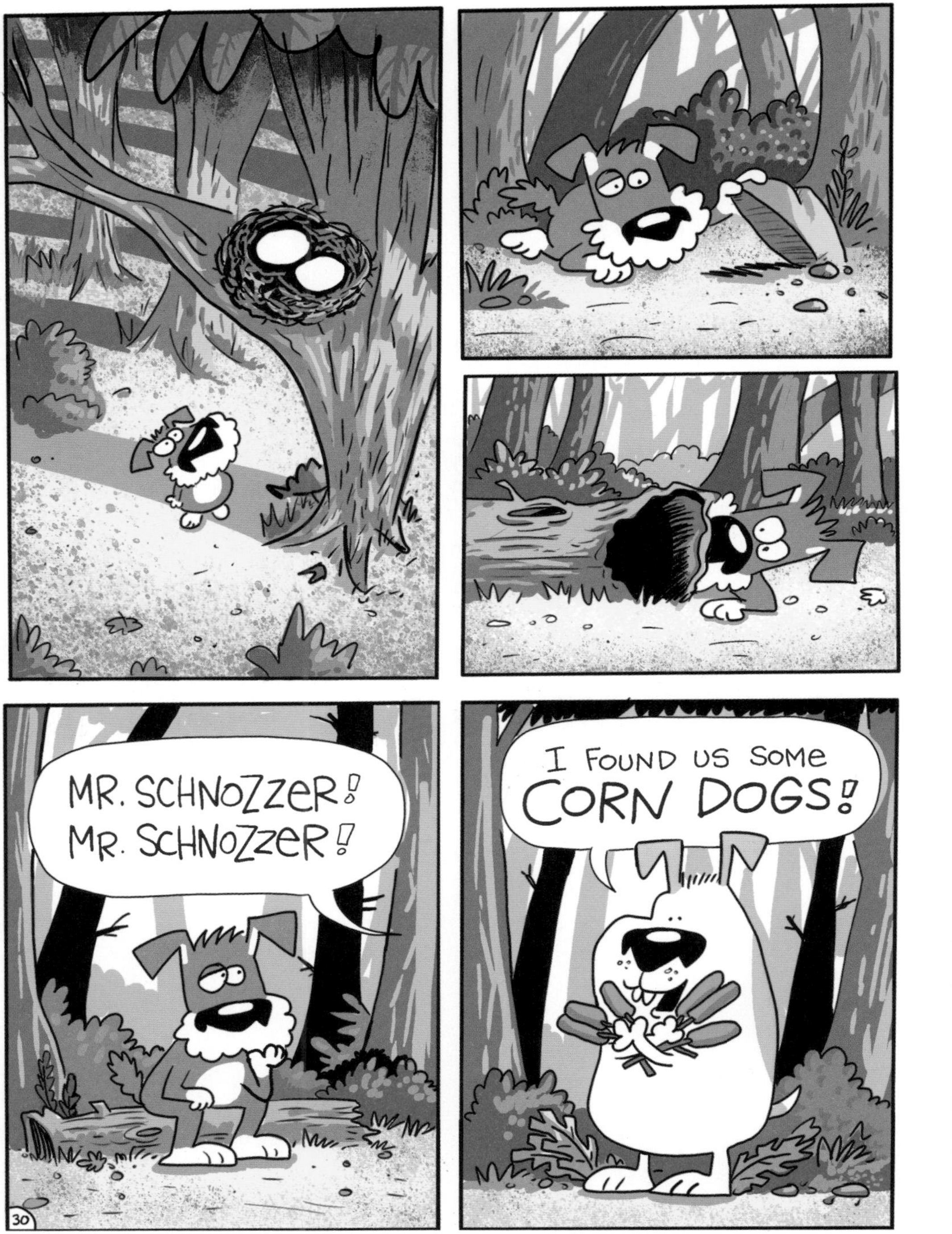
MR. SCHNOZZER!
MR. SCHNOZZER!
I FOUND US SOME CORN DOGS!

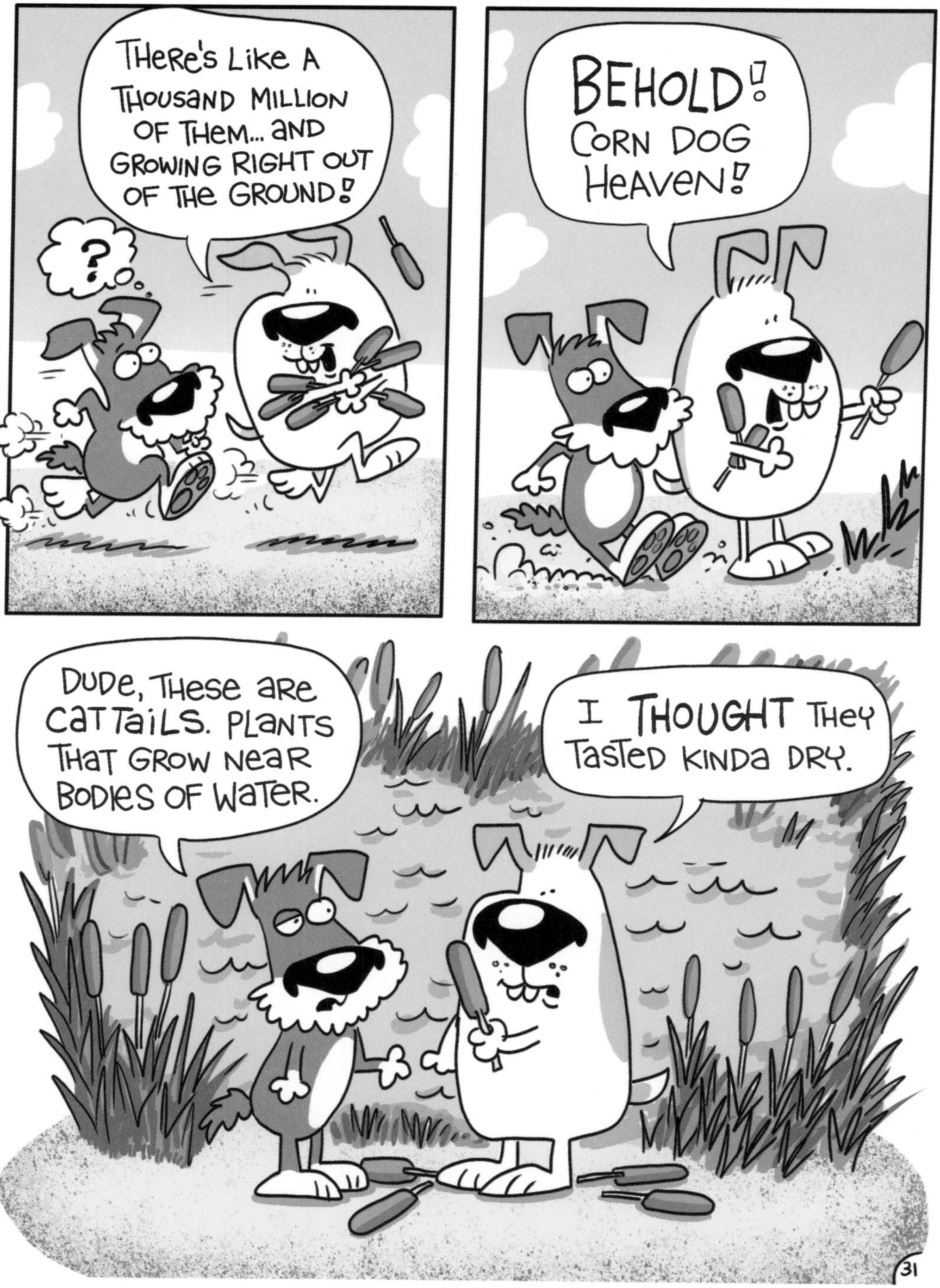
THERE'S LIKE A THOUSAND MILLION OF THEM... AND GROWING RIGHT OUT OF THE GROUND!
?
BEHOLD! CORN DOG HEAVEN!
DUDE, THESE ARE CATTAILS. PLANTS THAT GROW NEAR BODIES OF WATER.
I THOUGHT THEY TASTED KINDA DRY.

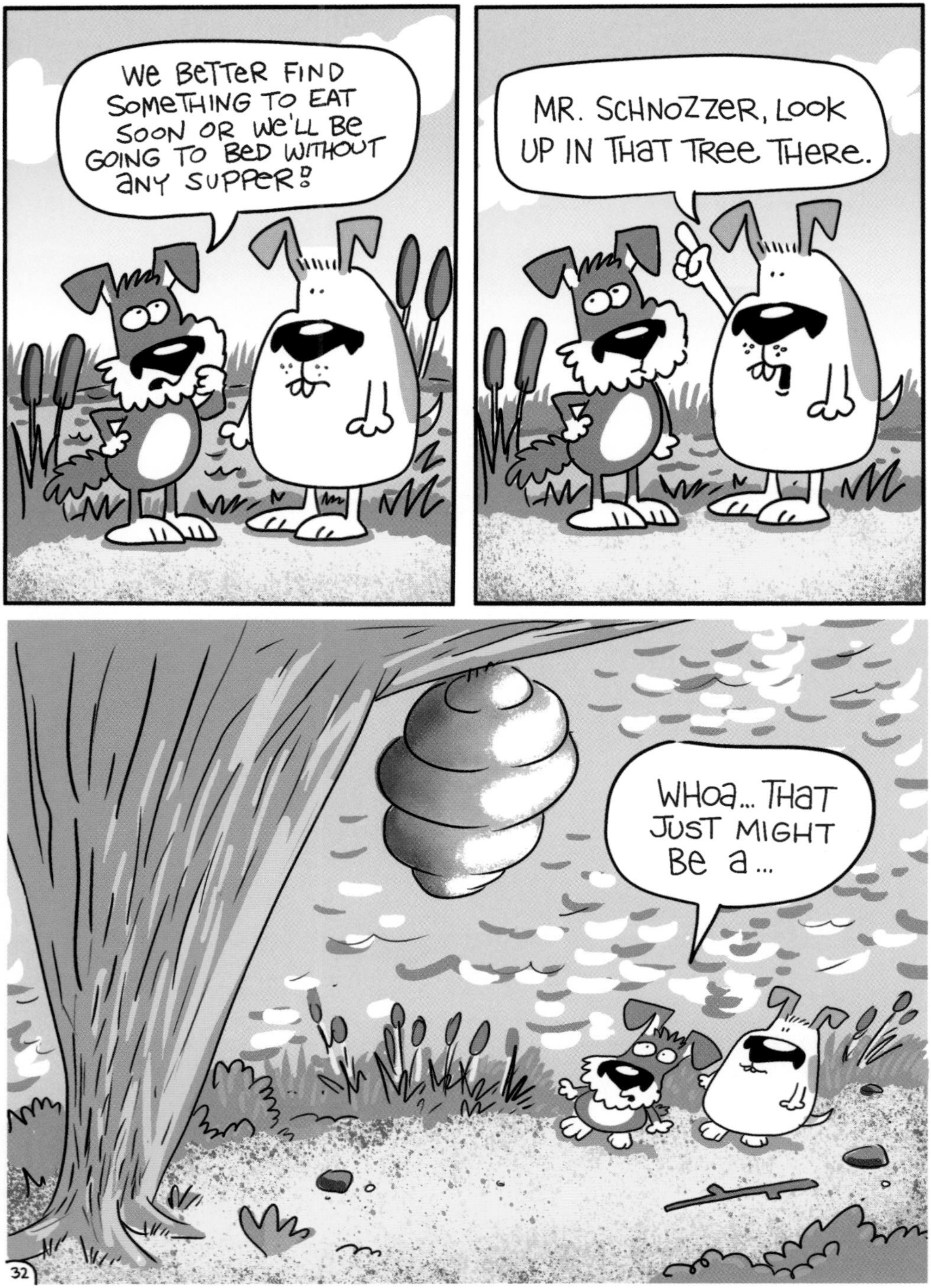
WE BETTER FIND SOMETHING TO EAT SOON OR WE'LL BE GOING TO BED WITHOUT ANY SUPPER!
MR. SCHNOZZER, LOOK UP IN THAT TREE THERE.
WHOA... THAT JUST MIGHT BE A...

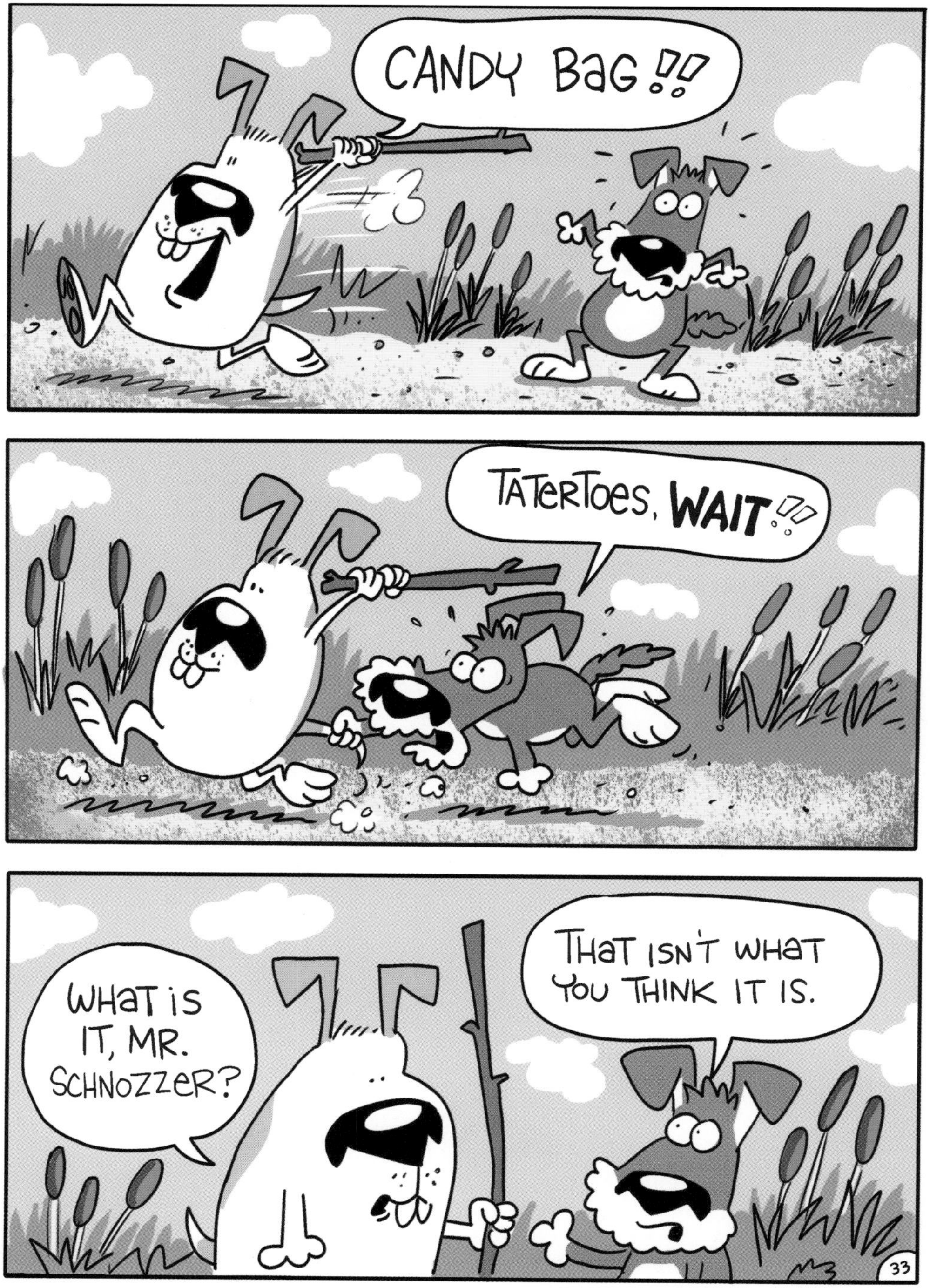
CANDY BAG!!!
TATERTOES, WAIT!!
WHAT IS IT, MR. SCHNOZZER?
THAT ISN'T WHAT YOU THINK IT IS.

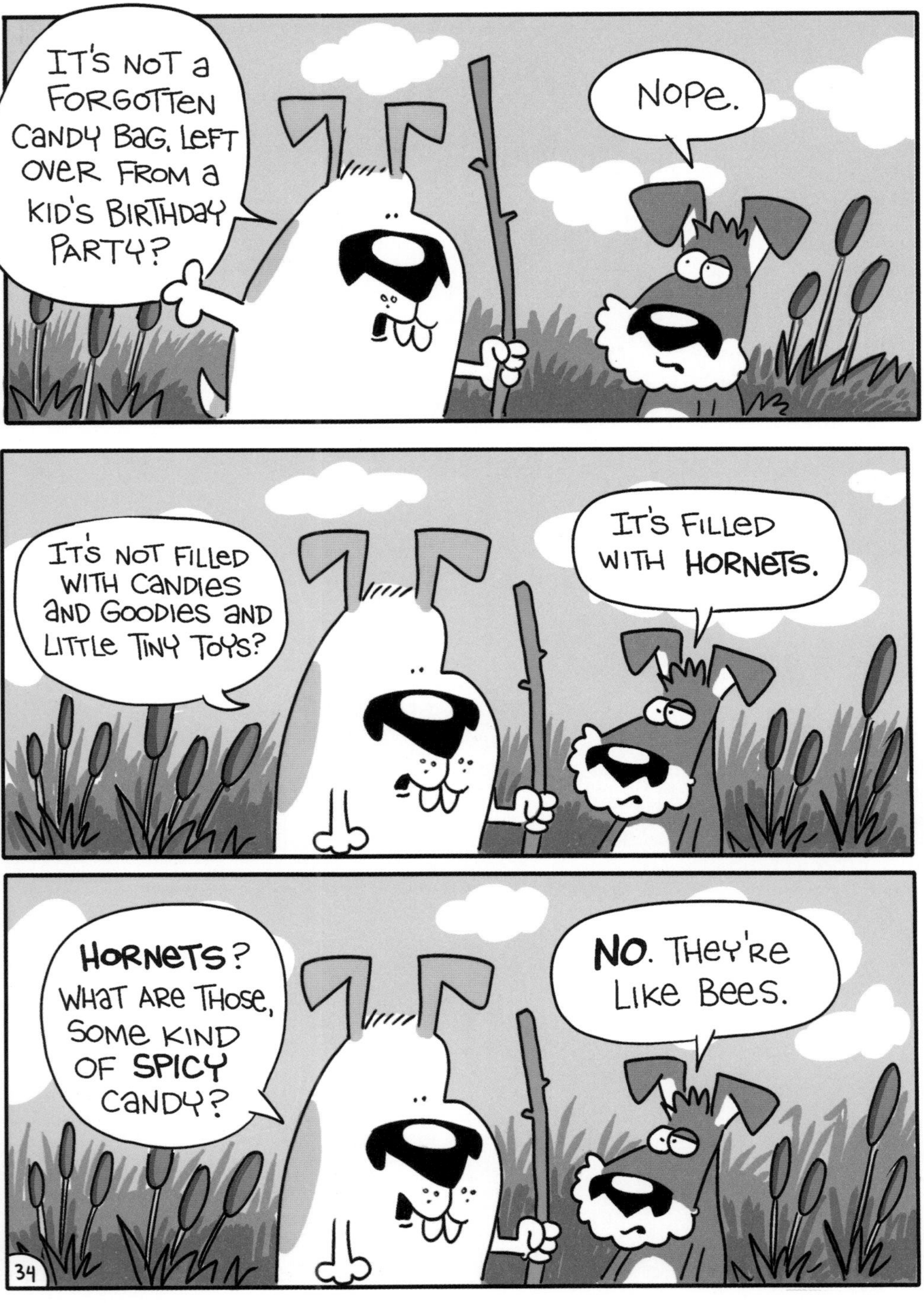
IT'S NOT a FORGOTTEN CANDY BAG, LEFT OVER FROM a KID'S BIRTHDAY PARTY?
NOPE.
IT'S NOT FILLED WITH CANDIES AND GOODIES AND LITTLE TINY TOYS?
IT'S FILLED WITH **HORNETS**.
HORNETS? WHAT ARE THOSE, SOME KIND OF **SPICY** CANDY?
NO. THEY'RE LIKE BEES.

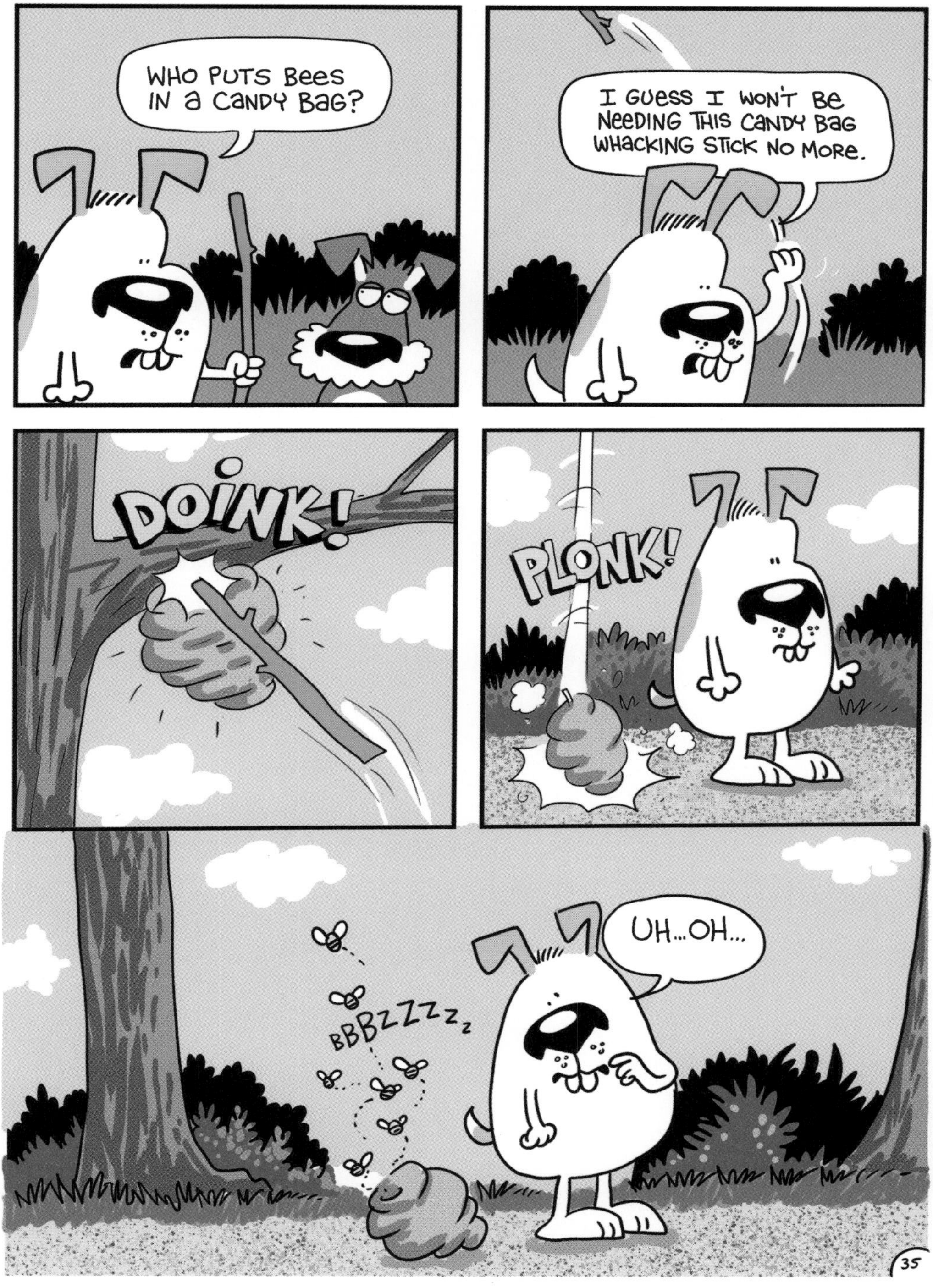

WHO PUTS Bees IN a CANDY BaG?
I GUESS I WON'T Be NEEDING THIS CANDY BaG WHACKING STICK NO MORe.
DOINK!
PLONK!
UH...OH...
BBBZZZZzz

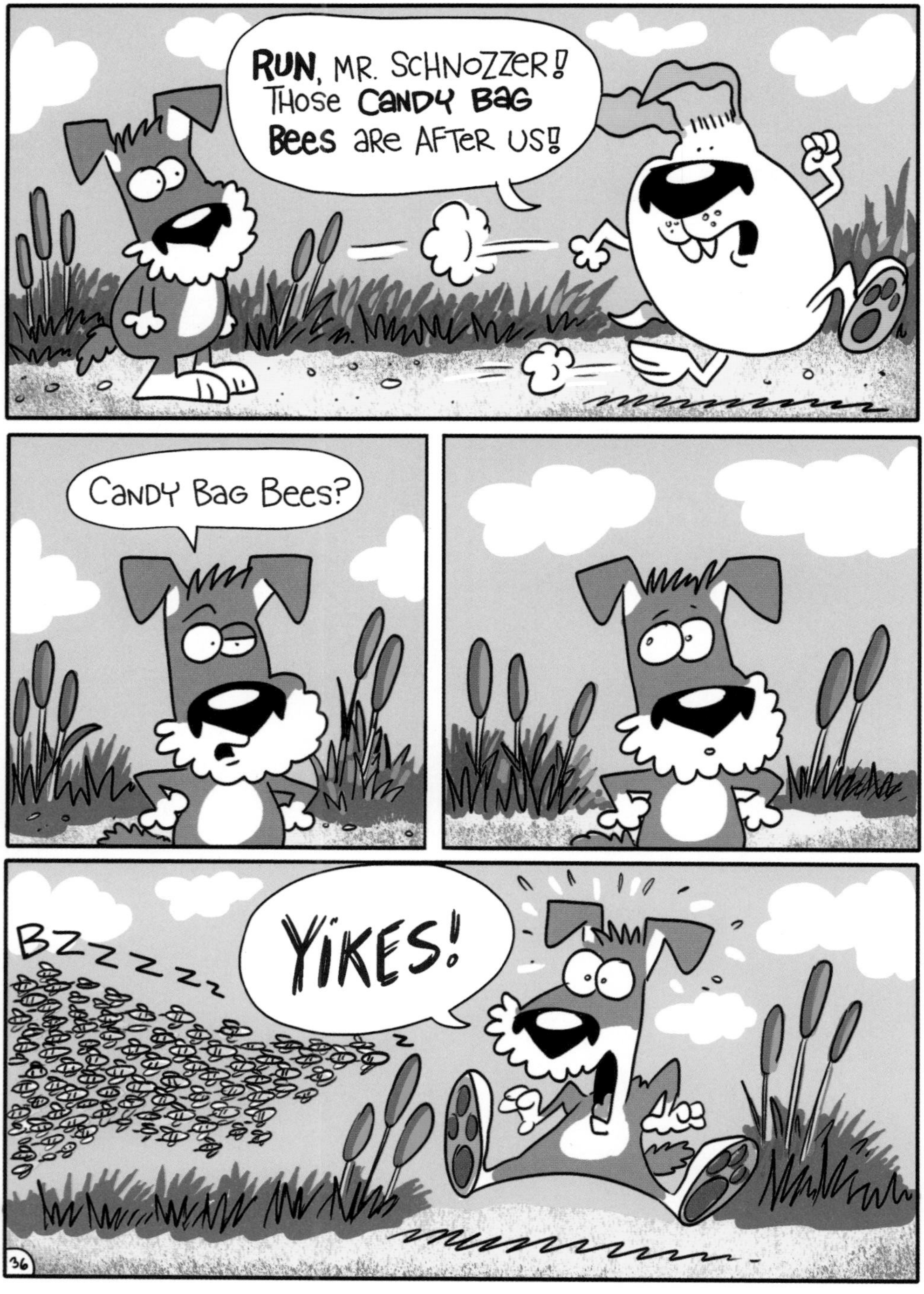
RUN, MR. SCHNOZZER! THOSE CANDY BAG BEES ARE AFTER US!
CANDY BAG BEES?
BZZZZZZ
YIKES!

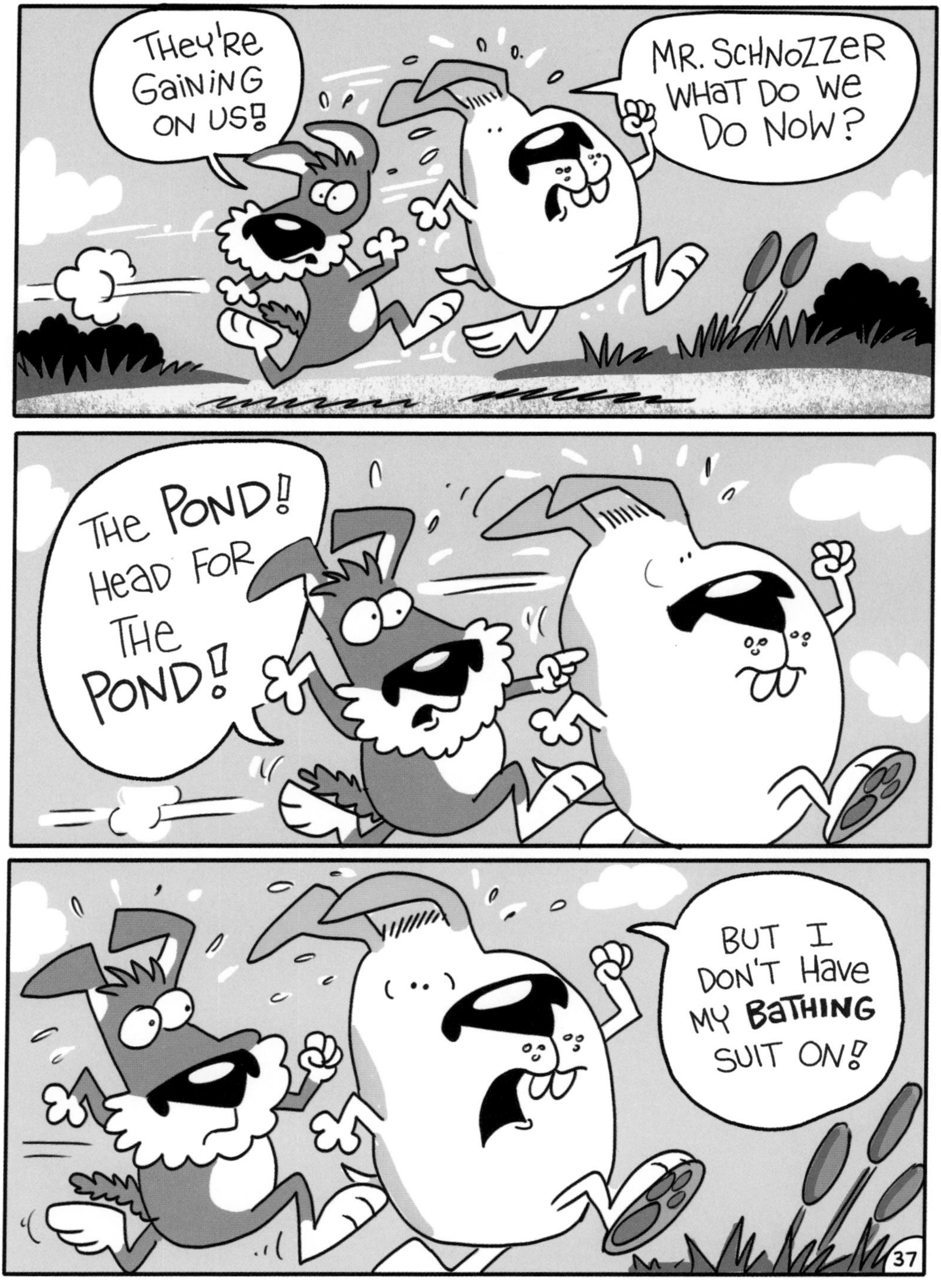
THEY'RE GAINING ON US!
MR. SCHNOZZER WHAT DO WE DO NOW?
THE POND! HEAD FOR THE POND!
BUT I DON'T HAVE MY BATHING SUIT ON!

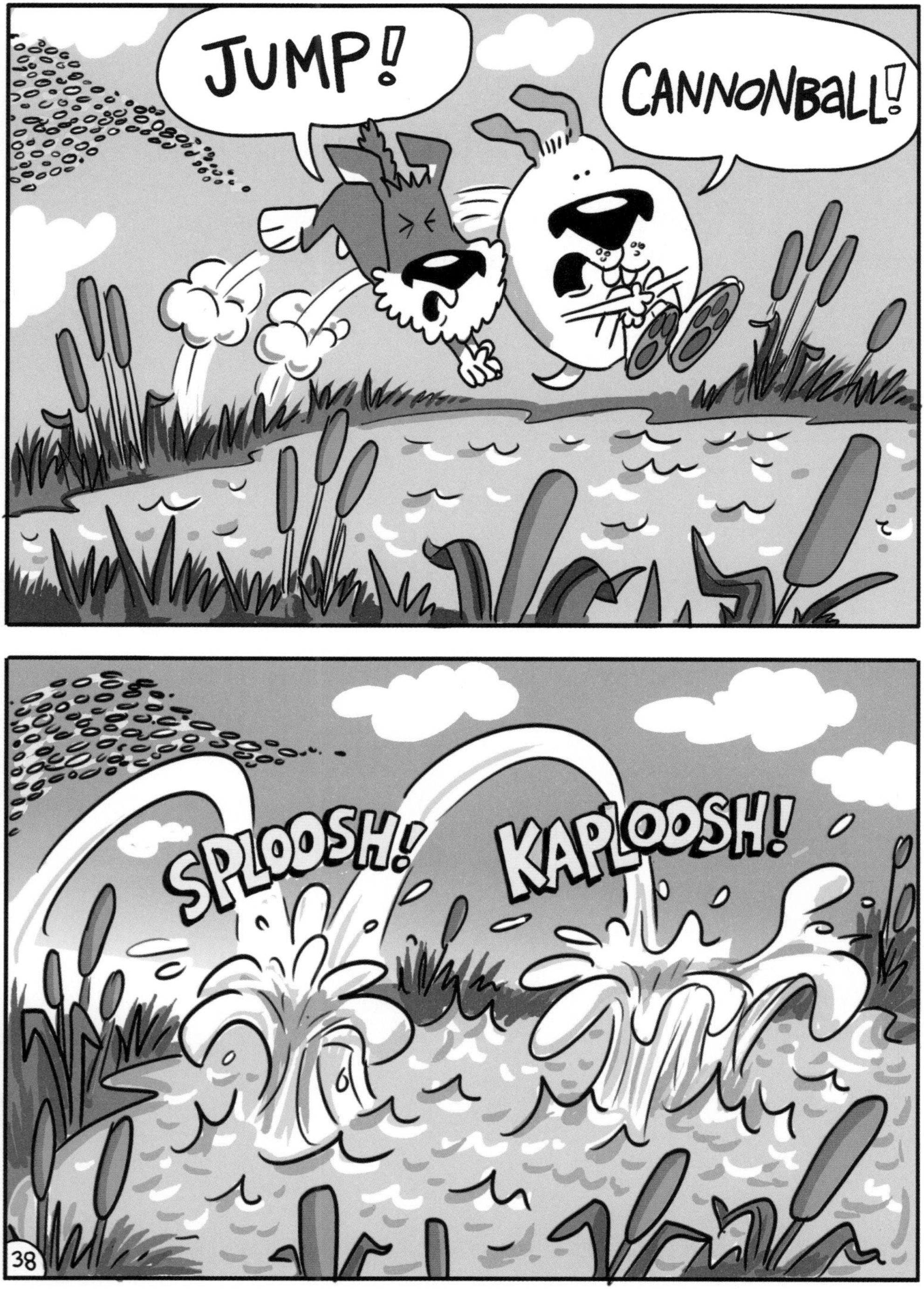
JUMP!
CANNONBALL!
SPLOOSH!
KAPLOOSH!

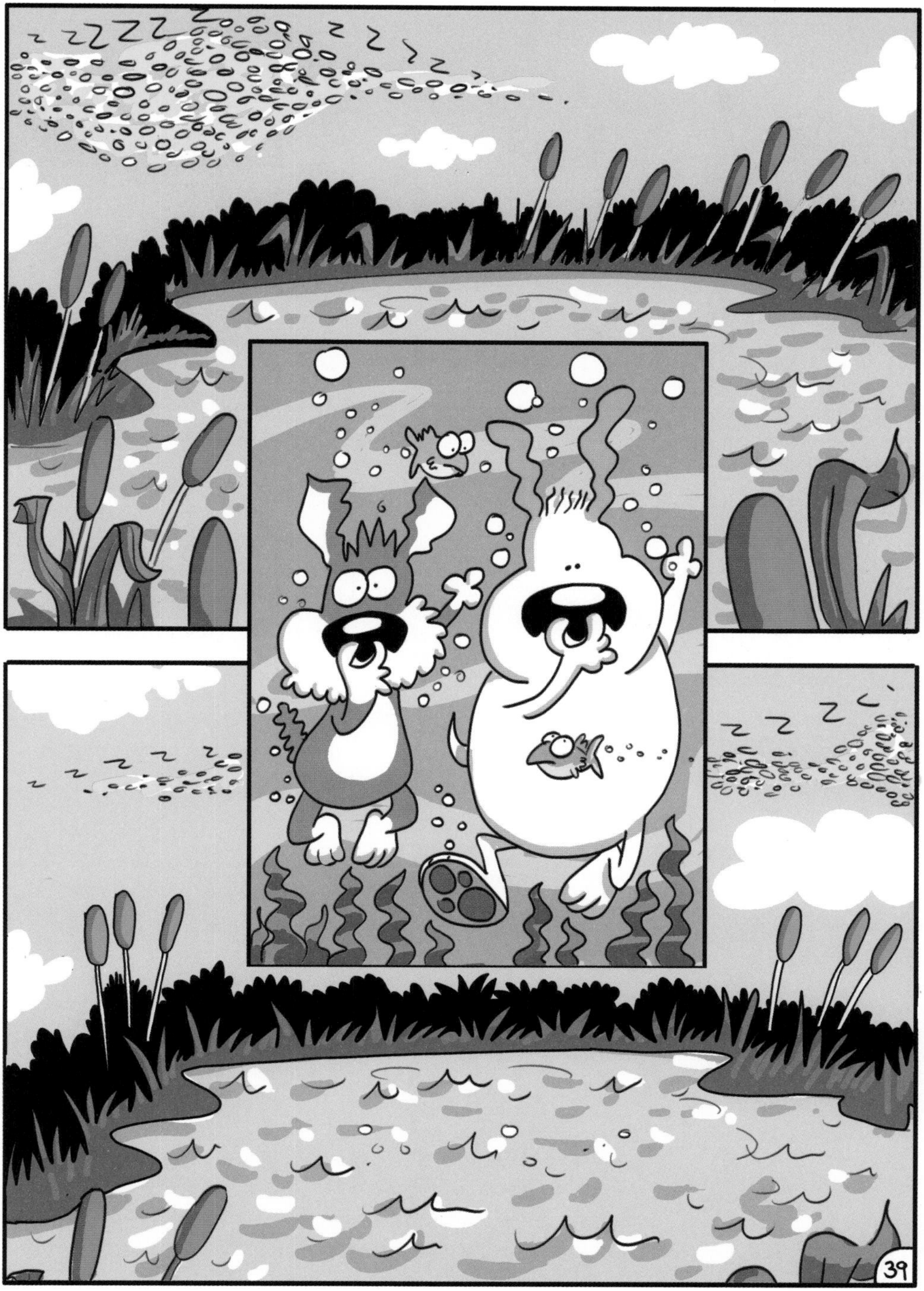

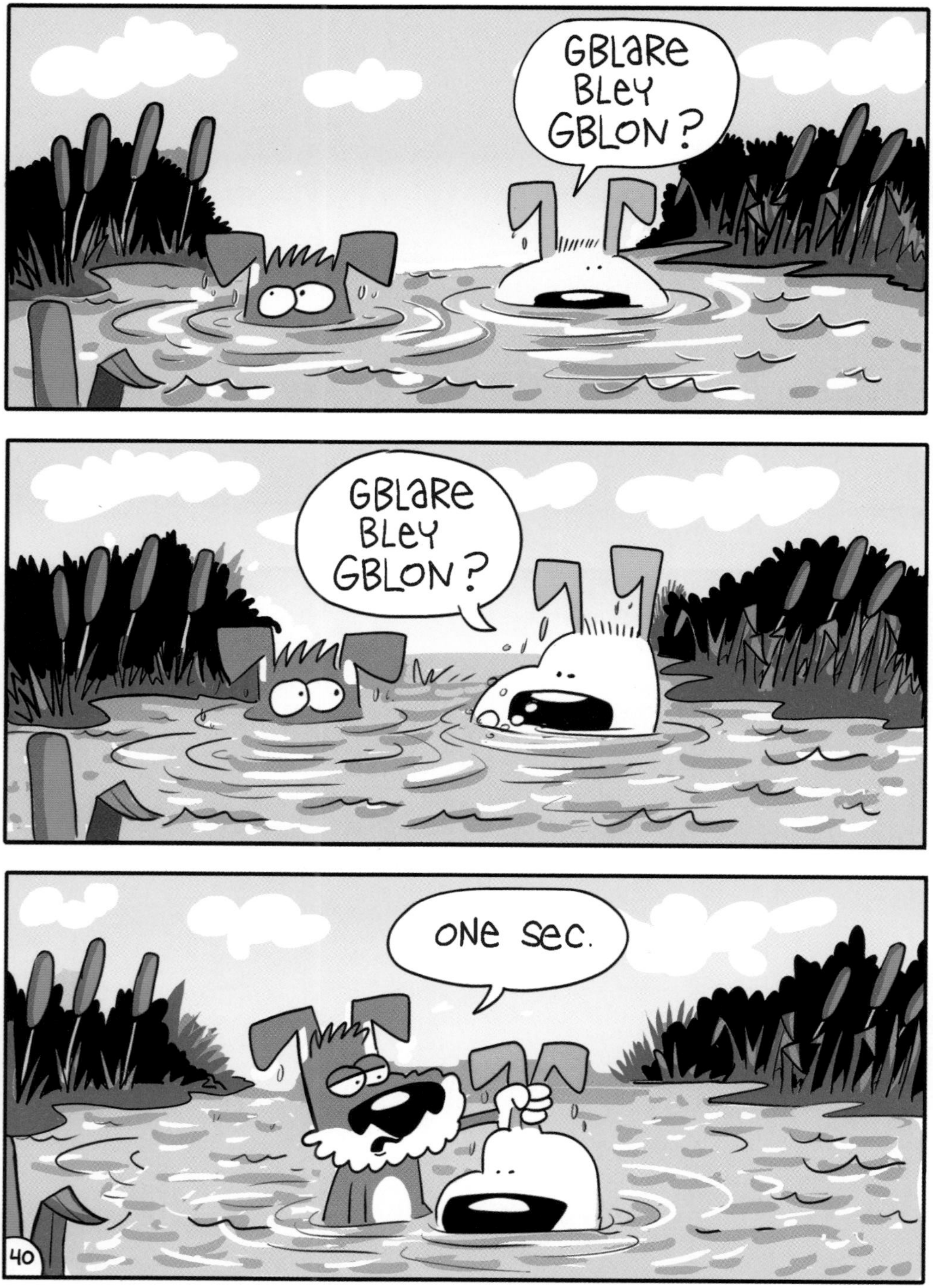
GBLare BLey GBLON?
GBLare BLey GBLON?
one sec.

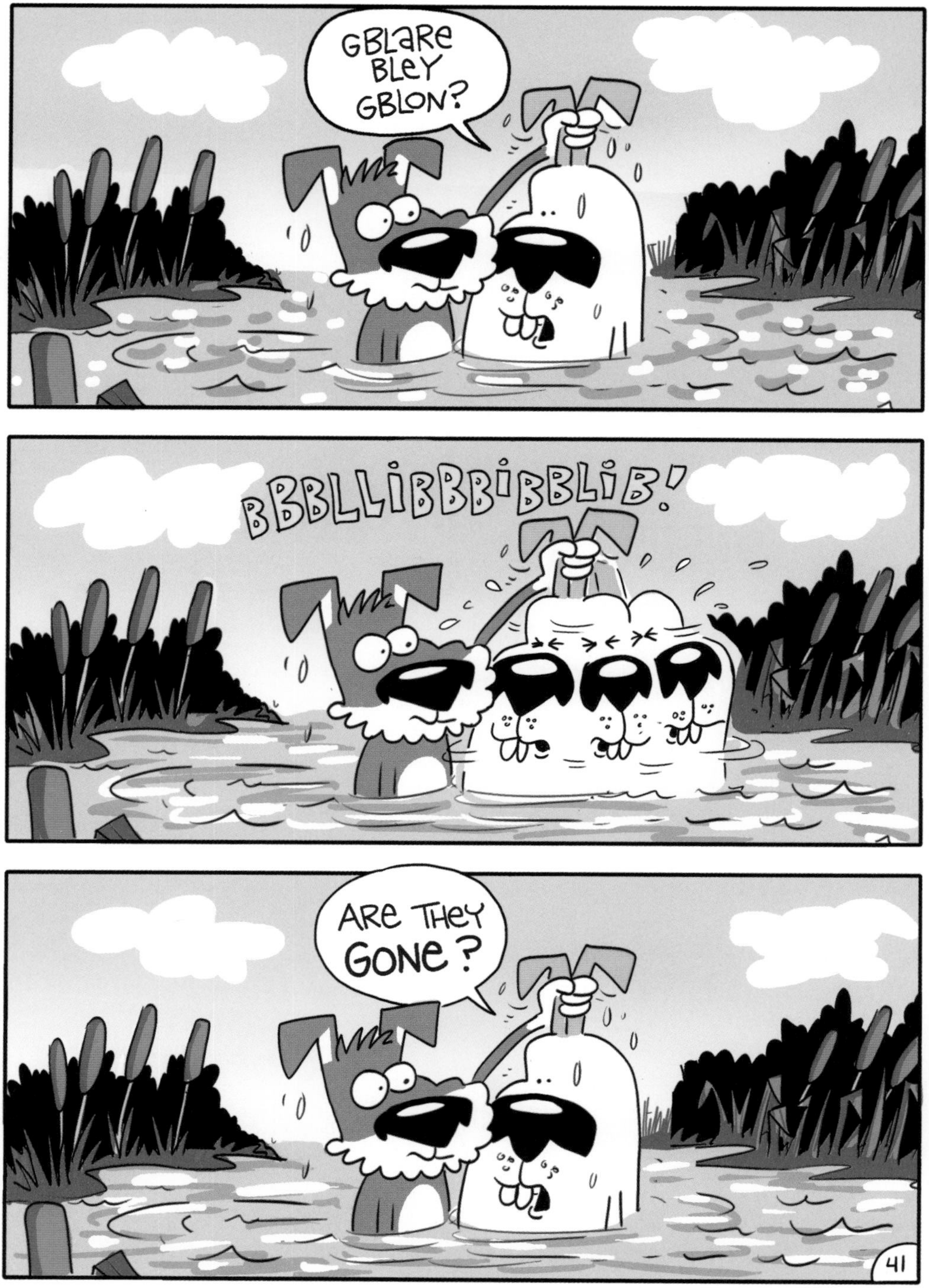
GBLARE BLEY GBLON?
BBBLLIBBBIBBLIB!
ARE THEY GONE?

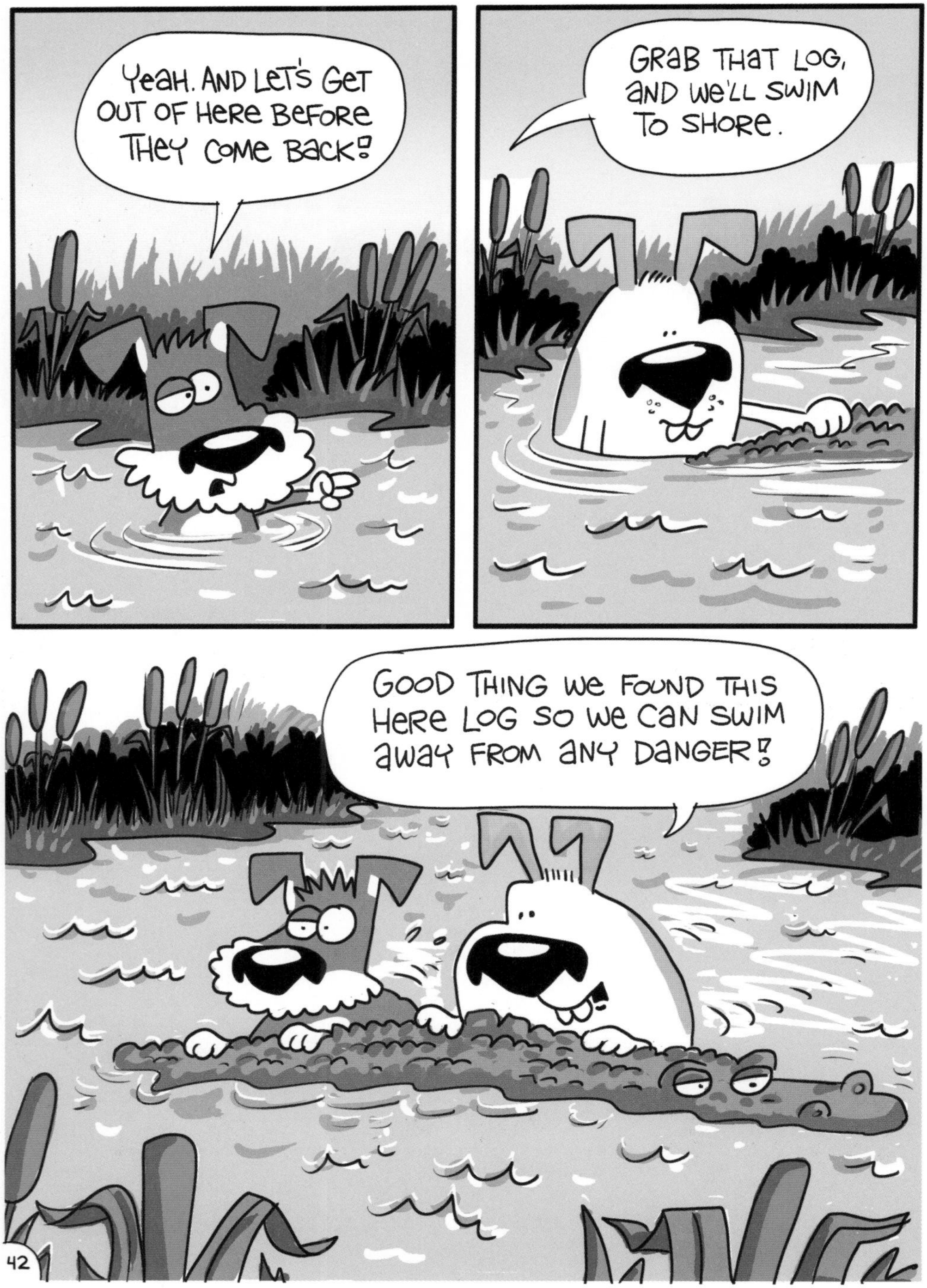
Yeah. AND LET'S GET OUT OF HERE BEFORE THEY COME BACK!
GRAB THAT LOG, AND WE'LL SWIM TO SHORE.
GOOD THING WE FOUND THIS HERE LOG SO WE CAN SWIM AWAY FROM ANY DANGER!

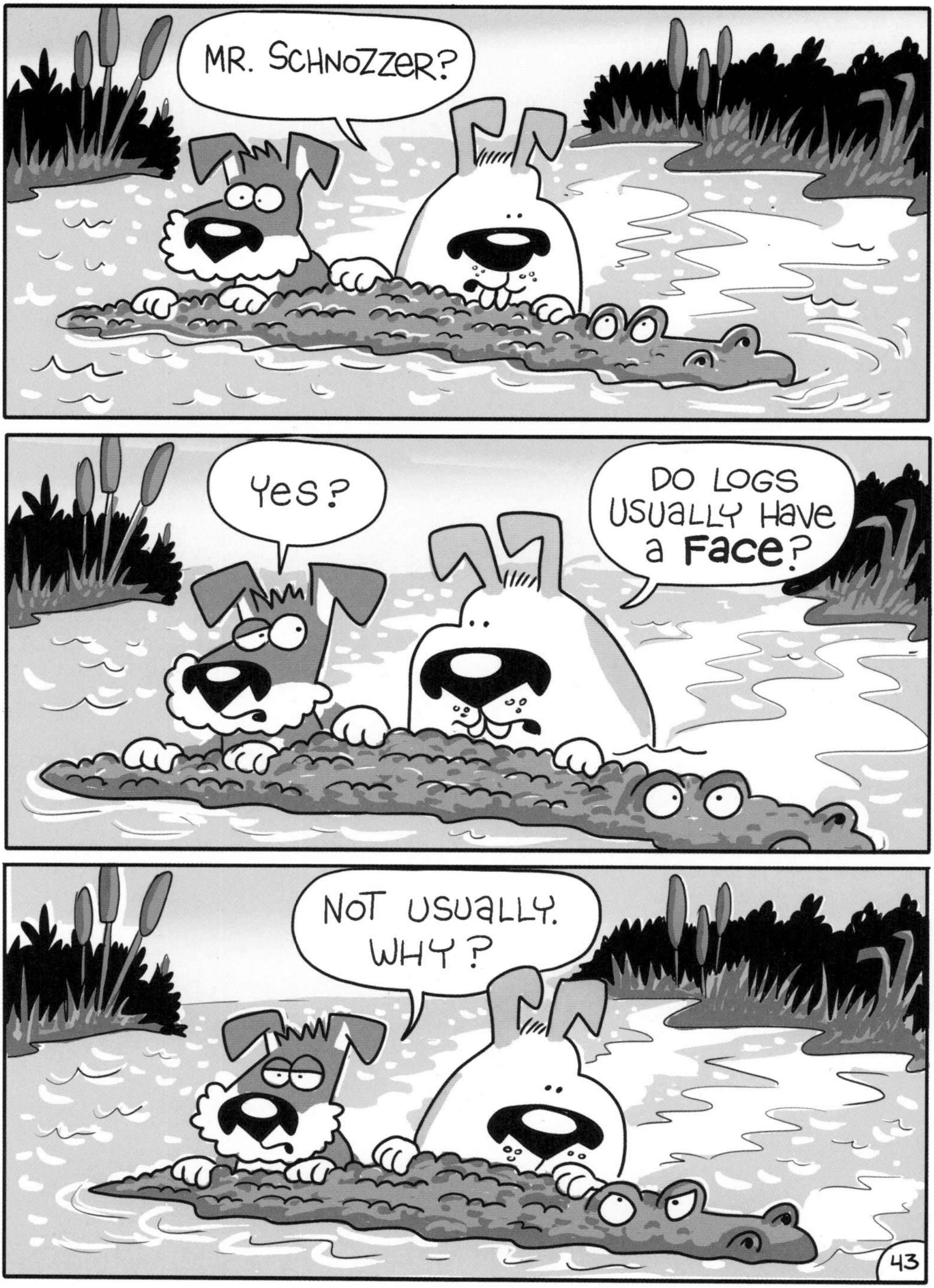
MR. SCHNOZZER?
YES?
DO LOGS USUALLY HAVE A FACE?
NOT USUALLY. WHY?

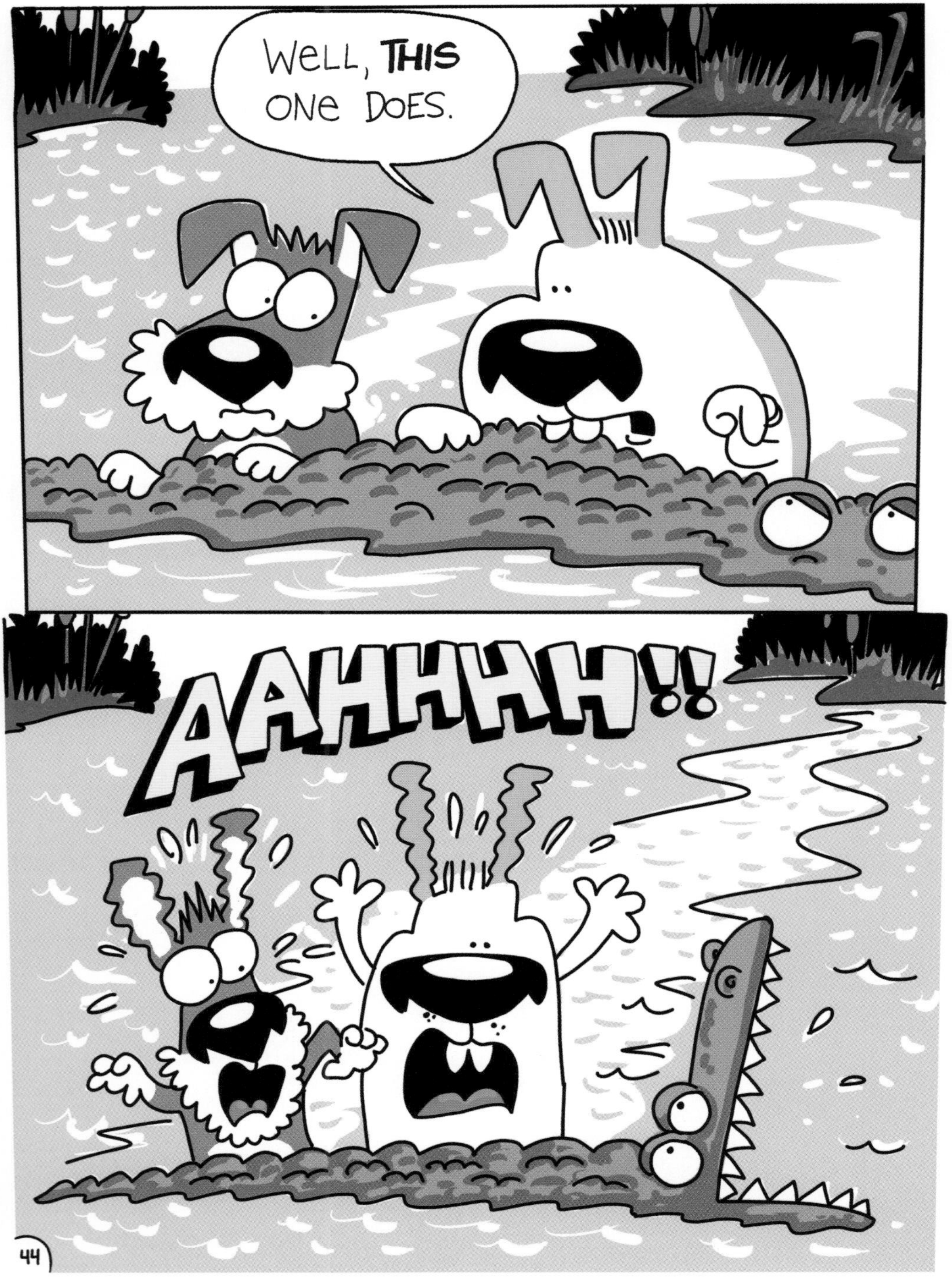
WELL, **THIS** ONE DOES.
AAHHHH!!

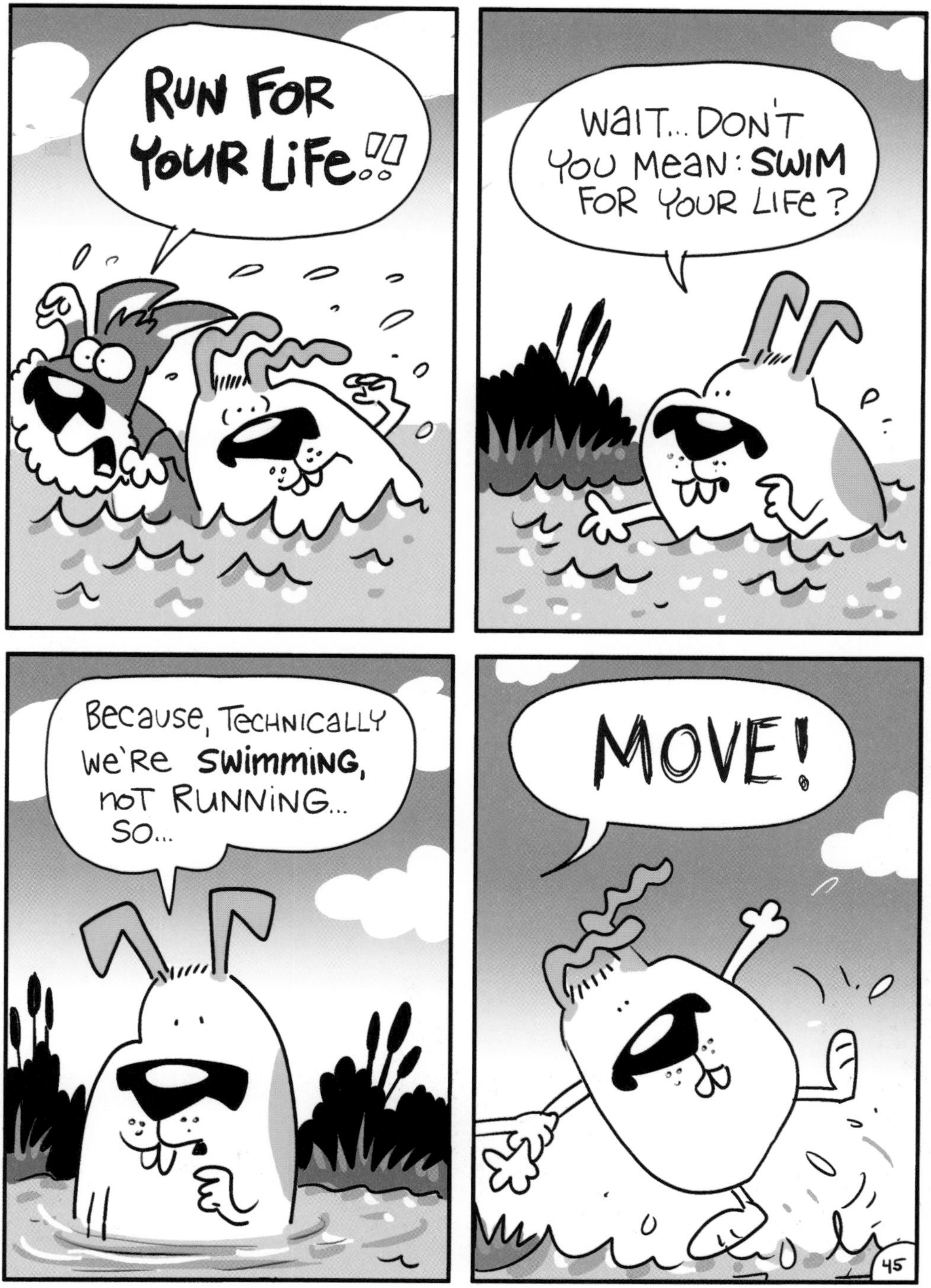
RUN FOR YOUR LIFE!!
WAIT... DON'T YOU MEAN: SWIM FOR YOUR LIFE?
BECAUSE, TECHNICALLY WE'RE SWIMMING, NOT RUNNING... SO...
MOVE!

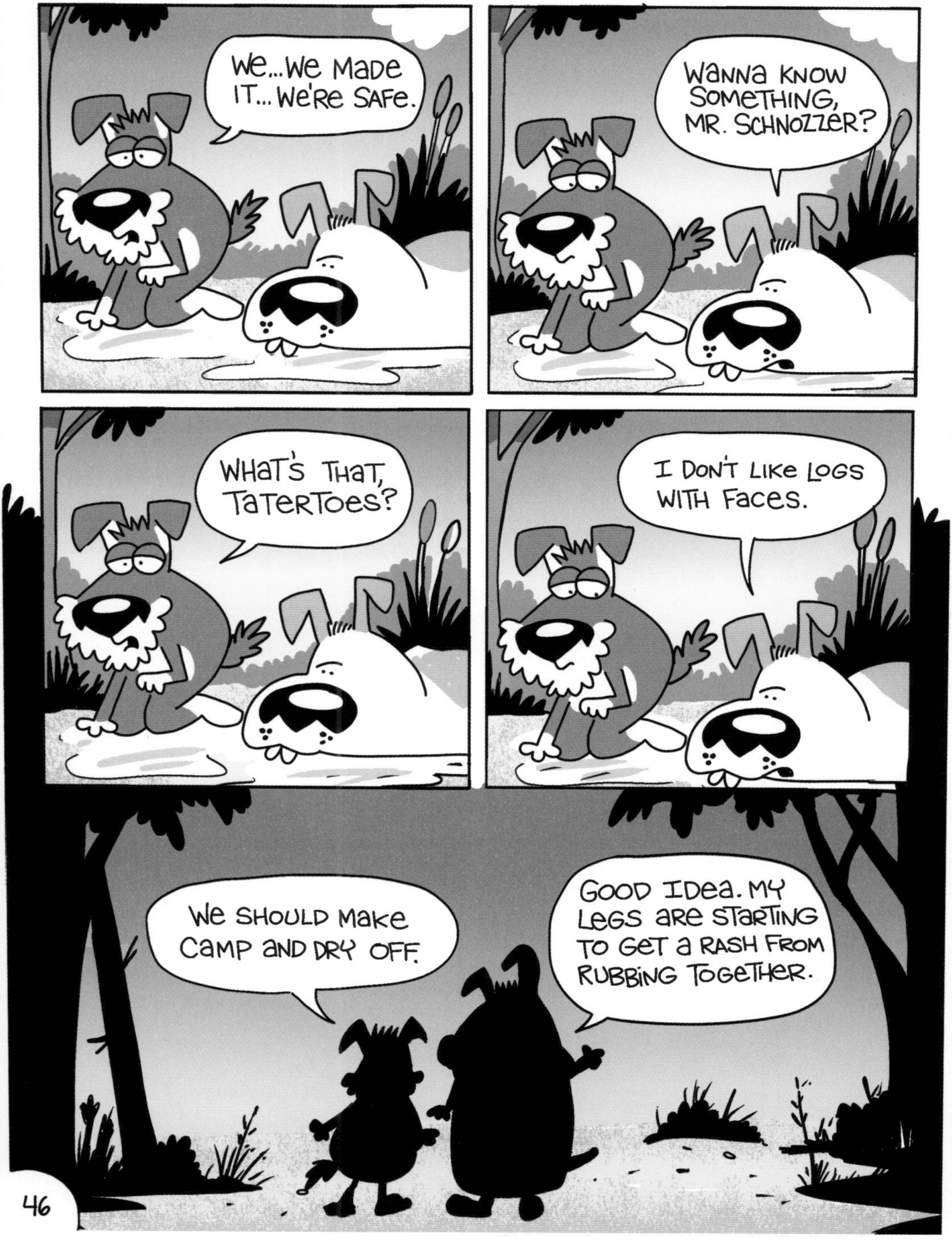

WE...WE MADE IT...WE'RE SAFE.
WANNA KNOW SOMETHING, MR. SCHNOZZER?
WHAT'S THAT, TATERTOES?
I DON'T LIKE LOGS WITH FACES.
WE SHOULD MAKE CAMP AND DRY OFF.
GOOD IDEA. MY LEGS ARE STARTING TO GET A RASH FROM RUBBING TOGETHER.

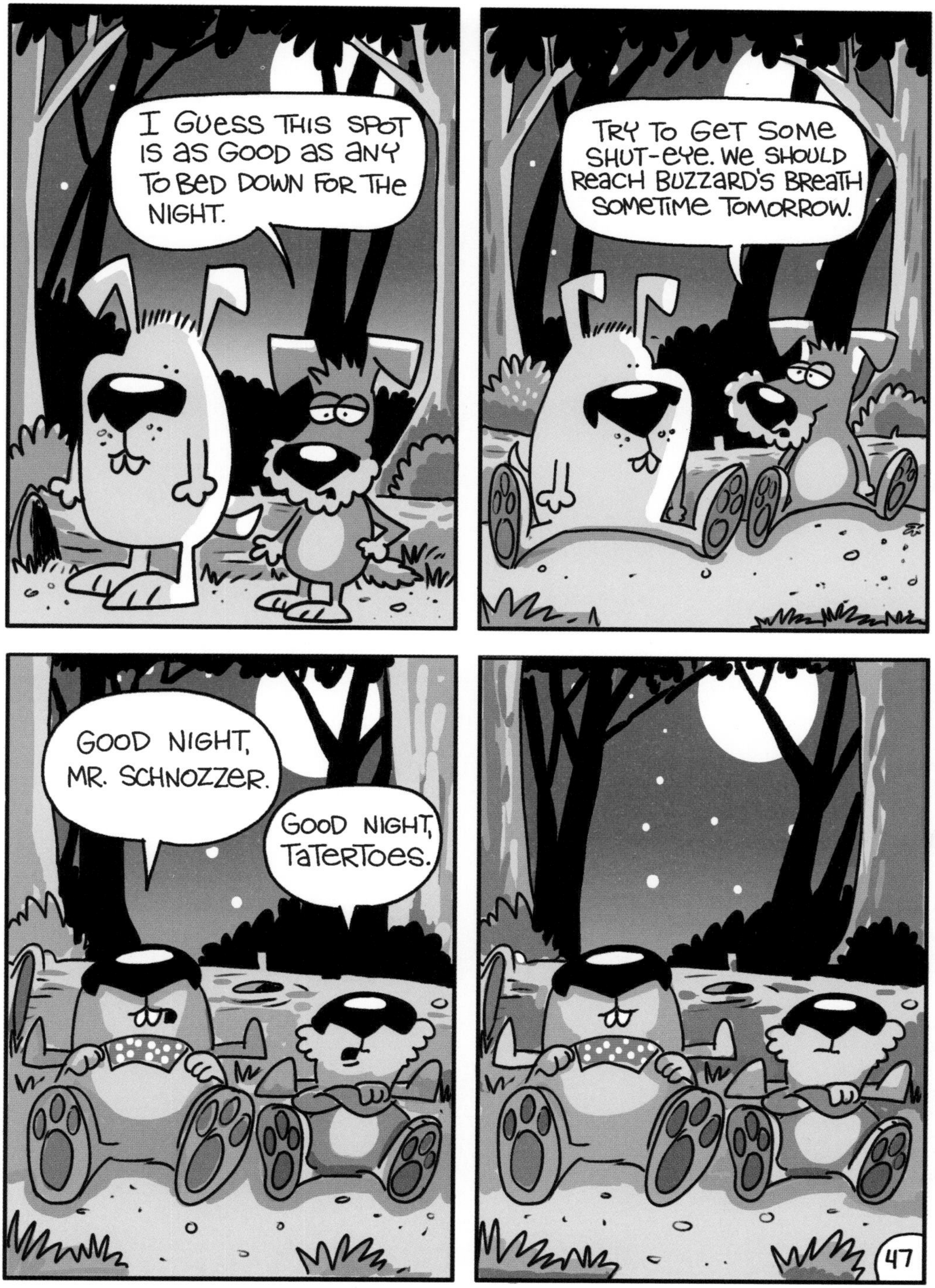
I GUESS THIS SPOT IS AS GOOD AS ANY TO BED DOWN FOR THE NIGHT.
TRY TO GET SOME SHUT-EYE. WE SHOULD REACH BUZZARD'S BREATH SOMETIME TOMORROW.
GOOD NIGHT, MR. SCHNOZZER.
GOOD NIGHT, TATERTOES.

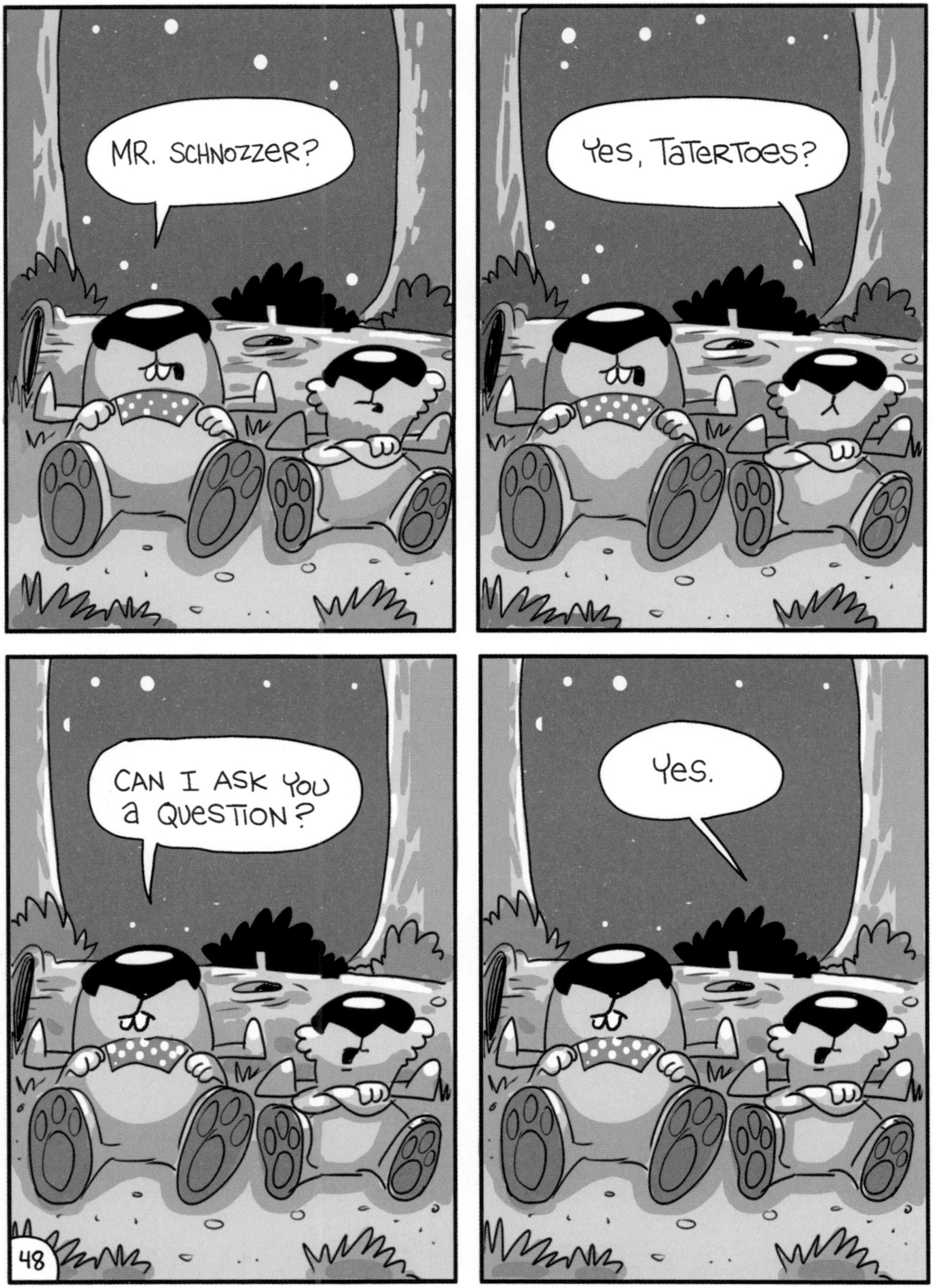
MR. SCHNOZZER?
YES, TATERTOES?
CAN I ASK YOU A QUESTION?
YES.

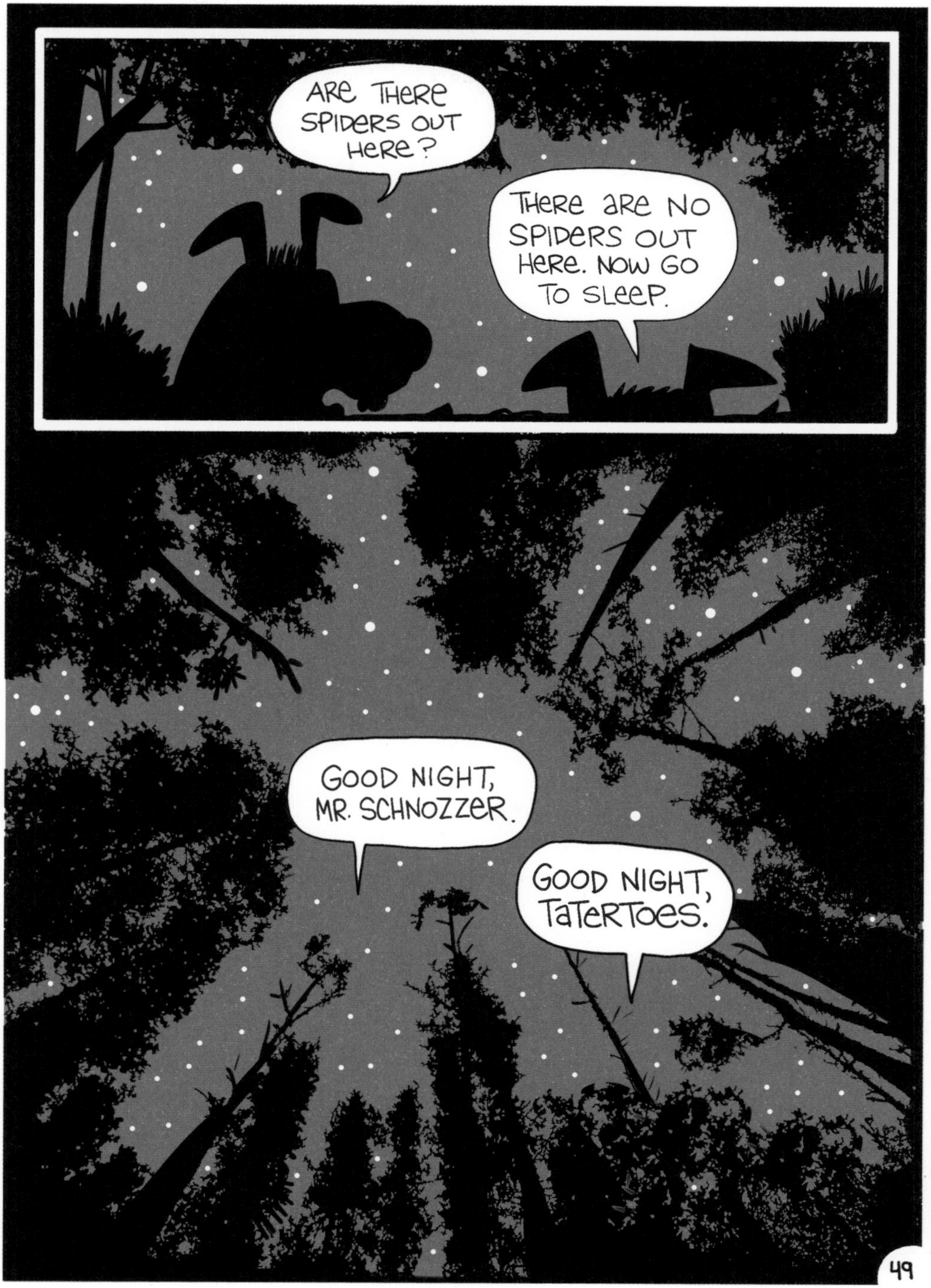
ARE THERE SPIDERS OUT HERE?
THERE ARE NO SPIDERS OUT HERE. NOW GO TO SLEEP.
GOOD NIGHT, MR. SCHNOZZER.
GOOD NIGHT, TATERTOES.

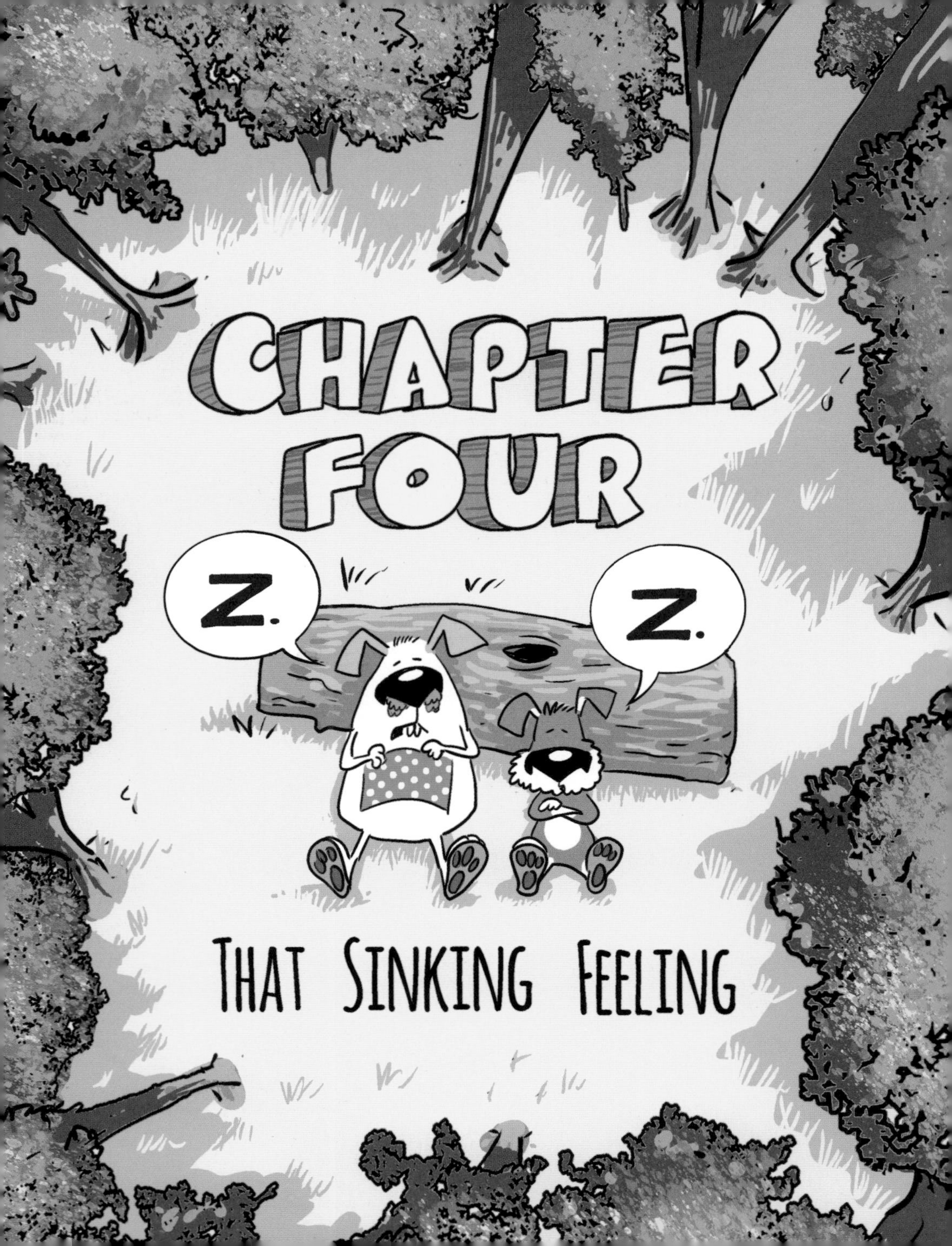
CHAPTER FOUR
Z.
Z.
THAT SINKING FEELING

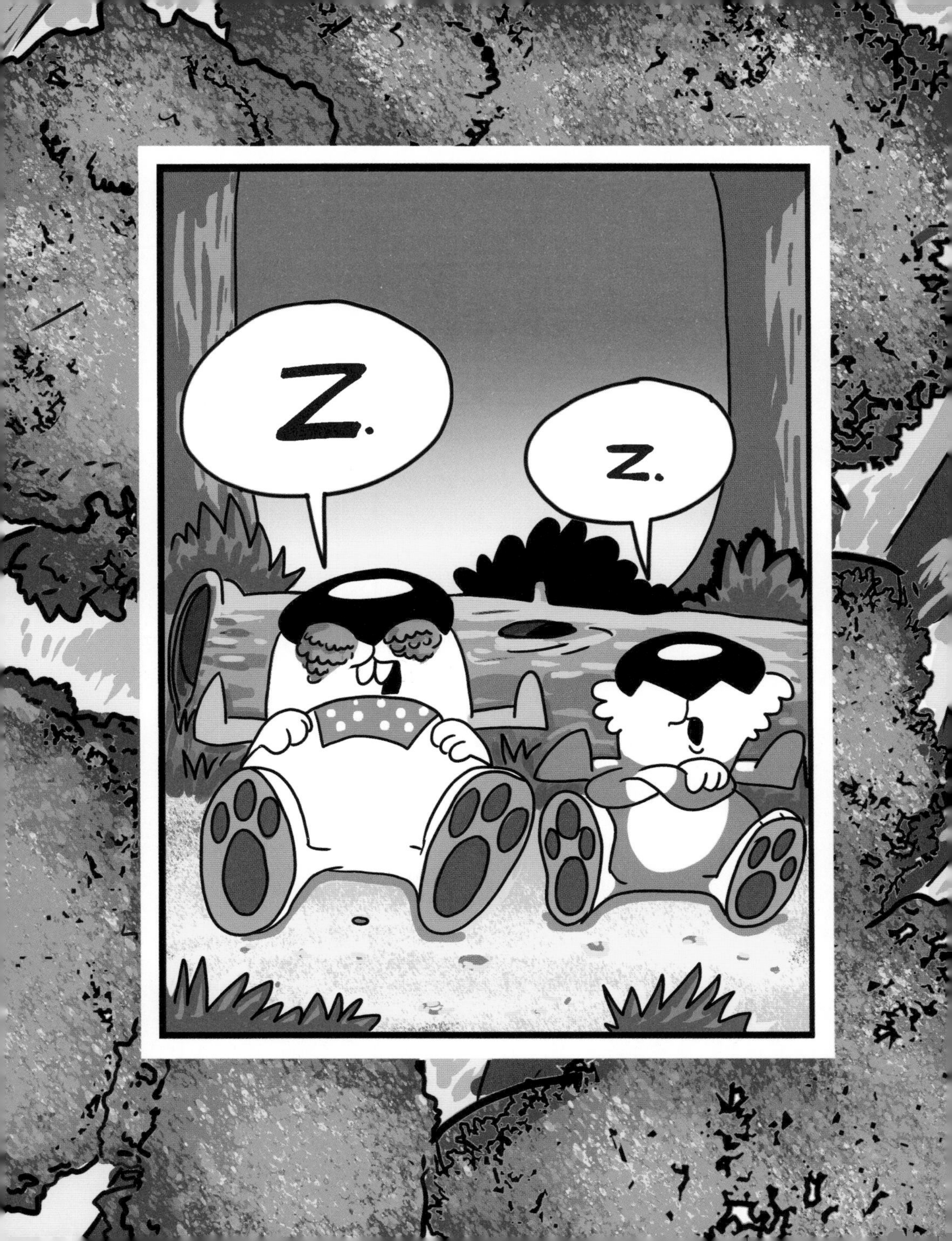
Z.
z.

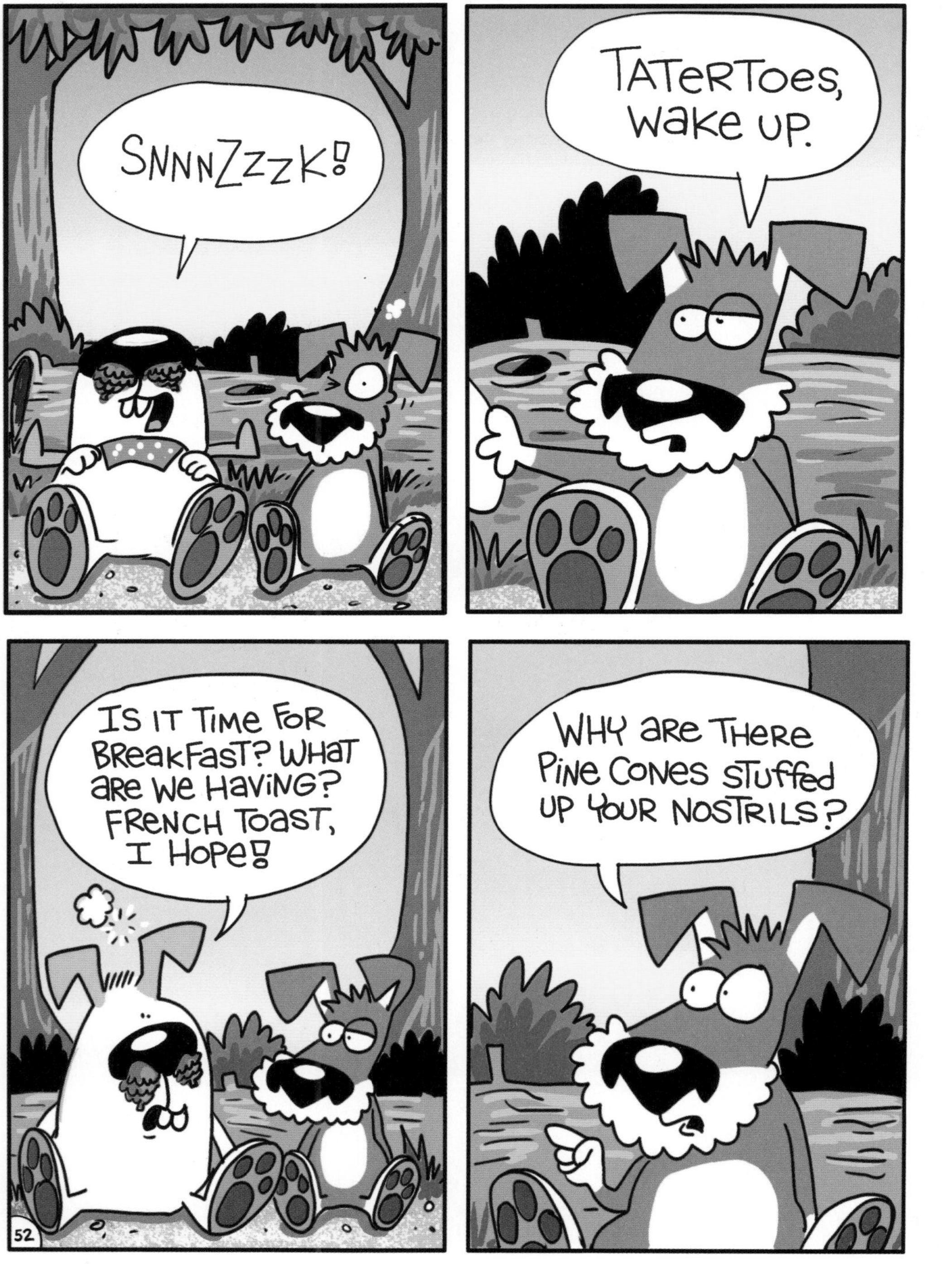
SNNNZzzK!
TATerToes, wake up.
IS IT TIME FOR BREAKFAST? WHAT ARE WE HAVING? FRENCH TOAST, I HOPE!
WHY are There Pine Cones stuffed up your nostrils?

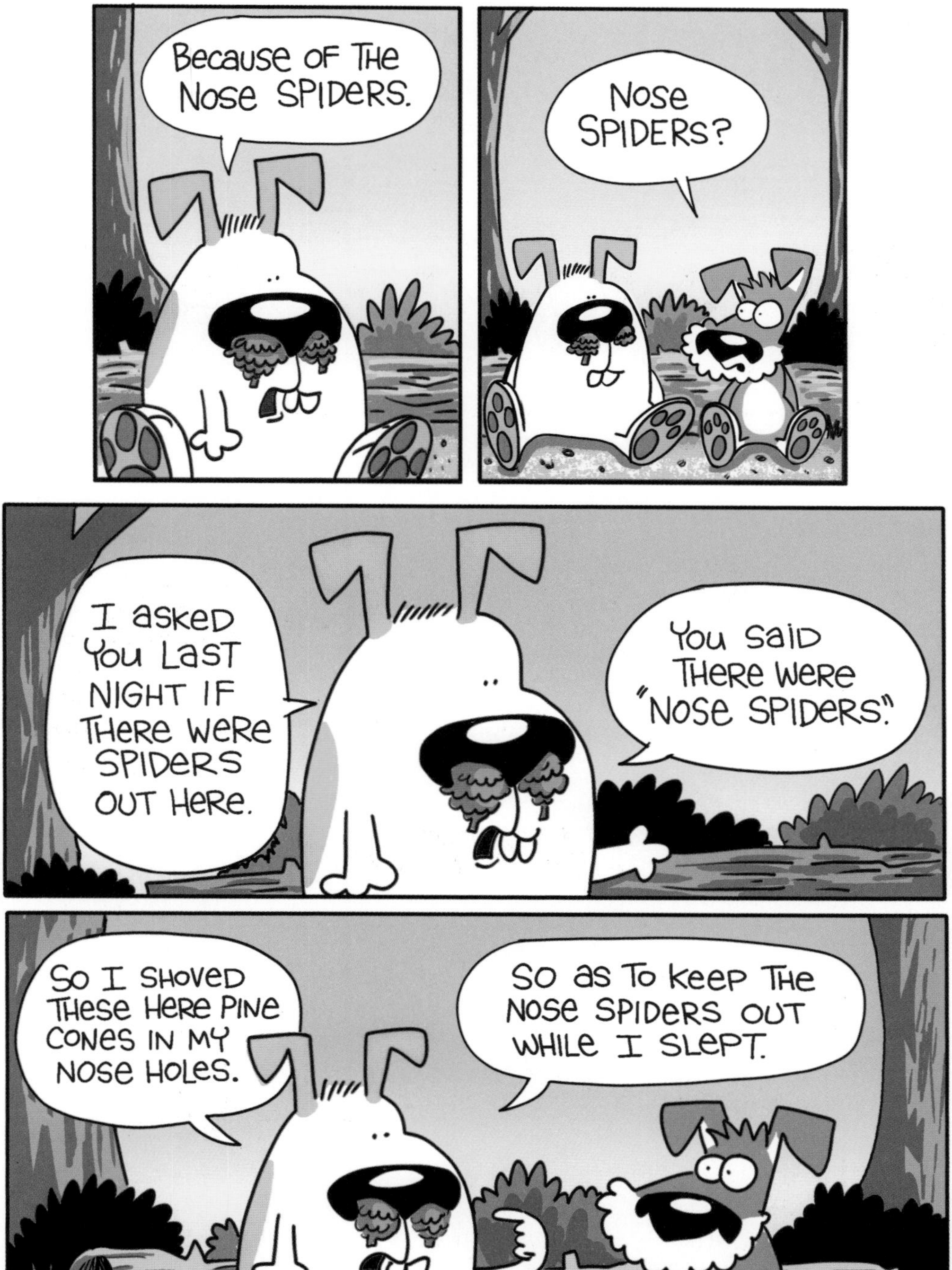
Because of The Nose SPIDERS.
Nose SPIDERS?
I asked You Last NIGHT IF There were SPIDERS OUT Here.
You said There were "Nose SPIDERS."
So I SHOVED These Here PINe CONes IN MY Nose Holes.
So as To keep The Nose SPIDERS OUT WHILe I SLePT.

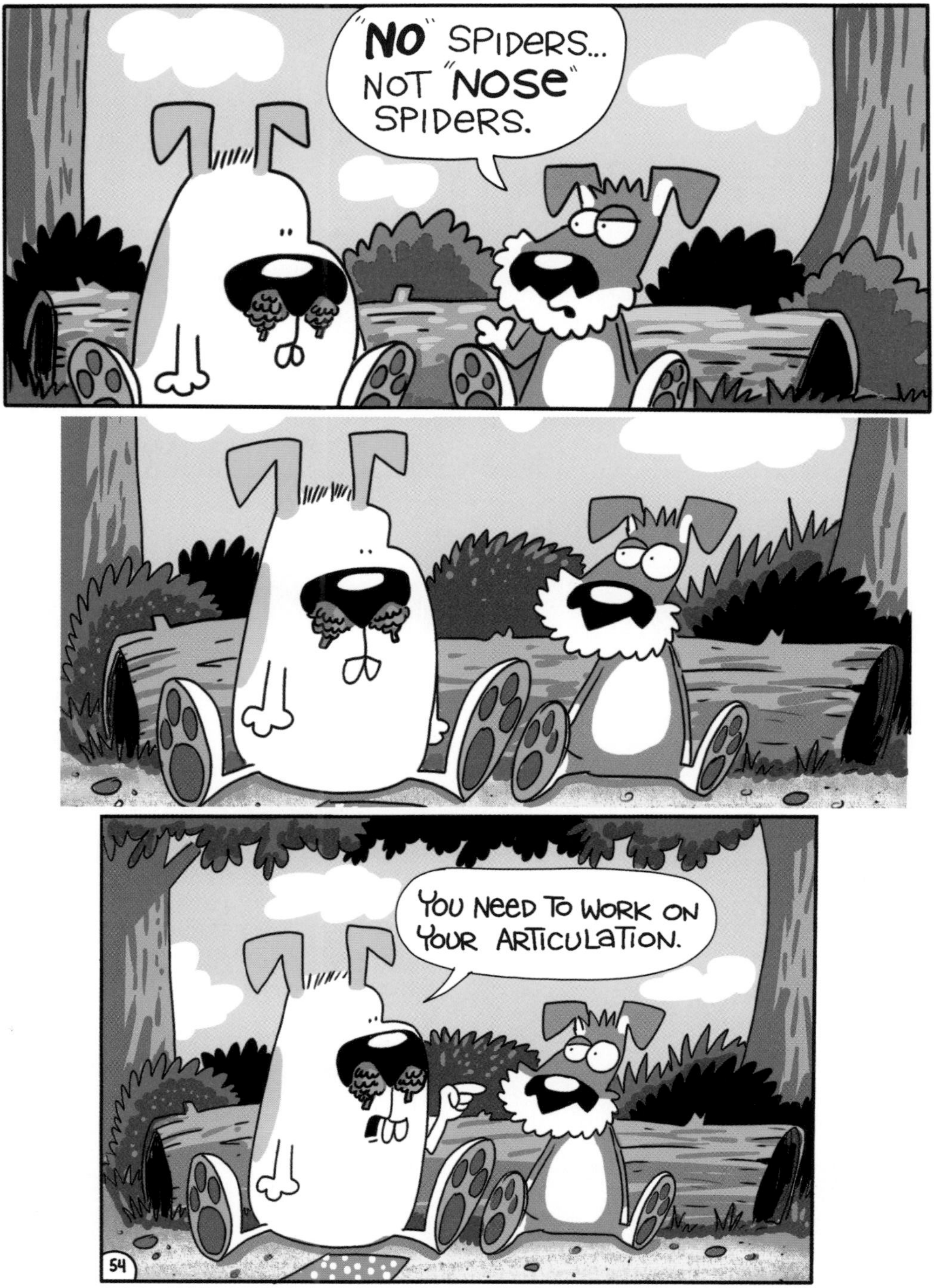
"NO" SPIDERS... NOT "NOSE" SPIDERS.
YOU NEED TO WORK ON YOUR ARTICULATION.

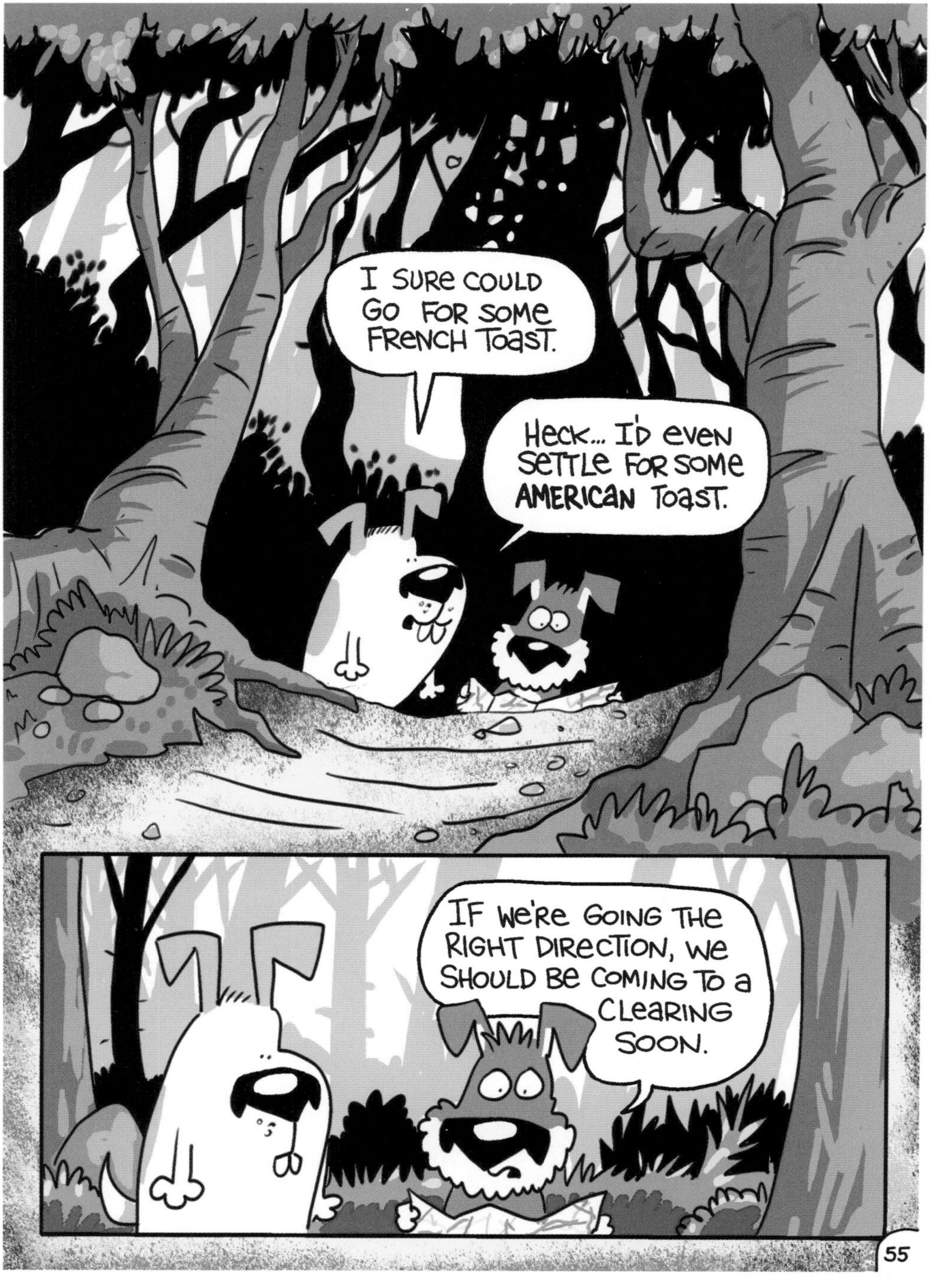
I SURE COULD GO FOR SOME FRENCH TOAST.
HECK... I'D EVEN SETTLE FOR SOME AMERICAN TOAST.
IF WE'RE GOING THE RIGHT DIRECTION, WE SHOULD BE COMING TO A CLEARING SOON.

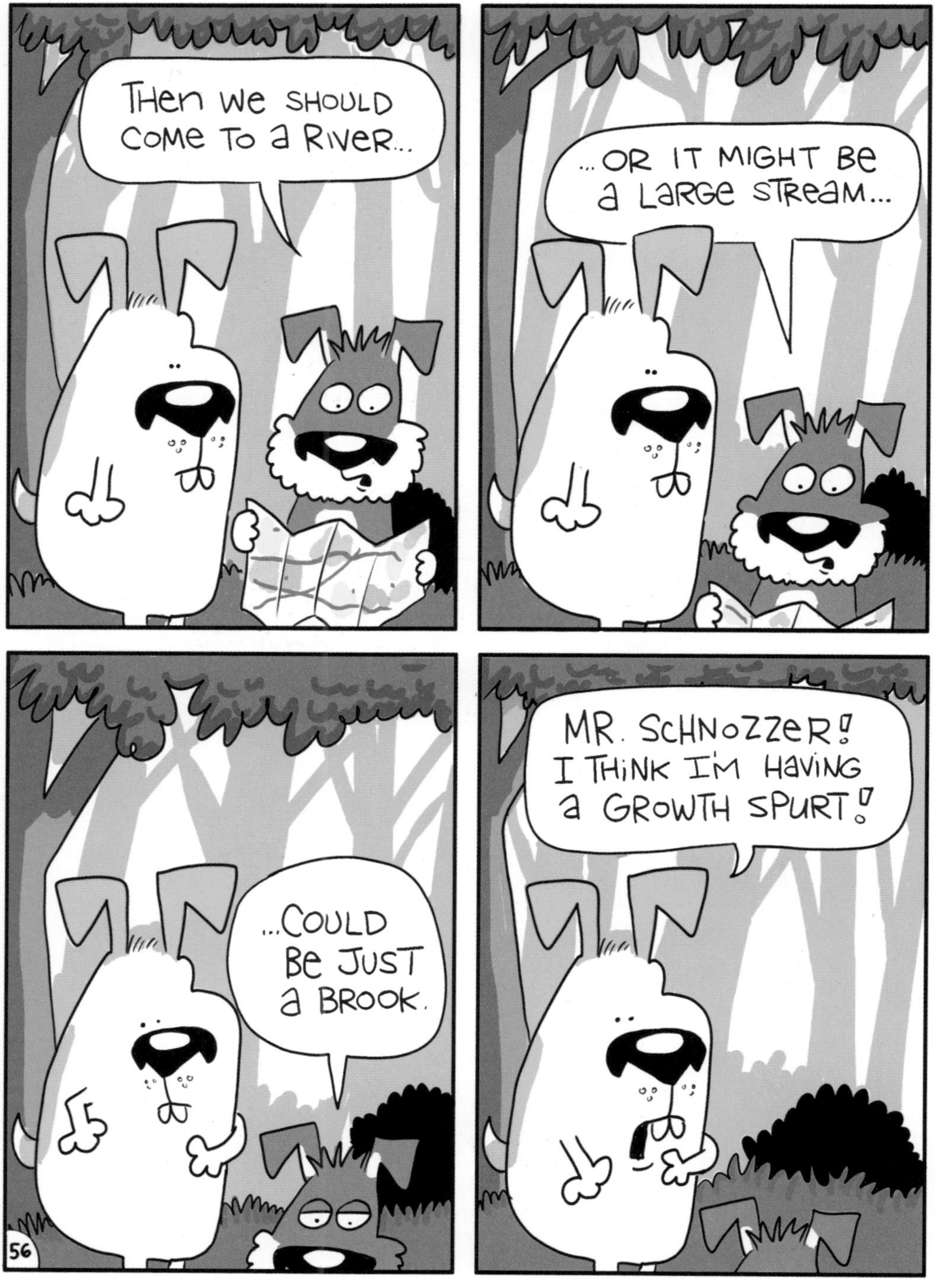
THEN WE SHOULD COME TO A RIVER...
...OR IT MIGHT BE A LARGE STREAM...
...COULD BE JUST A BROOK.
MR. SCHNOZZER! I THINK I'M HAVING A GROWTH SPURT!

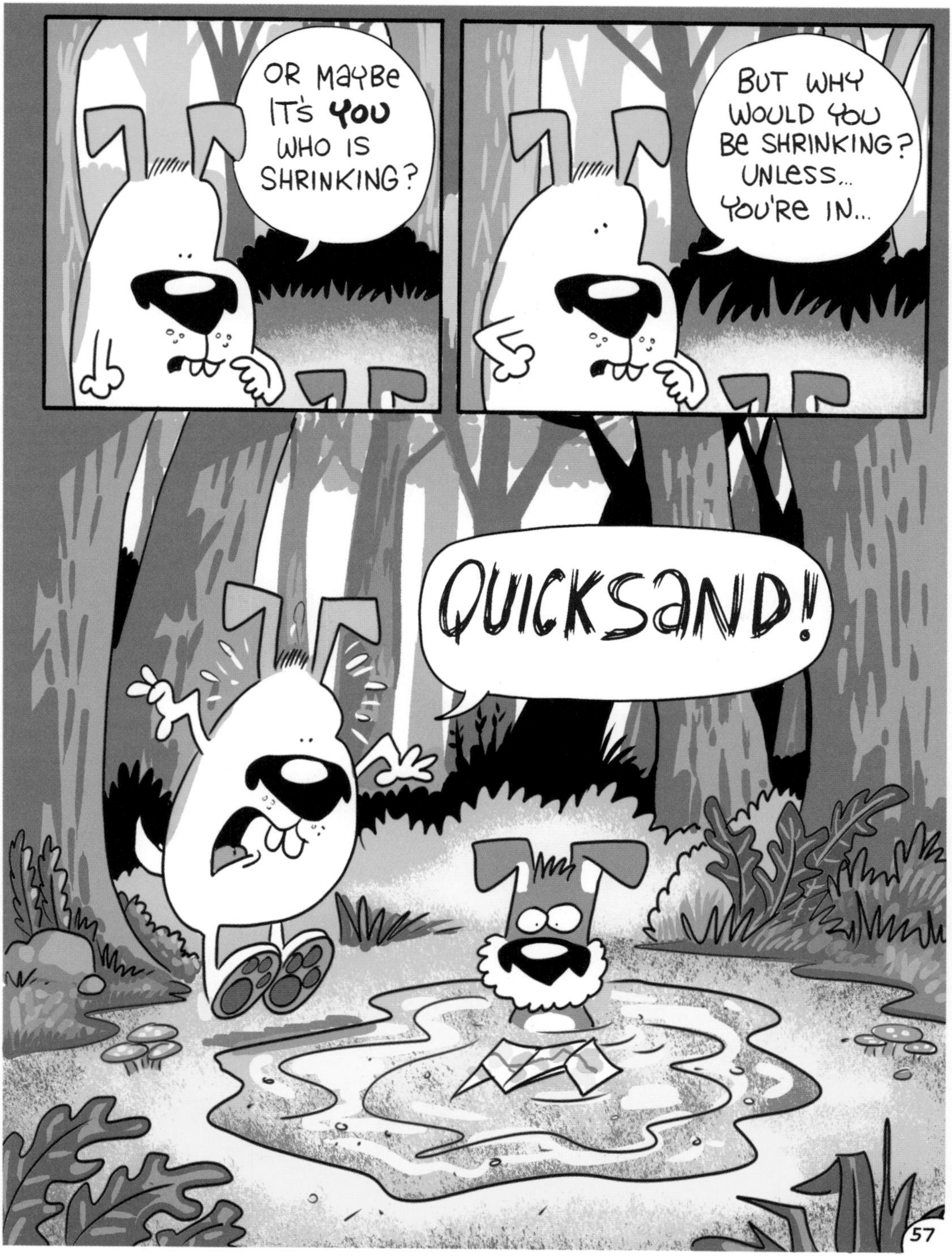
OR MAYBE IT'S **YOU** WHO IS SHRINKING?
BUT WHY WOULD YOU BE SHRINKING? UNLESS... YOU'RE IN...
QUICKSAND!

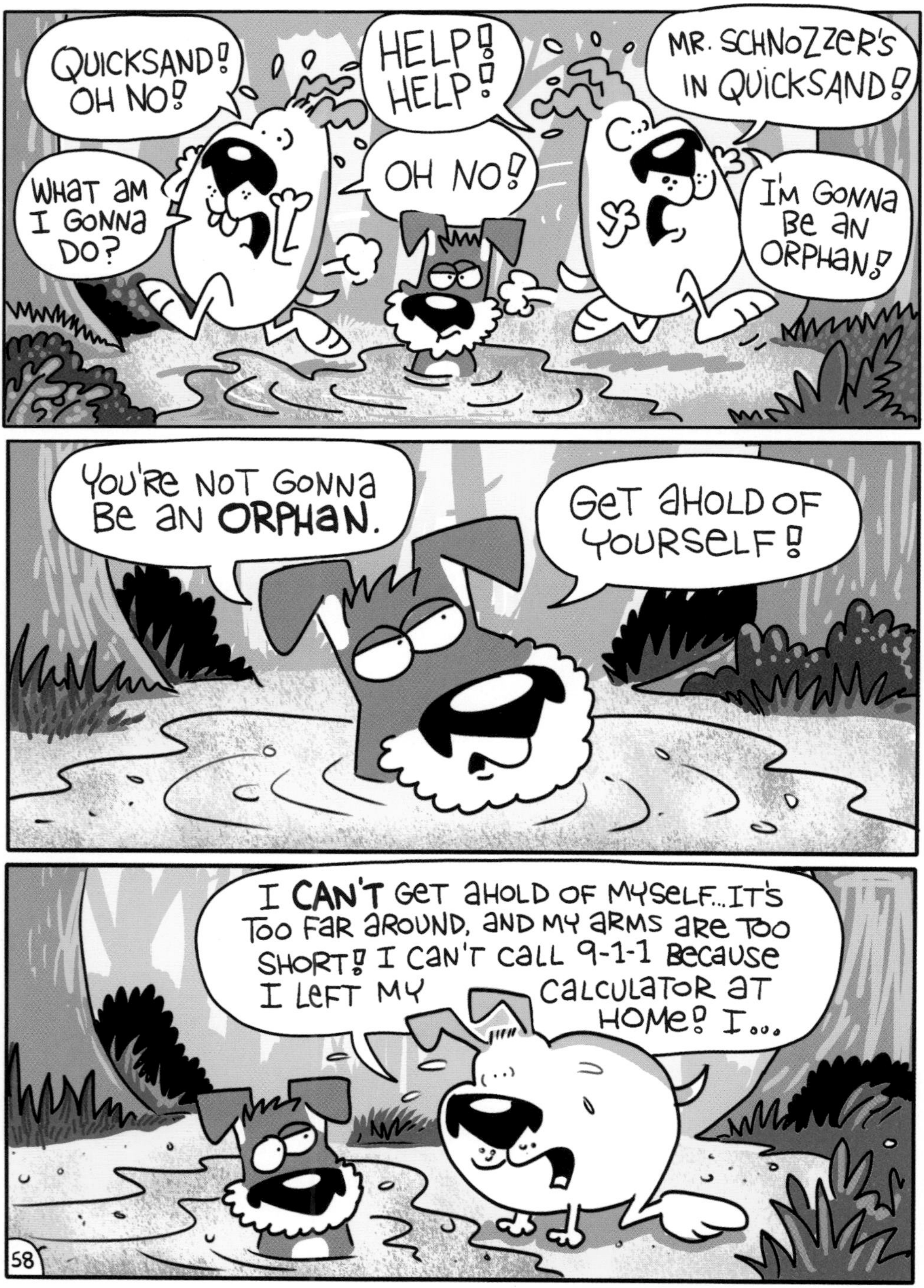
QUICKSAND! OH NO!
WHAT AM I GONNA DO?
HELP! HELP!
OH NO!
MR. SCHNOZZER'S IN QUICKSAND!
I'M GONNA BE AN ORPHAN!
YOU'RE NOT GONNA BE AN **ORPHAN**.
GET AHOLD OF YOURSELF!
I **CAN'T** GET AHOLD OF MYSELF...IT'S TOO FAR AROUND, AND MY ARMS ARE TOO SHORT! I CAN'T CALL 9-1-1 BECAUSE I LEFT MY CALCULATOR AT HOME! I...

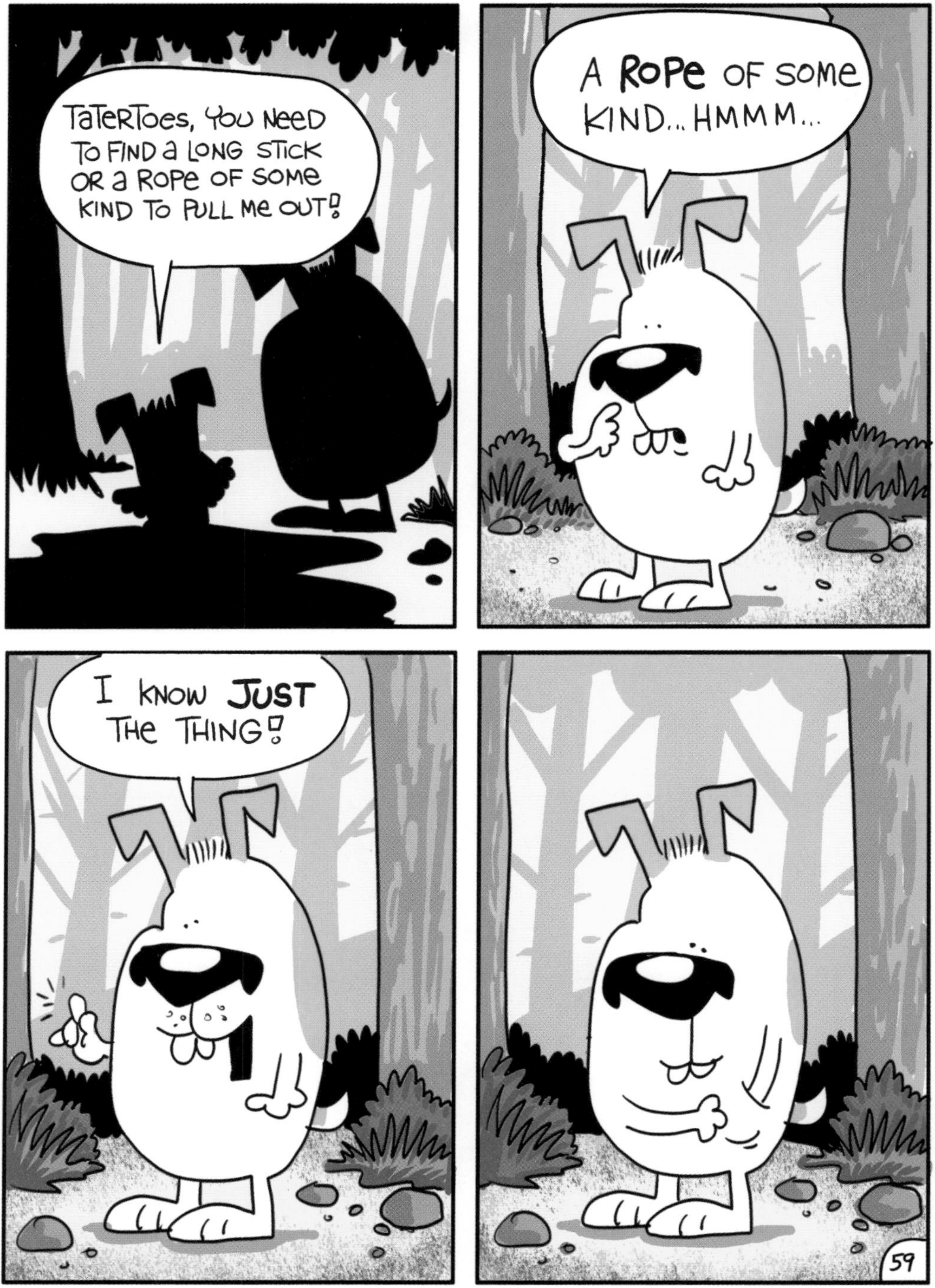
TATERTOES, YOU NEED TO FIND A LONG STICK OR A ROPE OF SOME KIND TO PULL ME OUT!
A **ROPE** OF SOME KIND... HMMM...
I KNOW **JUST** THE THING!

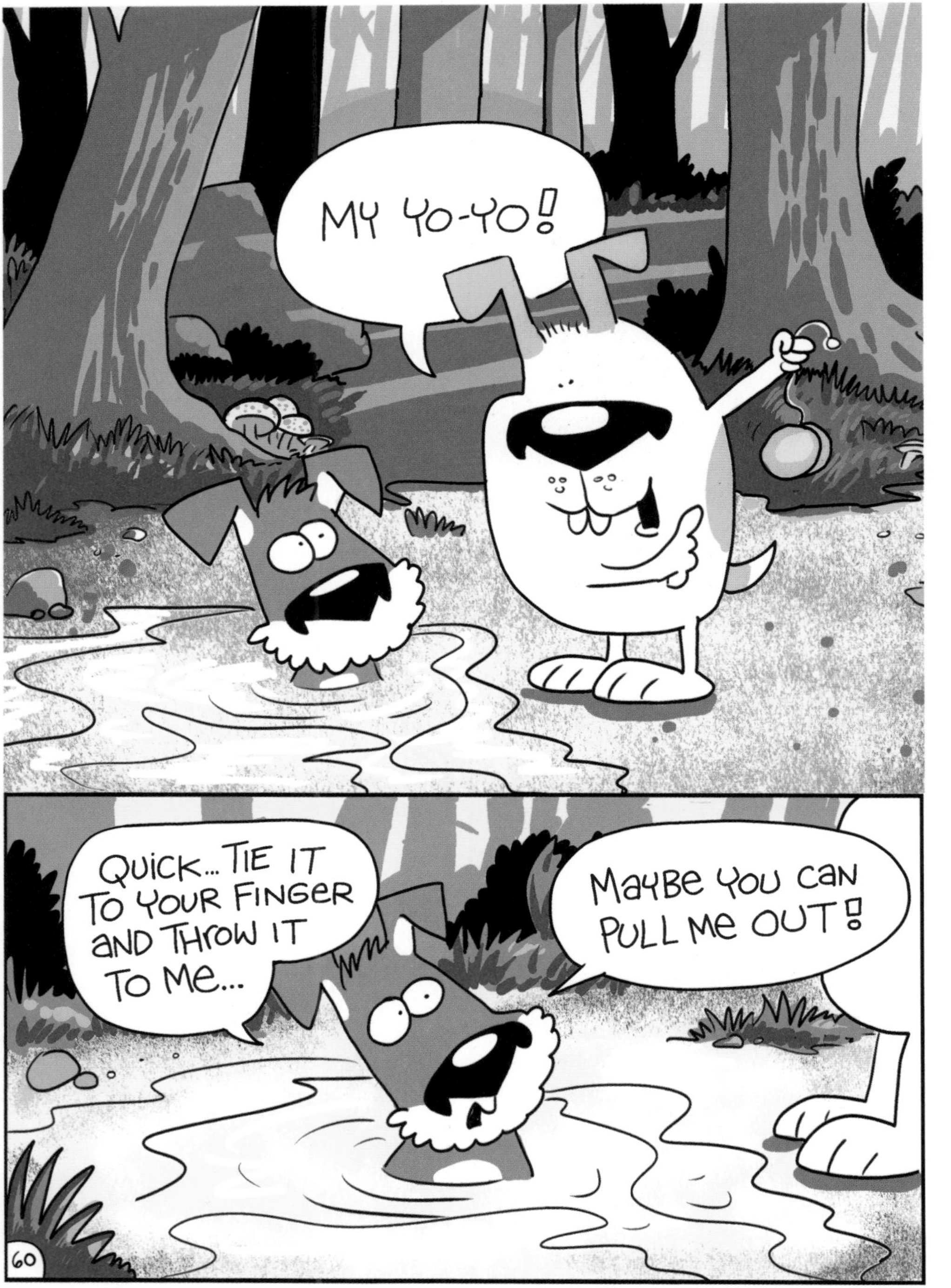
MY YO-YO!
QUICK... TIE IT TO YOUR FINGER AND THROW IT TO ME...
MAYBE YOU CAN PULL ME OUT!

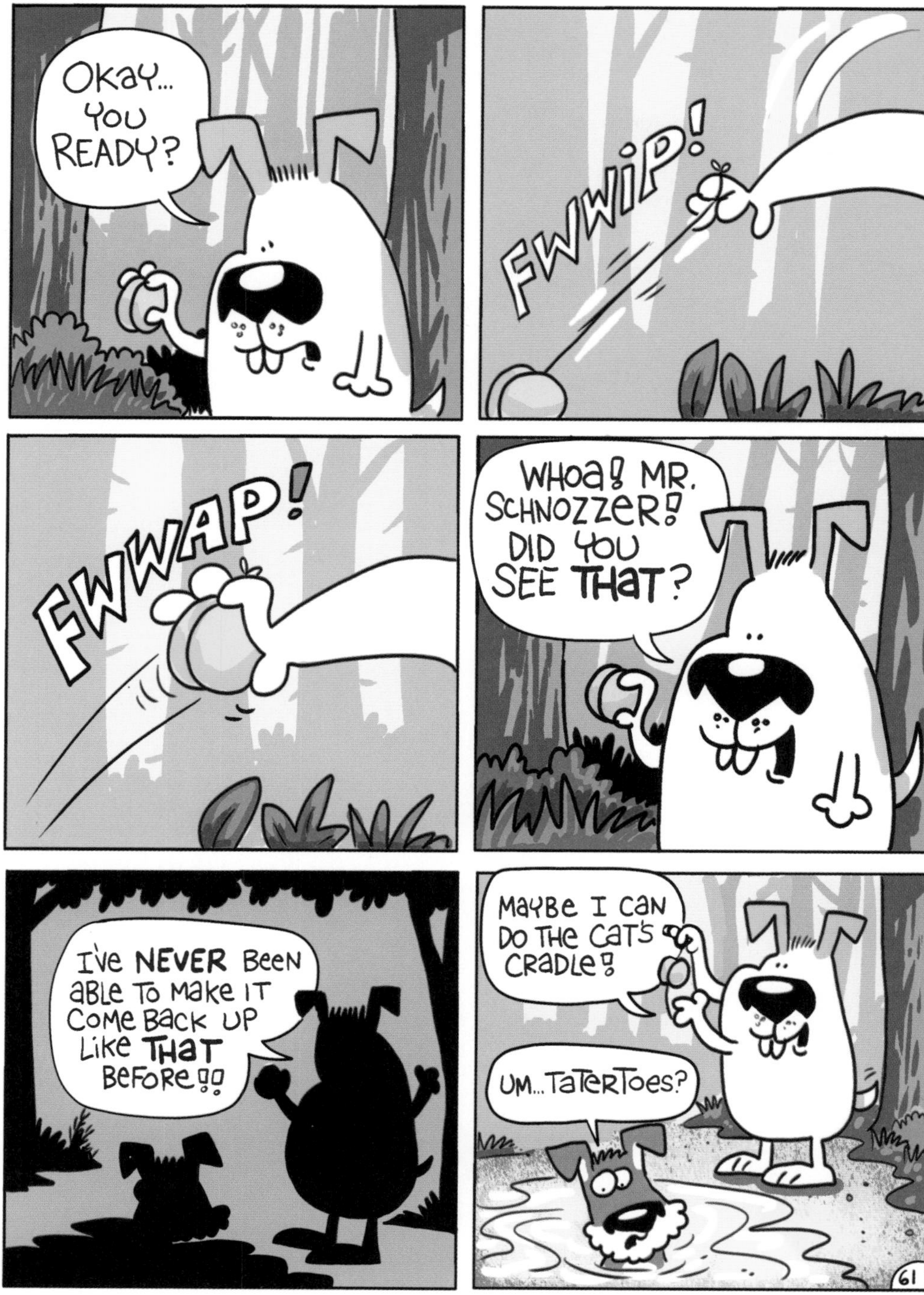
OKAY... YOU READY?
FWWIP!
FWWAP!
WHOA! MR. SCHNOZZER! DID YOU SEE THAT?
I'VE NEVER BEEN ABLE TO MAKE IT COME BACK UP LIKE THAT BEFORE!!
MAYBE I CAN DO THE CAT'S CRADLE!
UM... TATERTOES?

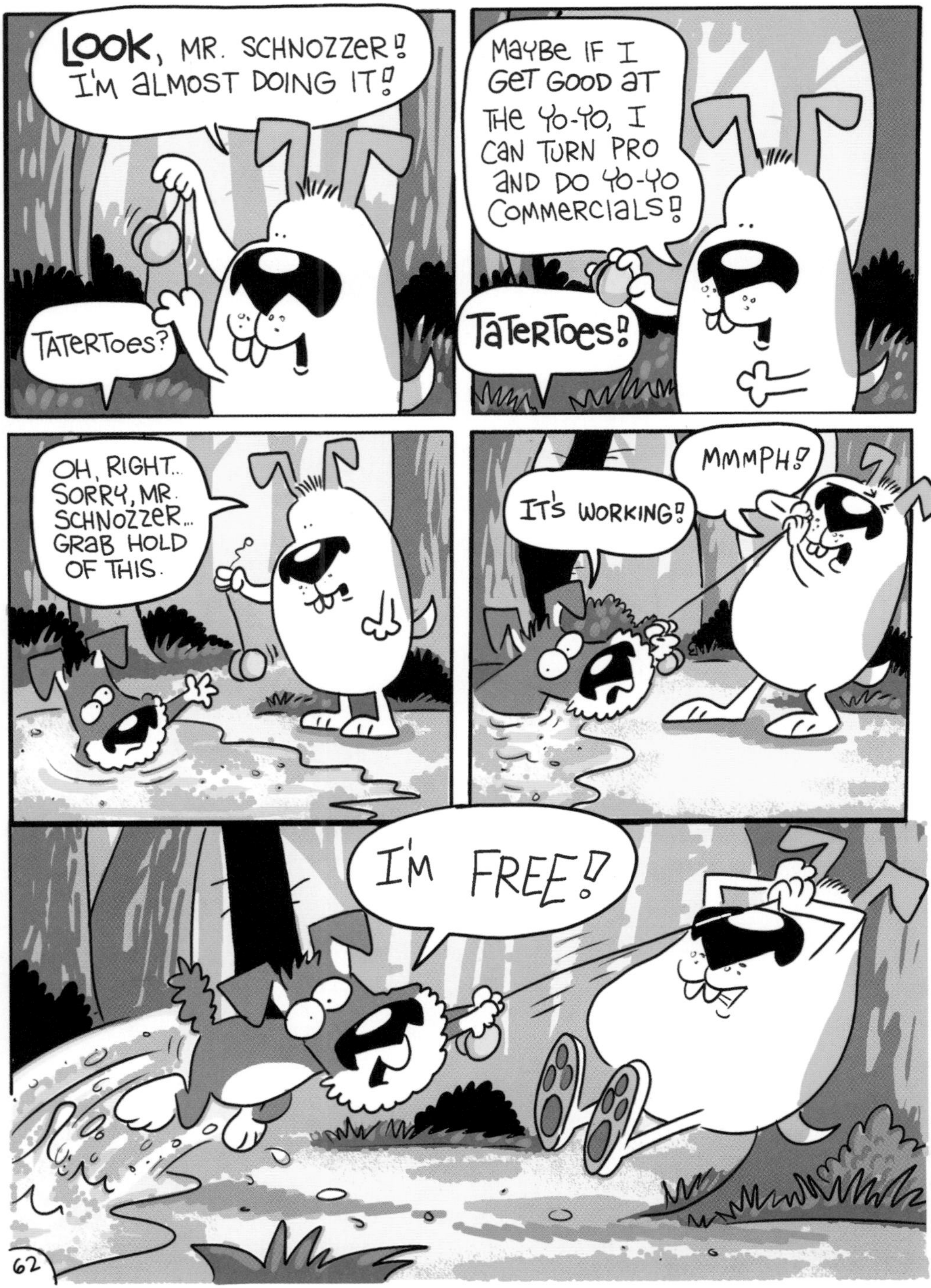
LOOK, MR. SCHNOZZER! I'M ALMOST DOING IT!
TATERTOES?
MAYBE IF I GET GOOD AT THE YO-YO, I CAN TURN PRO AND DO YO-YO COMMERCIALS!
TATERTOES!
OH, RIGHT... SORRY, MR. SCHNOZZER... GRAB HOLD OF THIS.
MMMPH!
IT'S WORKING!
I'M FREE!

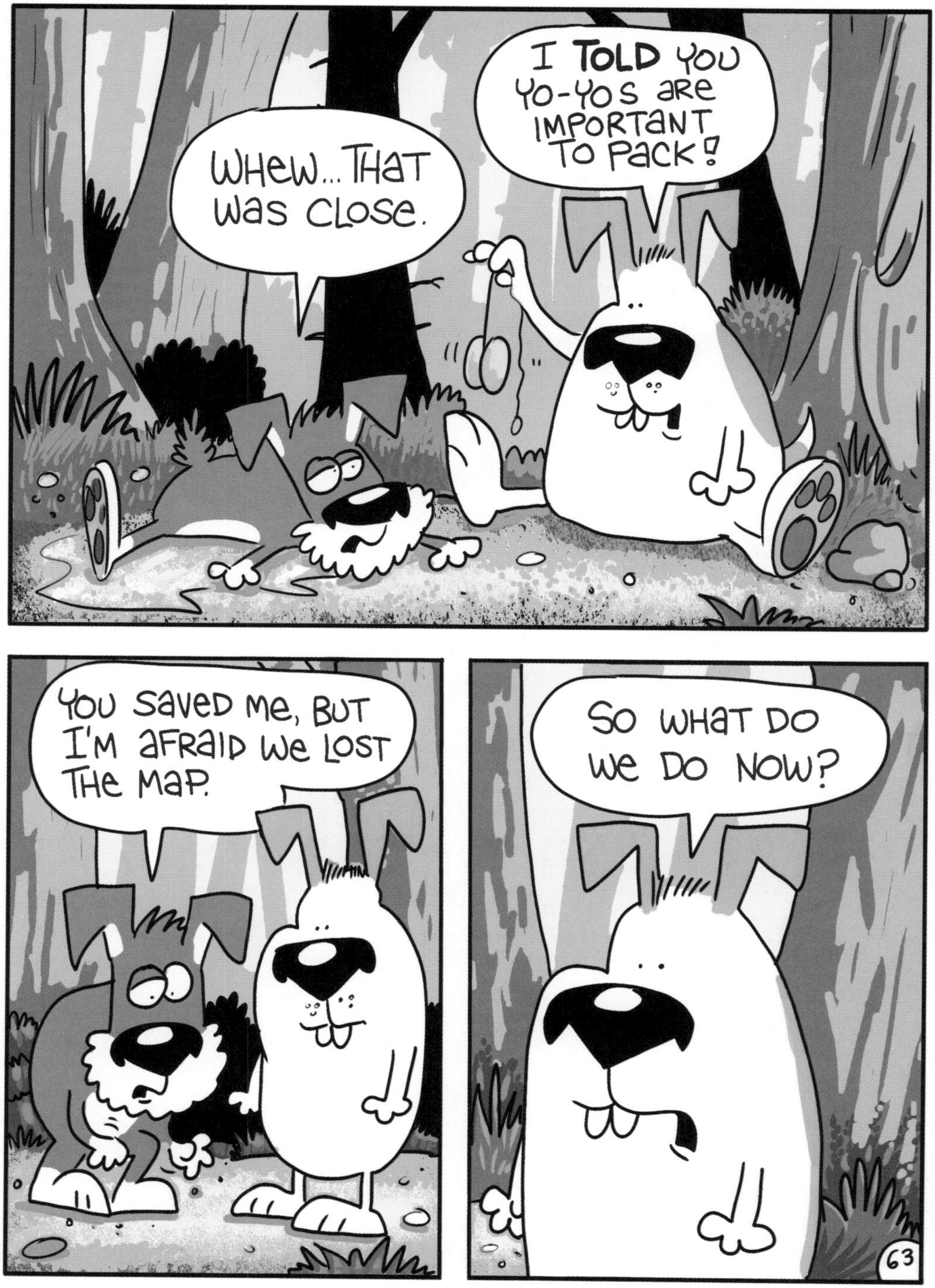
WHEW... THAT WAS CLOSE.
I TOLD YOU YO-YOS ARE IMPORTANT TO PACK!
YOU SAVED ME, BUT I'M AFRAID WE LOST THE MAP.
SO WHAT DO WE DO NOW?
63

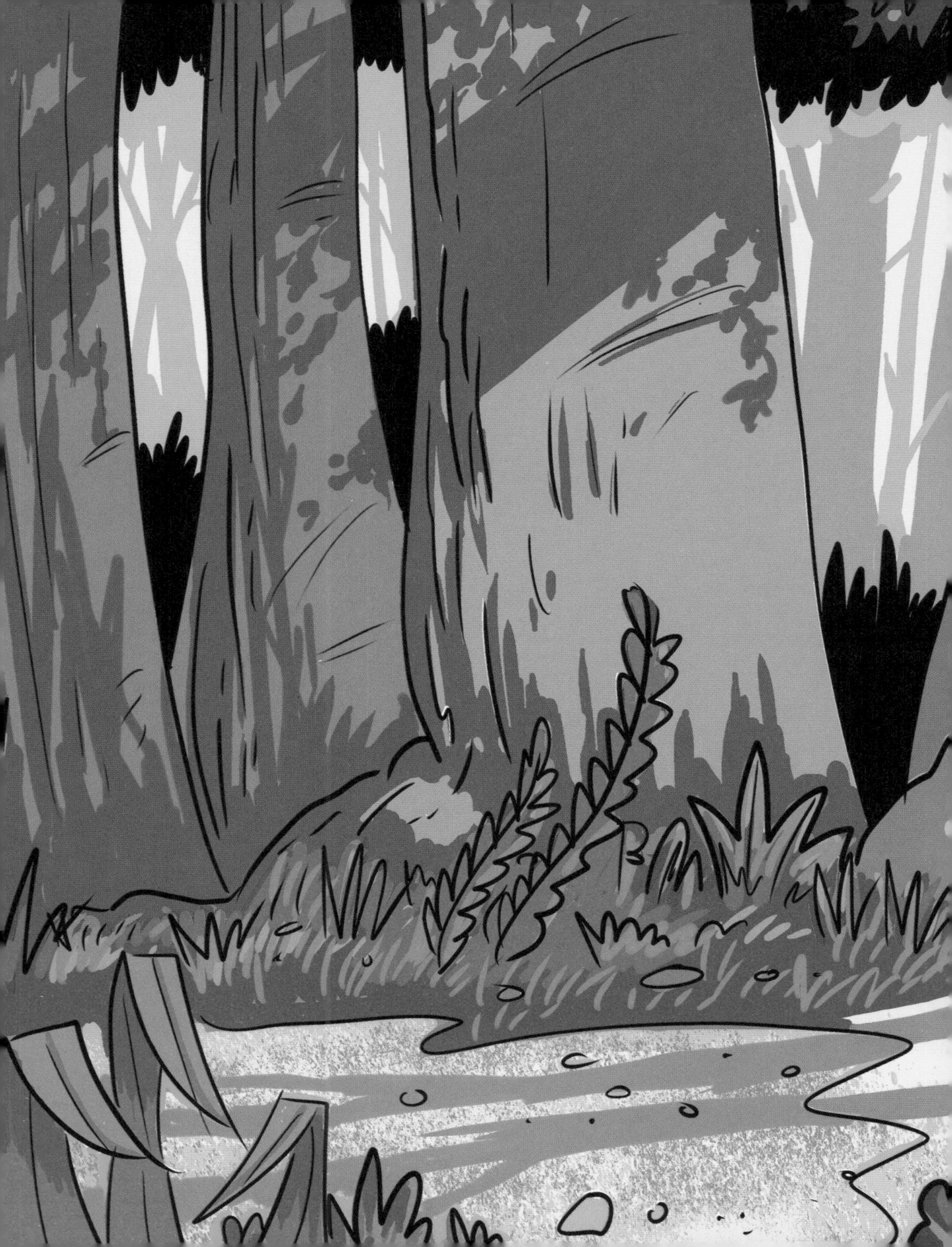

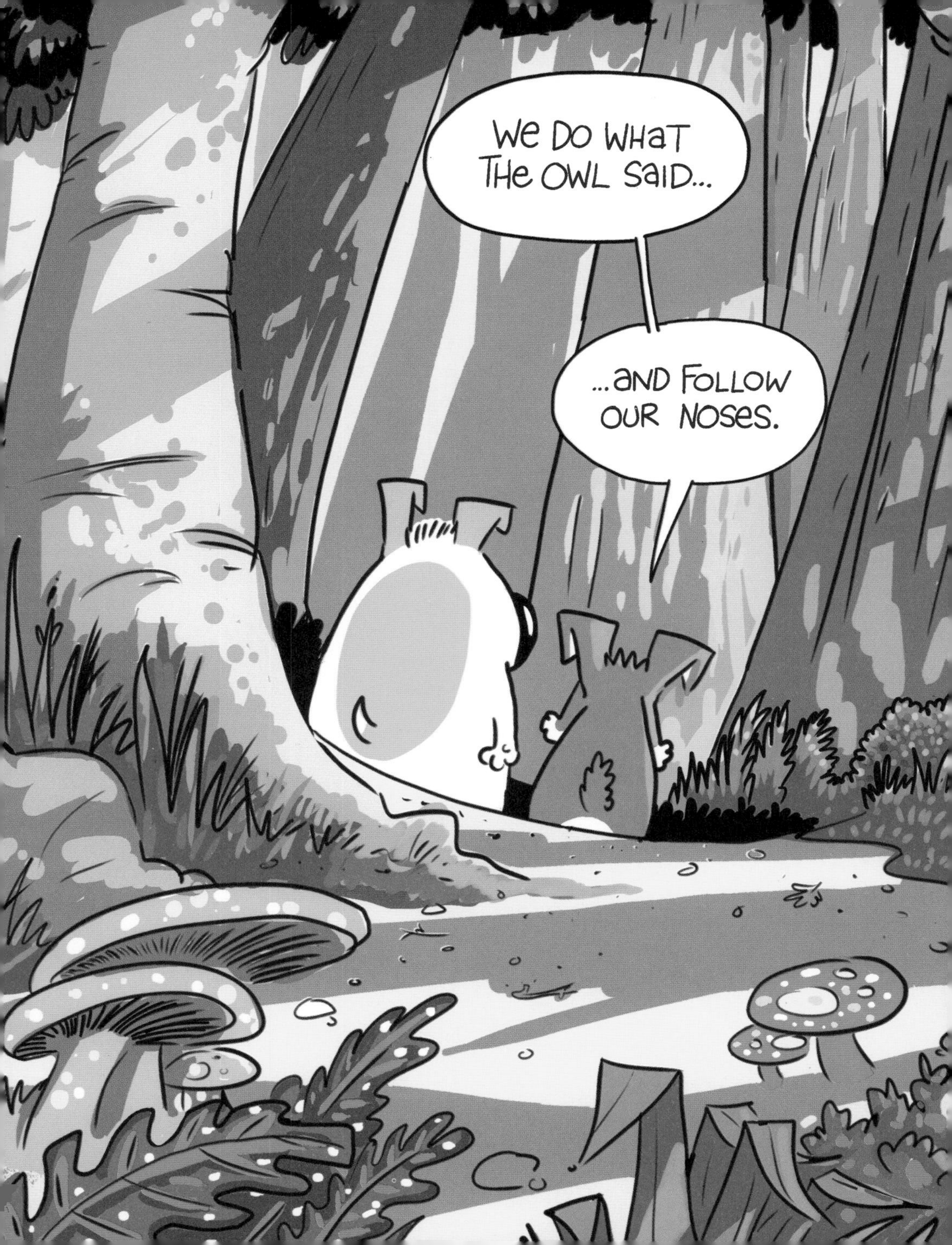
WE DO WHAT THE OWL SAID...
...AND FOLLOW OUR NOSES.

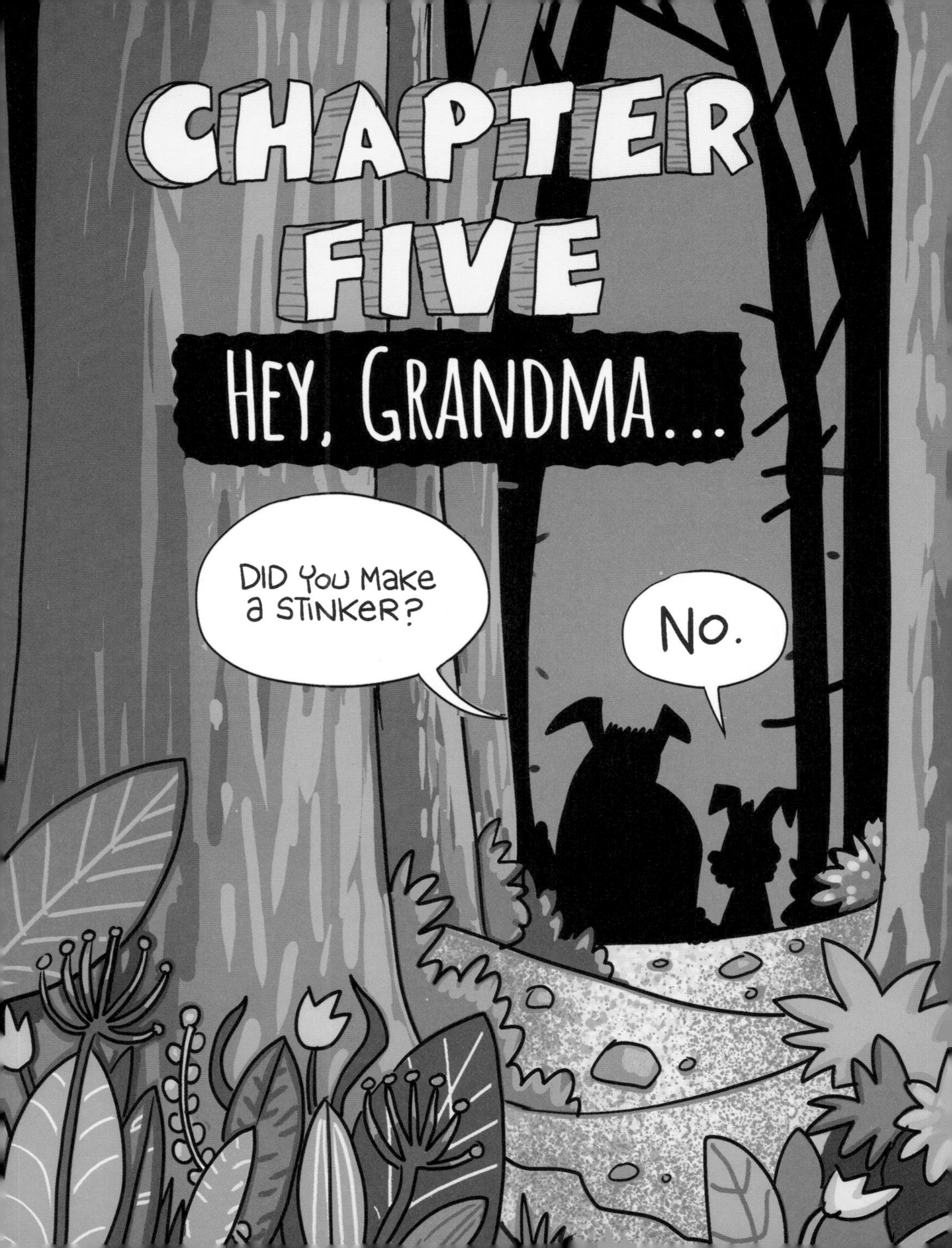
CHAPTER FIVE
HEY, GRANDMA...
DID YOU MAKE A STINKER?
NO.

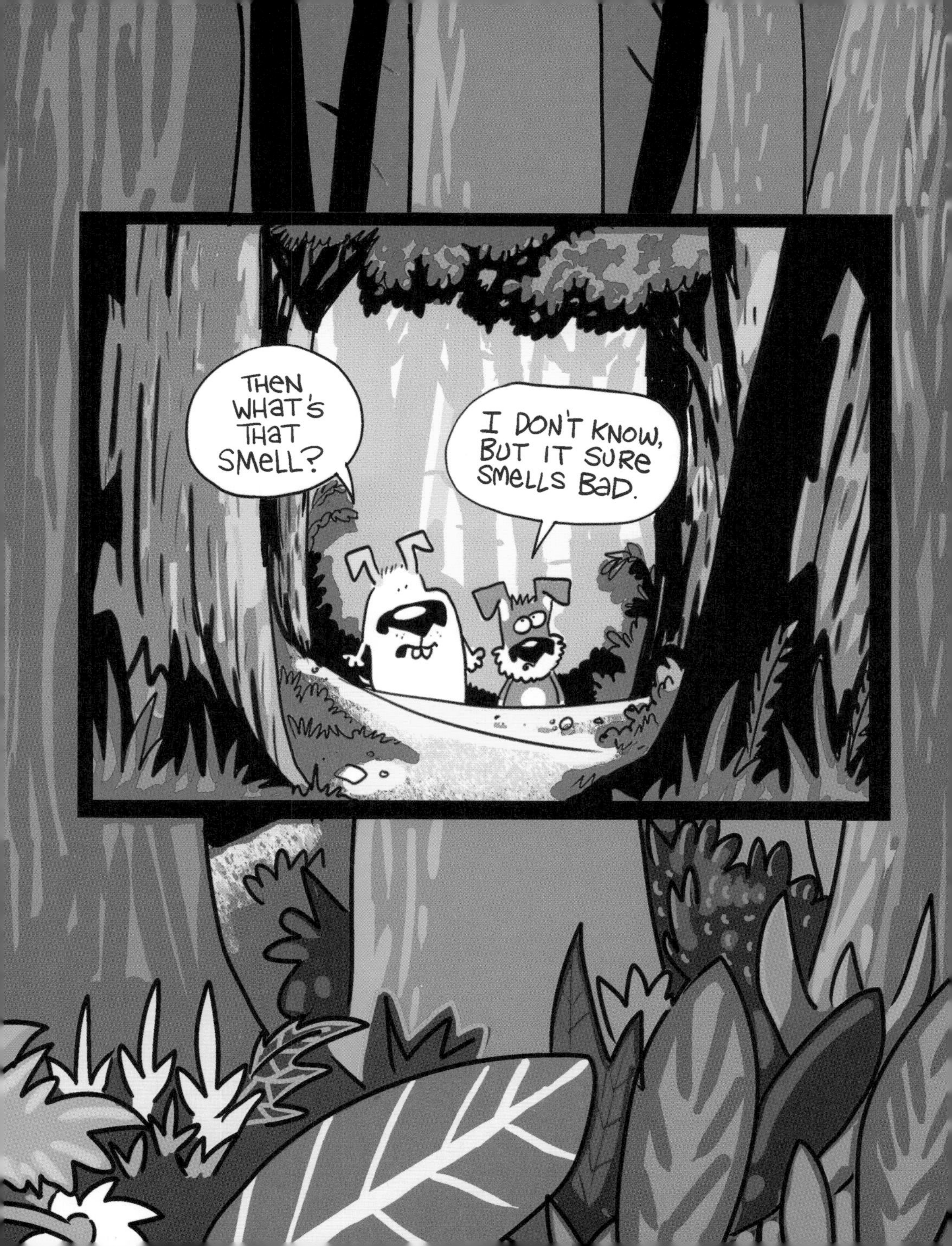
THEN WHAT'S THAT SMELL?
I DON'T KNOW, BUT IT SURE SMELLS BAD.

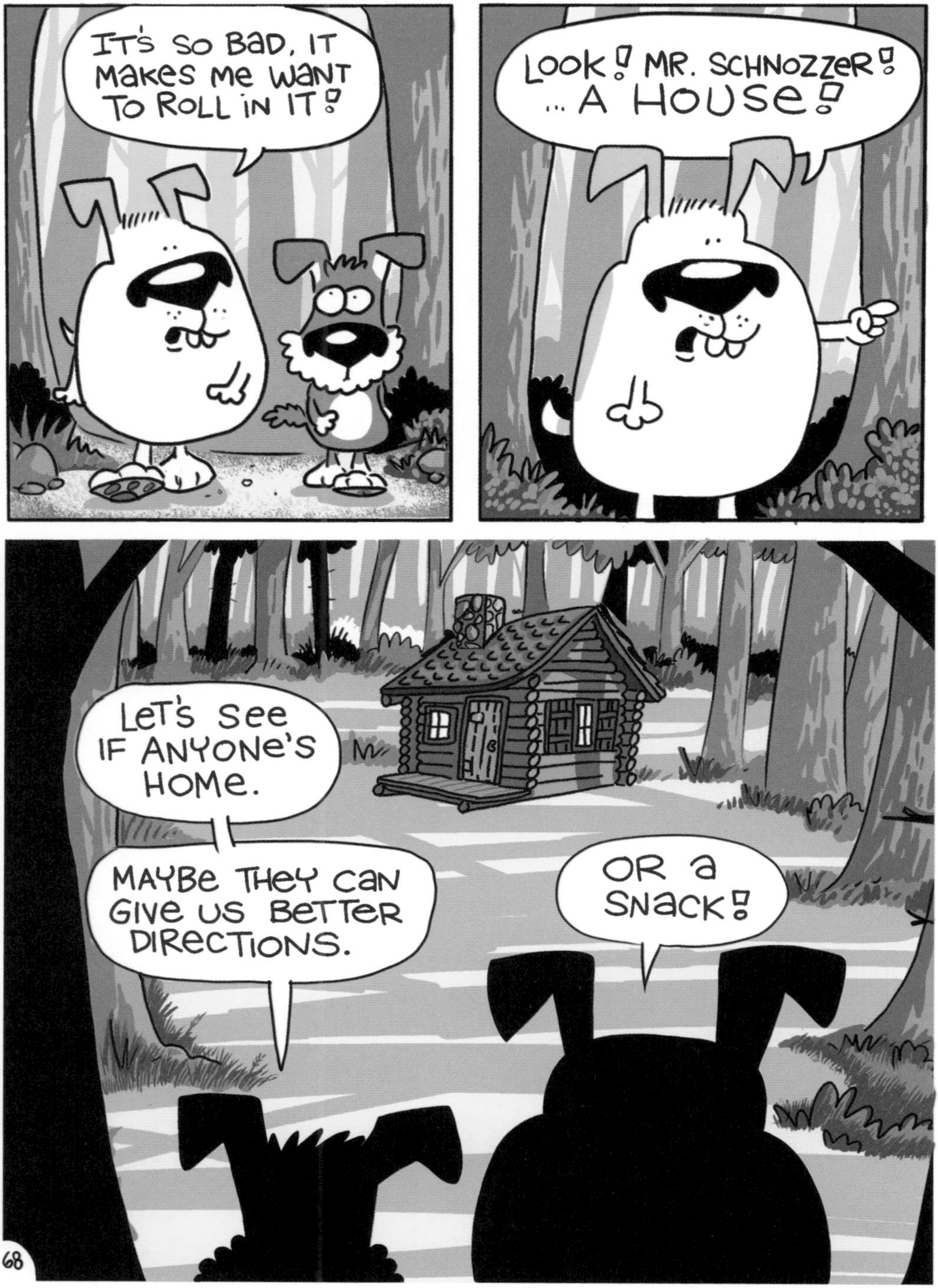
IT'S SO BAD, IT MAKES ME WANT TO ROLL IN IT!
LOOK! MR. SCHNOZZER! ...A HOUSE!
LET'S SEE IF ANYONE'S HOME.
MAYBE THEY CAN GIVE US BETTER DIRECTIONS.
OR A SNACK!

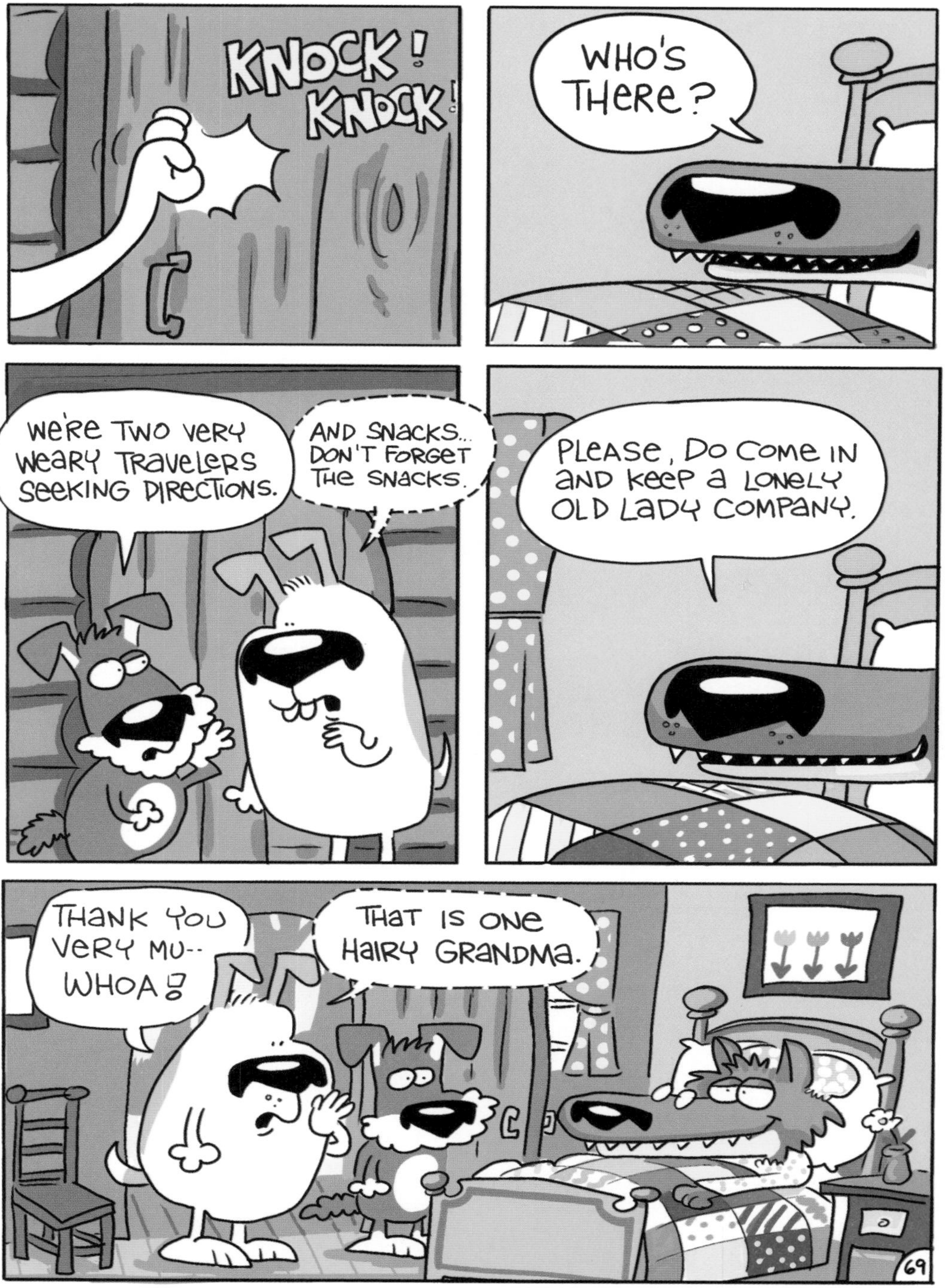
KNOCK! KNOCK!
WHO'S THERE?
WE'RE TWO VERY WEARY TRAVELERS SEEKING DIRECTIONS.
AND SNACKS... DON'T FORGET THE SNACKS.
PLEASE, DO COME IN AND KEEP A LONELY OLD LADY COMPANY.
THANK YOU VERY MU-- WHOA!?
THAT IS ONE HAIRY GRANDMA.

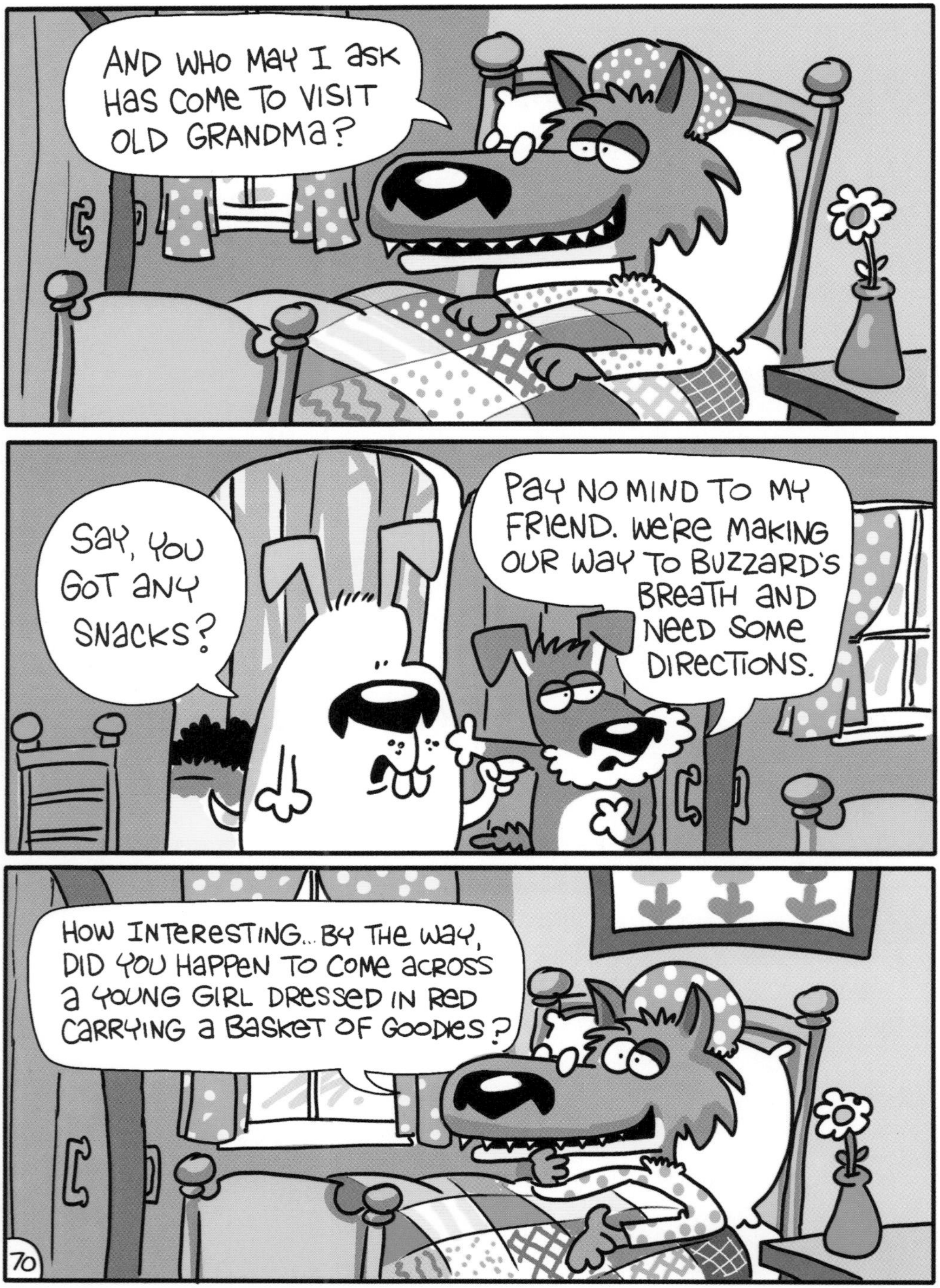
AND WHO MAY I ASK HAS COME TO VISIT OLD GRANDMA?
SAY, YOU GOT ANY SNACKS?
PAY NO MIND TO MY FRIEND. WE'RE MAKING OUR WAY TO BUZZARD'S BREATH AND NEED SOME DIRECTIONS.
HOW INTERESTING... BY THE WAY, DID YOU HAPPEN TO COME ACROSS A YOUNG GIRL DRESSED IN RED CARRYING A BASKET OF GOODIES?

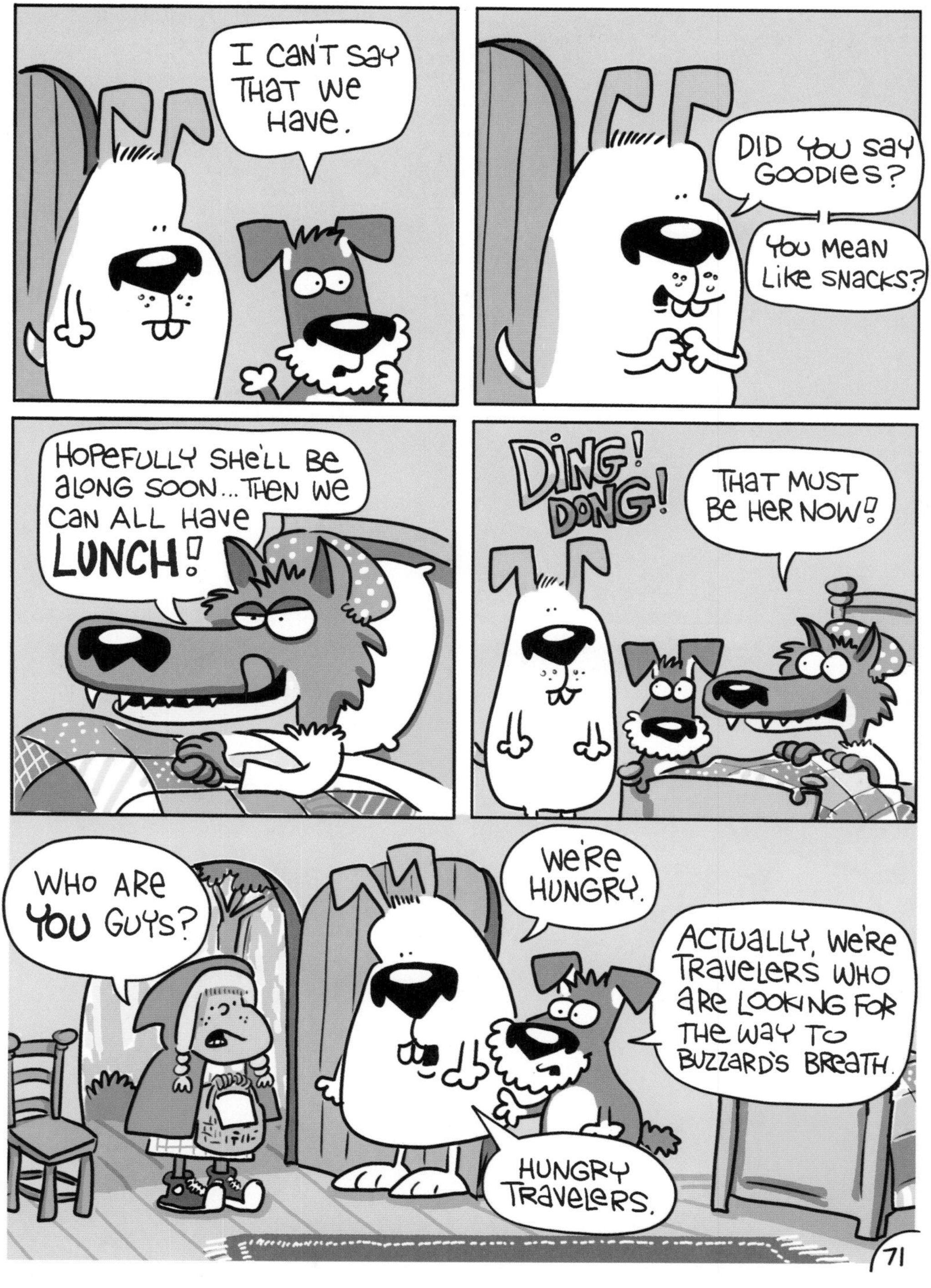
I CAN'T SAY THAT WE HAVE.
DID YOU SAY GOODIES?
YOU MEAN LIKE SNACKS?
HOPEFULLY SHE'LL BE ALONG SOON... THEN WE CAN ALL HAVE LUNCH!
DING! DONG!
THAT MUST BE HER NOW!
WHO ARE YOU GUYS?
WE'RE HUNGRY.
ACTUALLY, WE'RE TRAVELERS WHO ARE LOOKING FOR THE WAY TO BUZZARD'S BREATH.
HUNGRY TRAVELERS.

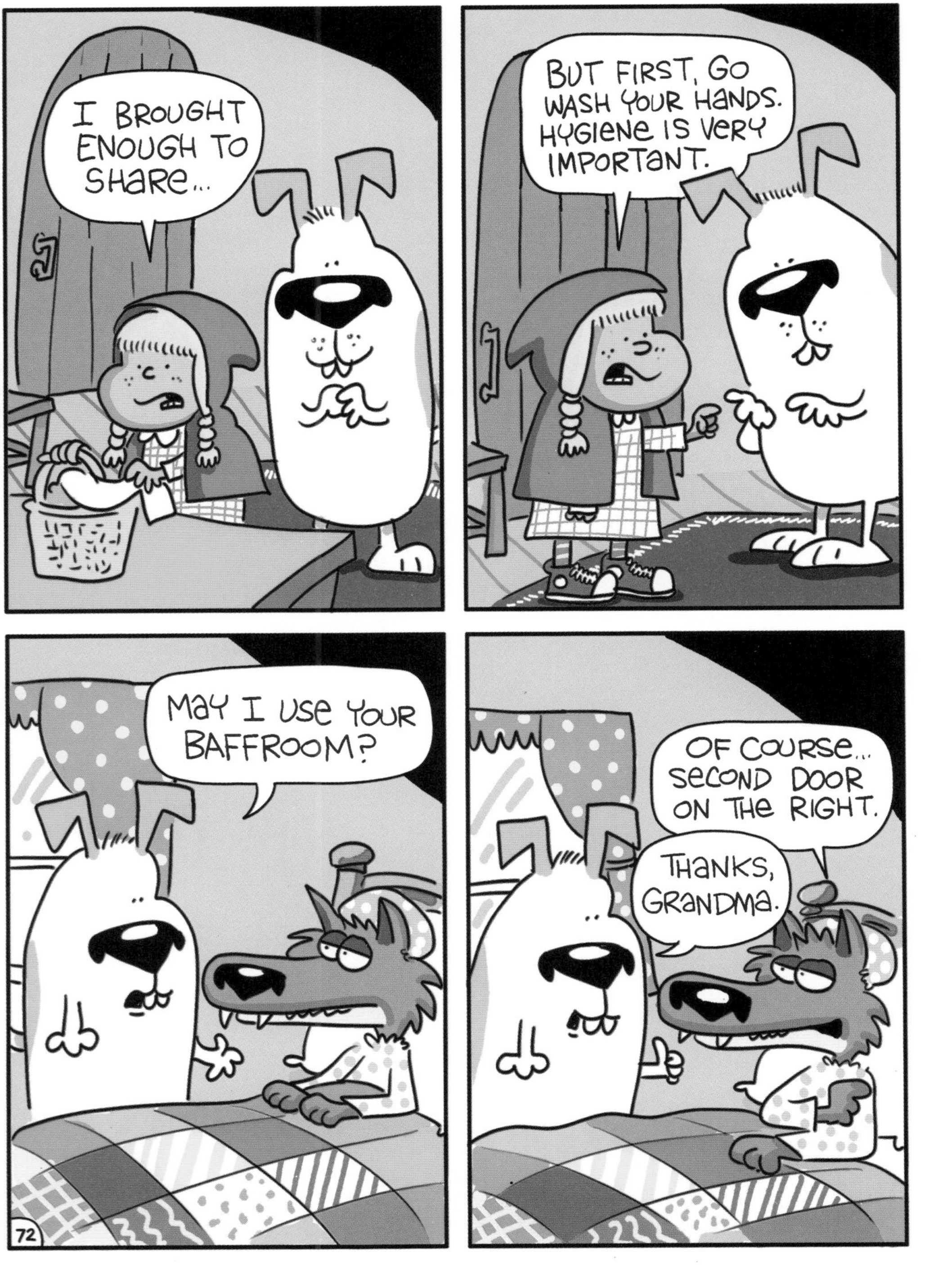

I BROUGHT ENOUGH TO SHARE...
BUT FIRST, GO WASH YOUR HANDS. HYGIENE IS VERY IMPORTANT.
MAY I USE YOUR BAFFROOM?
OF COURSE... SECOND DOOR ON THE RIGHT.
THANKS, GRANDMA.

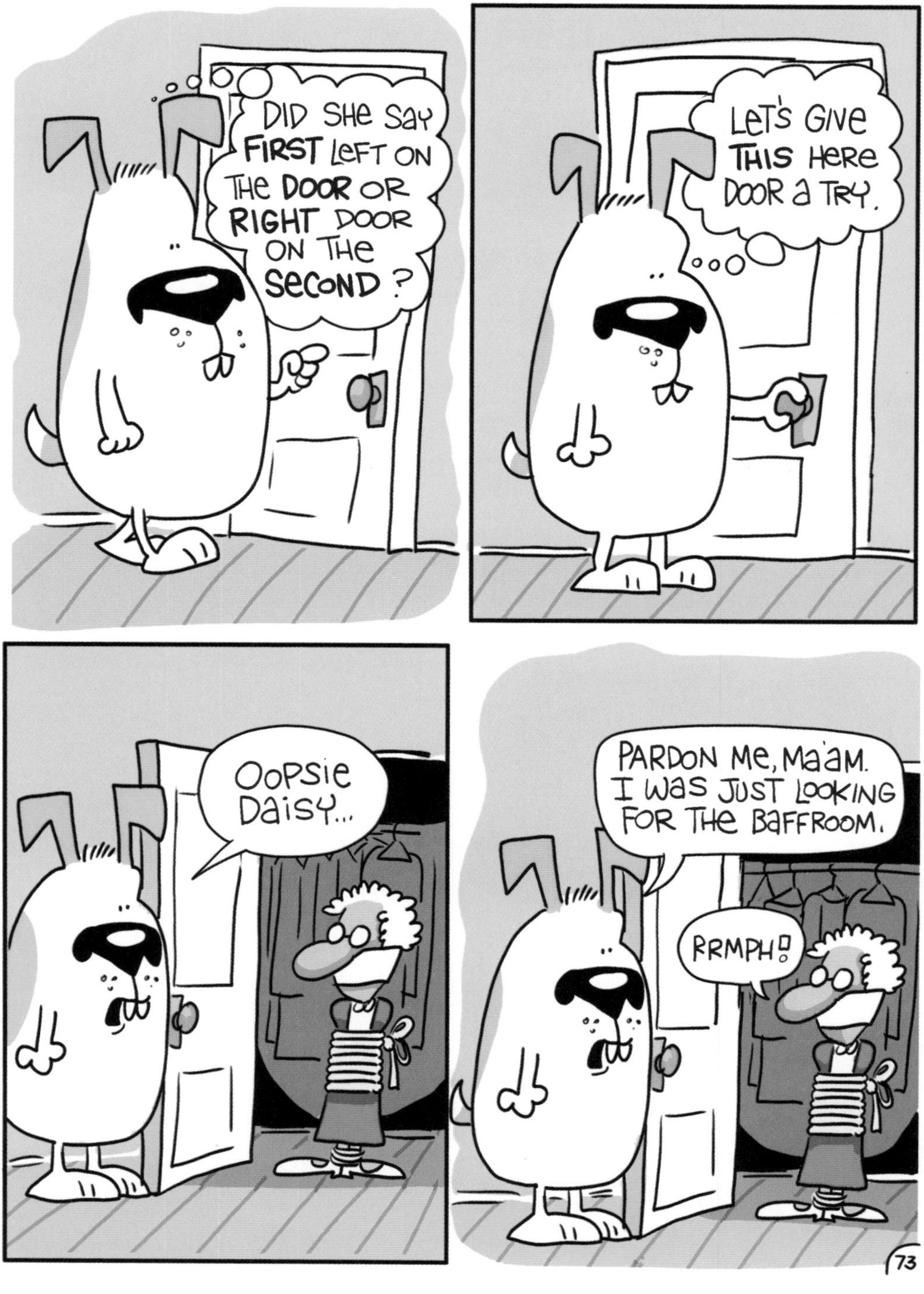
DID SHE SAY FIRST LEFT ON THE DOOR OR RIGHT DOOR ON THE SECOND ?
LET'S GIVE THIS HERE DOOR A TRY.
OOPSIE DAISY...
PARDON ME, MA'AM. I WAS JUST LOOKING FOR THE BAFFROOM.
RRMPH!!

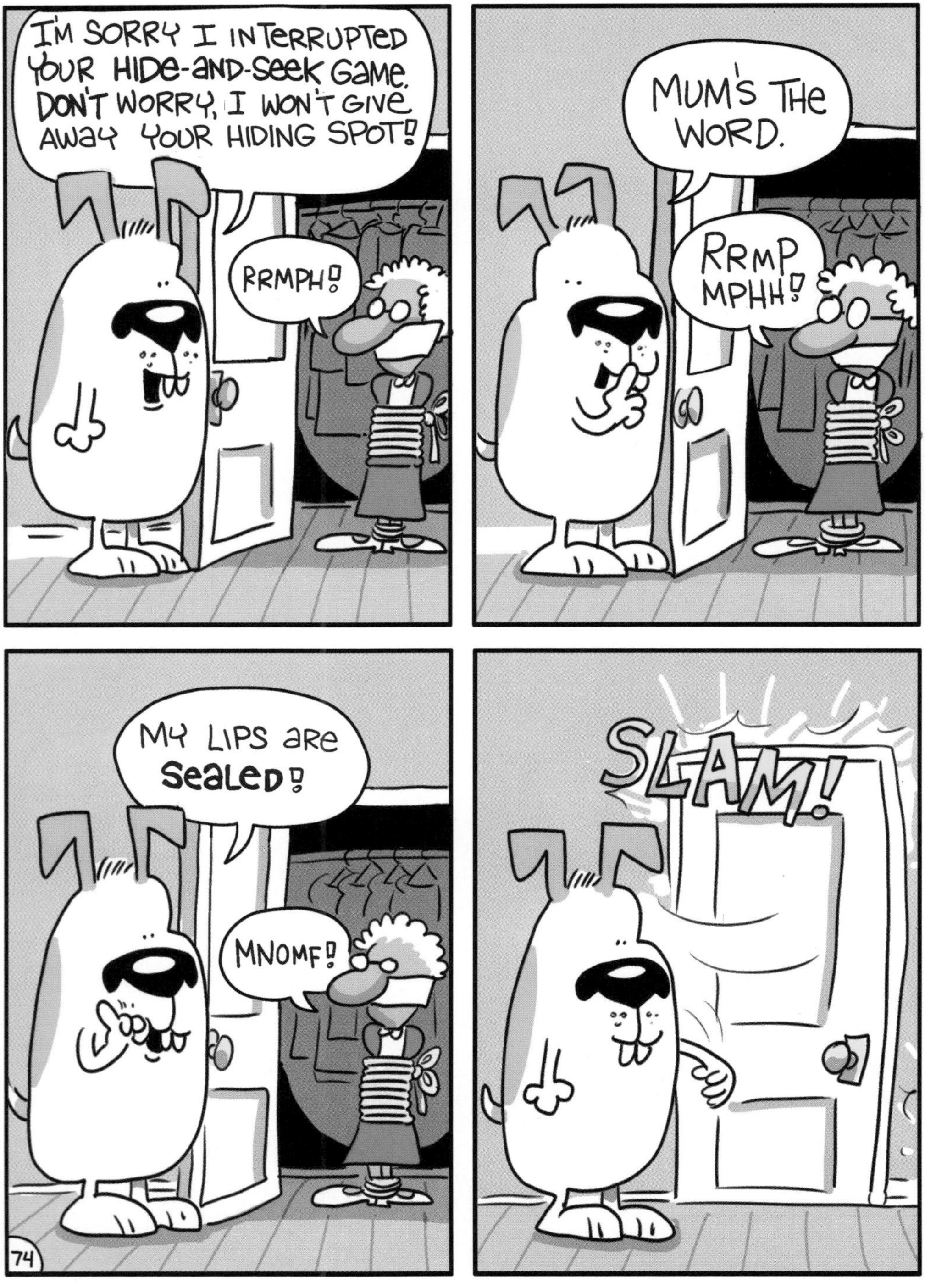
I'M SORRY I INTERRUPTED YOUR HIDE-AND-SEEK GAME. DON'T WORRY, I WON'T GIVE AWAY YOUR HIDING SPOT!
RRMPH!
MUM'S THE WORD.
RRMP MPHH!
MY LIPS ARE SEALED!
MNOMF!
SLAM!

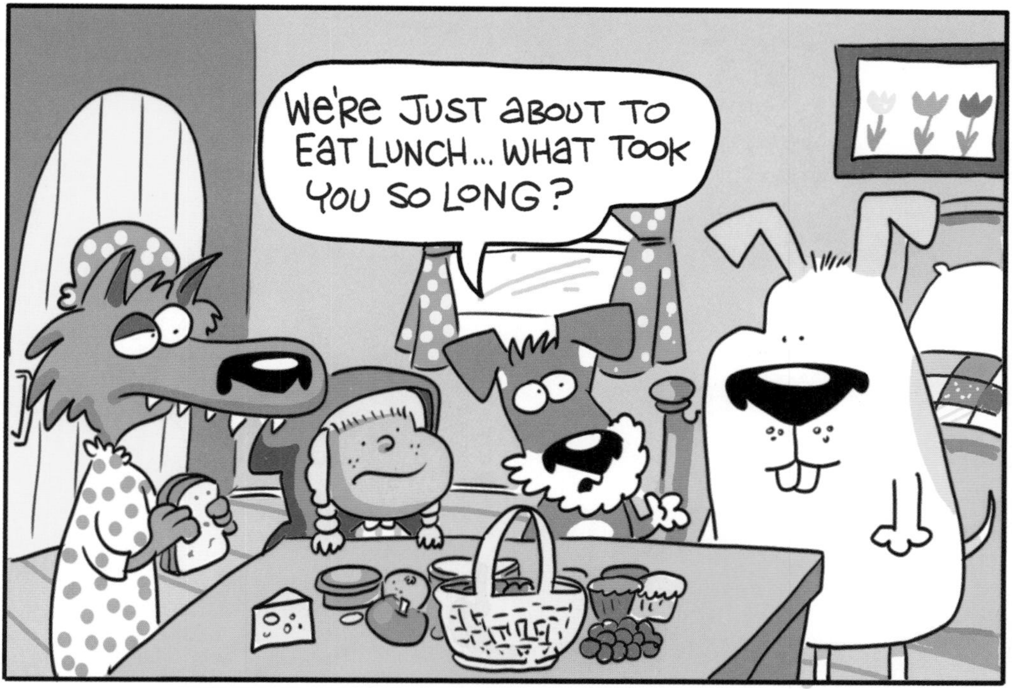
WE'RE JUST ABOUT TO EAT LUNCH... WHAT TOOK YOU SO LONG?

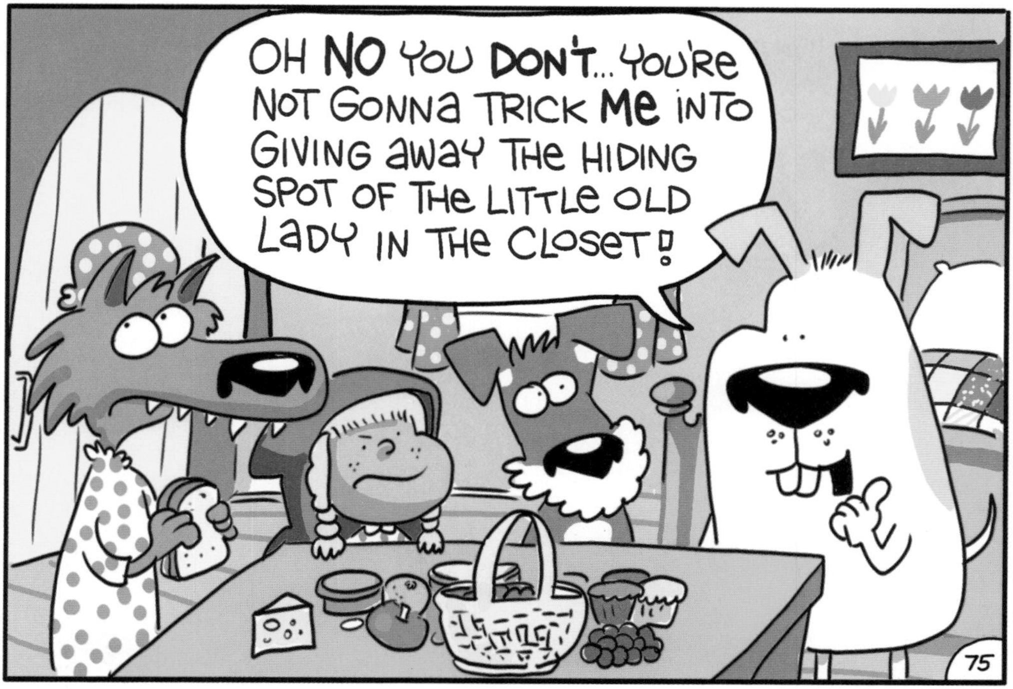
OH NO YOU DON'T... YOU'RE NOT GONNA TRICK ME INTO GIVING AWAY THE HIDING SPOT OF THE LITTLE OLD LADY IN THE CLOSET!

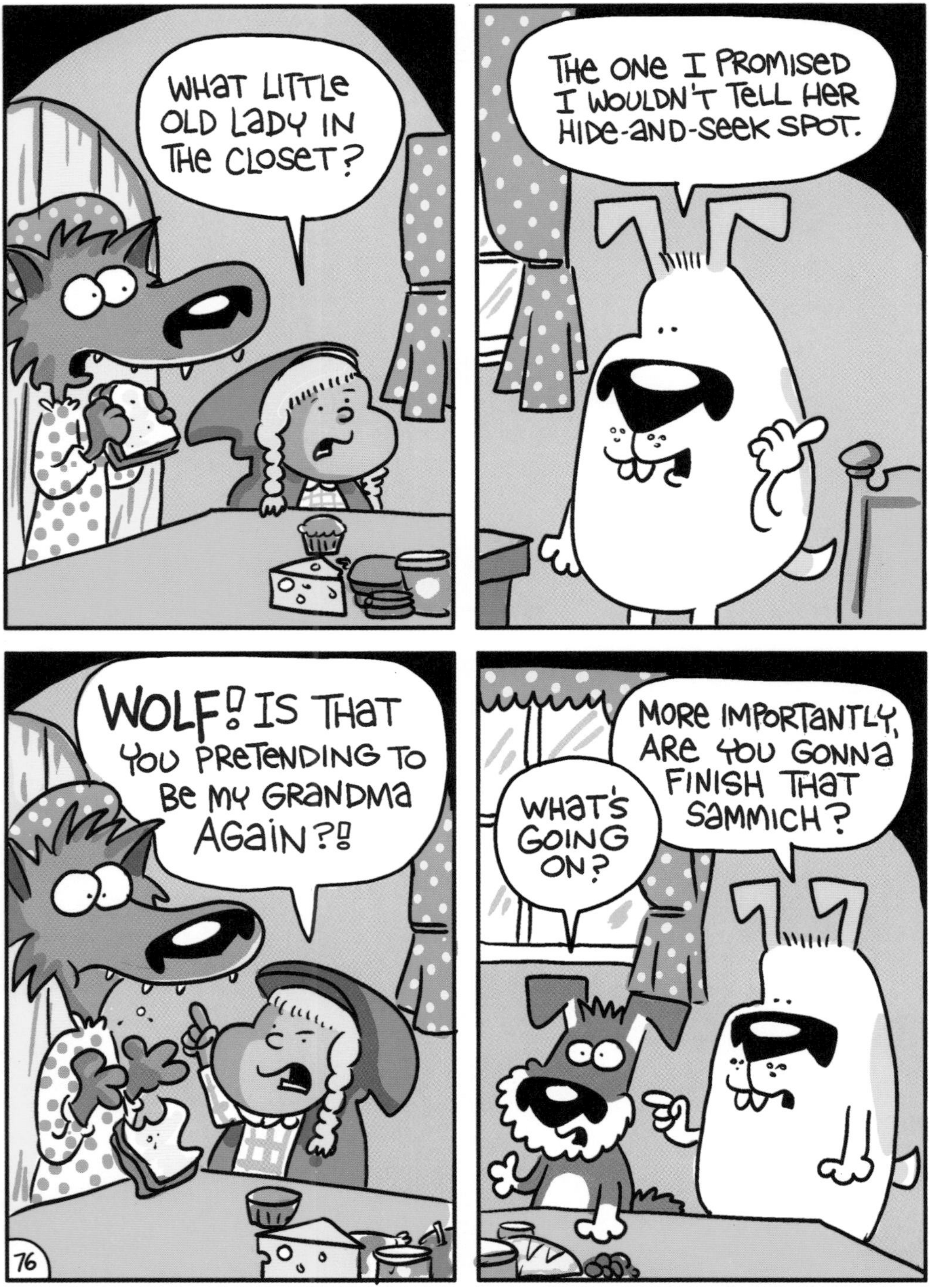
WHAT LITTLE OLD LADY IN THE CLOSET?
THE ONE I PROMISED I WOULDN'T TELL HER HIDE-AND-SEEK SPOT.
WOLF! IS THAT YOU PRETENDING TO BE MY GRANDMA AGAIN?!
WHAT'S GOING ON?
MORE IMPORTANTLY, ARE YOU GONNA FINISH THAT SAMMICH?

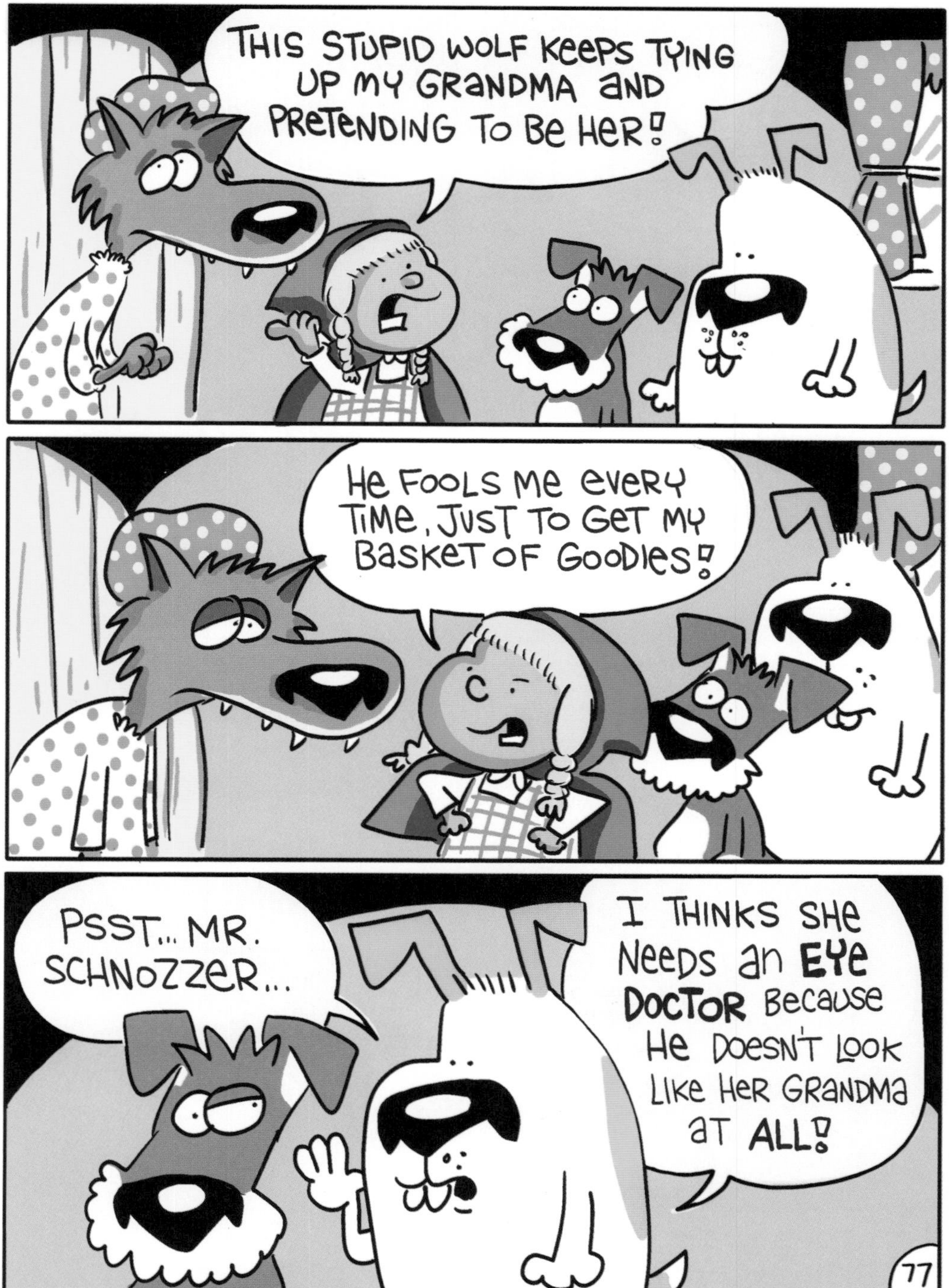
THIS STUPID WOLF KEEPS TYING UP MY GRANDMA AND PRETENDING TO BE HER!
HE FOOLS ME EVERY TIME, JUST TO GET MY BASKET OF GOODIES!
PSST... MR. SCHNOZZER...
I THINKS SHE NEEDS AN **EYE DOCTOR** BECAUSE HE DOESN'T LOOK LIKE HER GRANDMA AT **ALL**!

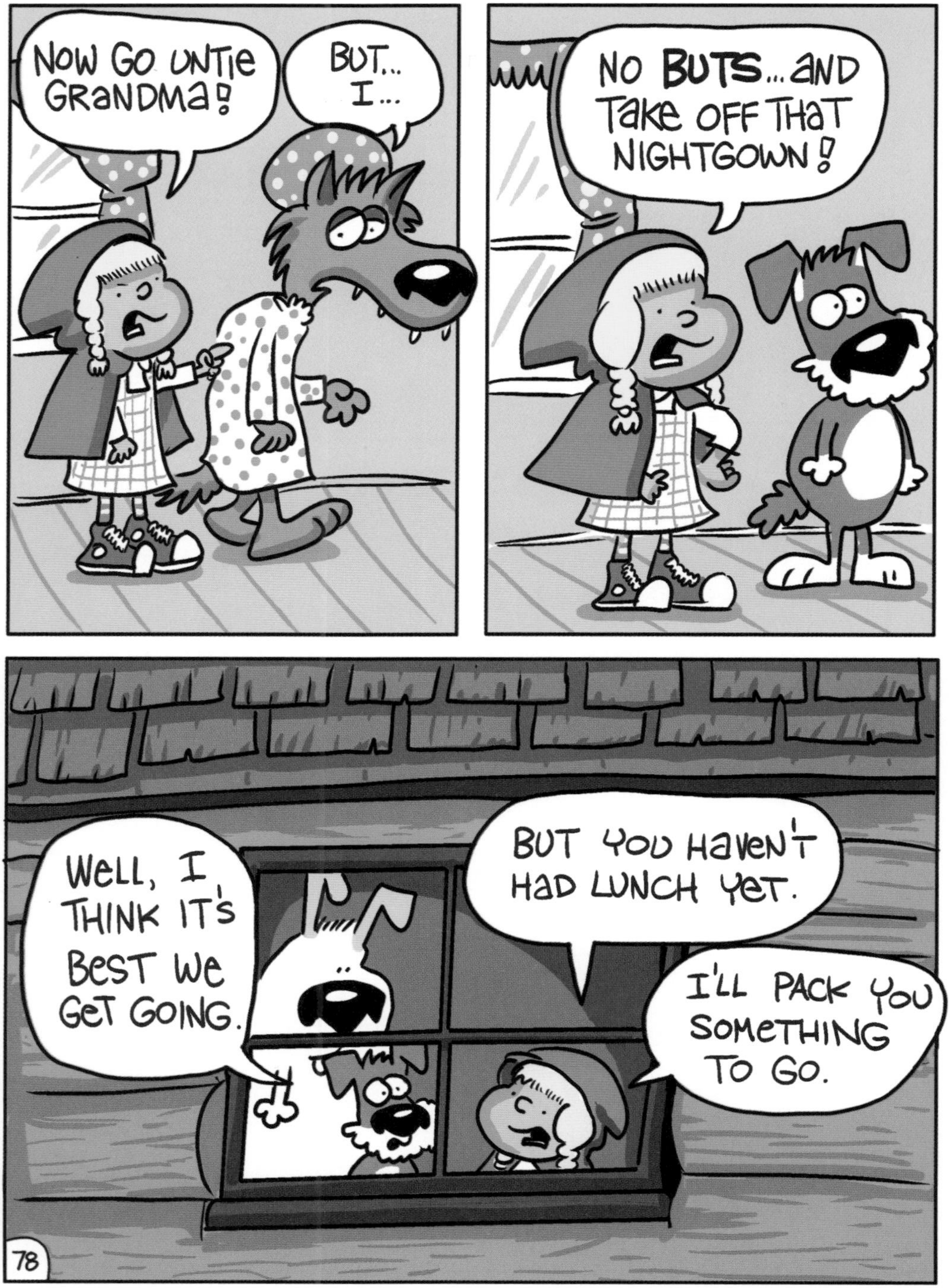
NOW GO UNTIE GRANDMA!
BUT... I...
NO BUTS... AND TAKE OFF THAT NIGHTGOWN!
WELL, I THINK IT'S BEST WE GET GOING.
BUT YOU HAVEN'T HAD LUNCH YET.
I'LL PACK YOU SOMETHING TO GO.

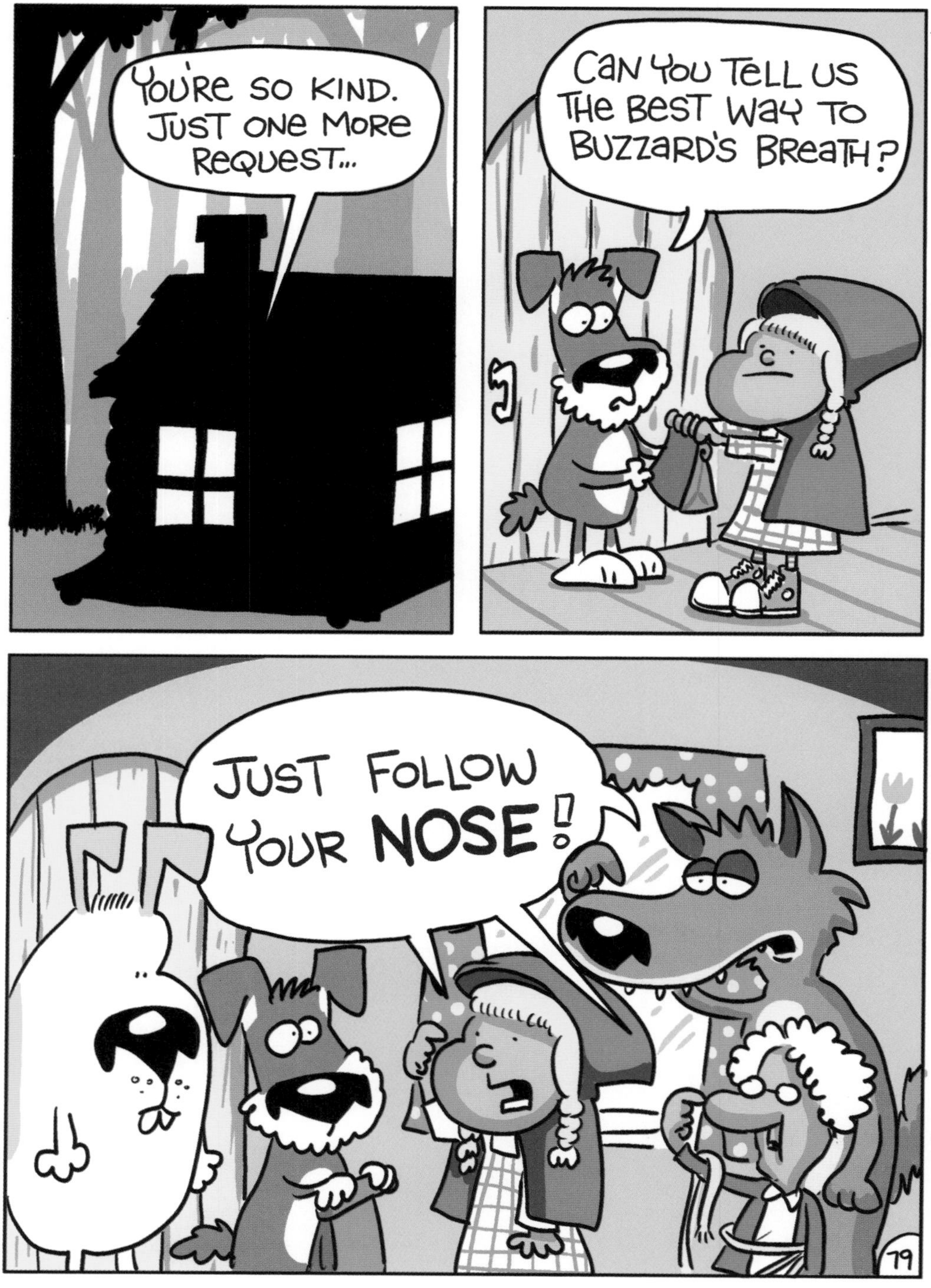
YOU'RE SO KIND. JUST ONE MORE REQUEST...
CAN YOU TELL US THE BEST WAY TO BUZZARD'S BREATH?
JUST FOLLOW YOUR NOSE!
79

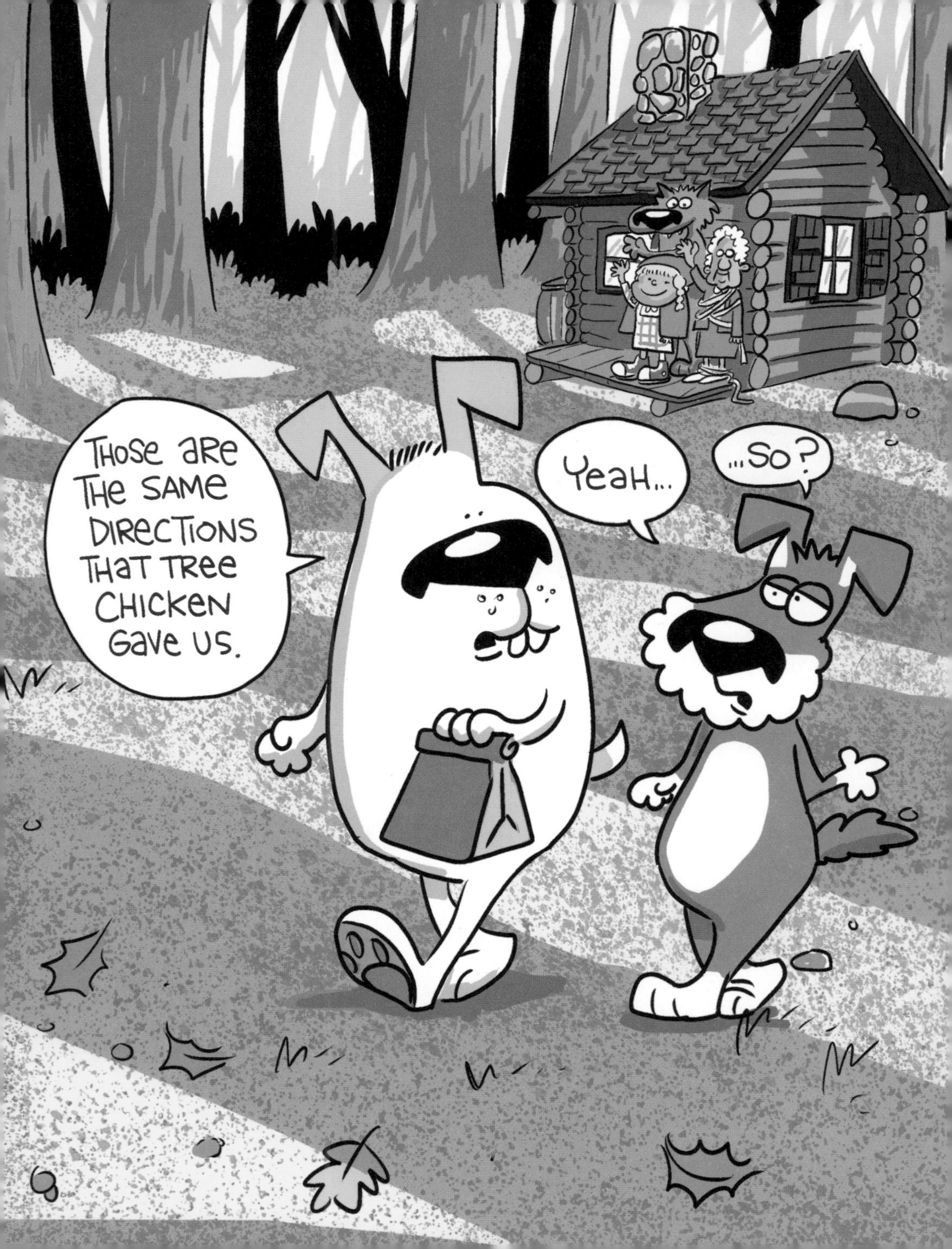
THOSE ARE THE SAME DIRECTIONS THAT TREE CHICKEN GAVE US.
YEAH...
...SO?

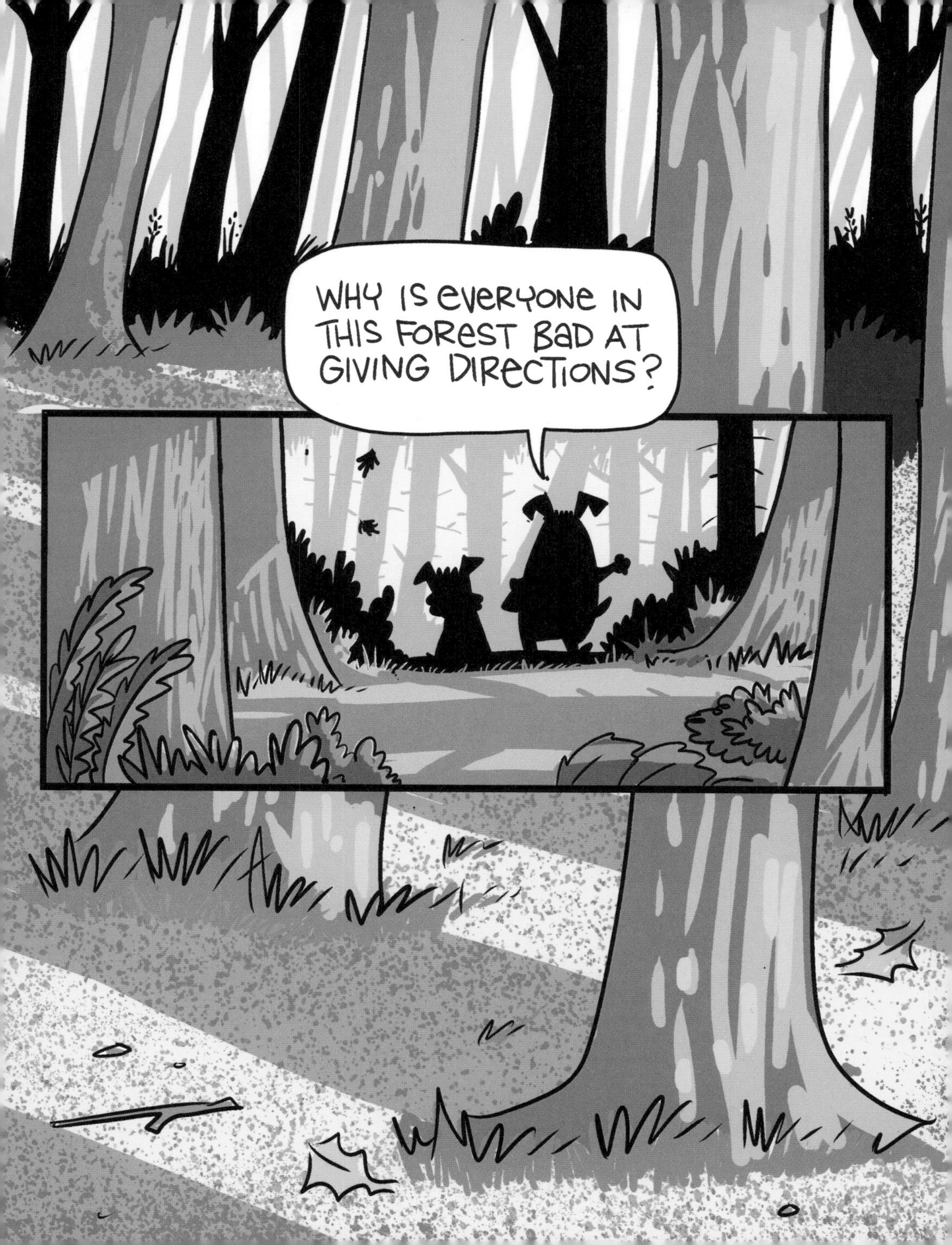
WHY IS EVERYONE IN THIS FOREST BAD AT GIVING DIRECTIONS?

CHAPTER SIX

GRIN AND BEAR IT

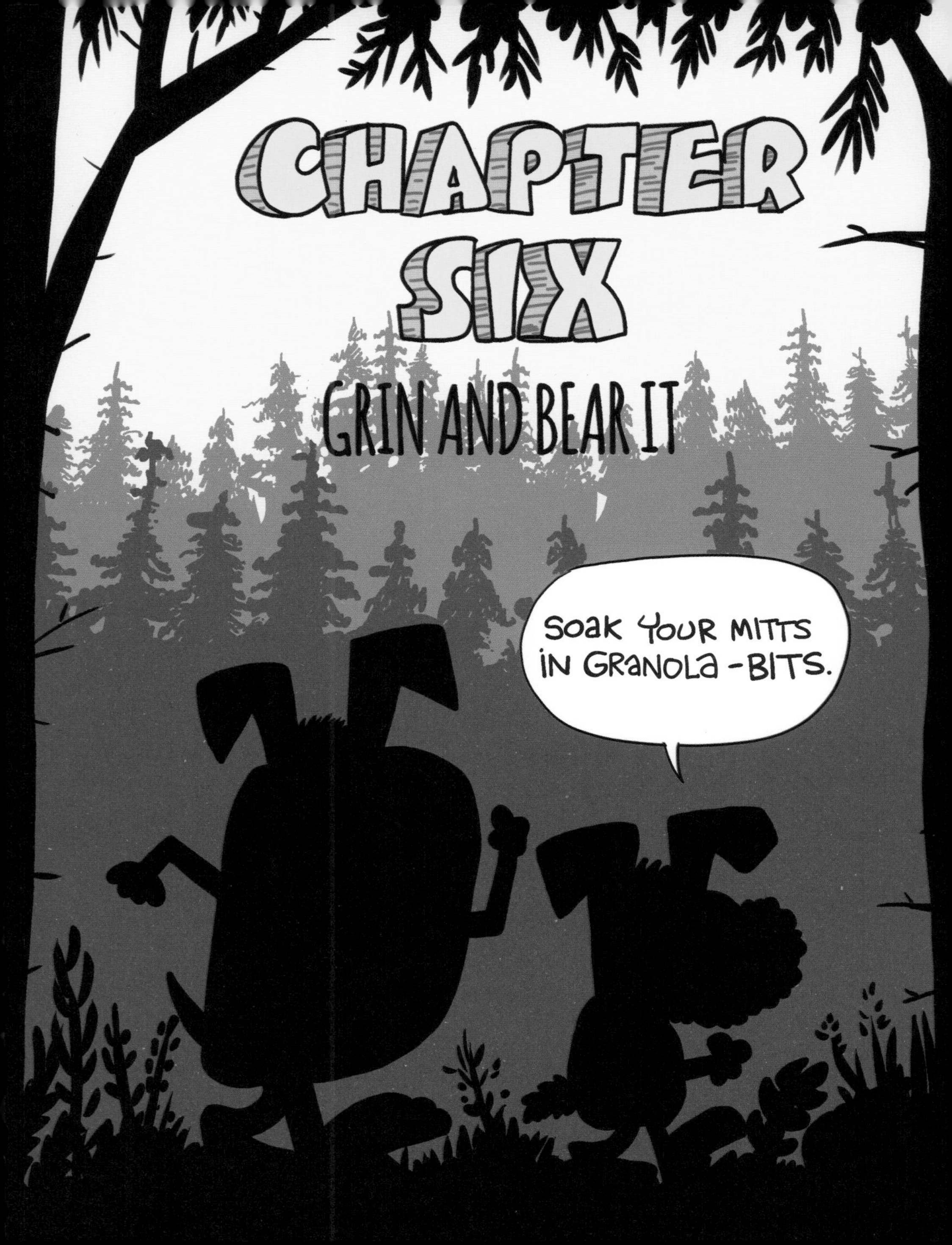
SOAK YOUR MITTS IN GRANOLA-BITS.

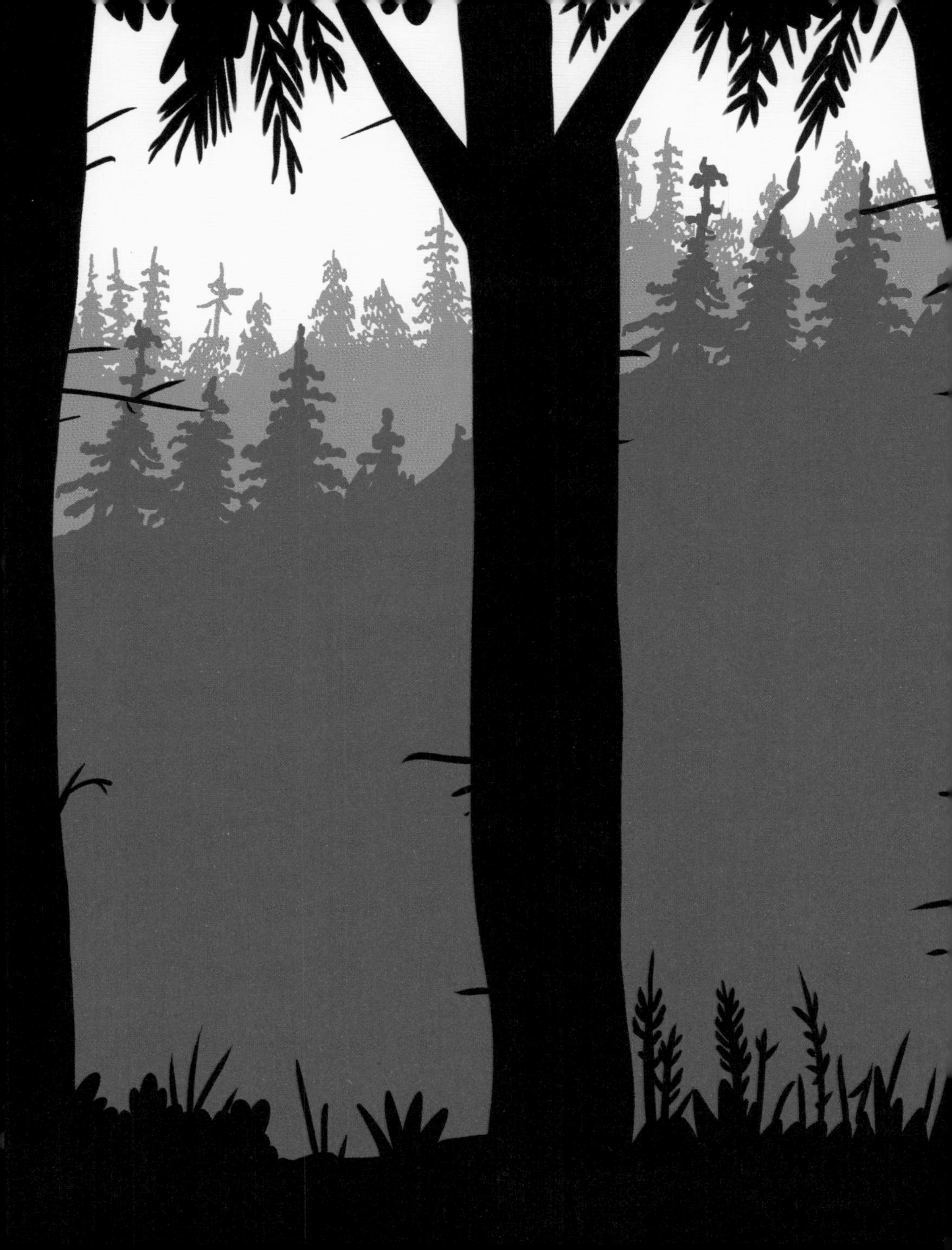

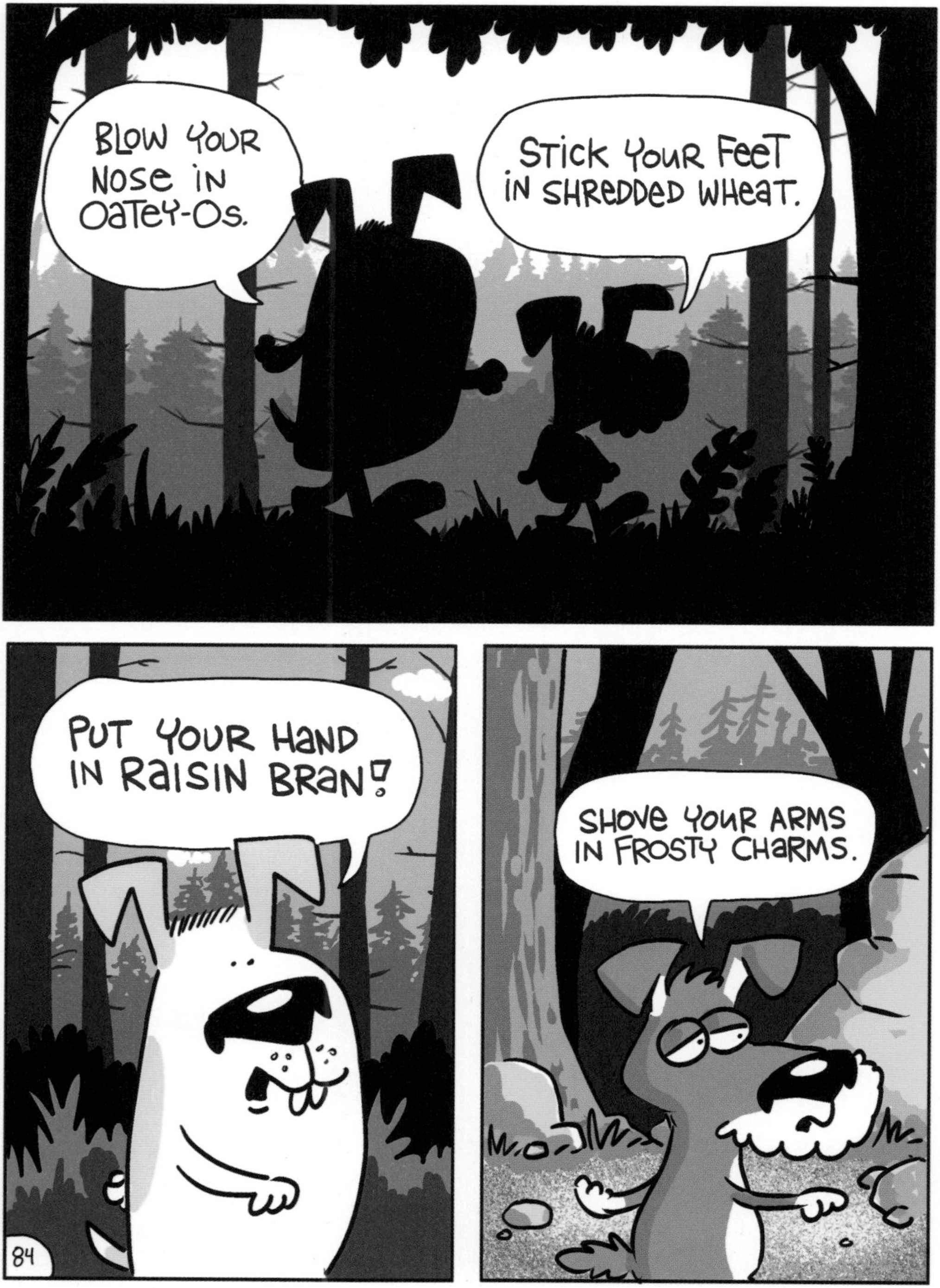
BLOW YOUR NOSE IN OATEY-OS.
STICK YOUR FEET IN SHREDDED WHEAT.
PUT YOUR HAND IN RAISIN BRAN!
SHOVE YOUR ARMS IN FROSTY CHARMS.

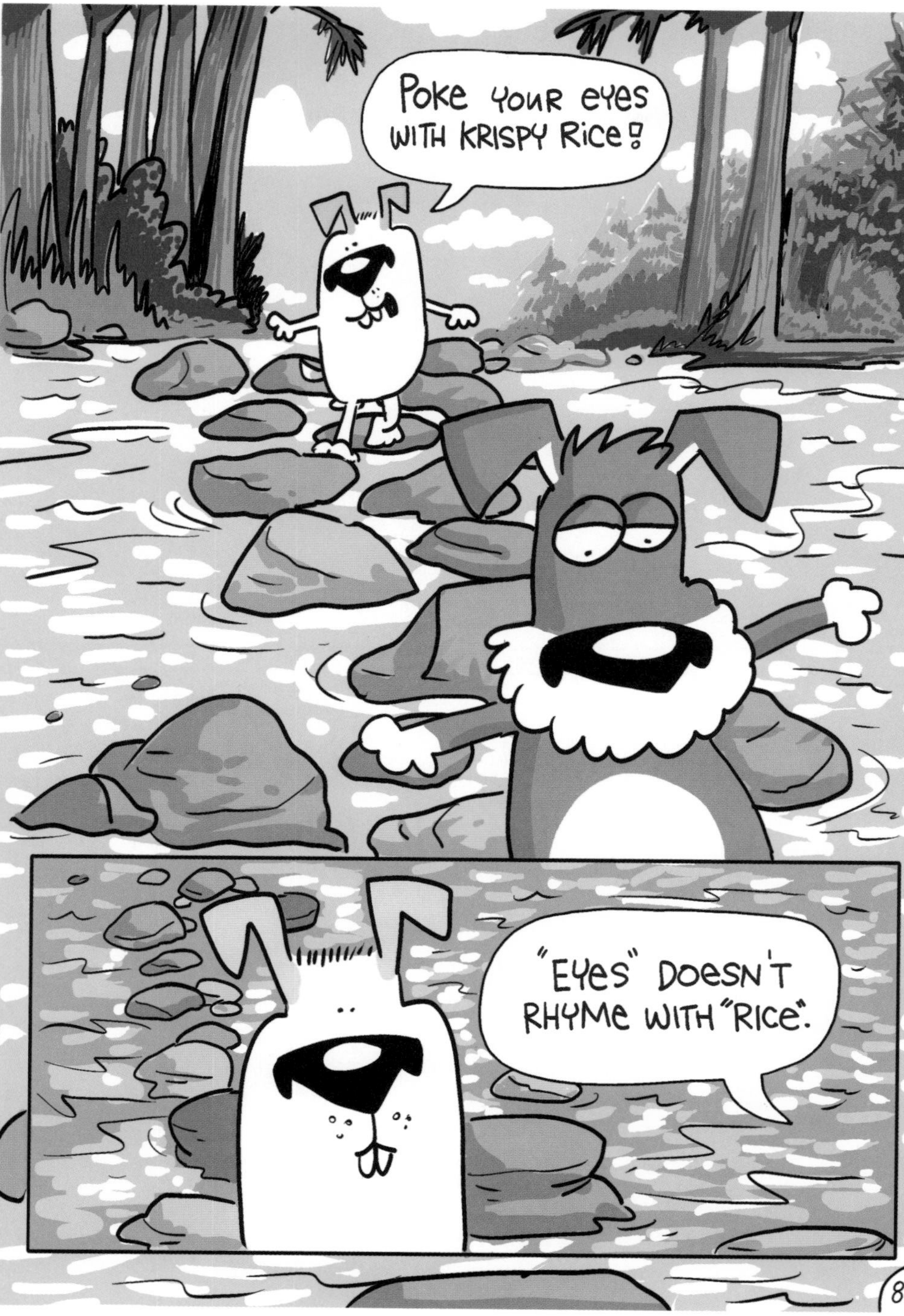
Poke your eyes with Krispy Rice!
"Eyes" doesn't rhyme with "Rice".

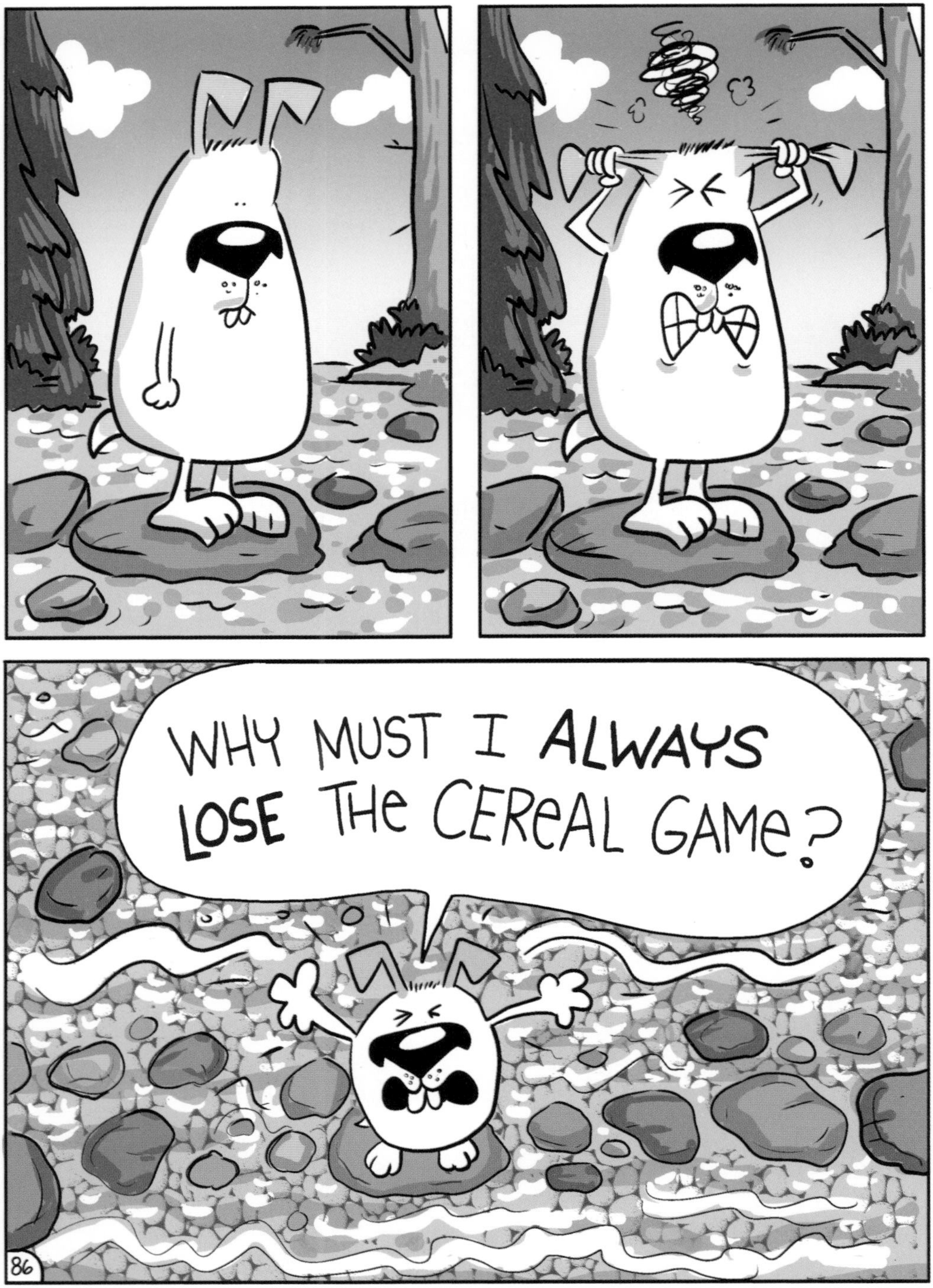
WHY MUST I ALWAYS LOSE THE CEREAL GAME?

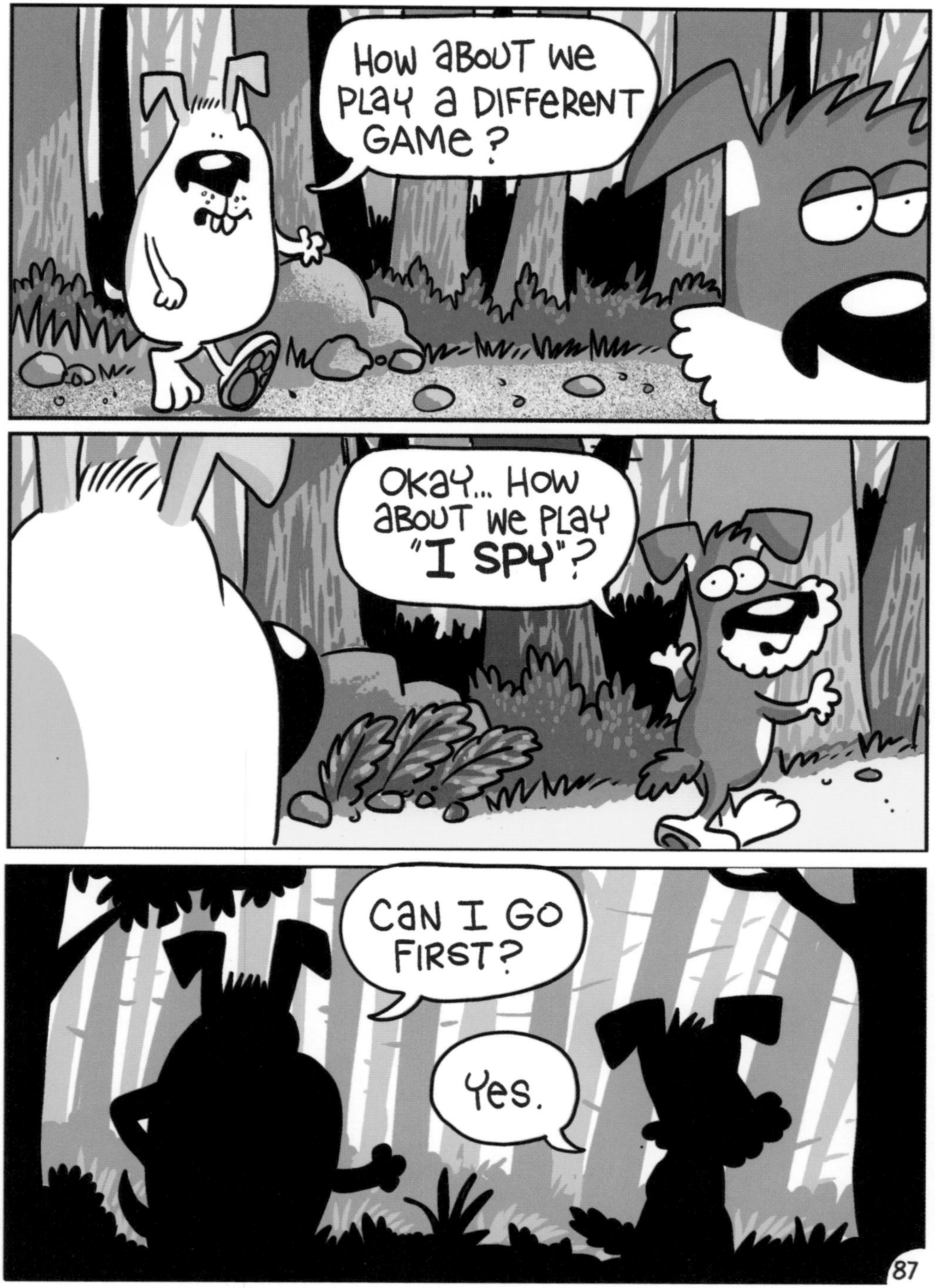
HOW ABOUT WE PLAY A DIFFERENT GAME?
OKAY... HOW ABOUT WE PLAY "I SPY"?
CAN I GO FIRST?
YES.

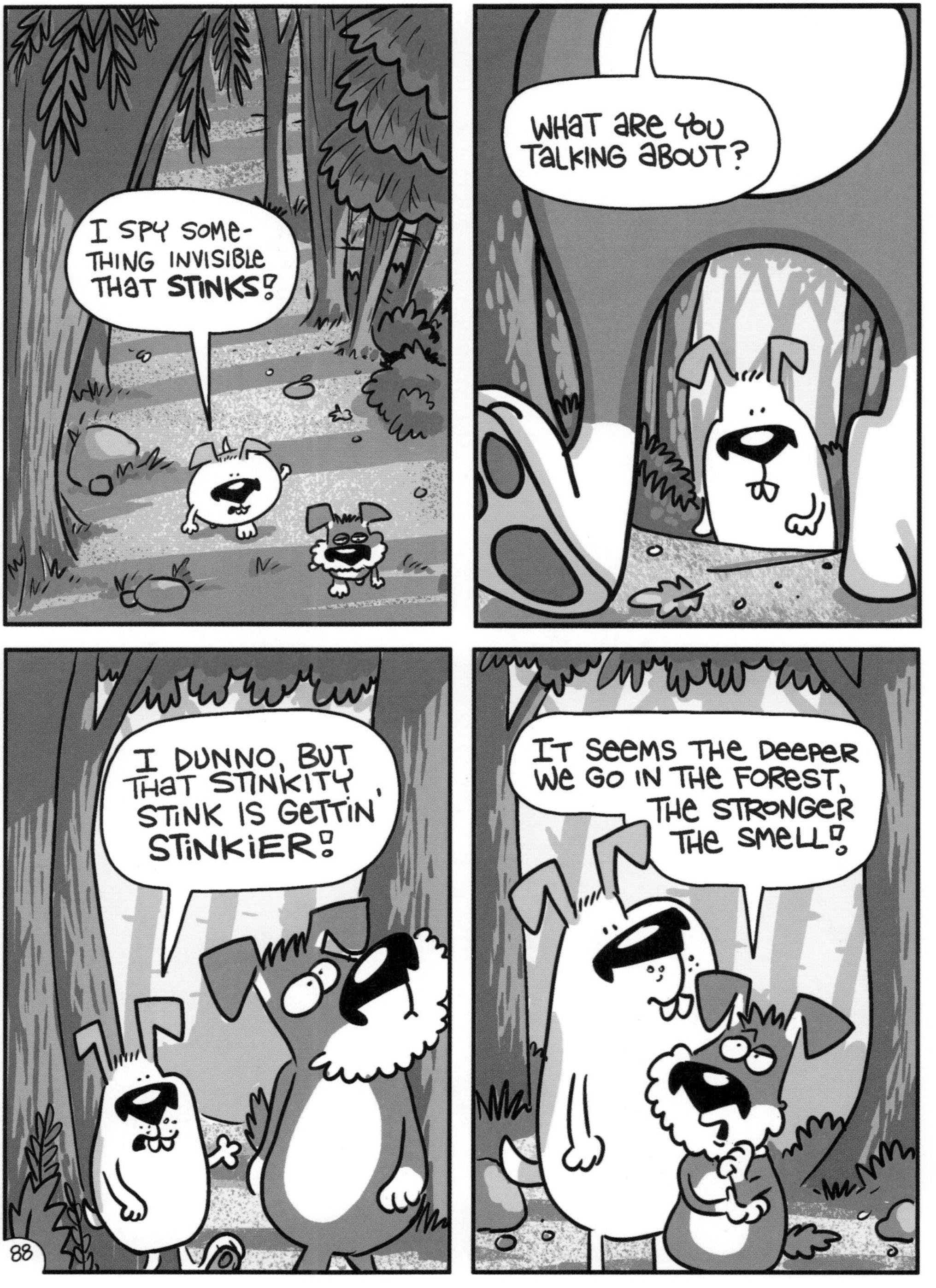
I SPY SOME-THING INVISIBLE THAT STINKS!
WHAT ARE YOU TALKING ABOUT?
I DUNNO, BUT THAT STINKITY STINK IS GETTIN' STINKIER!
IT SEEMS THE DEEPER WE GO IN THE FOREST, THE STRONGER THE SMELL!

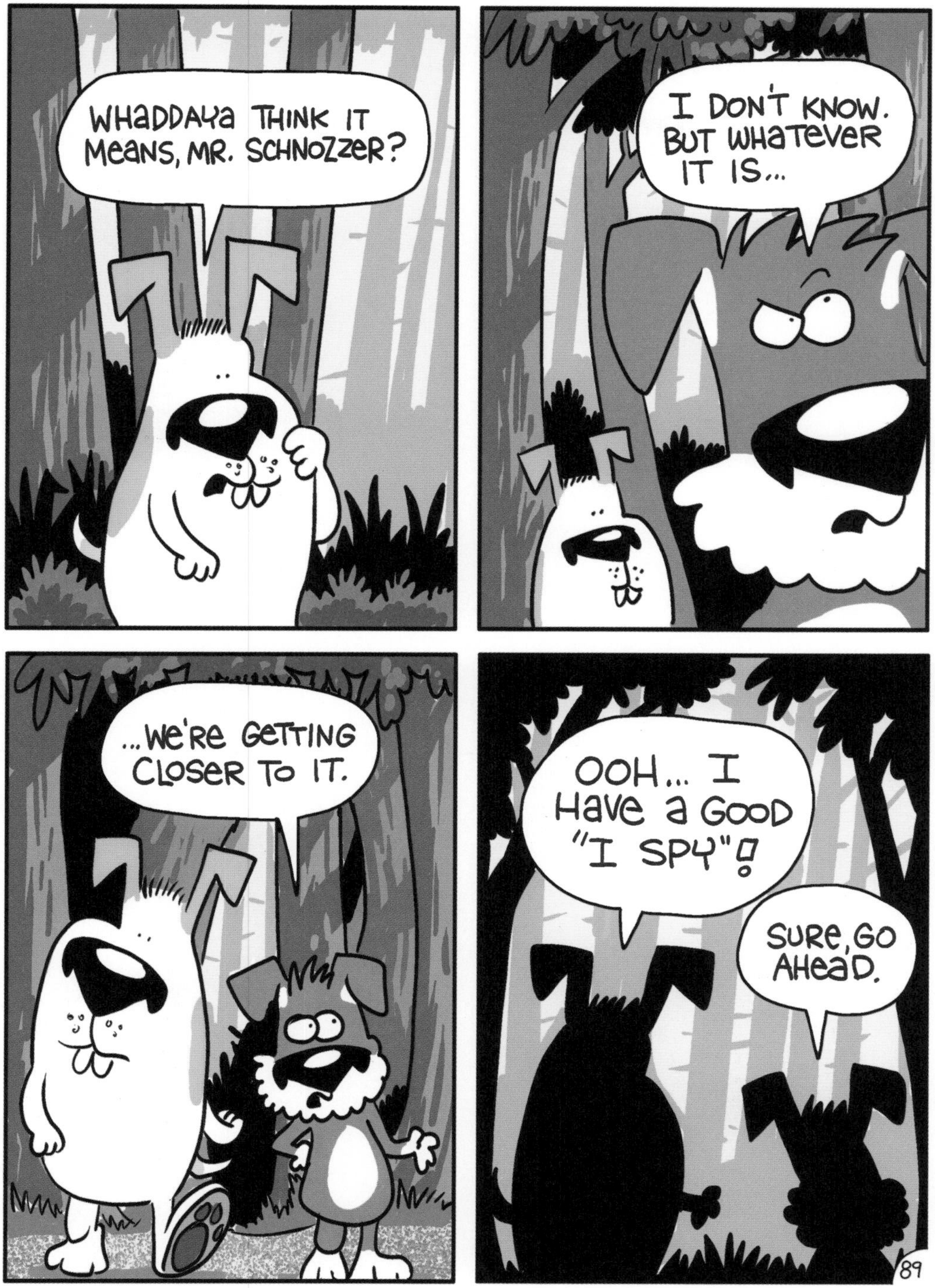
WHADDAYA THINK IT MEANS, MR. SCHNOZZER?
I DON'T KNOW. BUT WHATEVER IT IS...
...WE'RE GETTING CLOSER TO IT.
OOH... I HAVE A GOOD "I SPY"!
SURE, GO AHEAD.

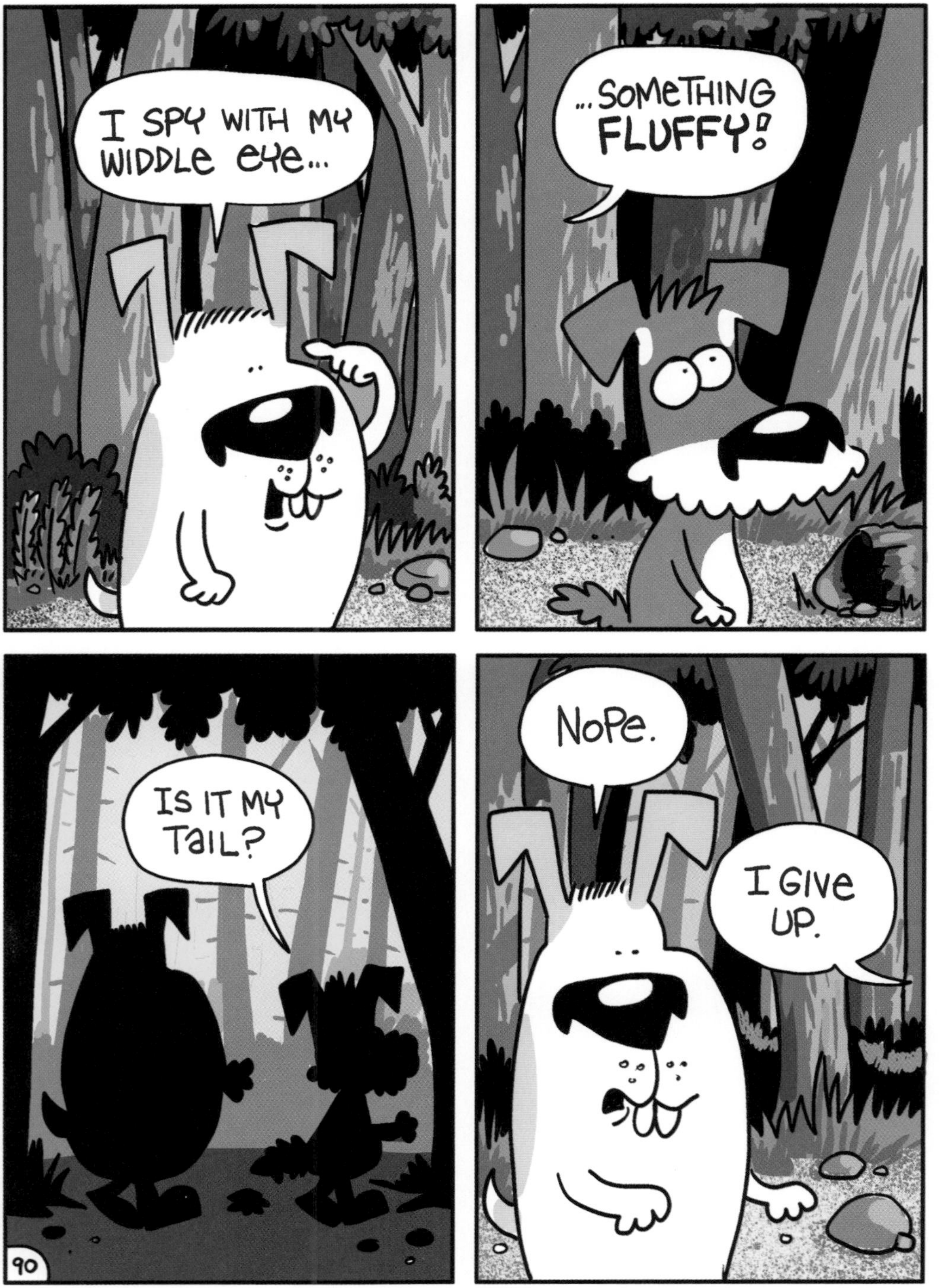

I SPY WITH MY WIDDLE EYE...
...SOMETHING FLUFFY!
IS IT MY TAIL?
NOPE.
I GIVE UP.
90

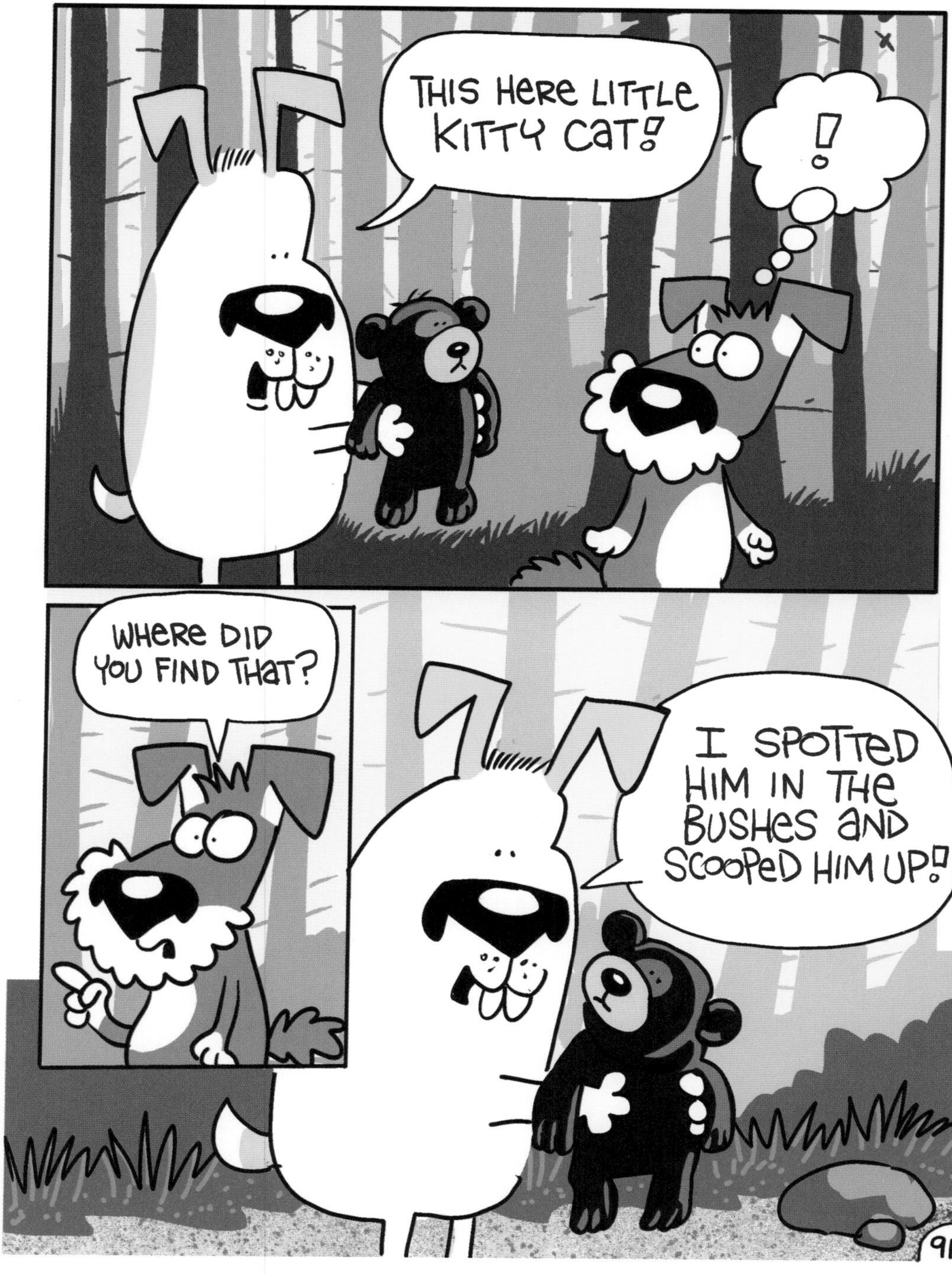
THIS HERE LITTLE KITTY CAT!
!
WHERE DID YOU FIND THAT?
I SPOTTED HIM IN THE BUSHES AND SCOOPED HIM UP!

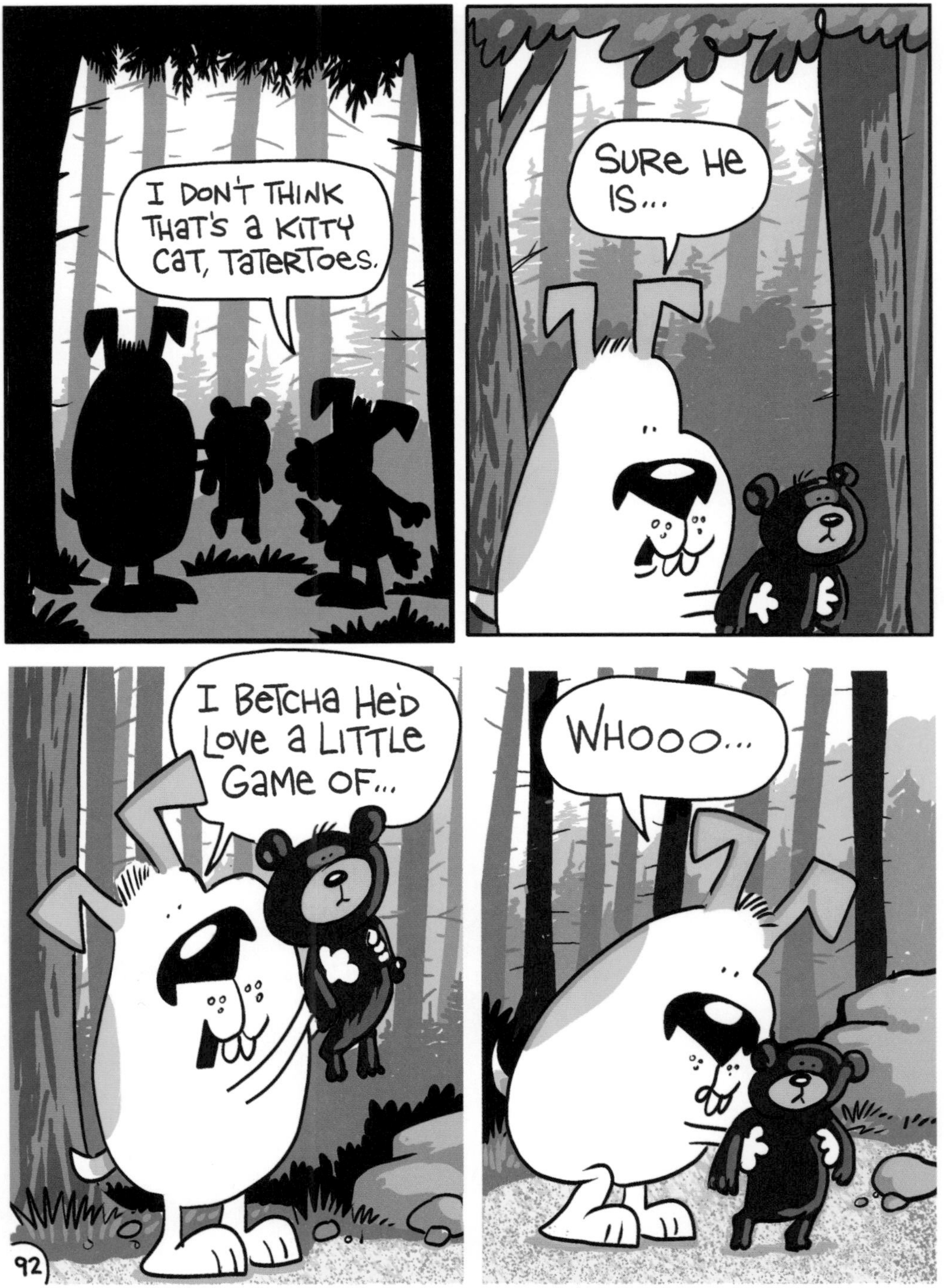
I DON'T THINK THAT'S a KITTY CAT, TaTeRToes.
SURe He IS...
I BeTCHa He'D Love a LITTLe Game OF...
WHOOO...

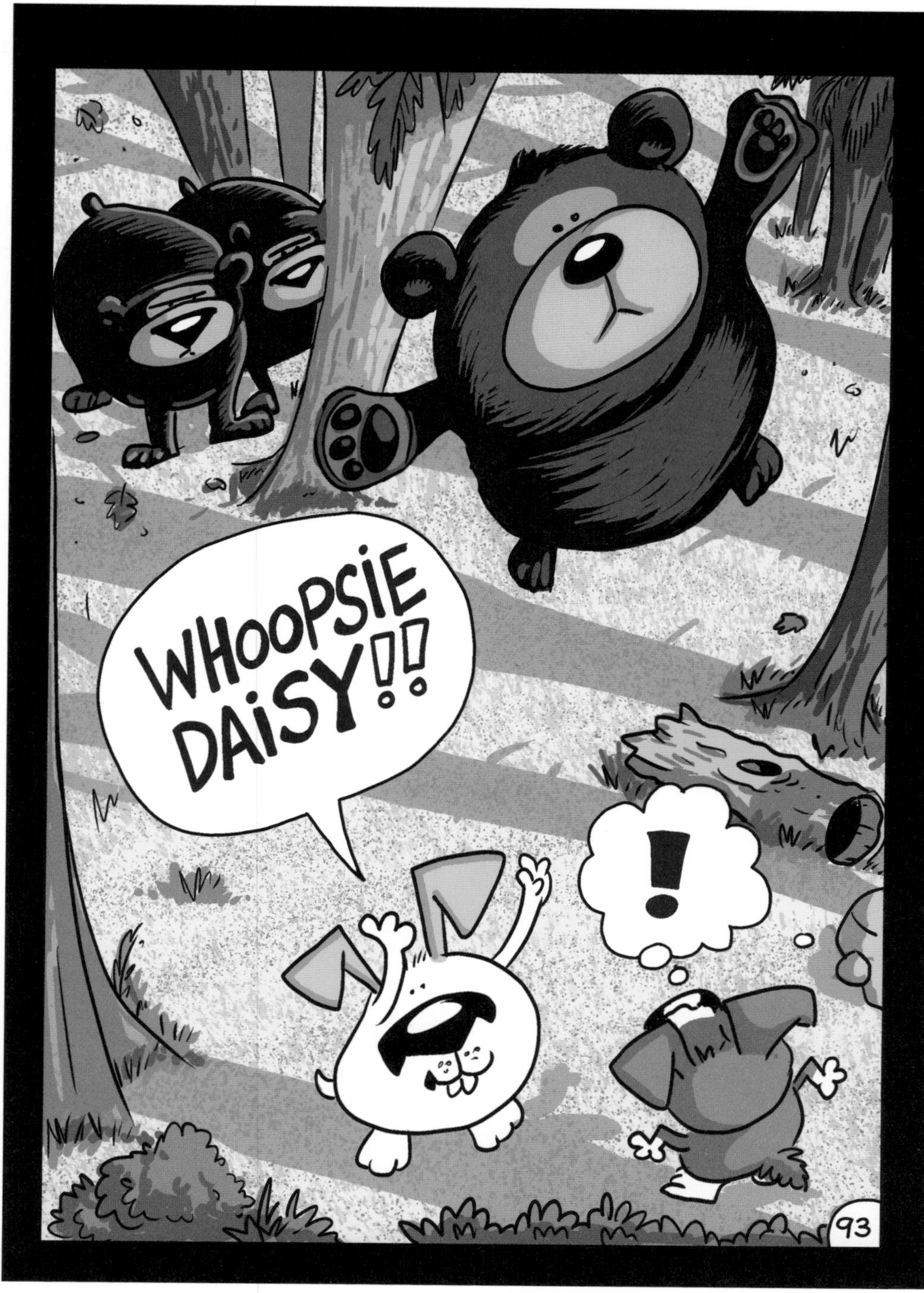
WHOOPSIE DAISY!!
!

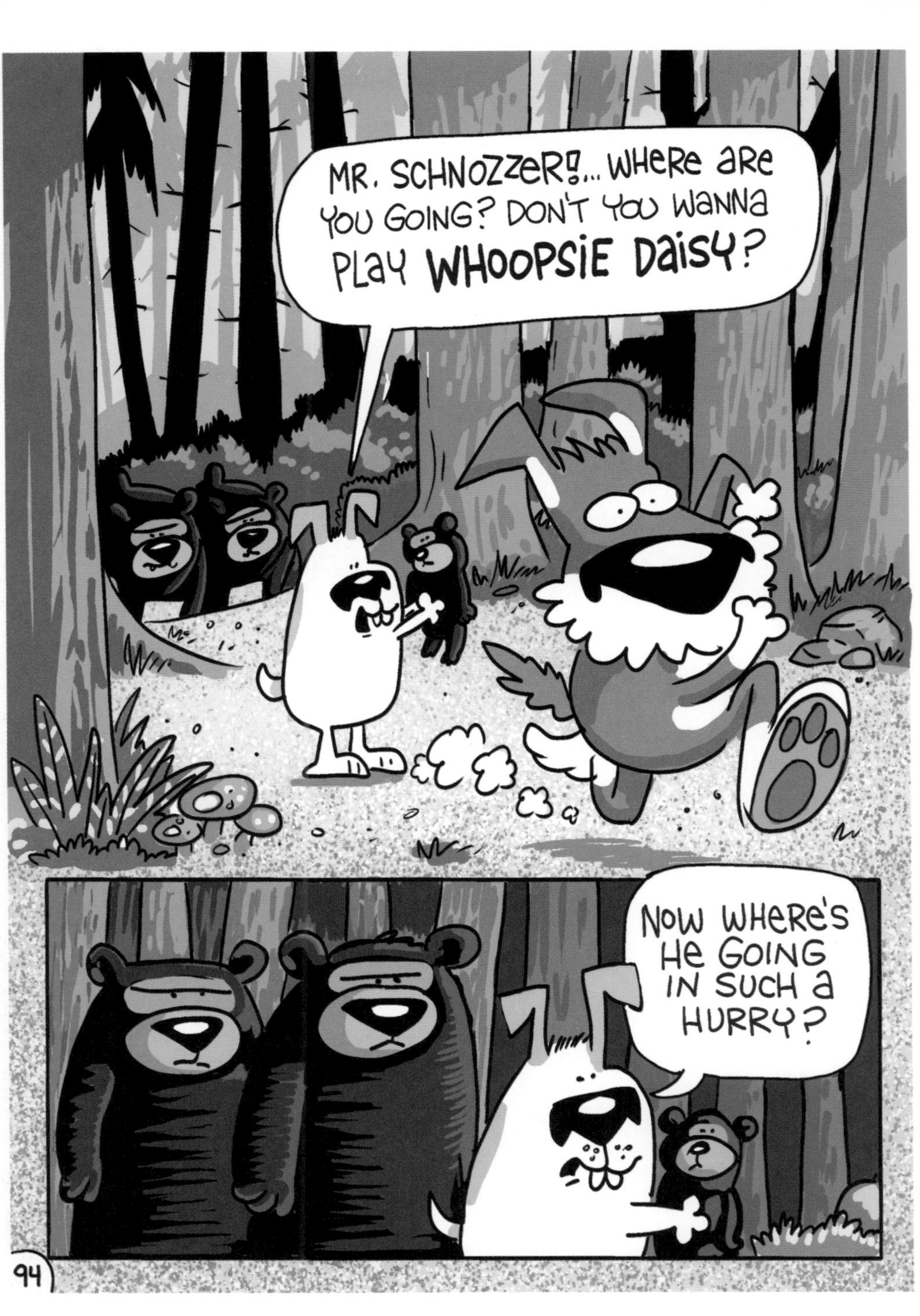
MR. SCHNOZZER!... WHERE ARE YOU GOING? DON'T YOU WANNA PLAY **WHOOPSIE DAISY**?
NOW WHERE'S HE GOING IN SUCH A HURRY?

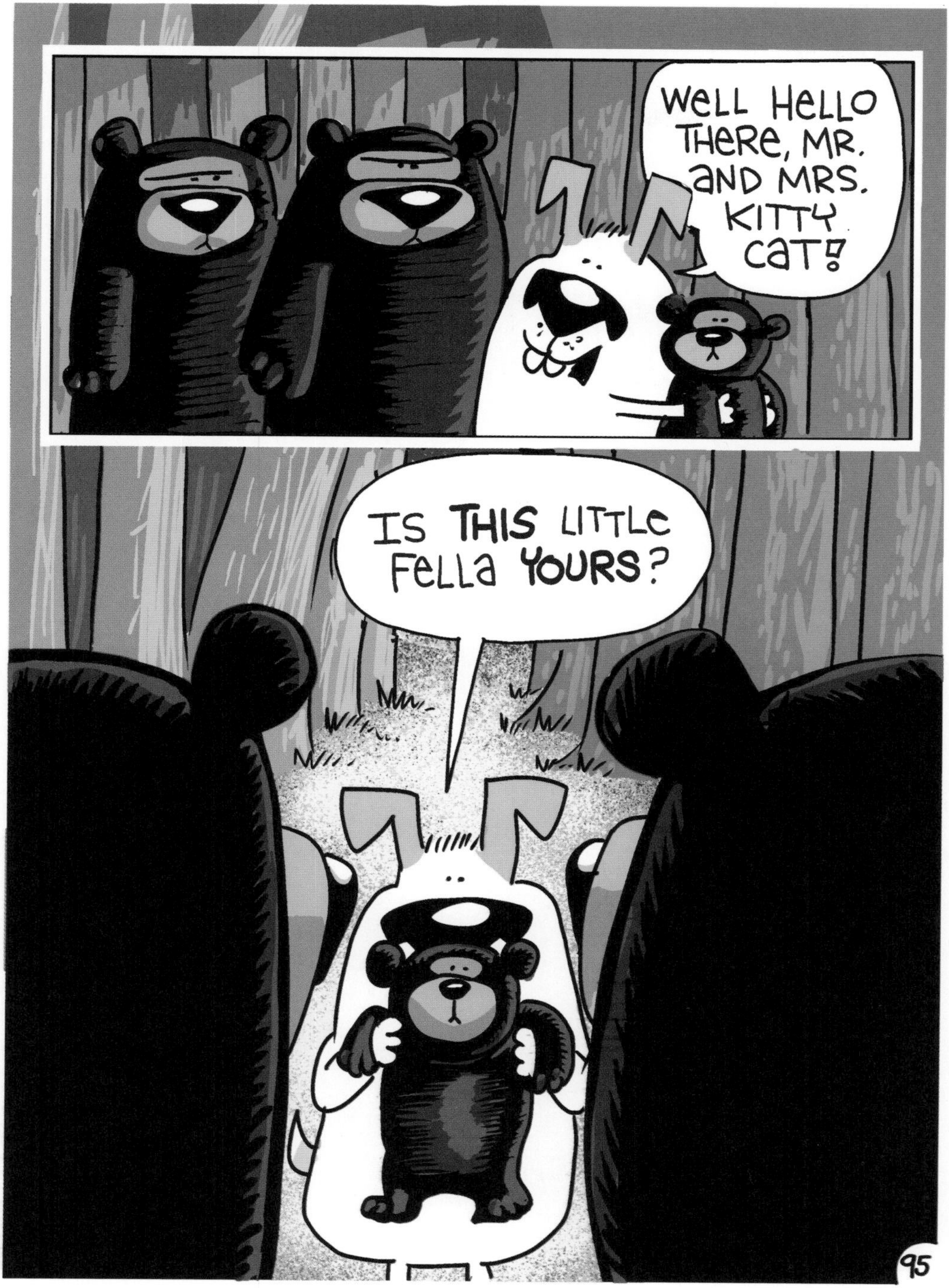
WELL HELLO THERE, MR. AND MRS. KITTY CAT!
IS THIS LITTLE FELLA YOURS?

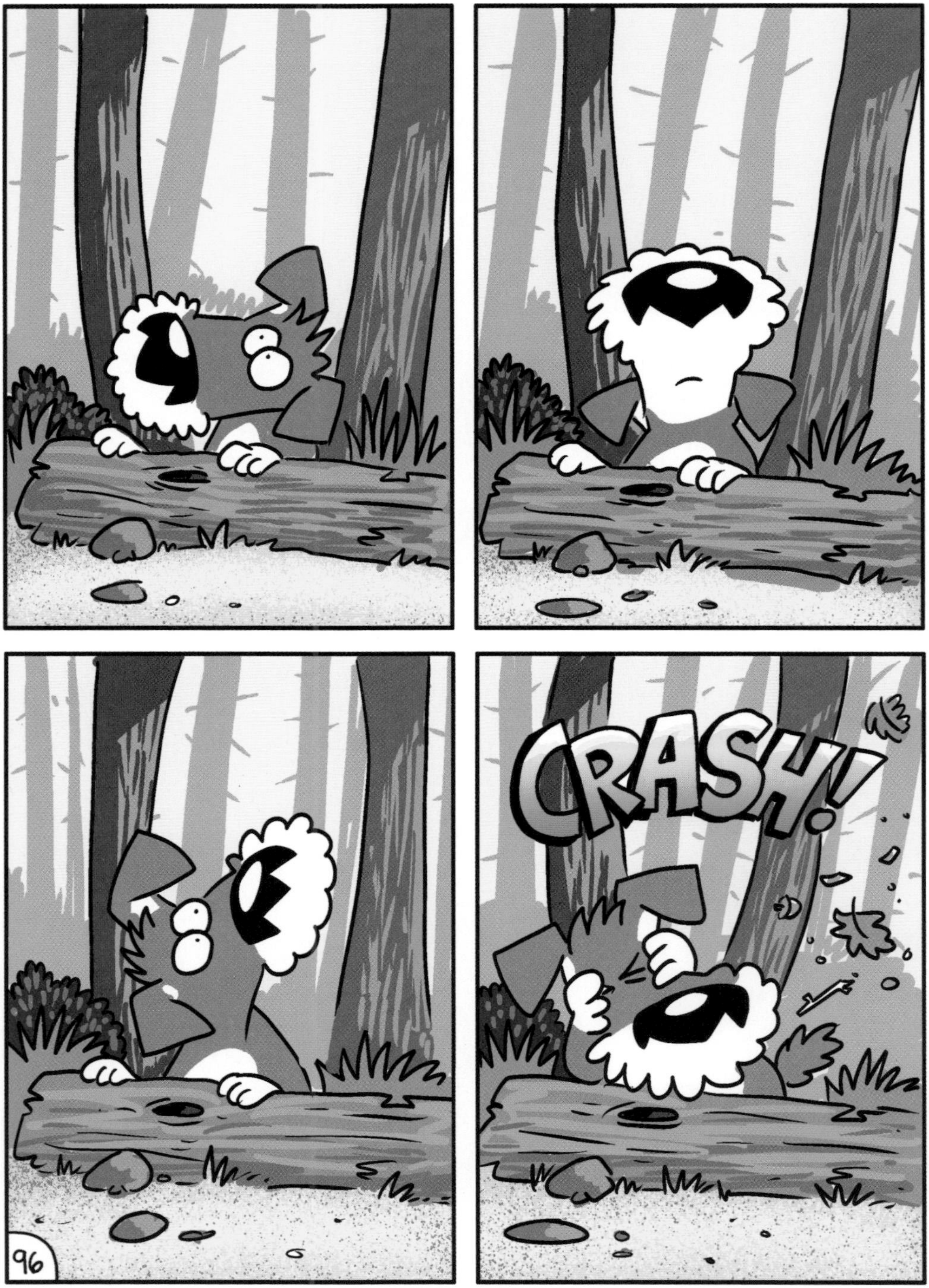
CRASH!

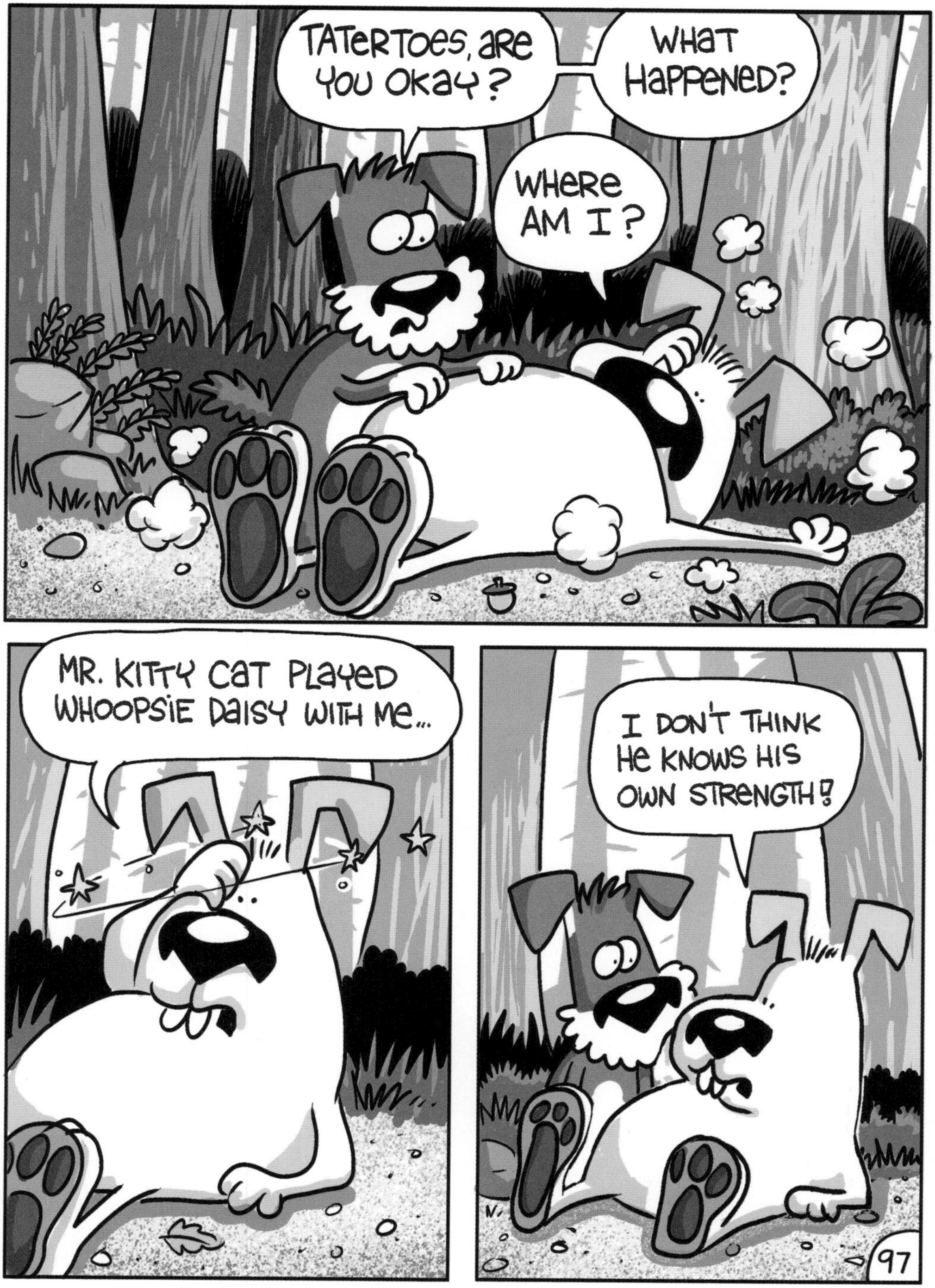
TATERTOES, ARE YOU OKAY?
WHAT HAPPENED?
WHERE AM I?
MR. KITTY CAT PLAYED WHOOPSIE DAISY WITH ME...
I DON'T THINK HE KNOWS HIS OWN STRENGTH!

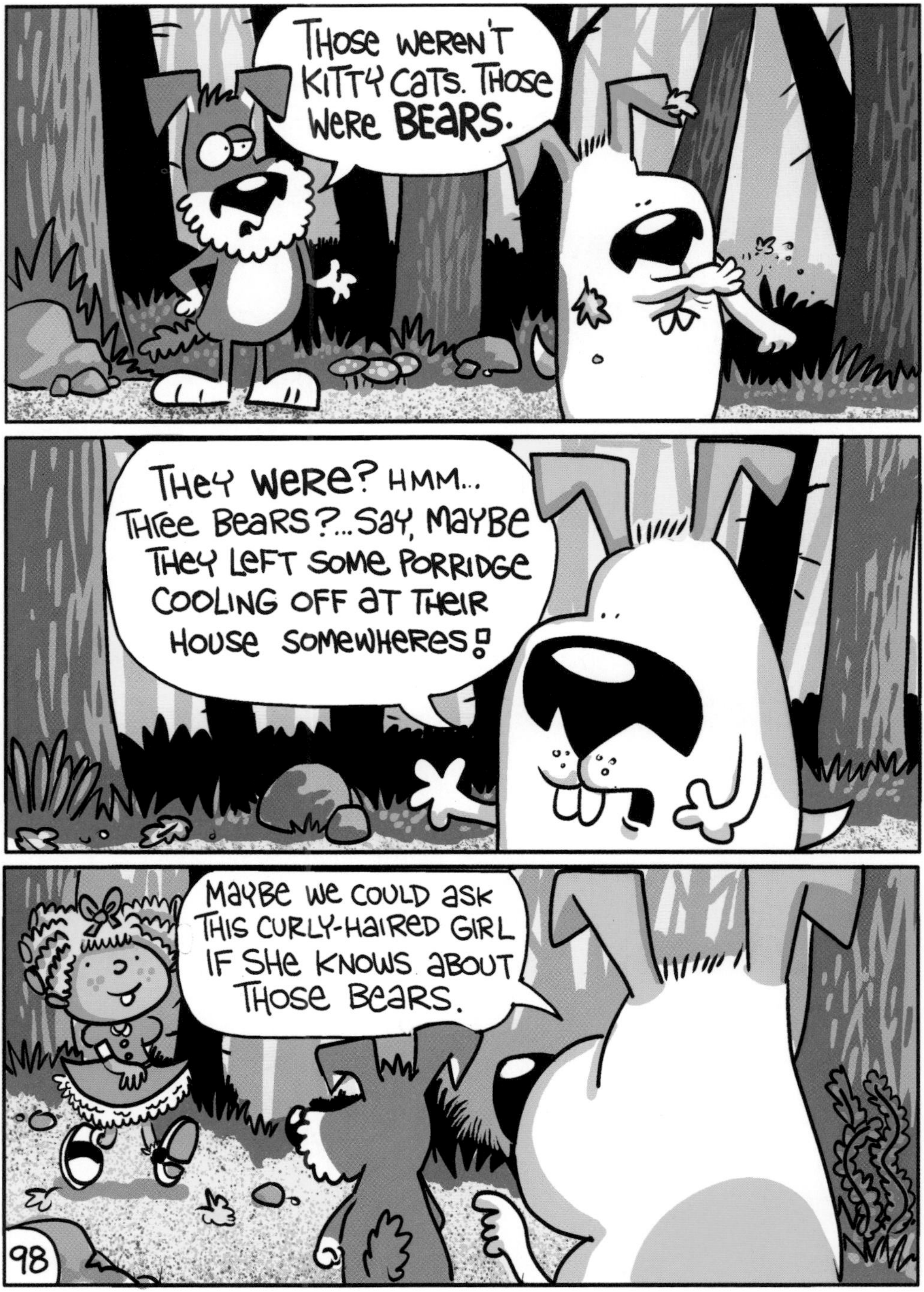
THOSE WEREN'T KITTY CATS. THOSE WERE BEARS.
THEY WERE? HMM... THREE BEARS?... SAY, MAYBE THEY LEFT SOME PORRIDGE COOLING OFF AT THEIR HOUSE SOMEWHERES!
MAYBE WE COULD ASK THIS CURLY-HAIRED GIRL IF SHE KNOWS ABOUT THOSE BEARS.

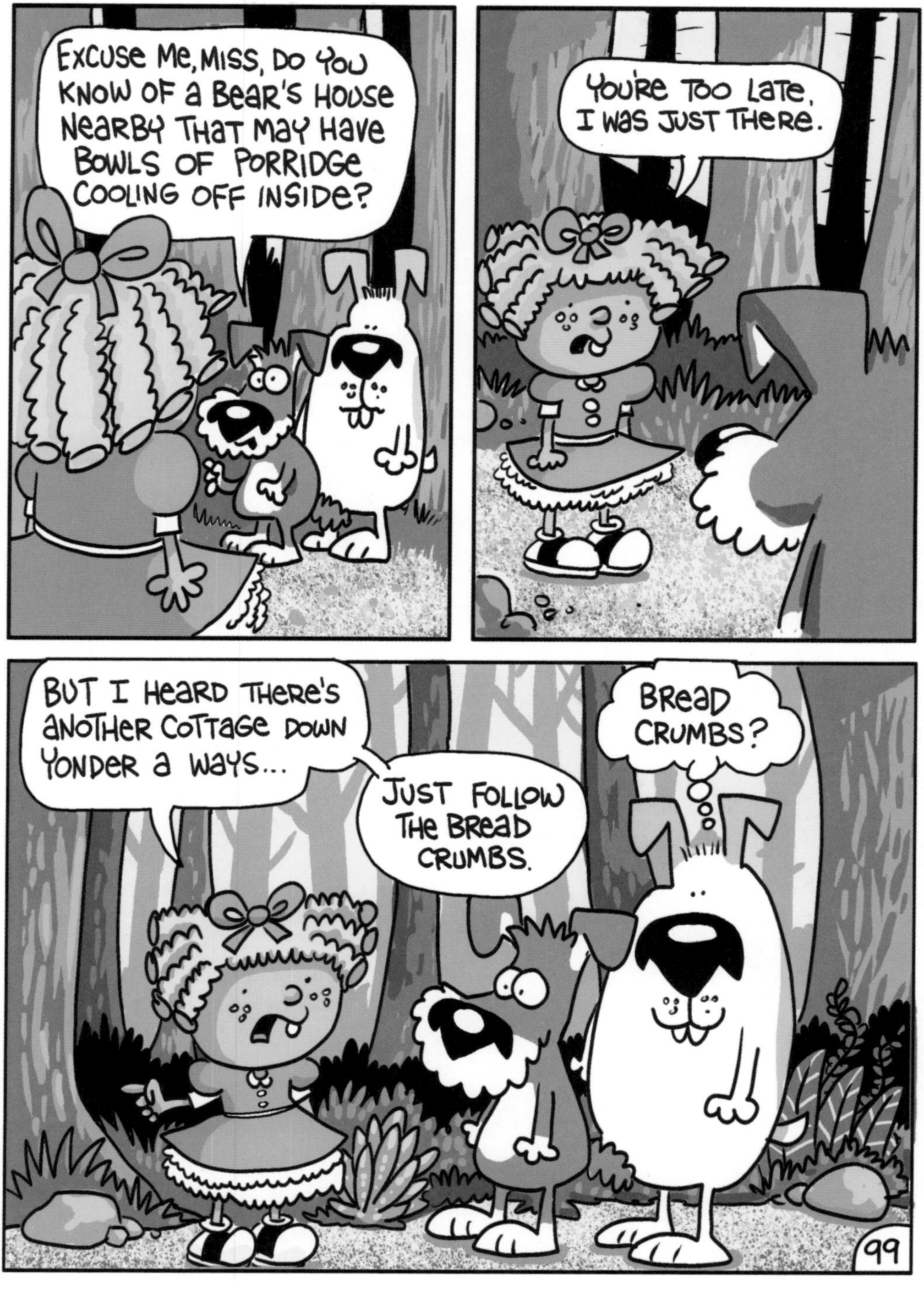
EXCUSE ME, MISS, DO YOU KNOW OF A BEAR'S HOUSE NEARBY THAT MAY HAVE BOWLS OF PORRIDGE COOLING OFF INSIDE?
YOU'RE TOO LATE. I WAS JUST THERE.
BUT I HEARD THERE'S ANOTHER COTTAGE DOWN YONDER A WAYS...
JUST FOLLOW THE BREAD CRUMBS.
BREAD CRUMBS?
99

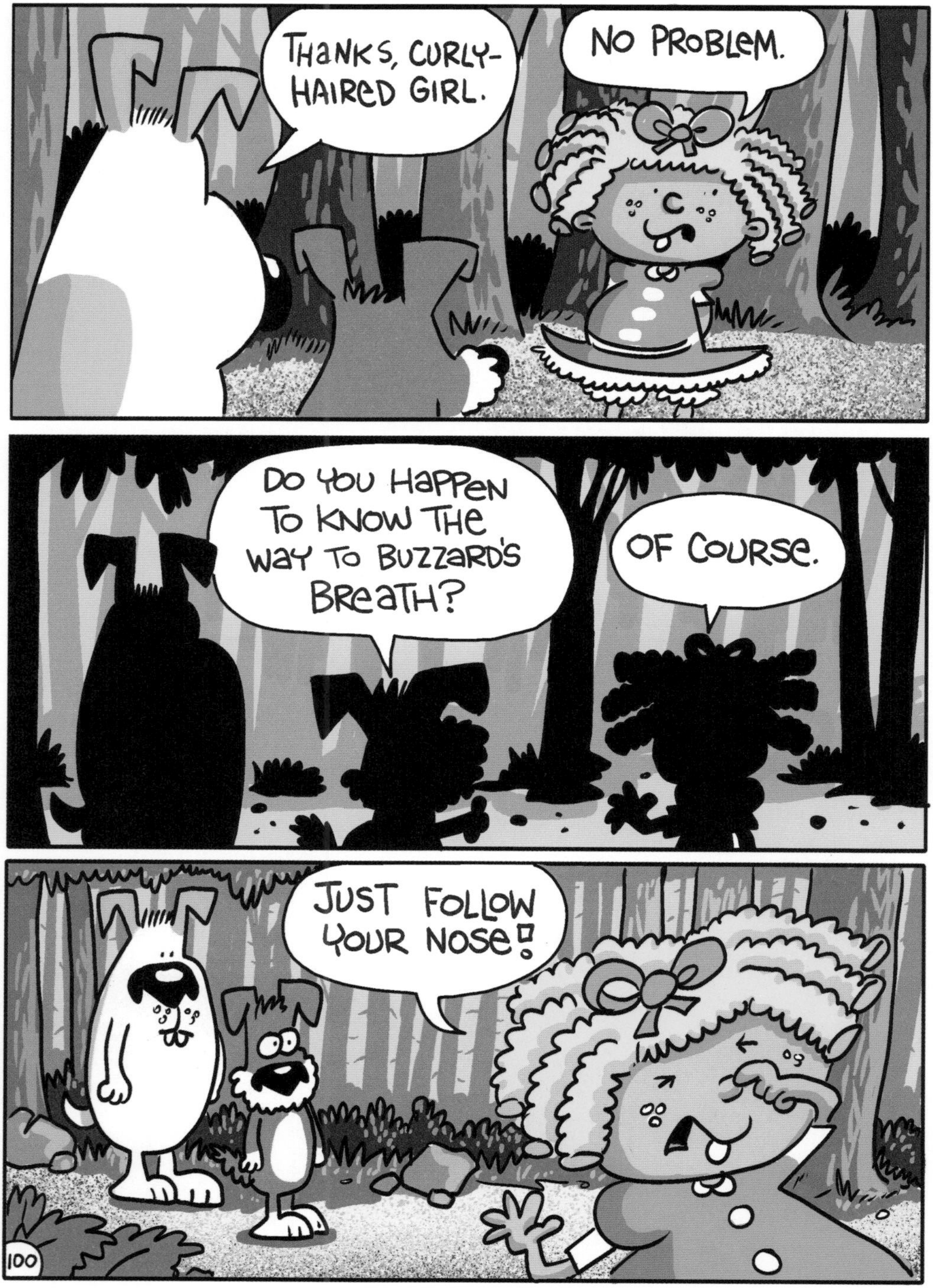

THANKS, CURLY-HAIRED GIRL.
NO PROBLEM.
DO YOU HAPPEN TO KNOW THE WAY TO BUZZARD'S BREATH?
OF COURSE.
JUST FOLLOW YOUR NOSE!

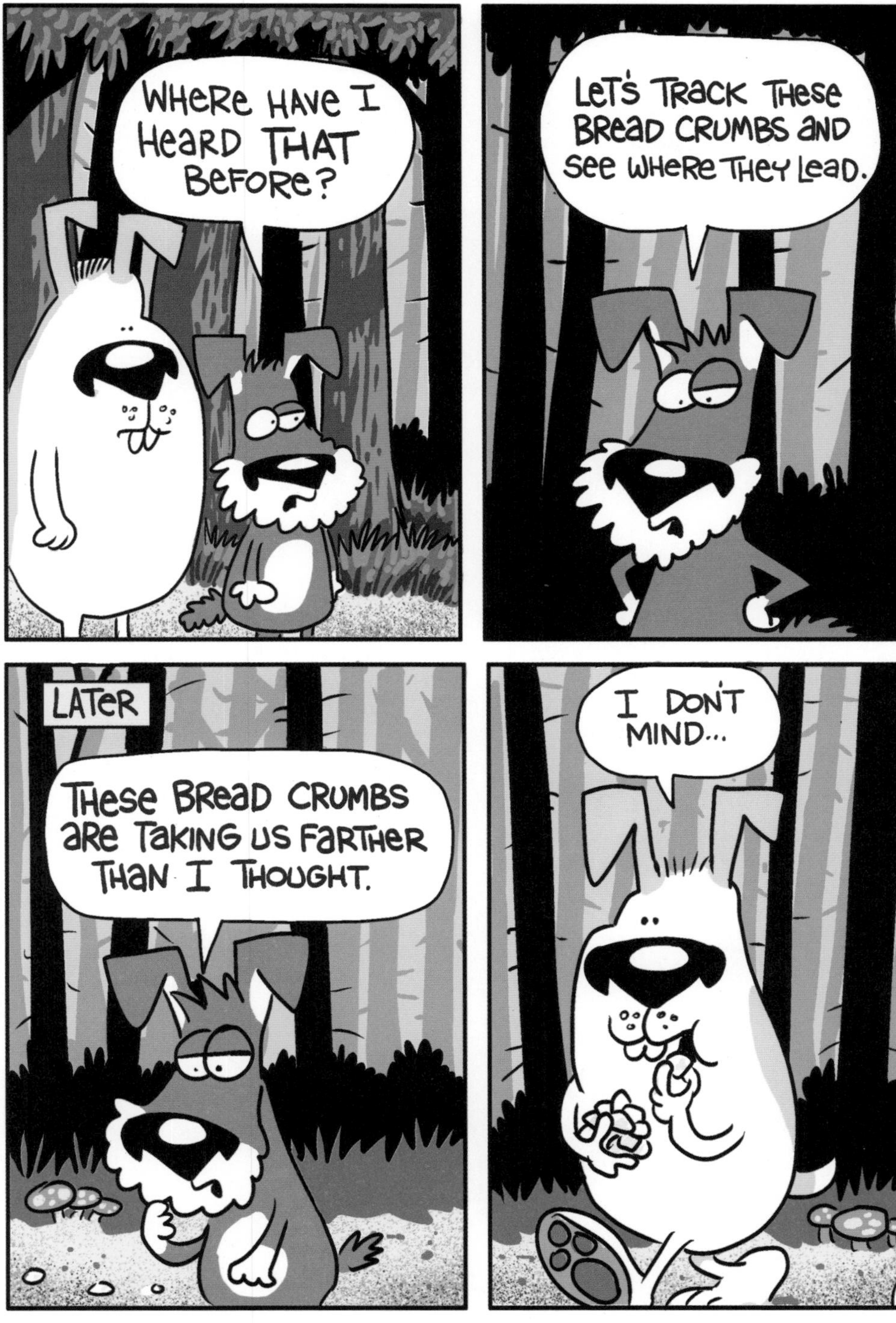
WHERE HAVE I HEARD THAT BEFORE?
LET'S TRACK THESE BREAD CRUMBS AND SEE WHERE THEY LEAD.
LATER
THESE BREAD CRUMBS ARE TAKING US FARTHER THAN I THOUGHT.
I DON'T MIND...

CHAPTER SEVEN

WHICH WAY DO WE GO?

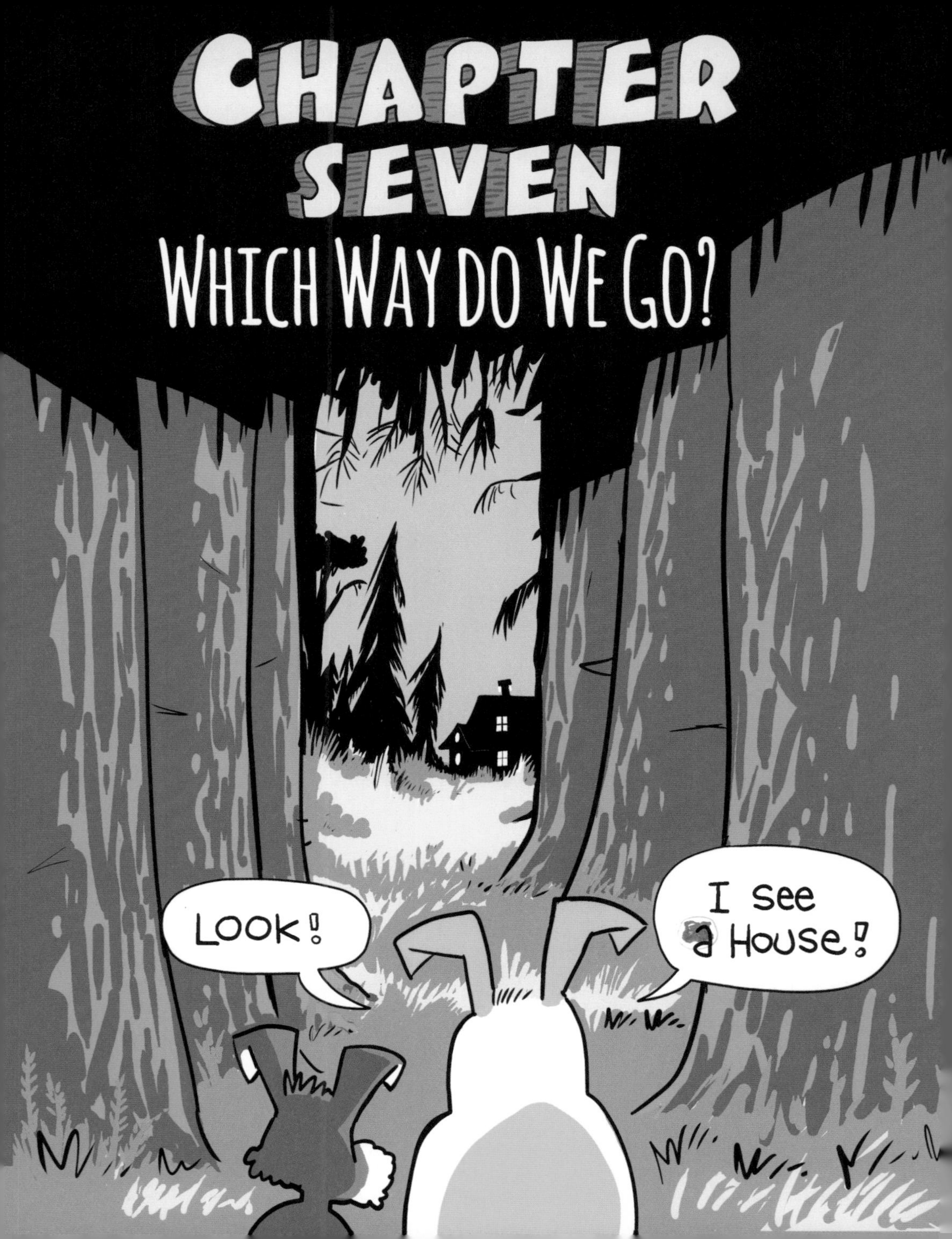
LOOK!
I see a House!

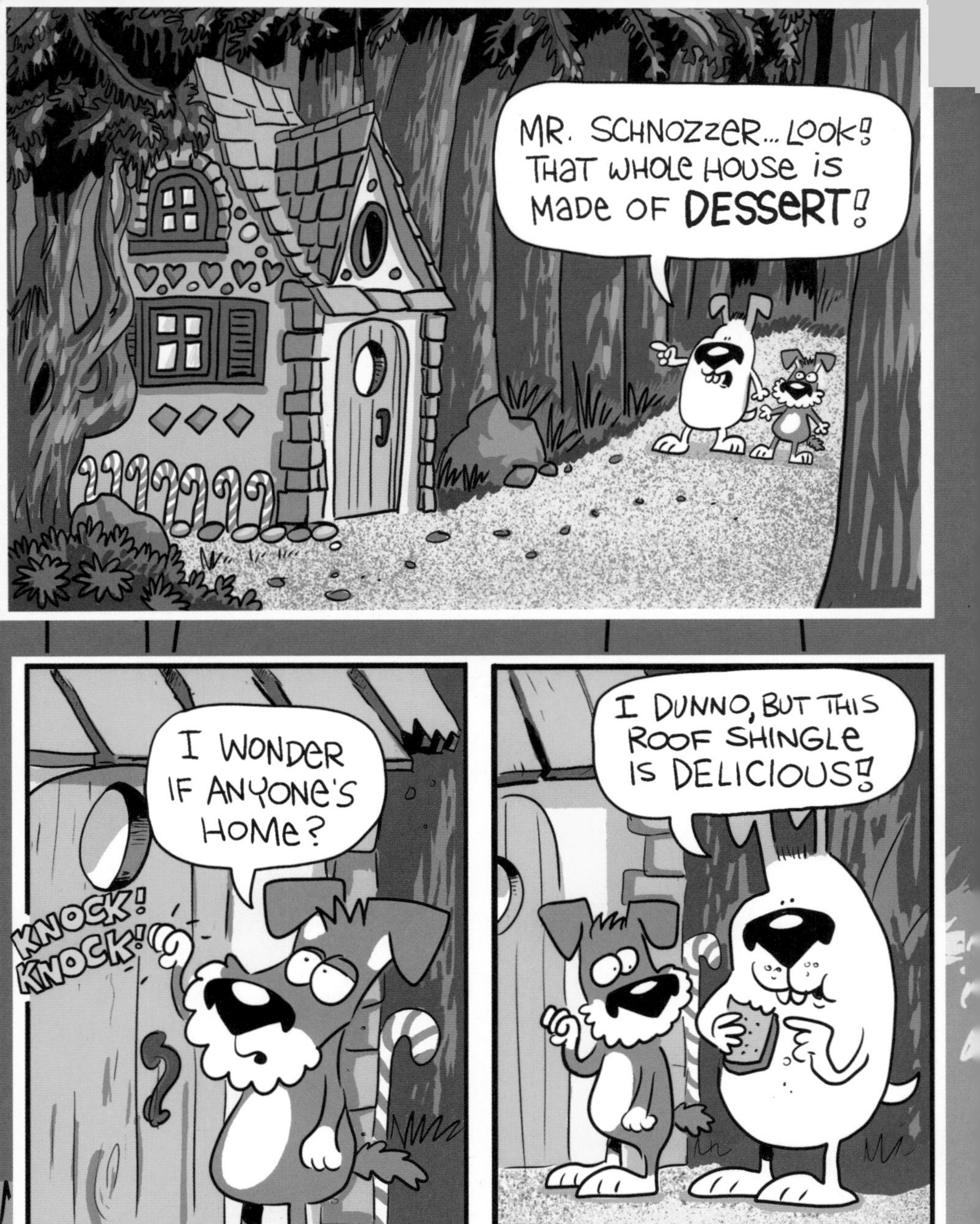
MR. SCHNOZZER... LOOK! THAT WHOLE HOUSE IS MADE OF DESSERT!
I WONDER IF ANYONE'S HOME?
KNOCK! KNOCK!
I DUNNO, BUT THIS ROOF SHINGLE IS DELICIOUS!

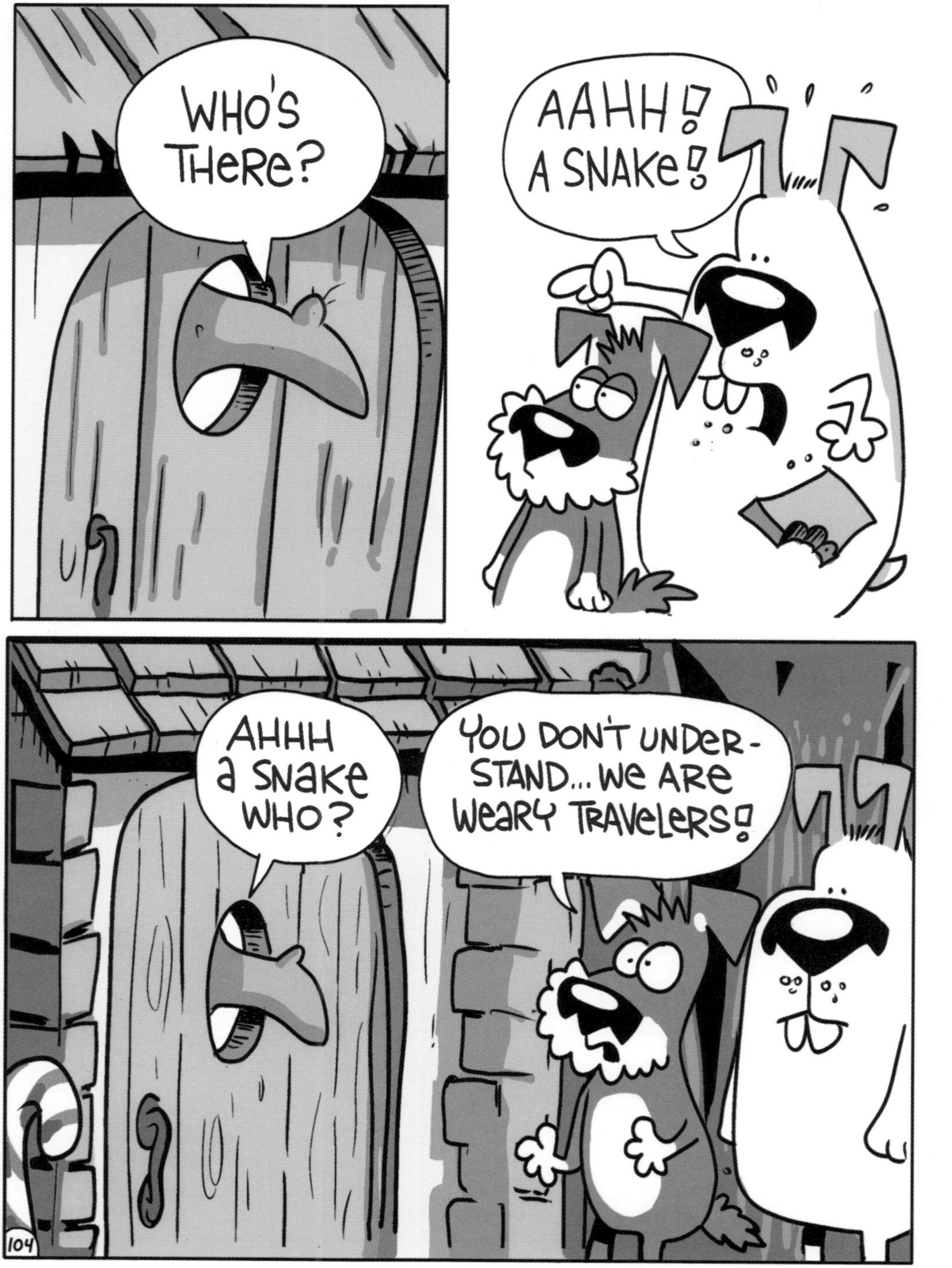
WHO'S THERE?
AAHH! A SNAKE!
AHHH a SNaKe WHO?
YOU DON'T UNDER-STAND... We ARe WeaRY TRAVeLeRS!

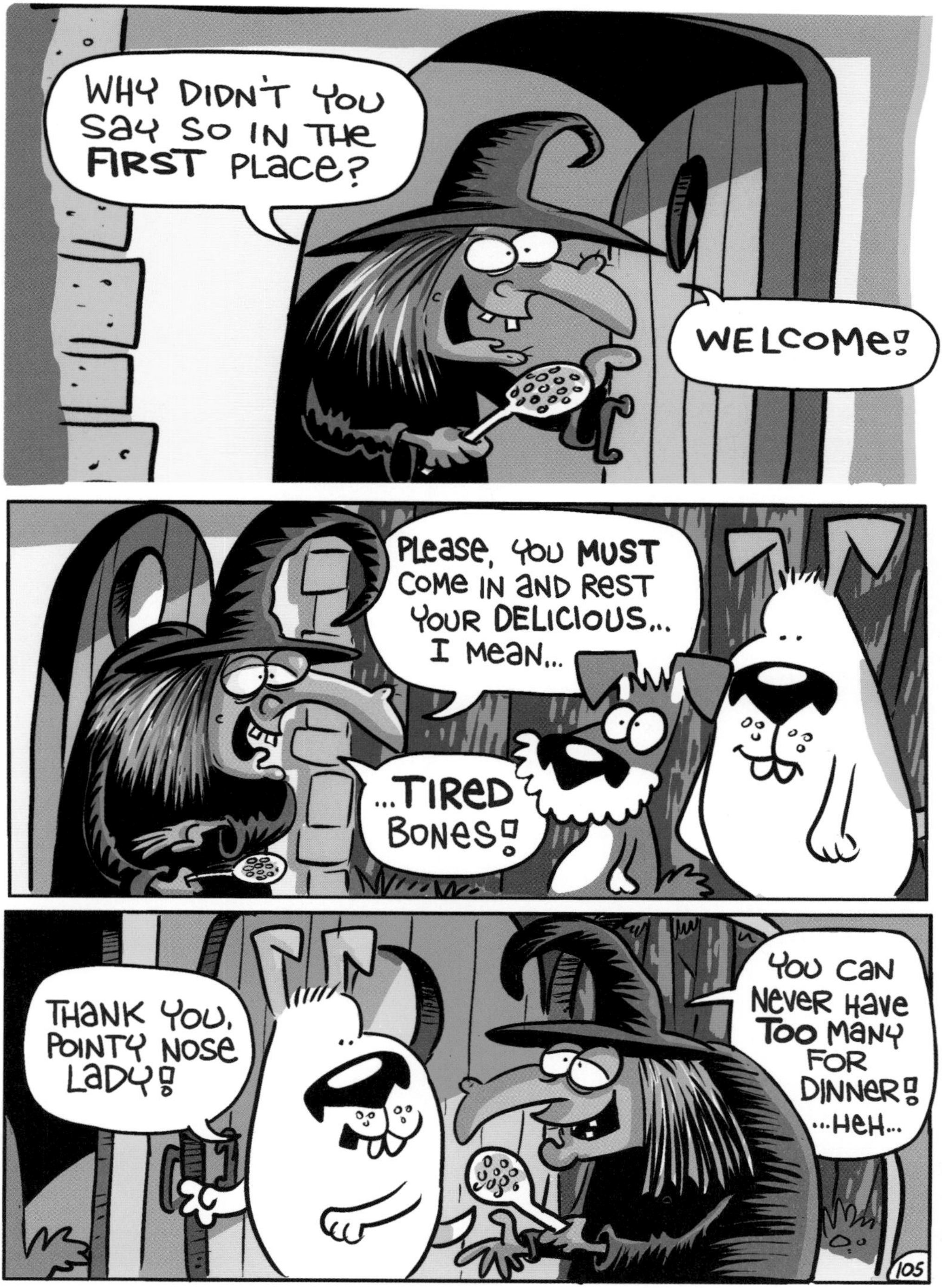
WHY DIDN'T YOU SAY SO IN THE FIRST PLACE?
WELCOME!
PLEASE, YOU MUST COME IN AND REST YOUR DELICIOUS... I MEAN...
...TIRED BONES!
THANK YOU, POINTY NOSE LADY!
YOU CAN NEVER HAVE TOO MANY FOR DINNER! ...HEH...

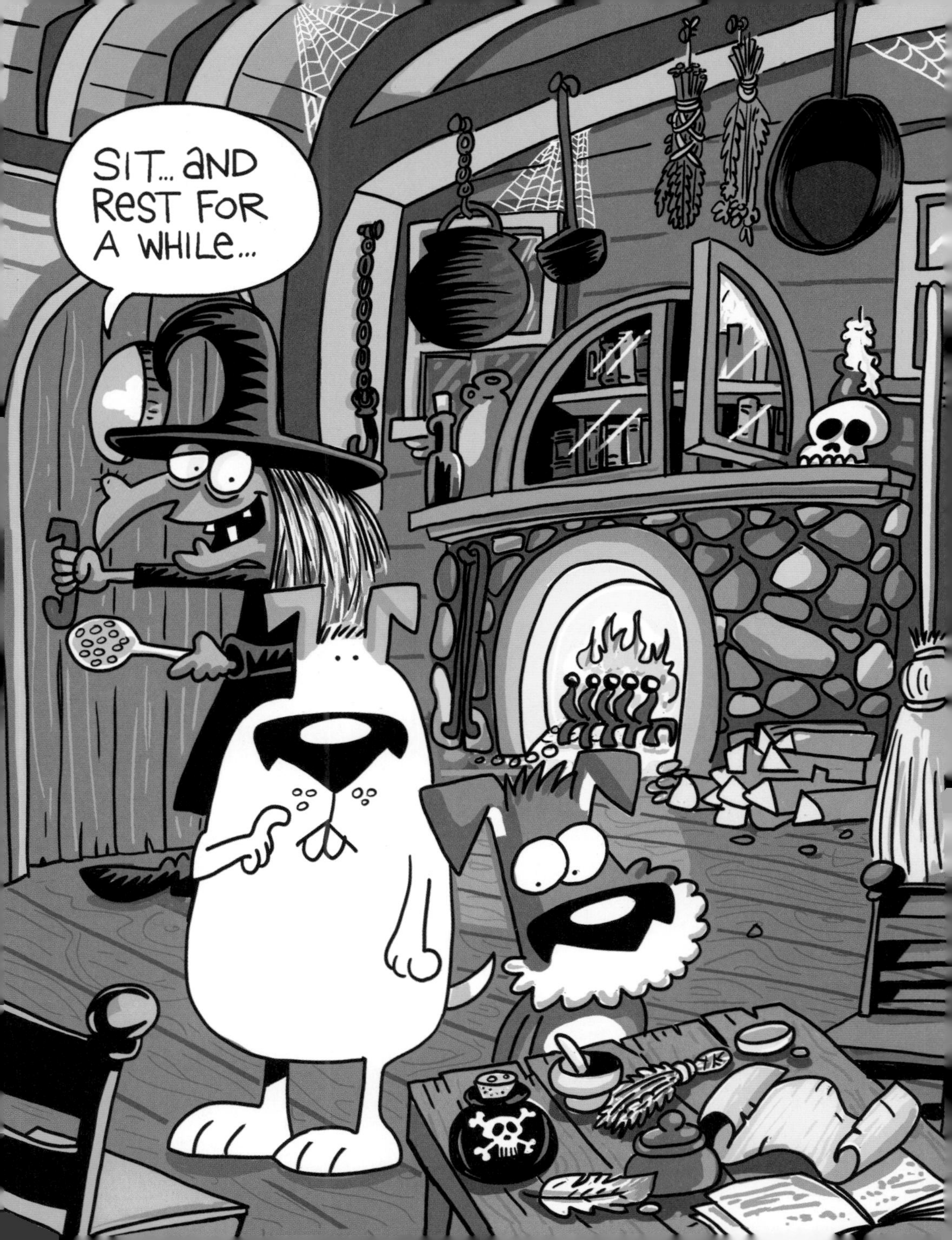
SIT... aND REST FOR A WHILE...

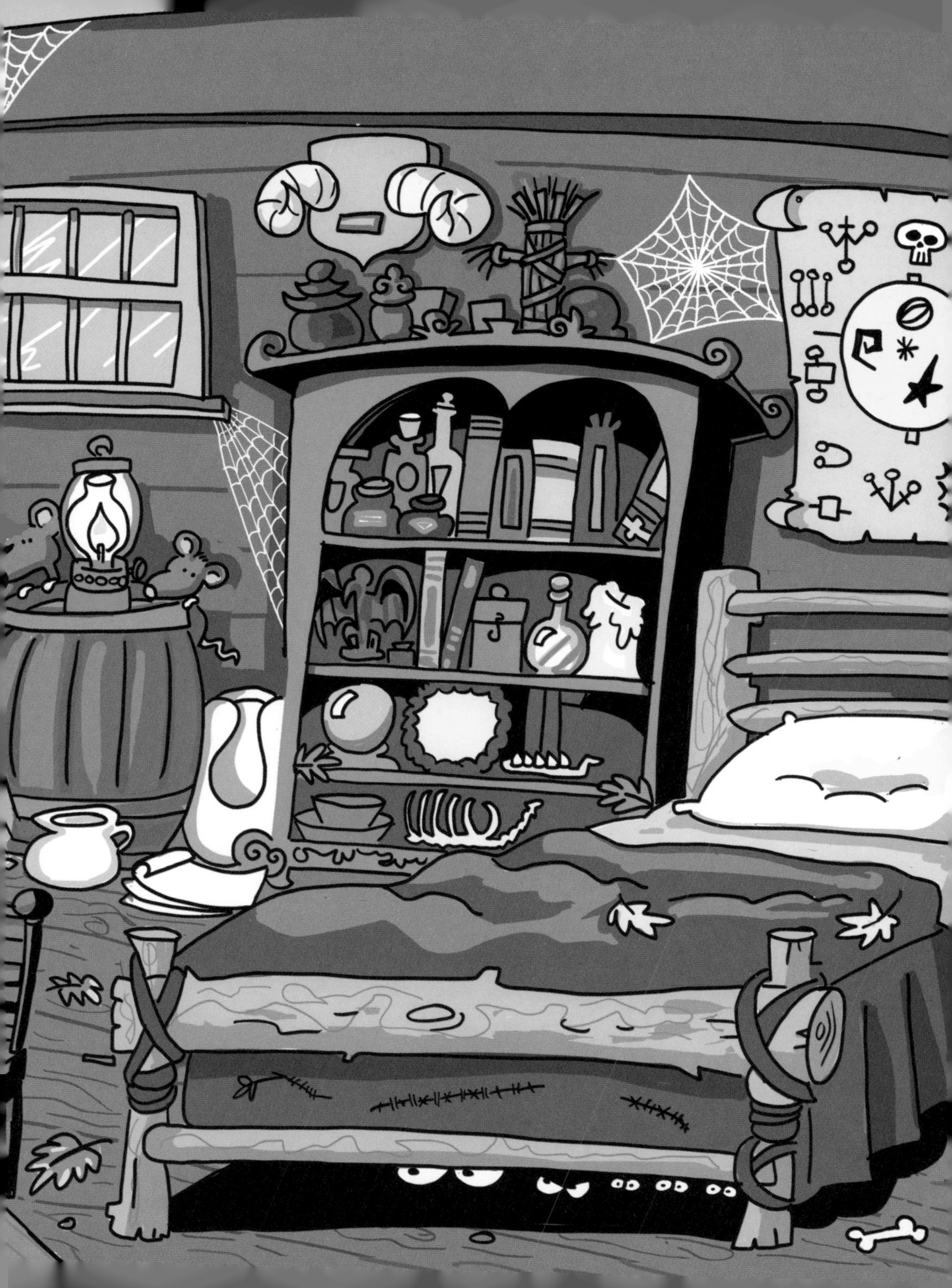

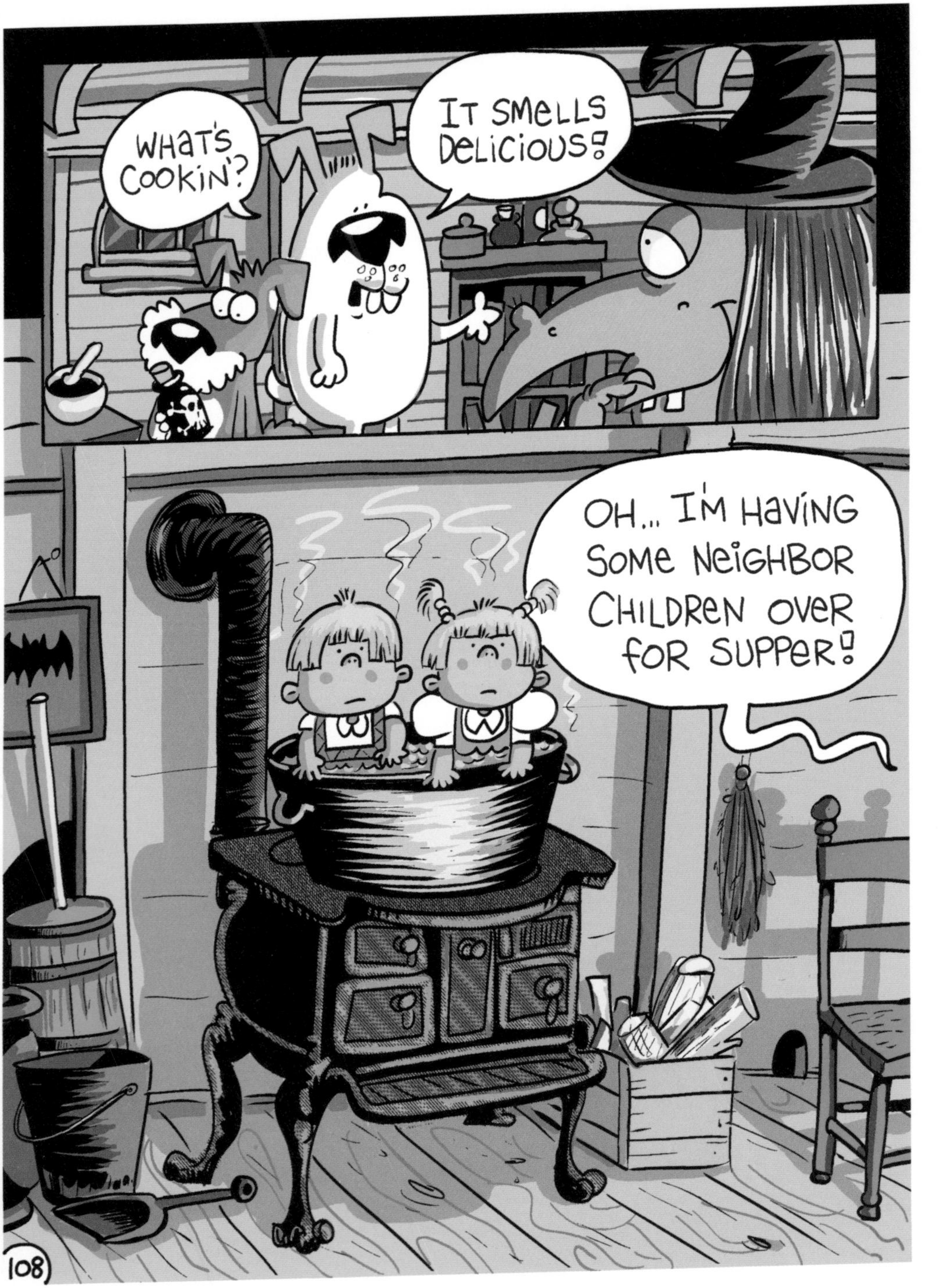
WHAT'S COOKIN'?
IT SMELLS DELICIOUS!
OH... I'M HAVING SOME NEIGHBOR CHILDREN OVER FOR SUPPER!

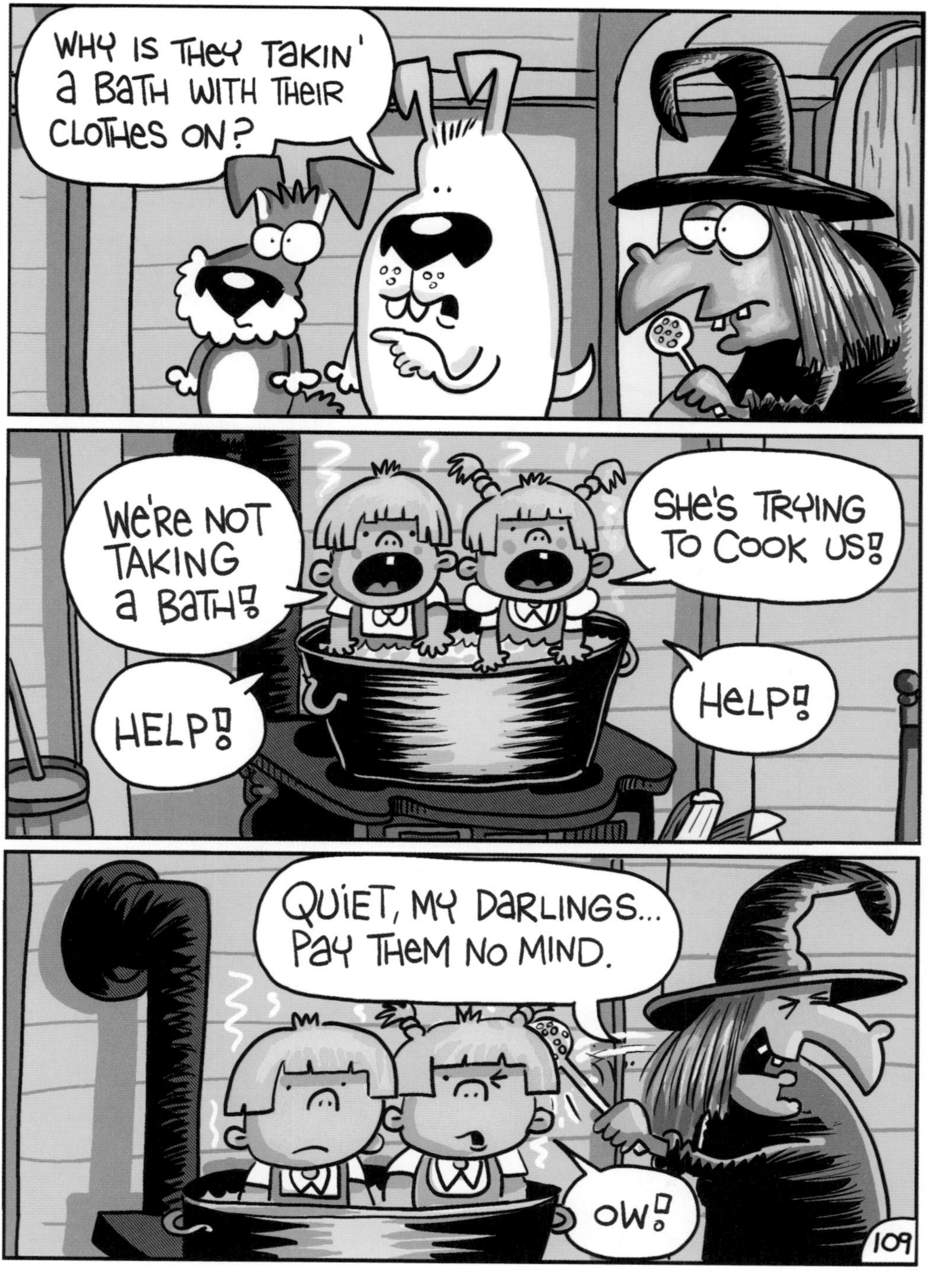
WHY IS THEY TAKIN' a BATH WITH THEIR CLOTHES ON?
WE'RE NOT TAKING a BATH!
SHE'S TRYING TO COOK US!
HELP!
HELP!
QUIET, MY DARLINGS... PAY THEM NO MIND.
OW!

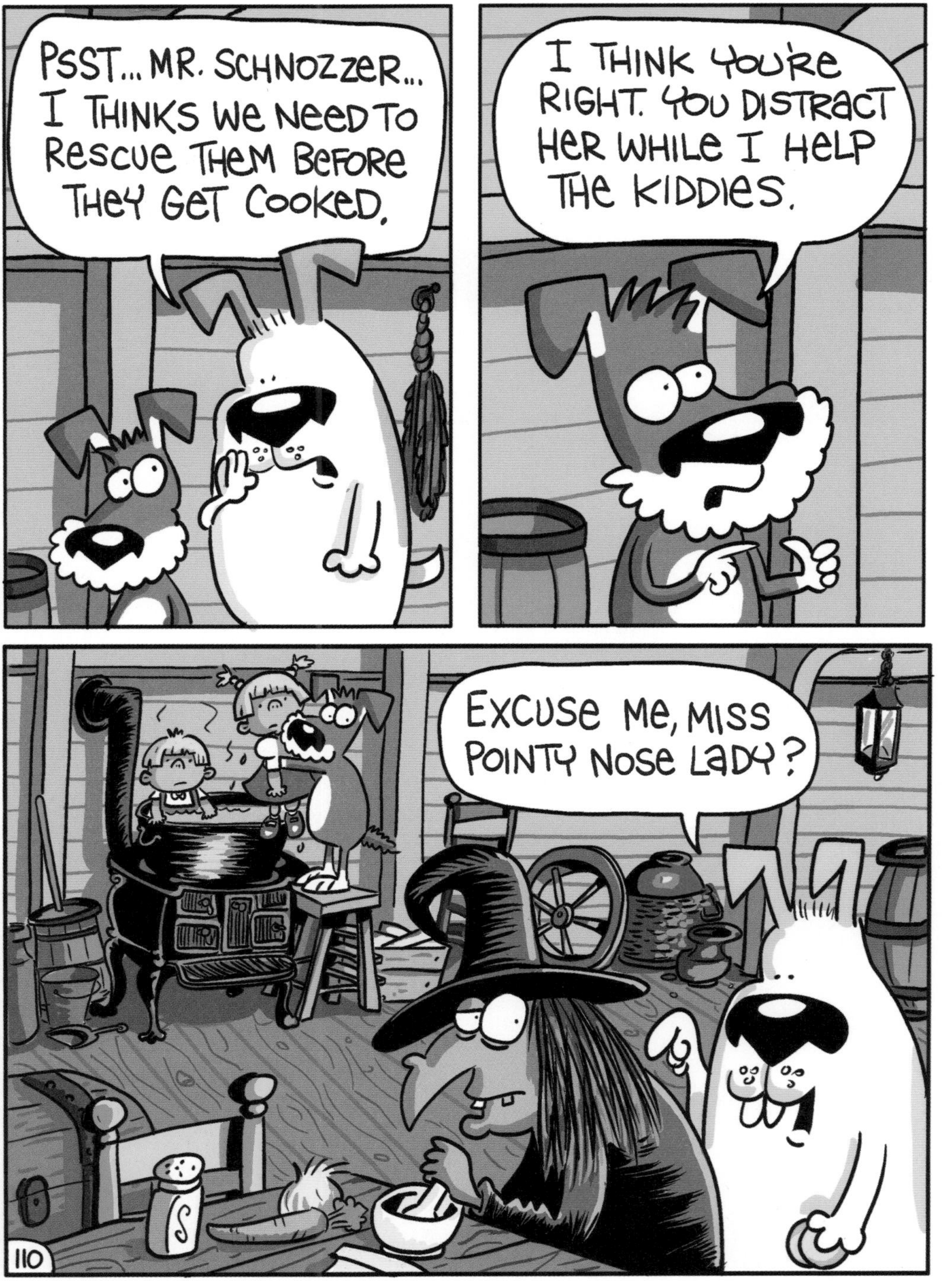
PSST... MR. SCHNOZZER... I THINKS WE NEED TO RESCUE THEM BEFORE THEY GET COOKED.
I THINK YOU'RE RIGHT. YOU DISTRACT HER WHILE I HELP THE KIDDIES.
EXCUSE ME, MISS POINTY NOSE LADY?
S

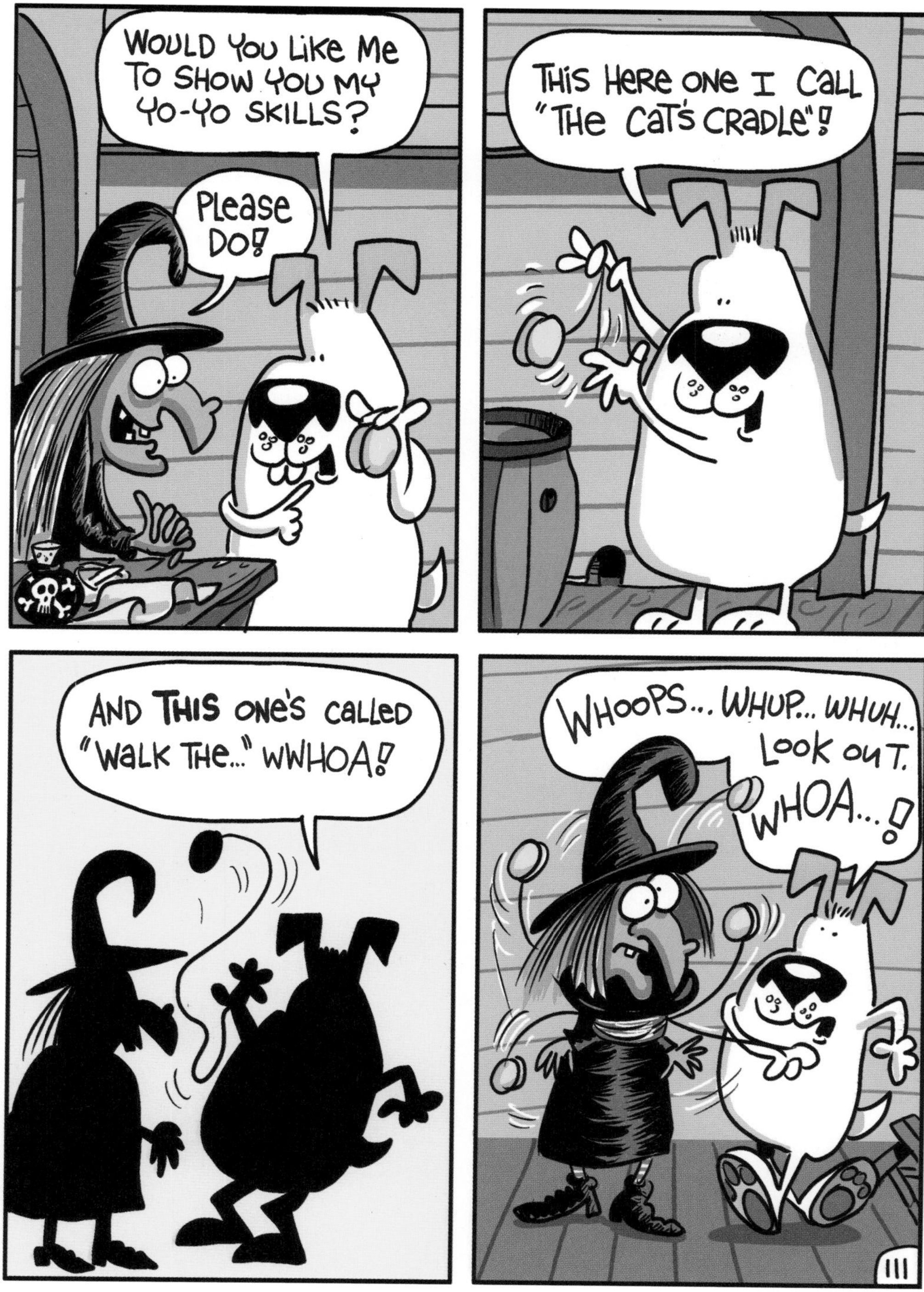
WOULD YOU LIKE ME TO SHOW YOU MY YO-YO SKILLS?
PLEASE DO!
THIS HERE ONE I CALL "THE CAT'S CRADLE"!
AND THIS ONE'S CALLED "WALK THE..." WWHOA!
WHOOPS... WHUP... WHUH... LOOK OUT. WHOA...!

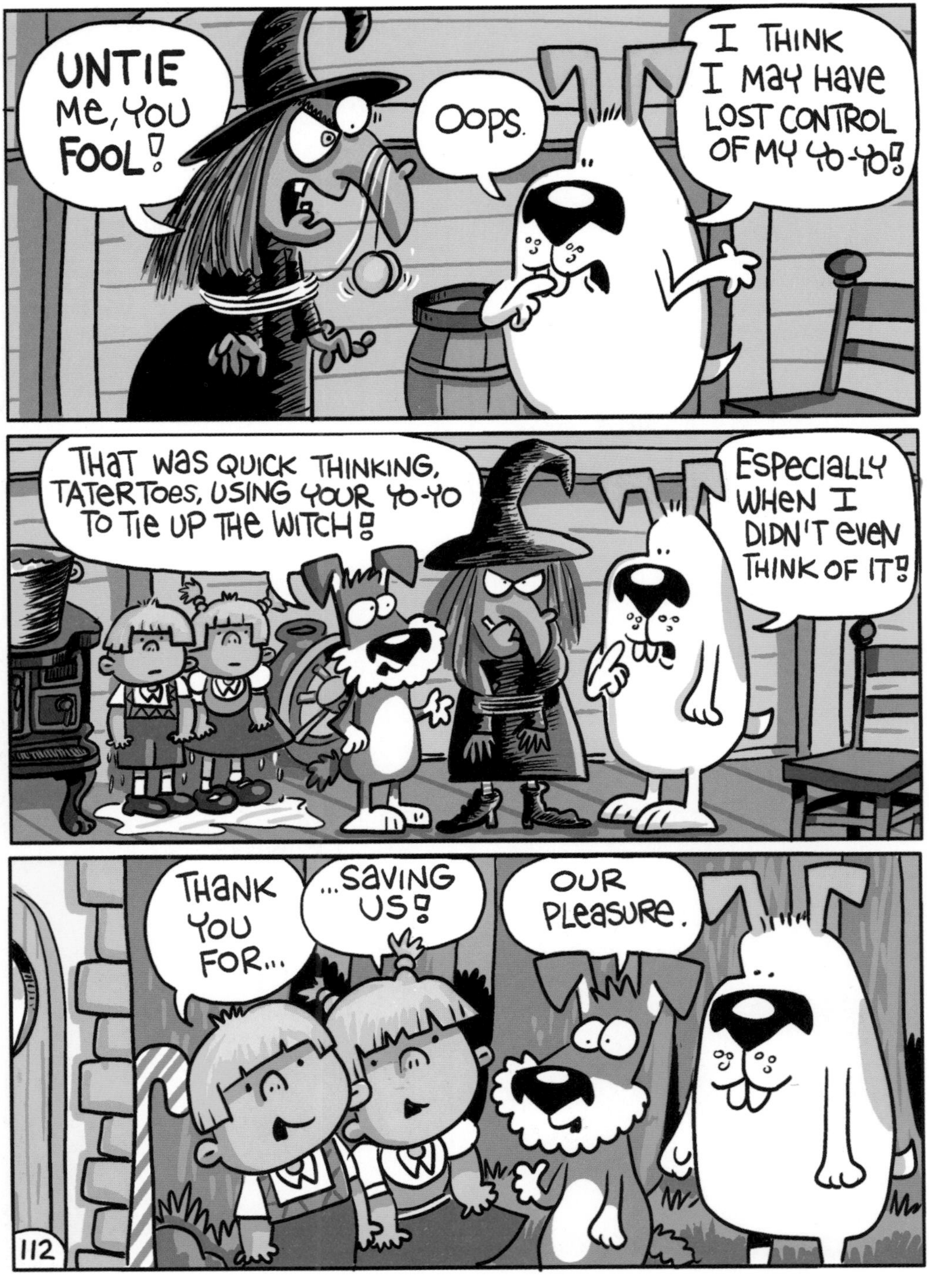
UNTIE Me, YOU FOOL!
OOPS.
I THINK I MAY HAVE LOST CONTROL OF MY YO-YO!
THAT WAS QUICK THINKING, TATERTOES, USING YOUR YO-YO TO TIE UP THE WITCH!
ESPECIALLY WHEN I DIDN'T EVEN THINK OF IT!
THANK YOU FOR...
...SAVING US!
OUR PLEASURE.

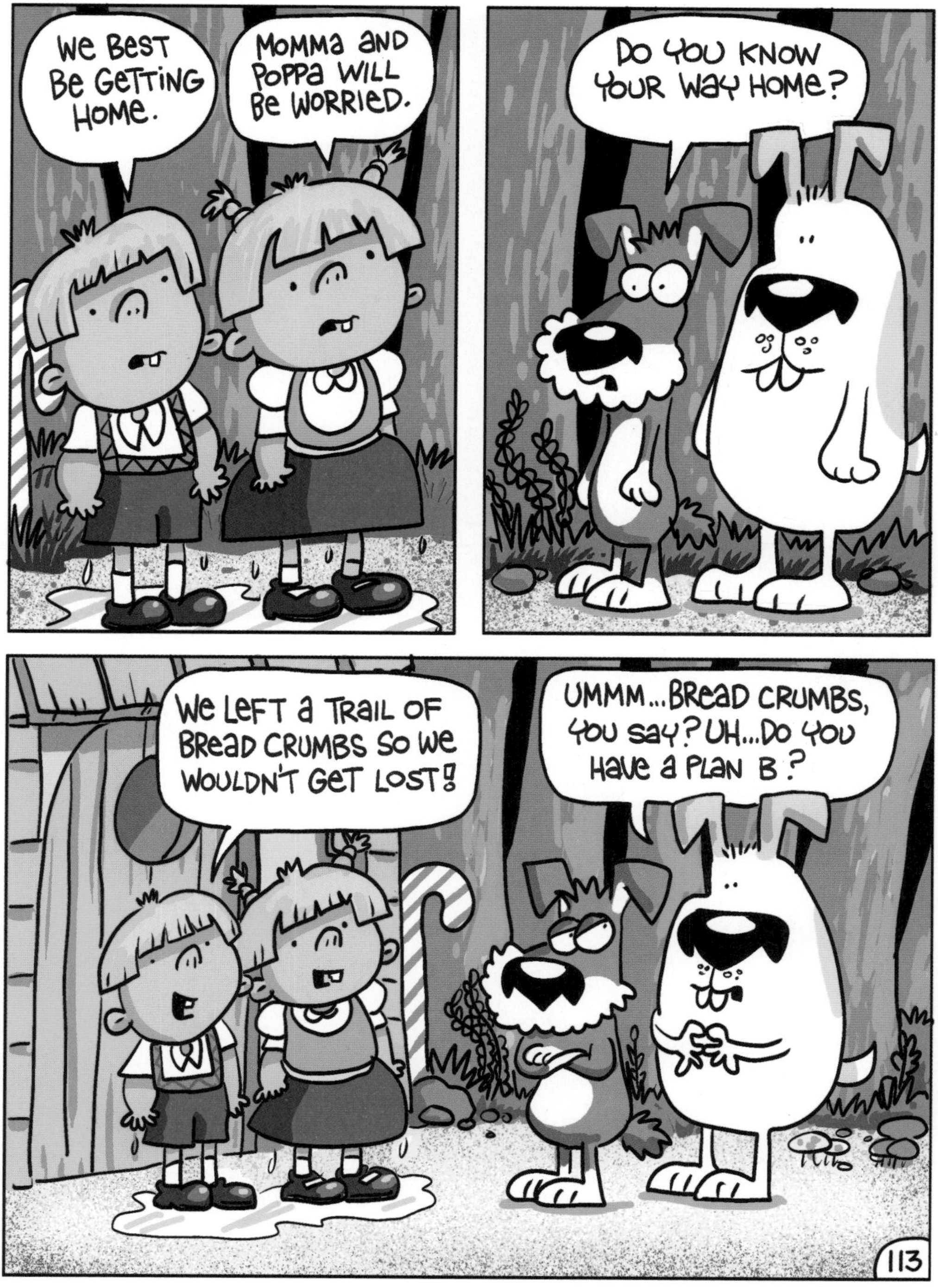
WE BEST BE GETTING HOME.
MOMMA AND POPPA WILL BE WORRIED.
DO YOU KNOW YOUR WAY HOME?
WE LEFT A TRAIL OF BREAD CRUMBS SO WE WOULDN'T GET LOST!
UMMM...BREAD CRUMBS, YOU SAY? UH...DO YOU HAVE A PLAN B?

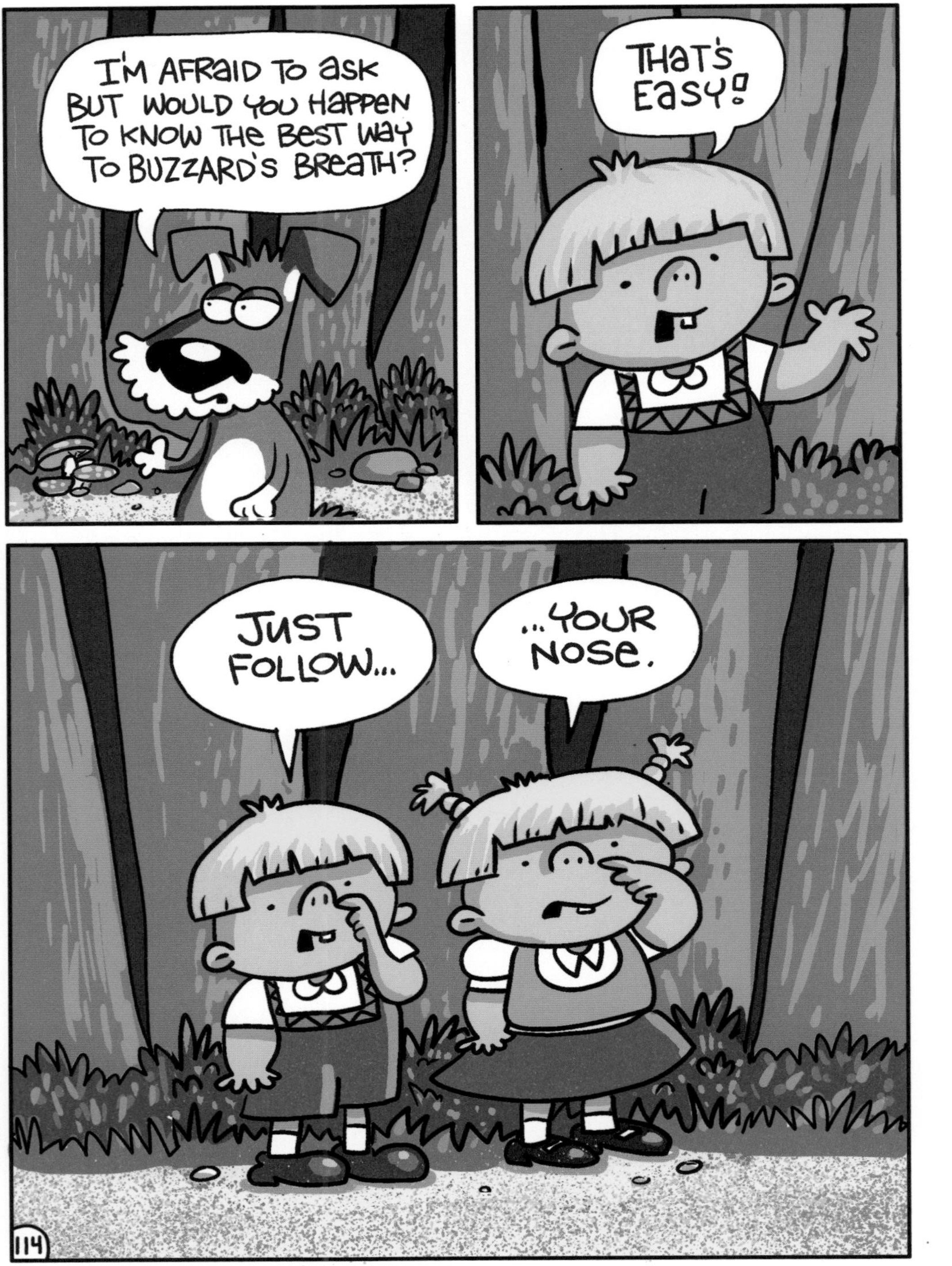
I'M AFRAID TO ASK BUT WOULD YOU HAPPEN TO KNOW THE BEST WAY TO BUZZARD'S BREATH?
THAT'S EASY!
JUST FOLLOW...
...YOUR NOSE.

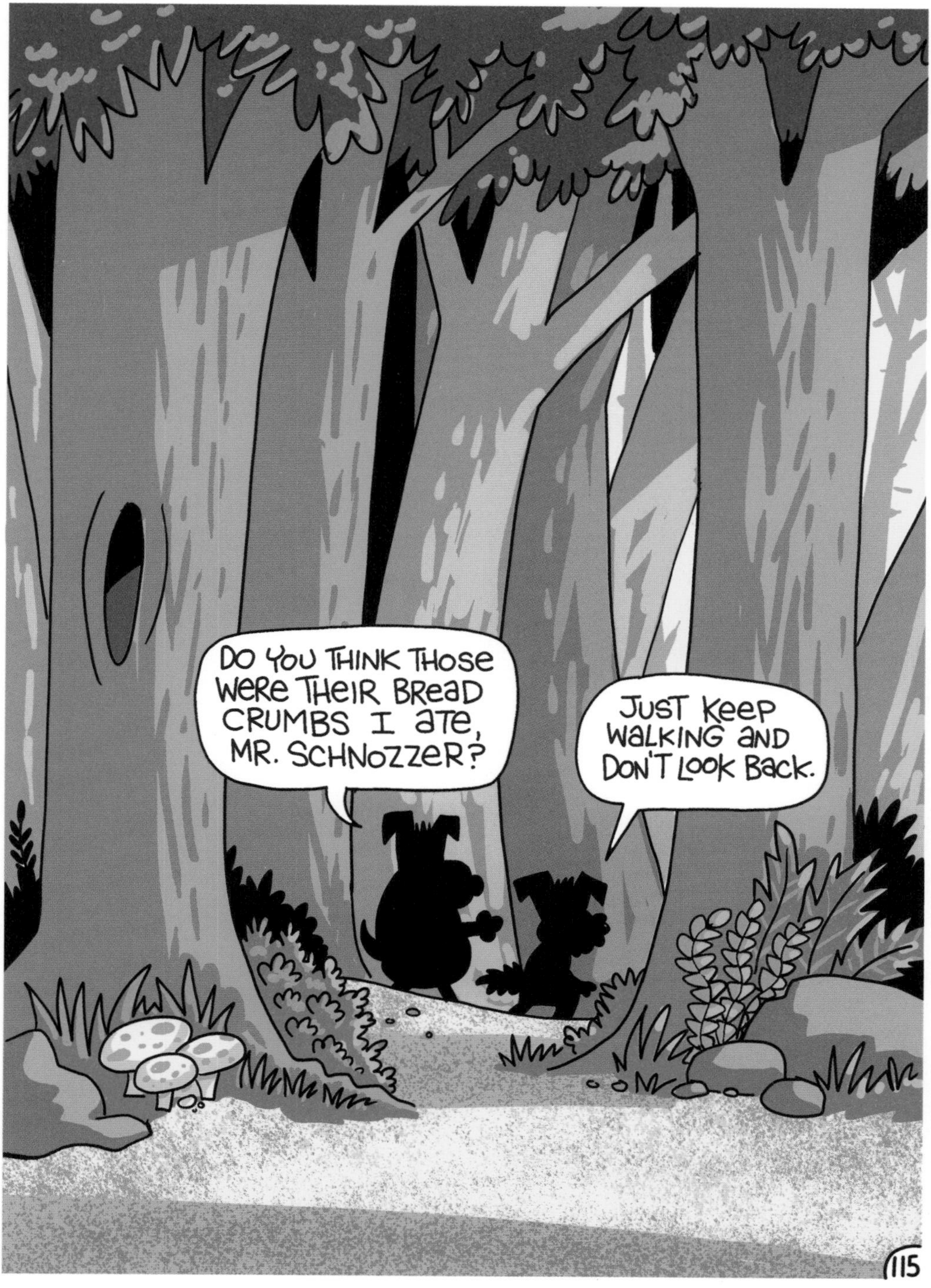
DO YOU THINK THOSE WERE THEIR BREAD CRUMBS I ATE, MR. SCHNOZZER?
JUST KEEP WALKING AND DON'T LOOK BACK.

CHAPTER EIGHT

HOME STINK HOME

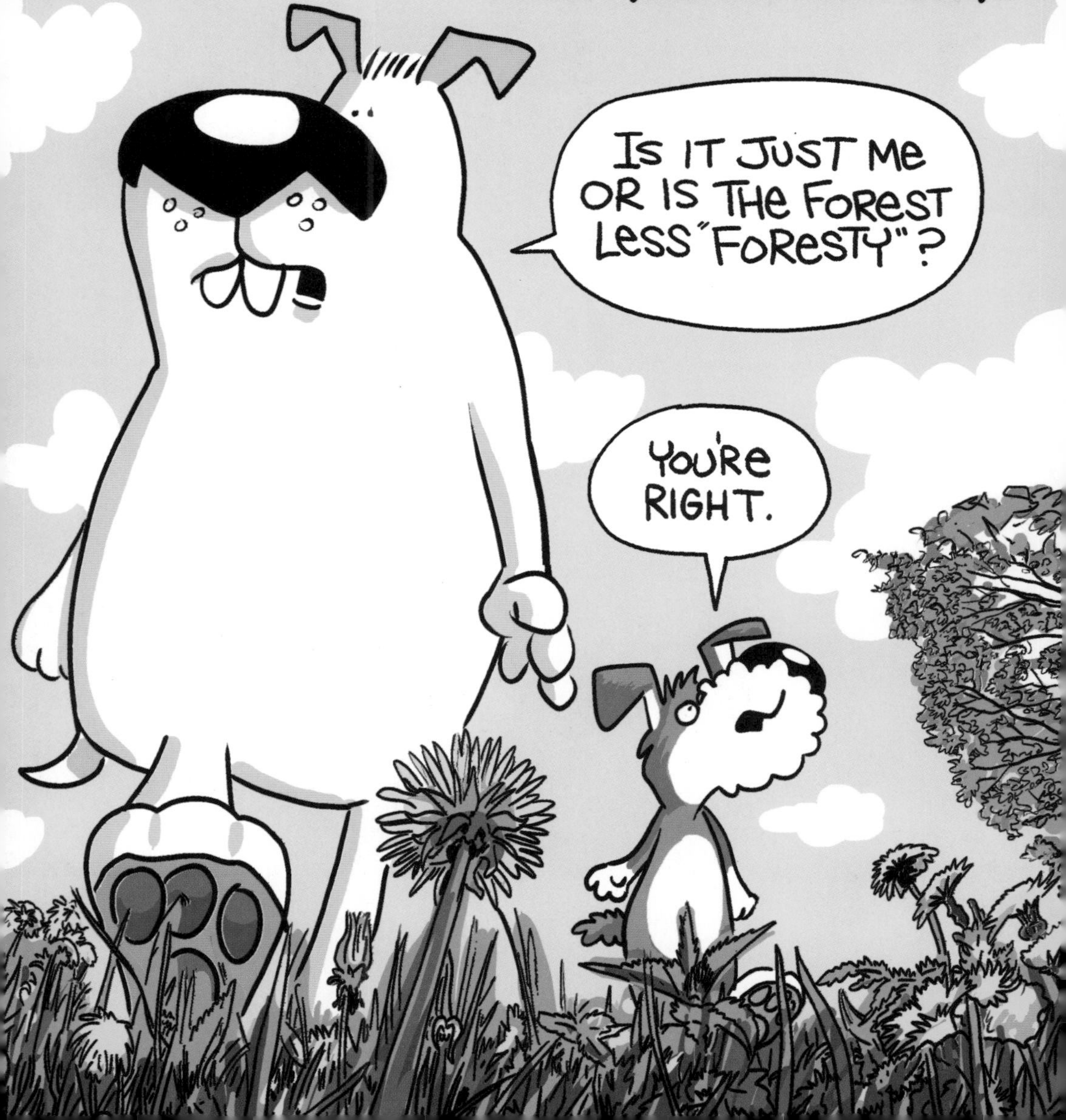
IS IT JUST ME OR IS THE FOREST LESS "FORESTY"?
YOU'RE RIGHT.

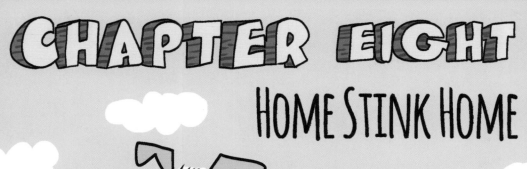

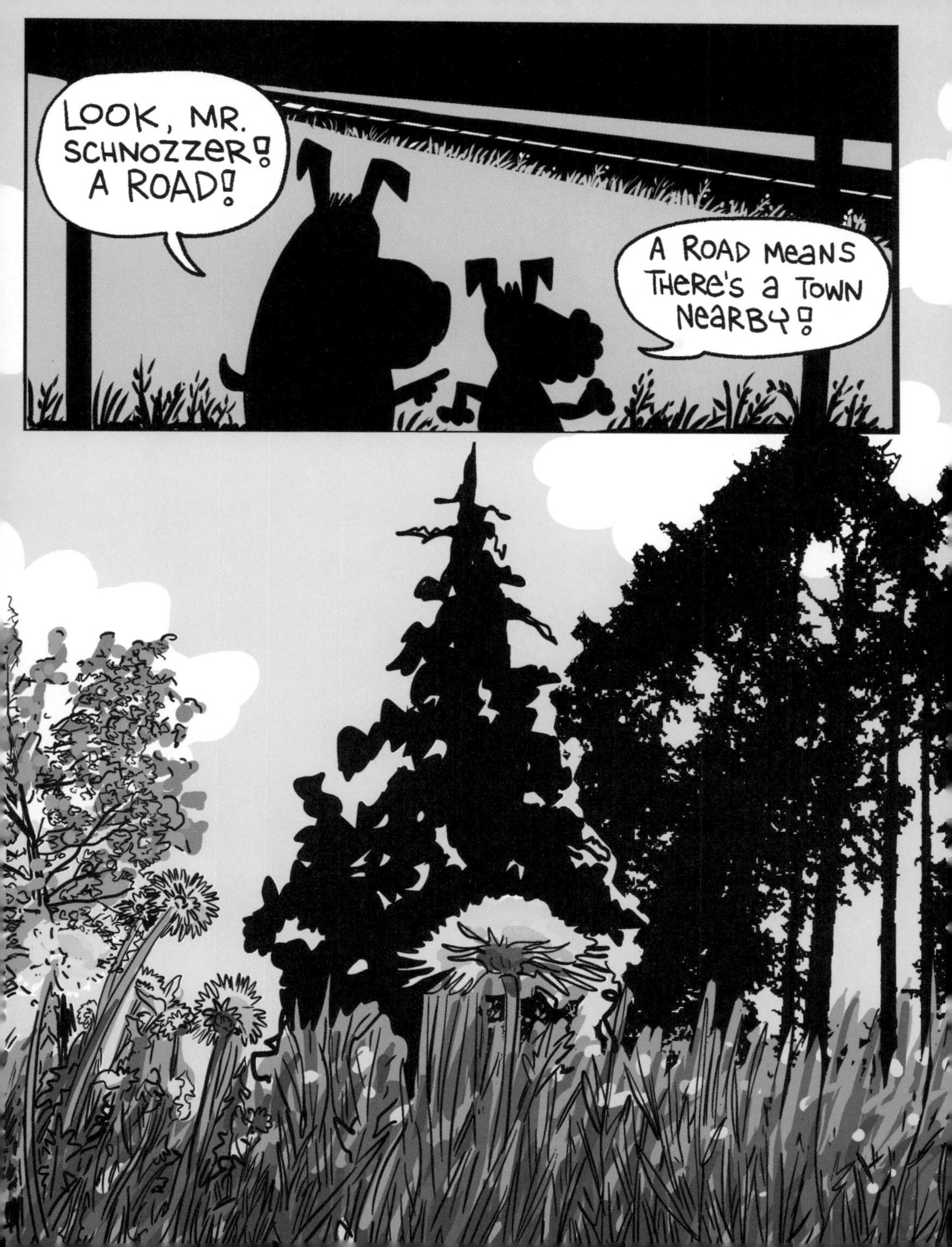
LOOK, MR. SCHNOZZER! A ROAD!
A ROAD MEANS THERE'S A TOWN NEARBY!

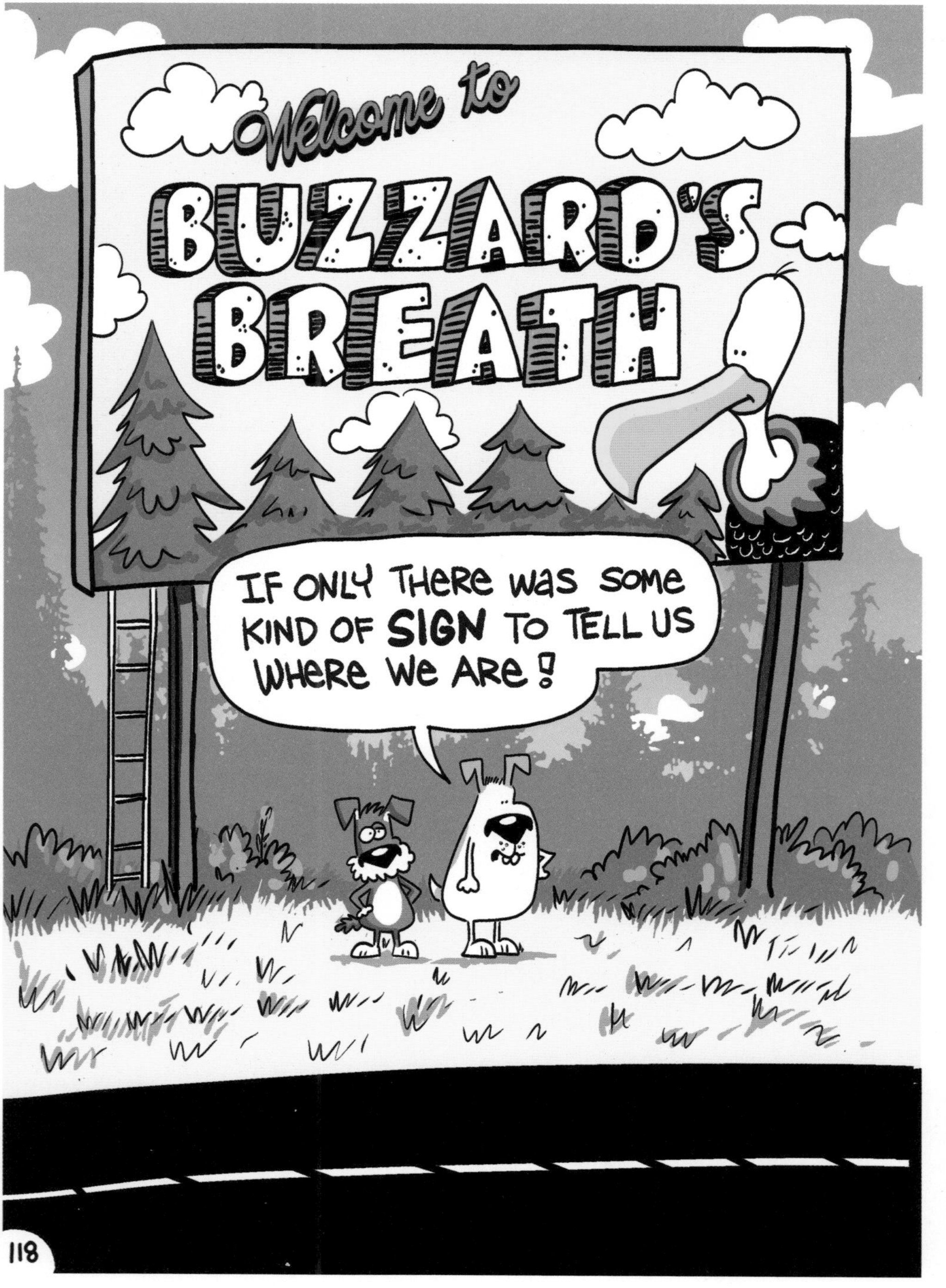
Welcome to
BUZZARD'S BREATH
IF ONLY THERE WAS SOME KIND OF **SIGN** TO TELL US WHERE WE ARE!

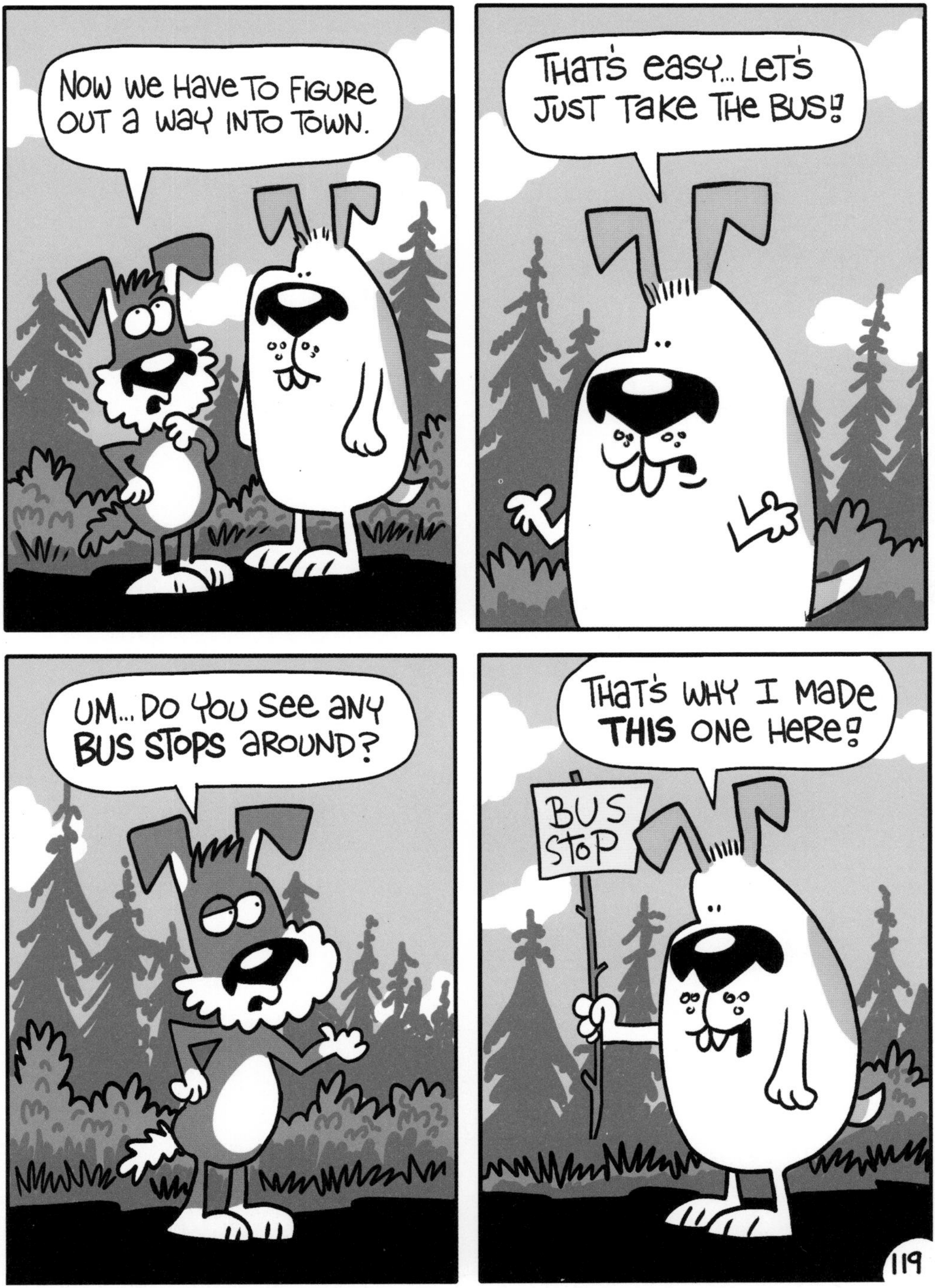
NOW WE HAVE TO FIGURE OUT A WAY INTO TOWN.
THAT'S EASY... LET'S JUST TAKE THE BUS!
UM... DO YOU SEE ANY BUS STOPS AROUND?
THAT'S WHY I MADE THIS ONE HERE!
BUS STOP

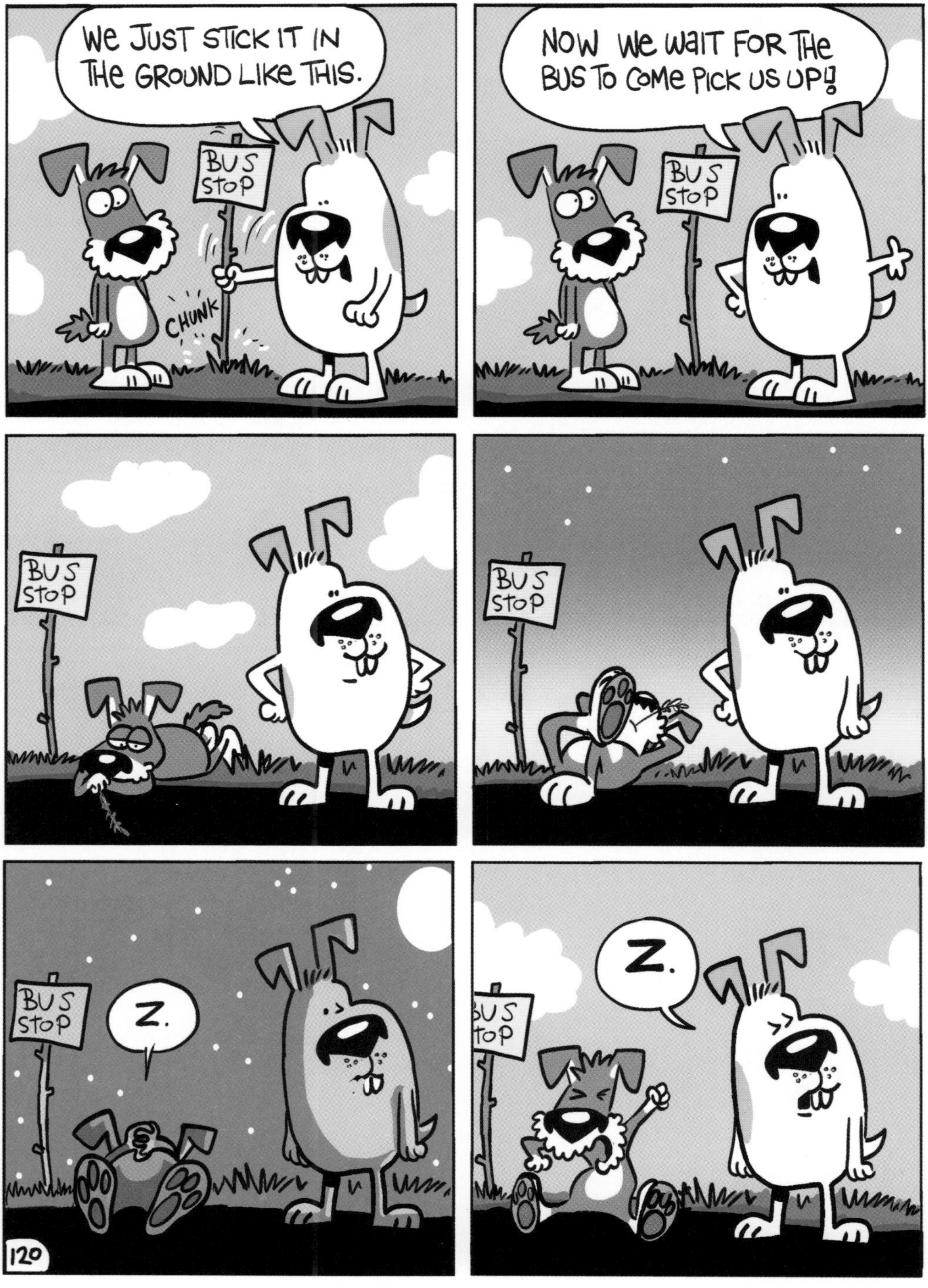
WE JUST STICK IT IN THE GROUND LIKE THIS.
BUS STOP
CHUNK
NOW WE WAIT FOR THE BUS TO COME PICK US UP!!
BUS STOP
BUS STOP
BUS STOP
BUS STOP
Z.
Z.

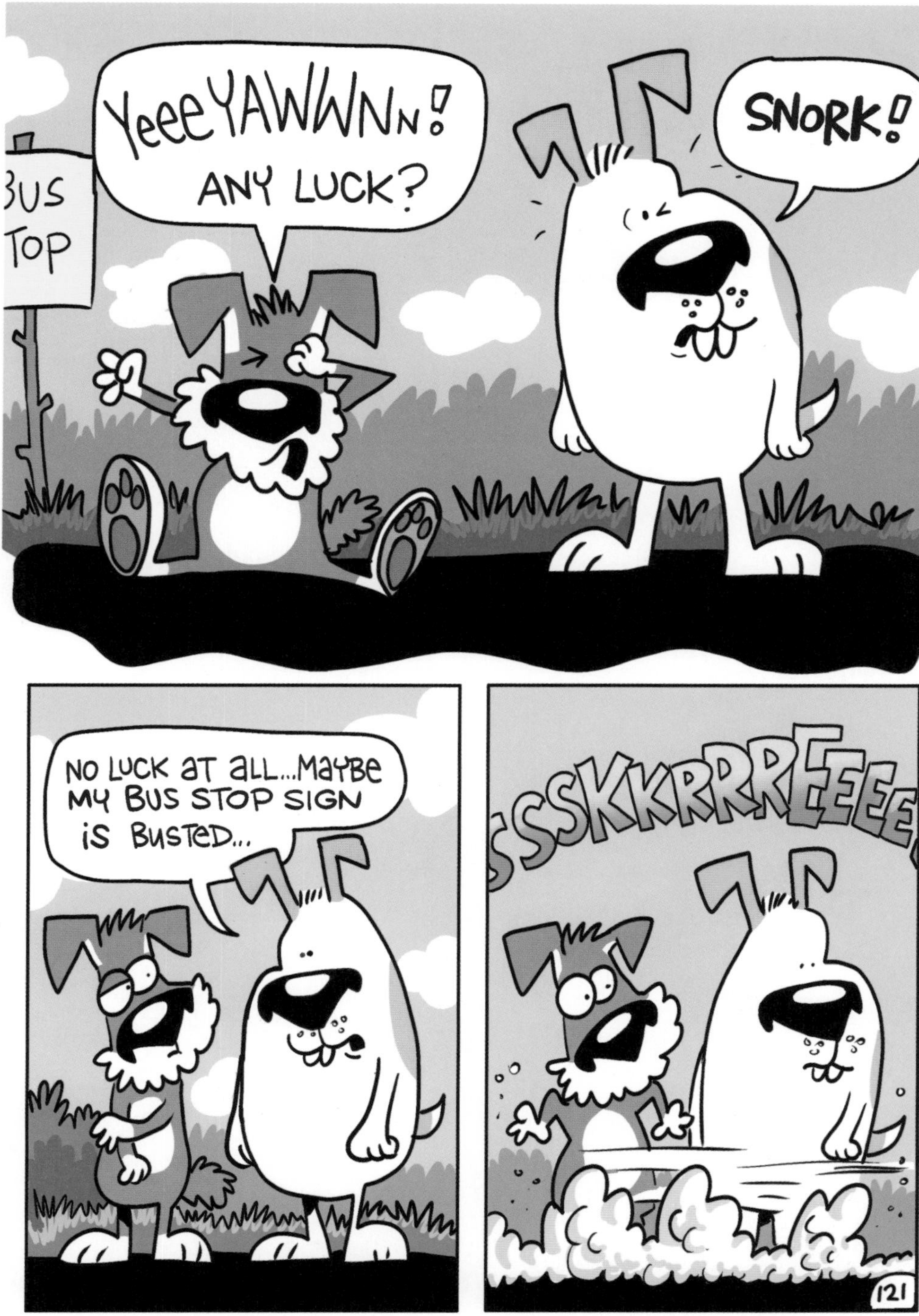
BUS
TOP
YeeeYAWWNn!
ANY LUCK?
SNORK!
NO LUCK aT aLL...MaYBe MY BUS STOP SIGN iS BUSTeD...
SSSKKRRREEEE

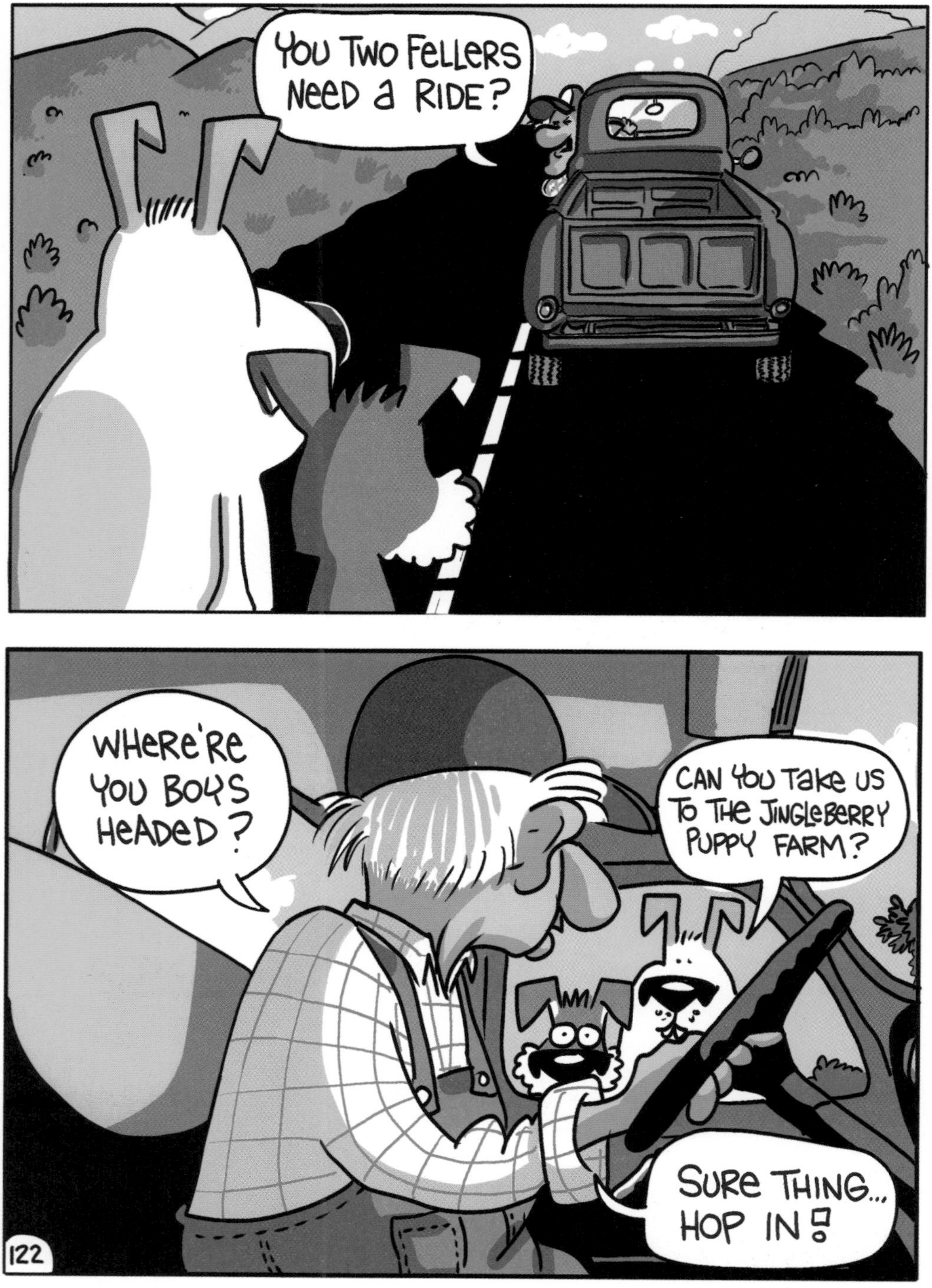
YOU TWO FELLERS NEED A RIDE?
WHERE'RE YOU BOYS HEADED?
CAN YOU TAKE US TO THE JINGLEBERRY PUPPY FARM?
SURE THING... HOP IN!

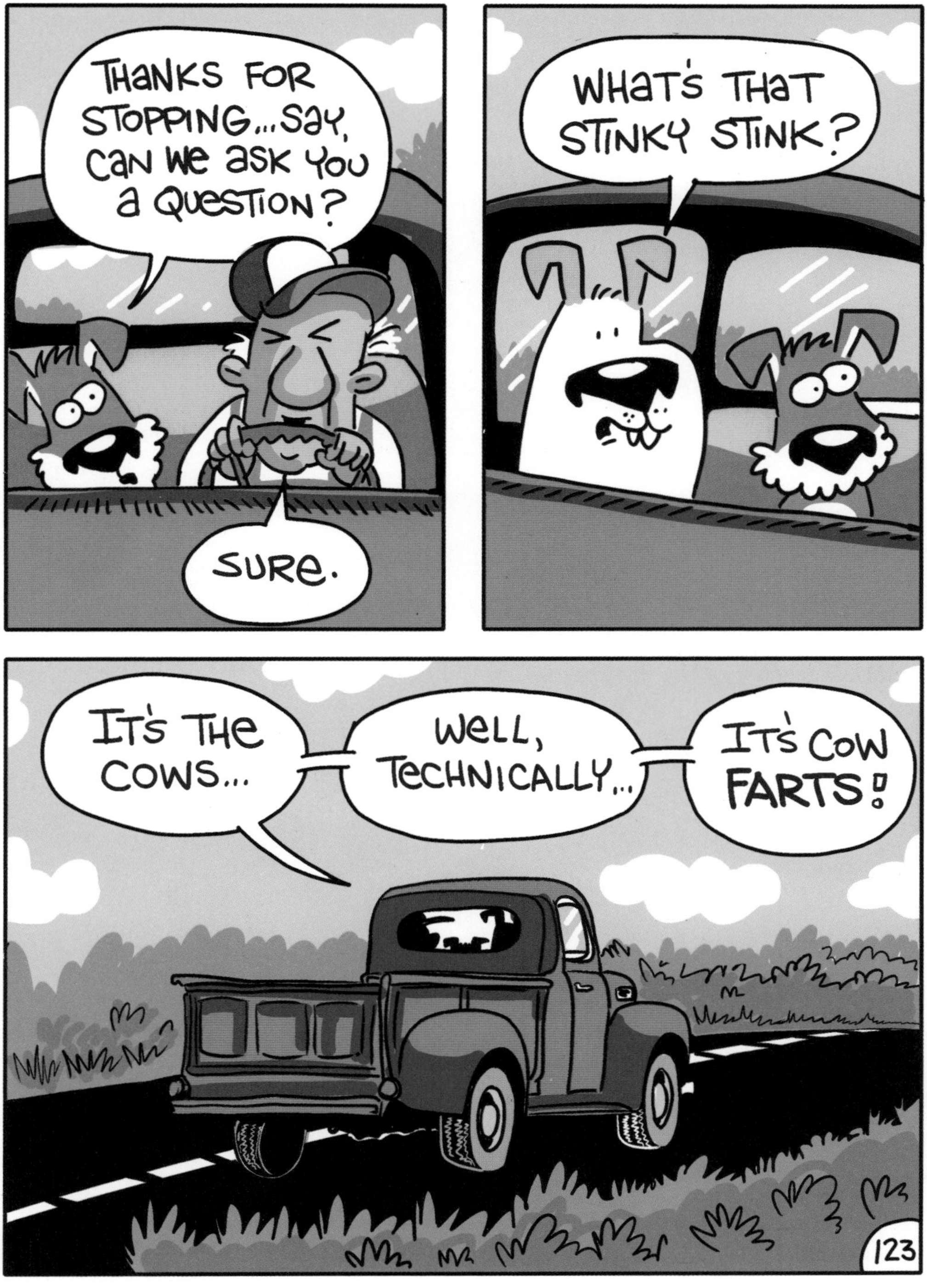
THANKS FOR STOPPING...SAY, CAN WE ASK YOU A QUESTION?
SURE.
WHAT'S THAT STINKY STINK?
IT'S THE COWS...
WELL, TECHNICALLY...
IT'S COW FARTS!

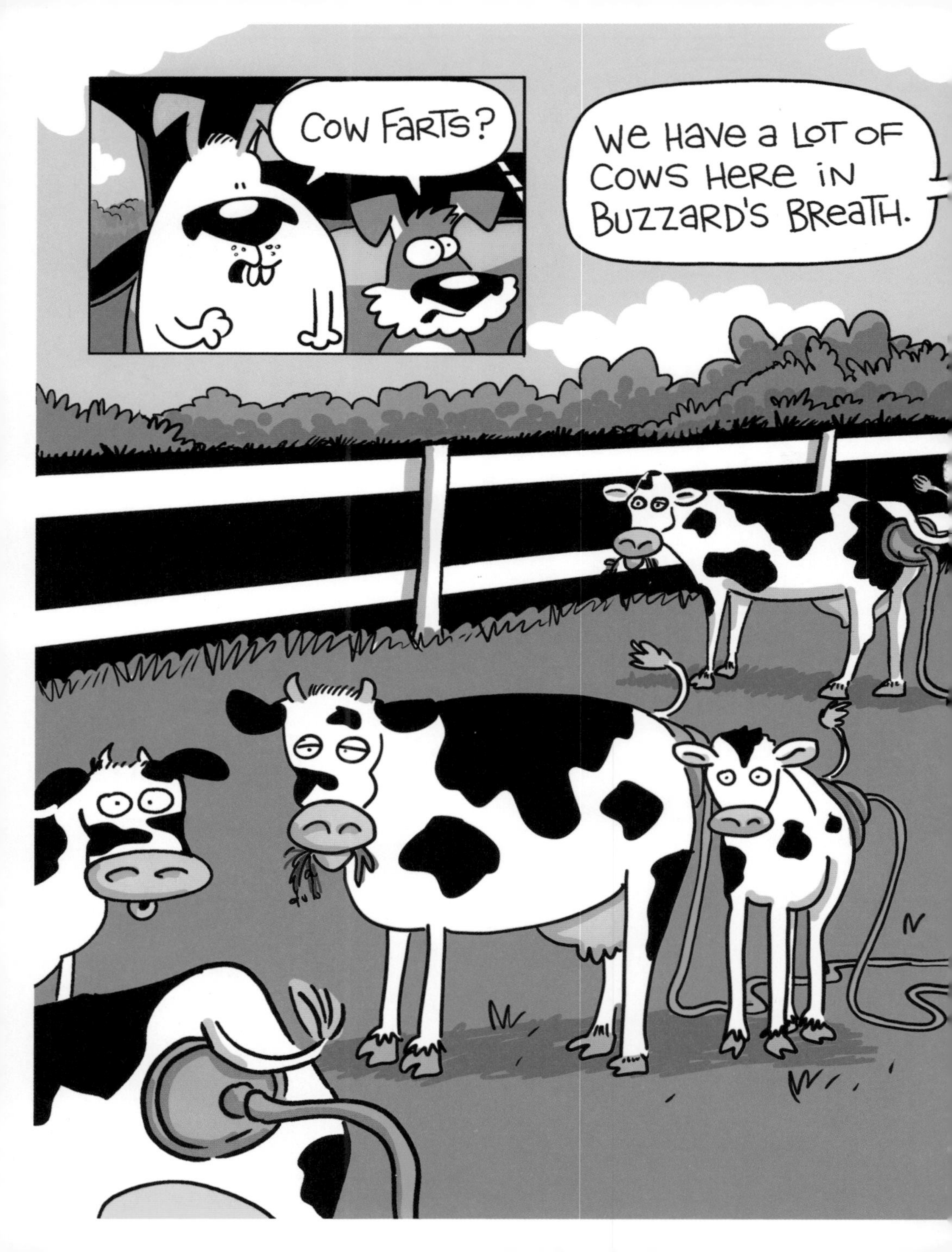
COW FARTS?
WE HAVE A LOT OF COWS HERE IN BUZZARD'S BREATH.

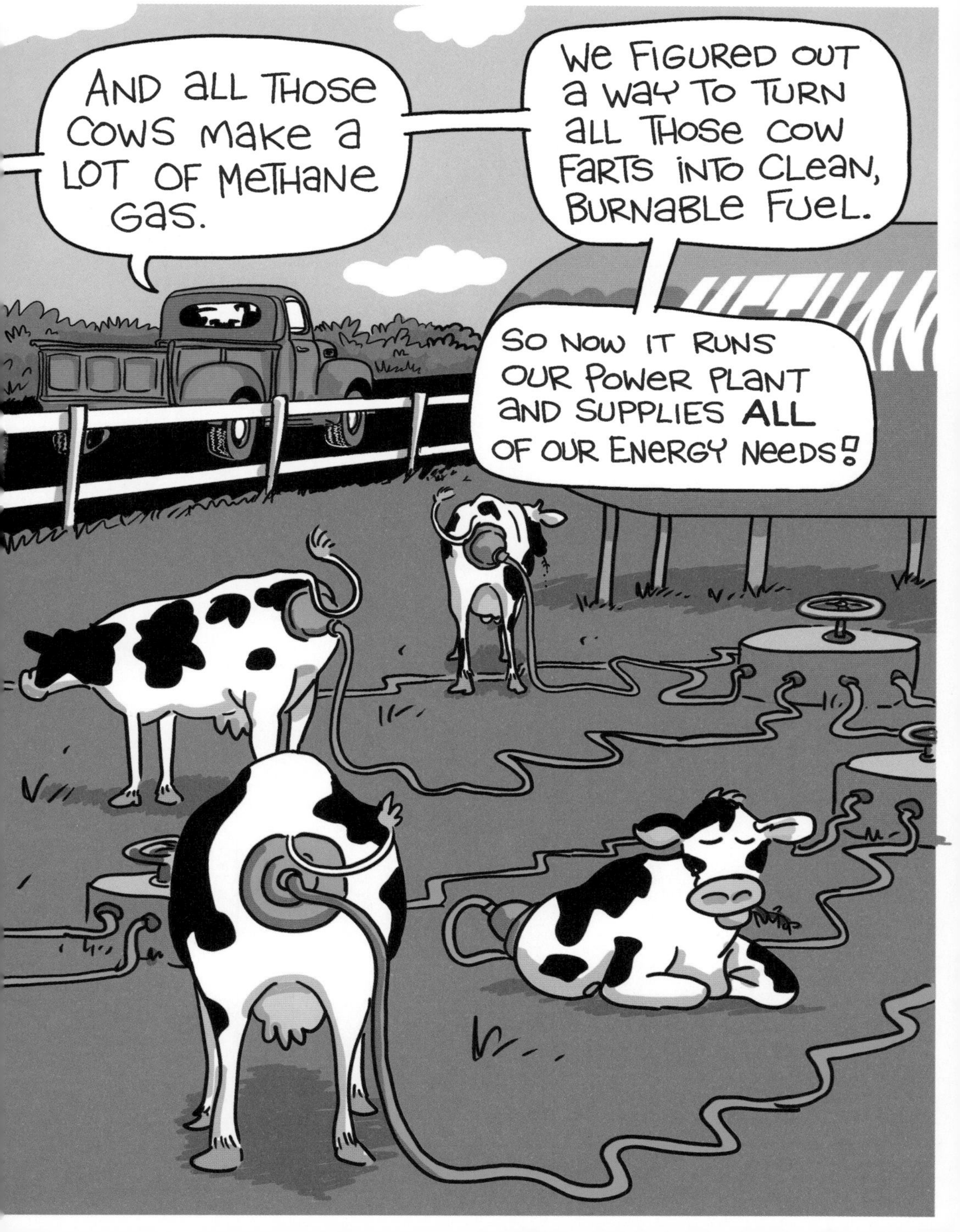
AND ALL THOSE COWS MAKE A LOT OF METHANE GAS.
WE FIGURED OUT A WAY TO TURN ALL THOSE COW FARTS INTO CLEAN, BURNABLE FUEL.
SO NOW IT RUNS OUR POWER PLANT AND SUPPLIES **ALL** OF OUR ENERGY NEEDS!

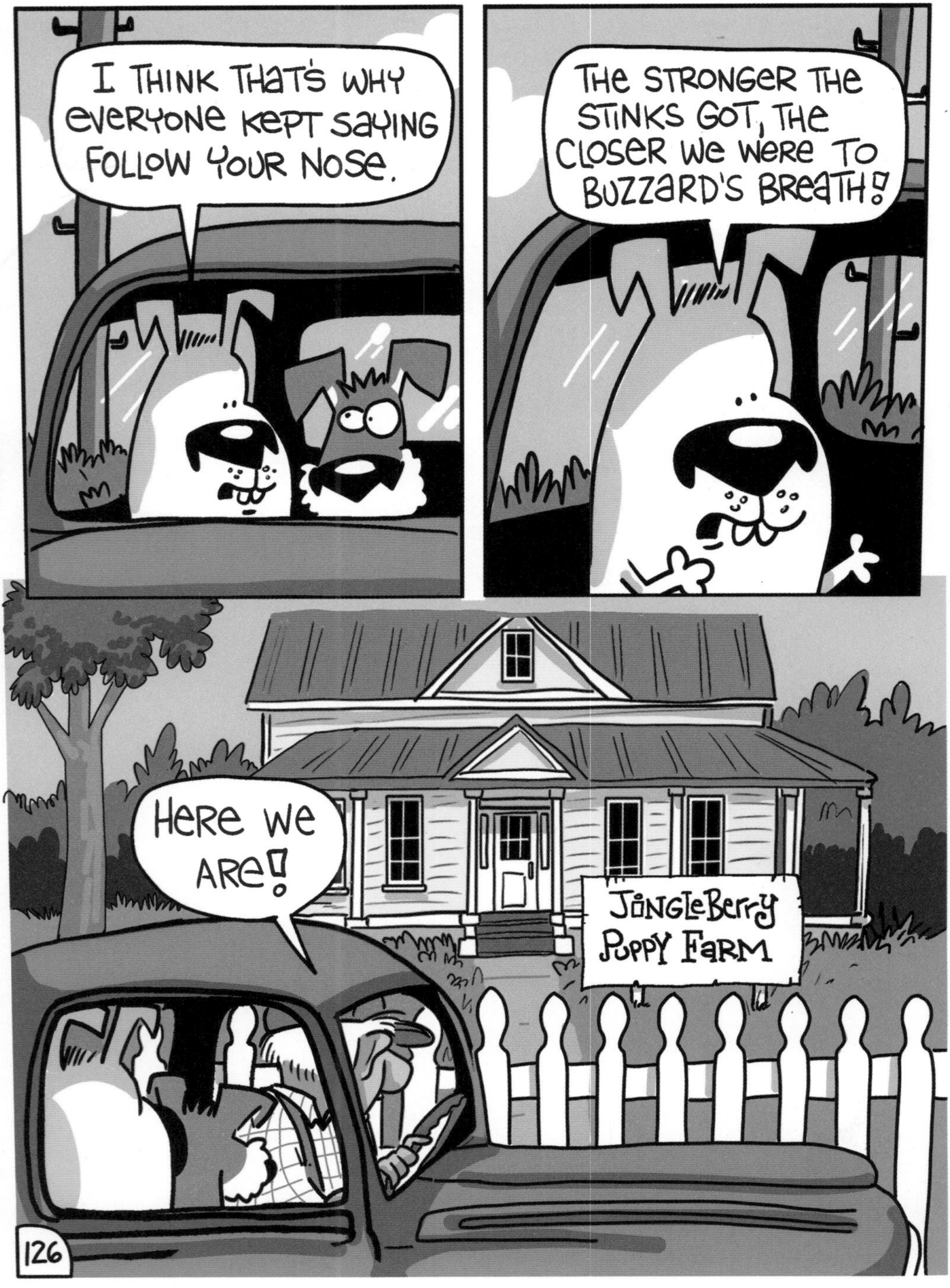
I THINK THAT'S WHY EVERYONE KEPT SAYING FOLLOW YOUR NOSE.
THE STRONGER THE STINKS GOT, THE CLOSER WE WERE TO BUZZARD'S BREATH!
HERE WE ARE!
JINGLEBERRY PUPPY FARM

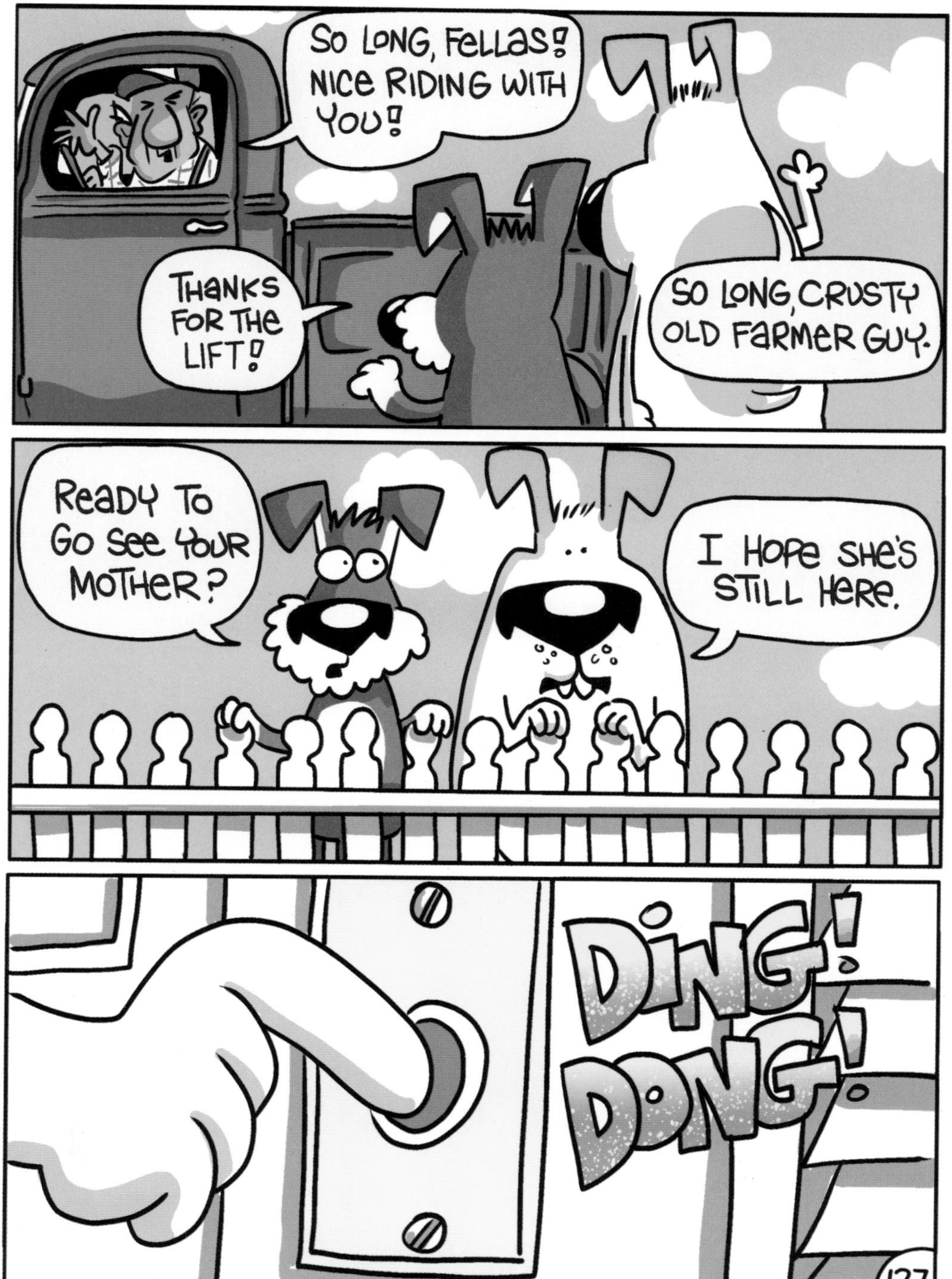

SO LONG, FELLAS! NICE RIDING WITH YOU!
THANKS FOR THE LIFT!
SO LONG, CRUSTY OLD FARMER GUY.
READY TO GO SEE YOUR MOTHER?
I HOPE SHE'S STILL HERE.
DING! DONG!

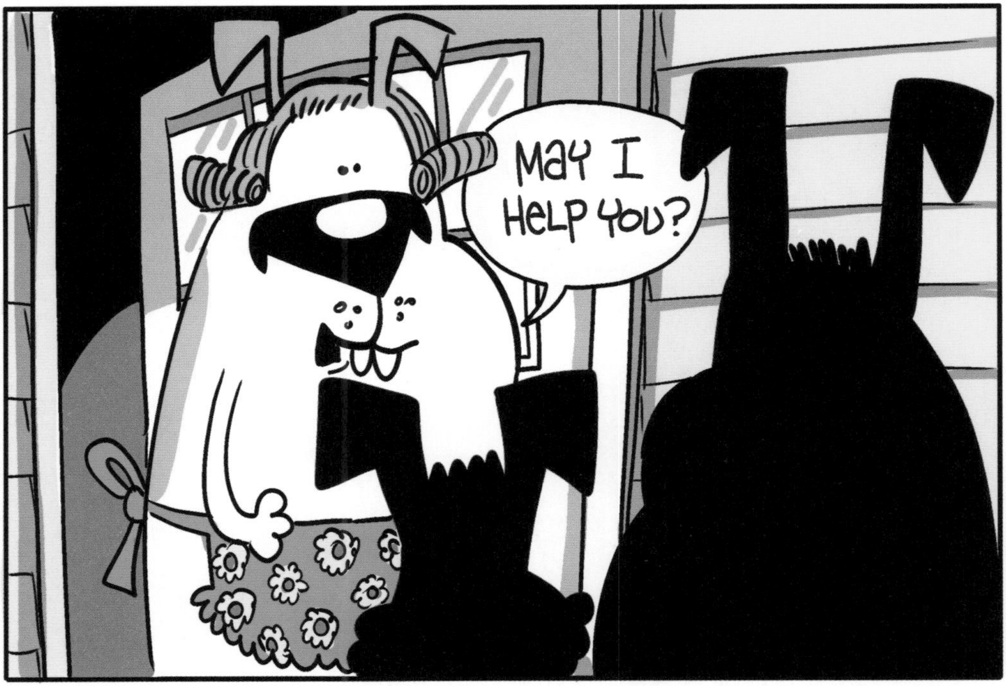
MAY I HELP YOU?

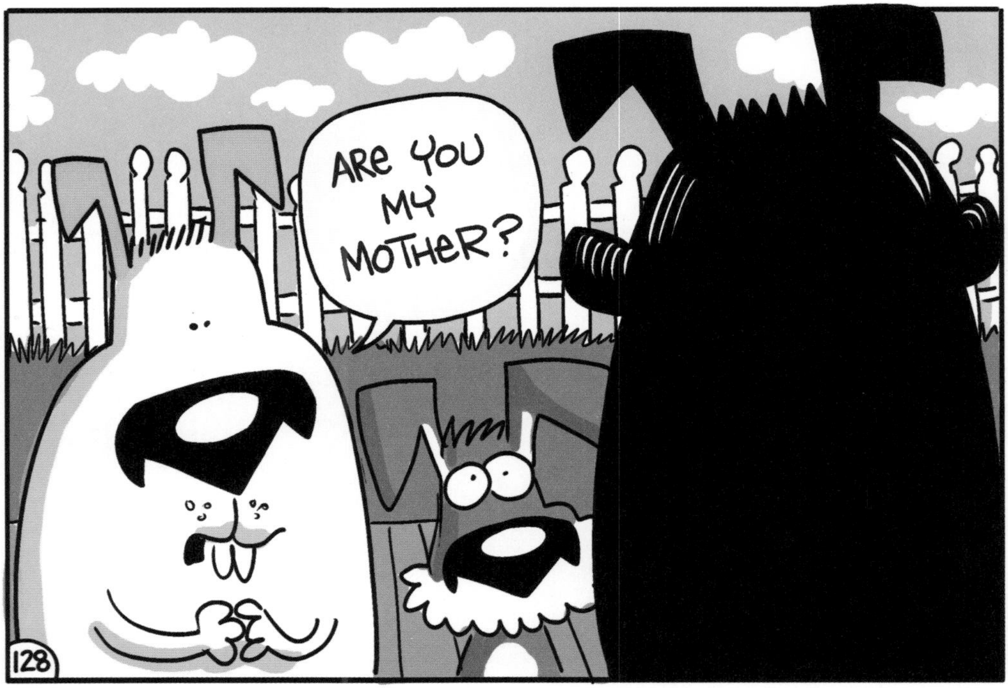
ARE YOU MY MOTHER?

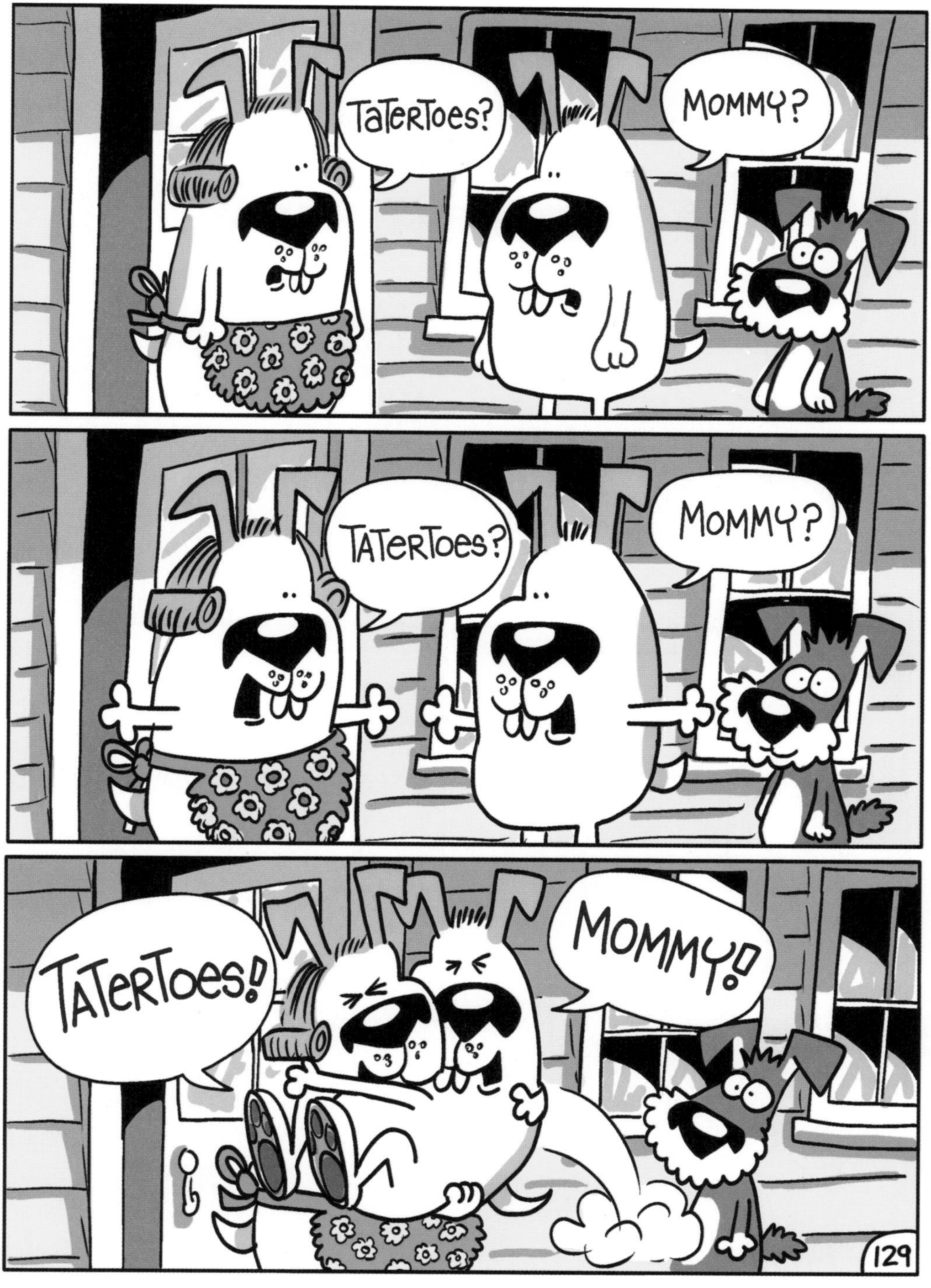
TaTerToes?
MOMMY?
TATerToes?
MOMMY?
TATerToes!
MOMMY!

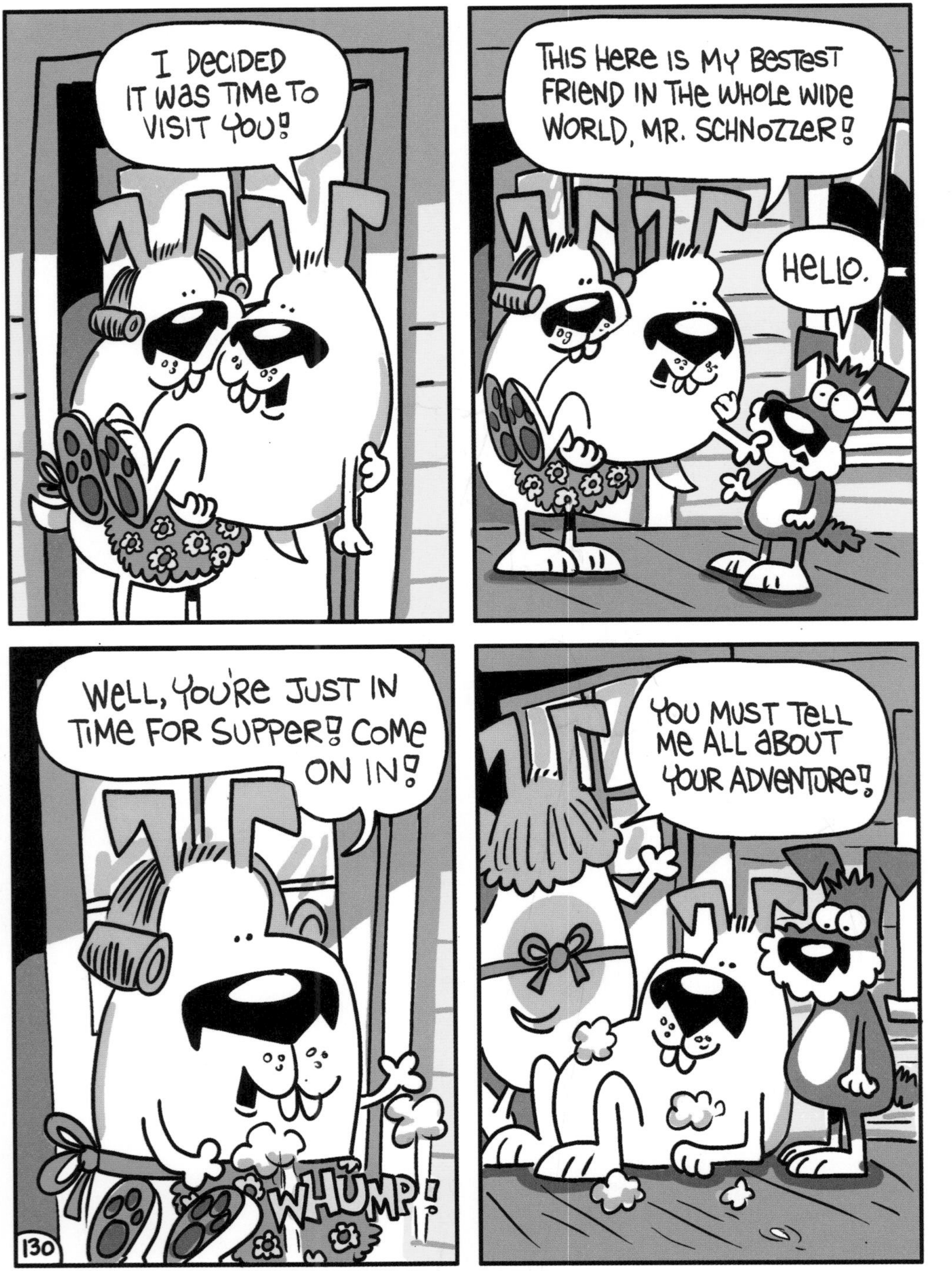
I DECIDED IT WAS TIME TO VISIT YOU!
THIS HERE IS MY BESTEST FRIEND IN THE WHOLE WIDE WORLD, MR. SCHNOZZER!
HELLO.
WELL, YOU'RE JUST IN TIME FOR SUPPER! COME ON IN!
WHUMP!
YOU MUST TELL ME ALL ABOUT YOUR ADVENTURE!

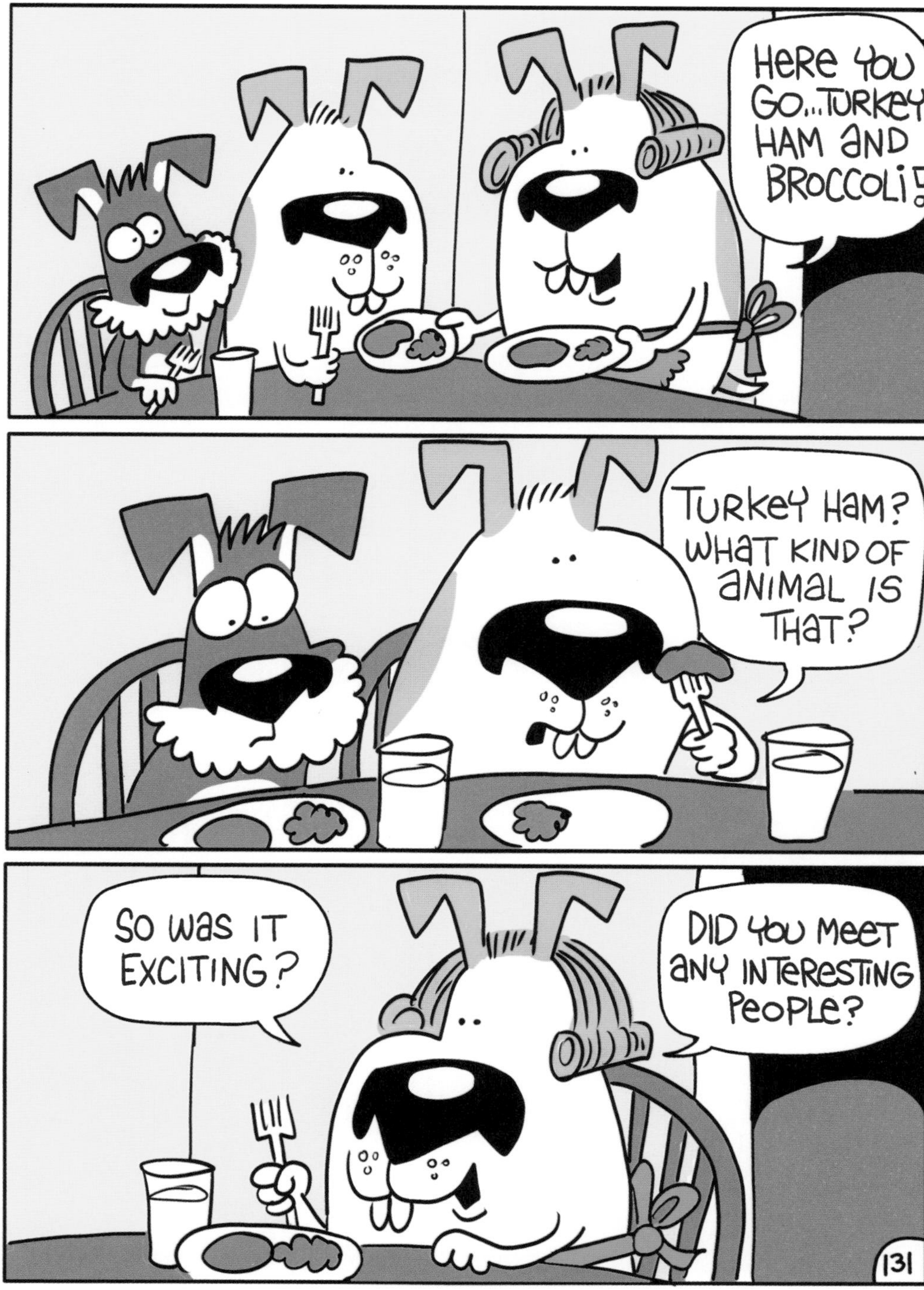
HERE YOU GO...TURKEY HAM AND BROCCOLI!
TURKEY HAM? WHAT KIND OF ANIMAL IS THAT?
SO WAS IT EXCITING?
DID YOU MEET ANY INTERESTING PEOPLE?

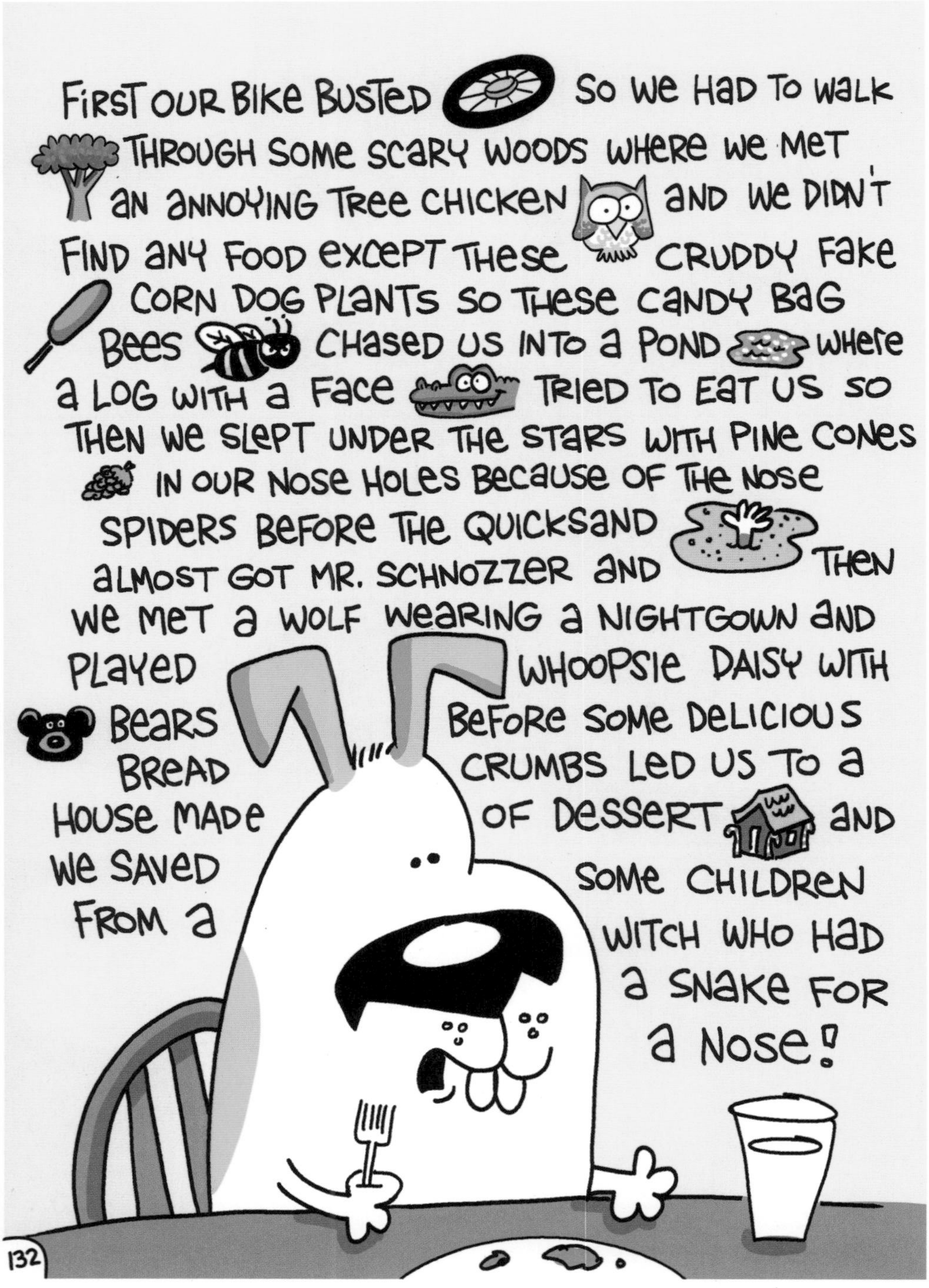
FIRST OUR BIKE BUSTED SO WE HAD TO WALK THROUGH SOME SCARY WOODS WHERE WE MET AN ANNOYING TREE CHICKEN AND WE DIDN'T FIND ANY FOOD EXCEPT THESE CRUDDY FAKE CORN DOG PLANTS SO THESE CANDY BAG BEES CHASED US INTO A POND WHERE A LOG WITH A FACE TRIED TO EAT US SO THEN WE SLEPT UNDER THE STARS WITH PINE CONES IN OUR NOSE HOLES BECAUSE OF THE NOSE SPIDERS BEFORE THE QUICKSAND ALMOST GOT MR. SCHNOZZER AND THEN WE MET A WOLF WEARING A NIGHTGOWN AND PLAYED WHOOPSIE DAISY WITH BEARS BEFORE SOME DELICIOUS BREAD CRUMBS LED US TO A HOUSE MADE OF DESSERT AND WE SAVED SOME CHILDREN FROM A WITCH WHO HAD A SNAKE FOR A NOSE!

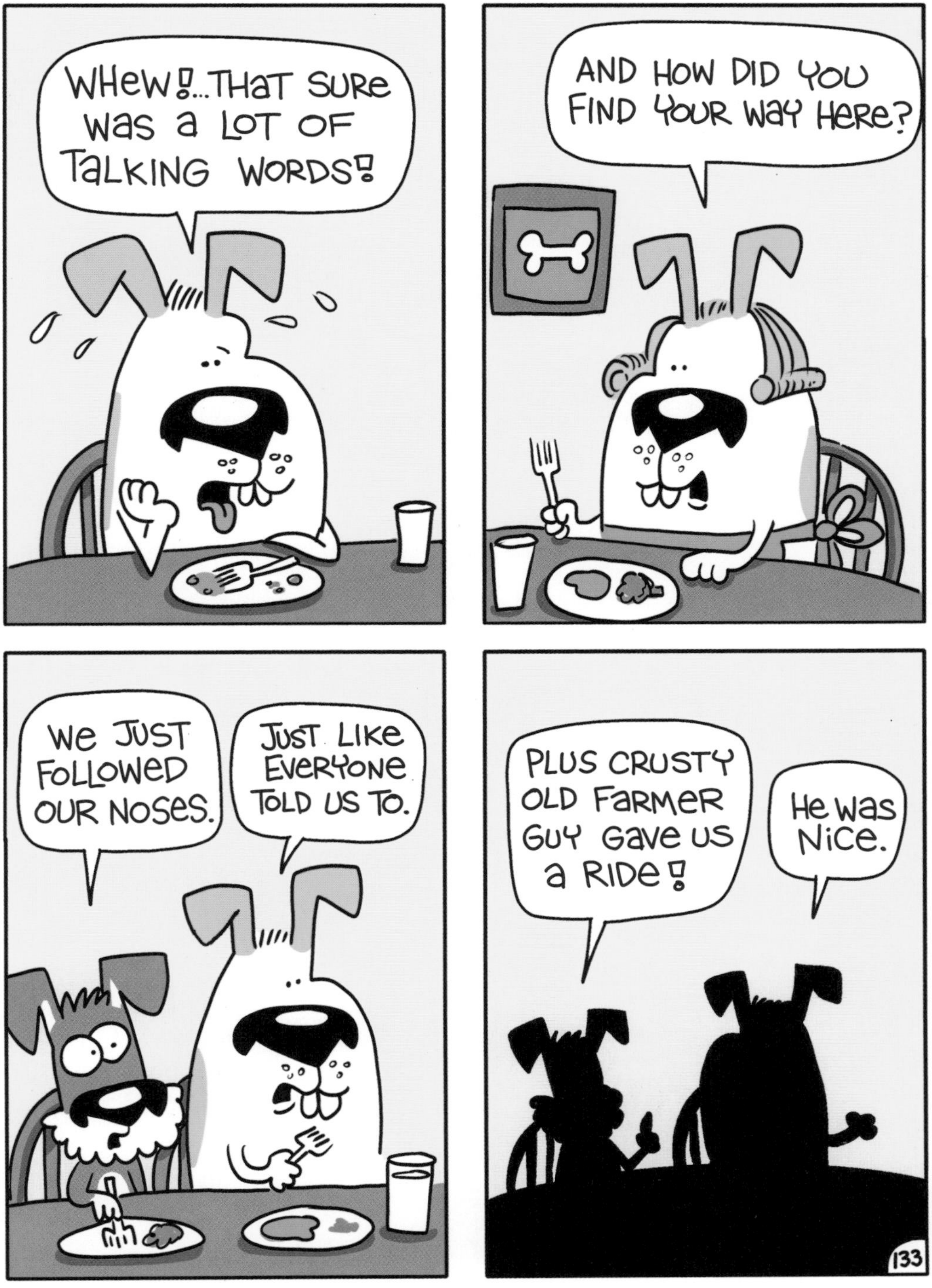
WHEW!...THAT SURE WAS A LOT OF TALKING WORDS!
AND HOW DID YOU FIND YOUR WAY HERE?
WE JUST FOLLOWED OUR NOSES.
JUST LIKE EVERYONE TOLD US TO.
PLUS CRUSTY OLD FARMER GUY GAVE US A RIDE!
HE WAS NICE.
133

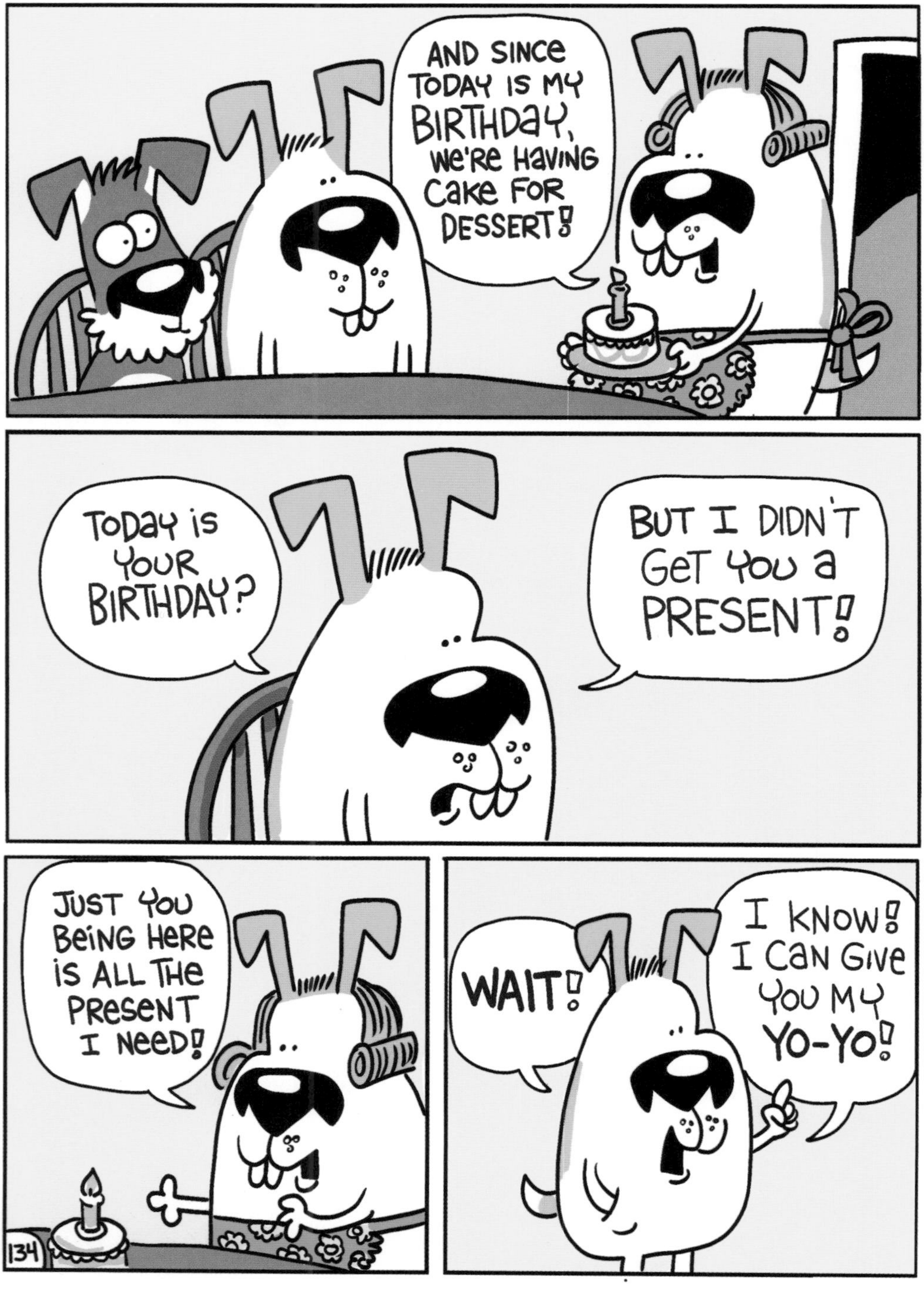
AND SINCE TODAY IS MY BIRTHDAY, WE'RE HAVING CAKE FOR DESSERT!
TODAY IS YOUR BIRTHDAY?
BUT I DIDN'T GET YOU A PRESENT!
JUST YOU BEING HERE IS ALL THE PRESENT I NEED!
WAIT!
I KNOW! I CAN GIVE YOU MY YO-YO!

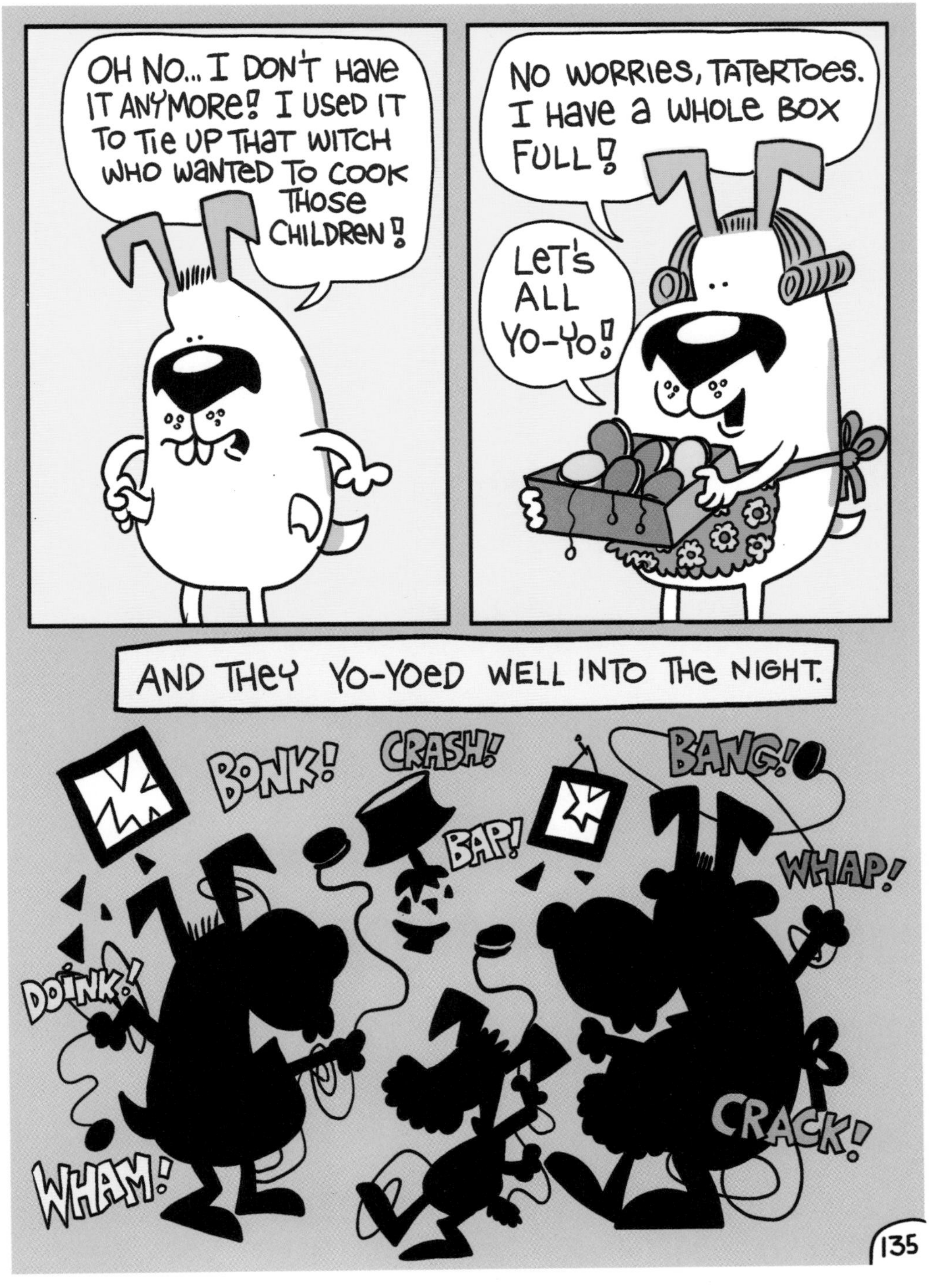
OH NO... I DON'T HAVE IT ANYMORE! I USED IT TO TIE UP THAT WITCH WHO WANTED TO COOK THOSE CHILDREN!
NO WORRIES, TATERTOES. I HAVE A WHOLE BOX FULL!
LET'S ALL YO-YO!
AND THEY YO-YOED WELL INTO THE NIGHT.
BONK!
CRASH!
BANG!
BAP!
WHAP!
DOINK!
CRACK!
WHAM!

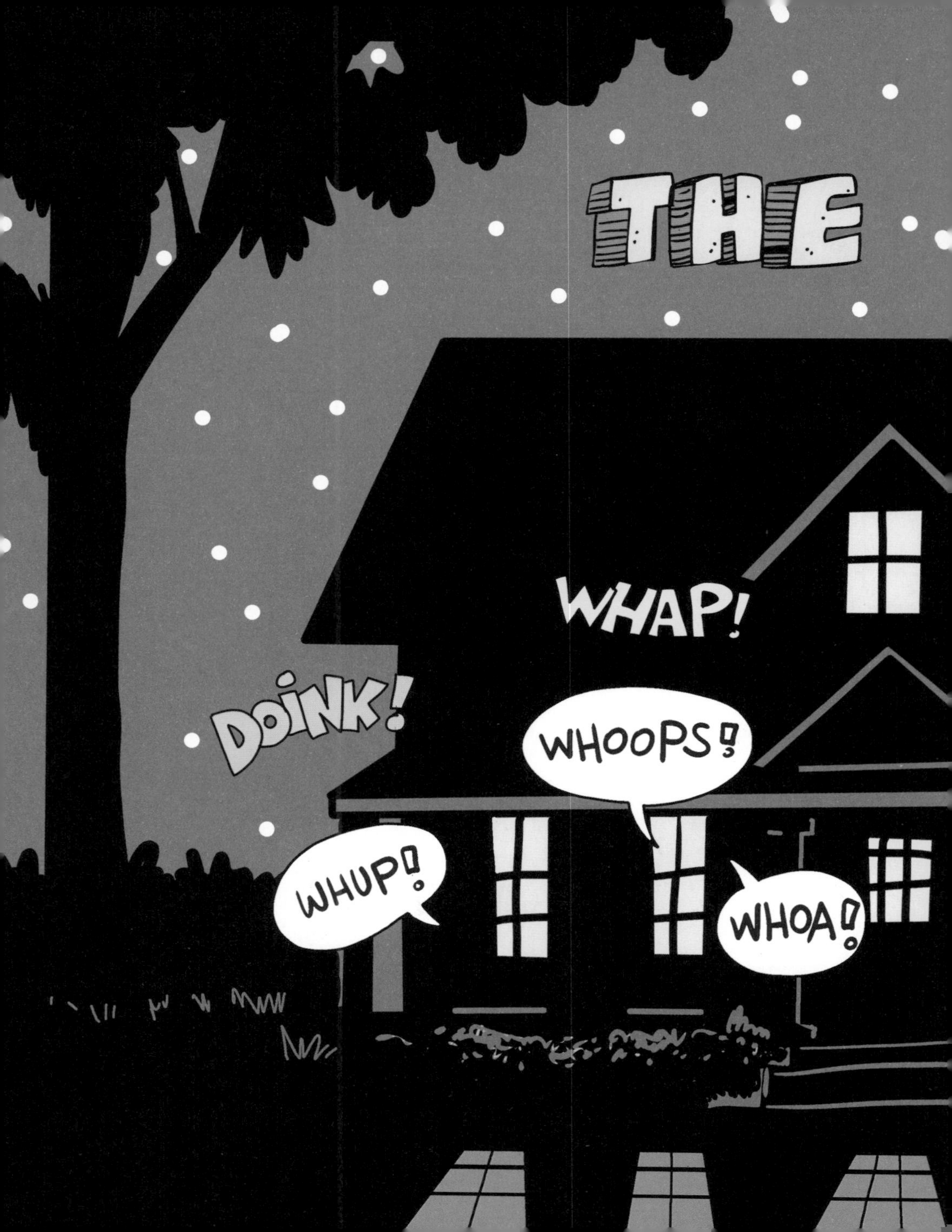
THE
WHAP!
DOINK!
WHOOPS!
WHUP!
WHOA!

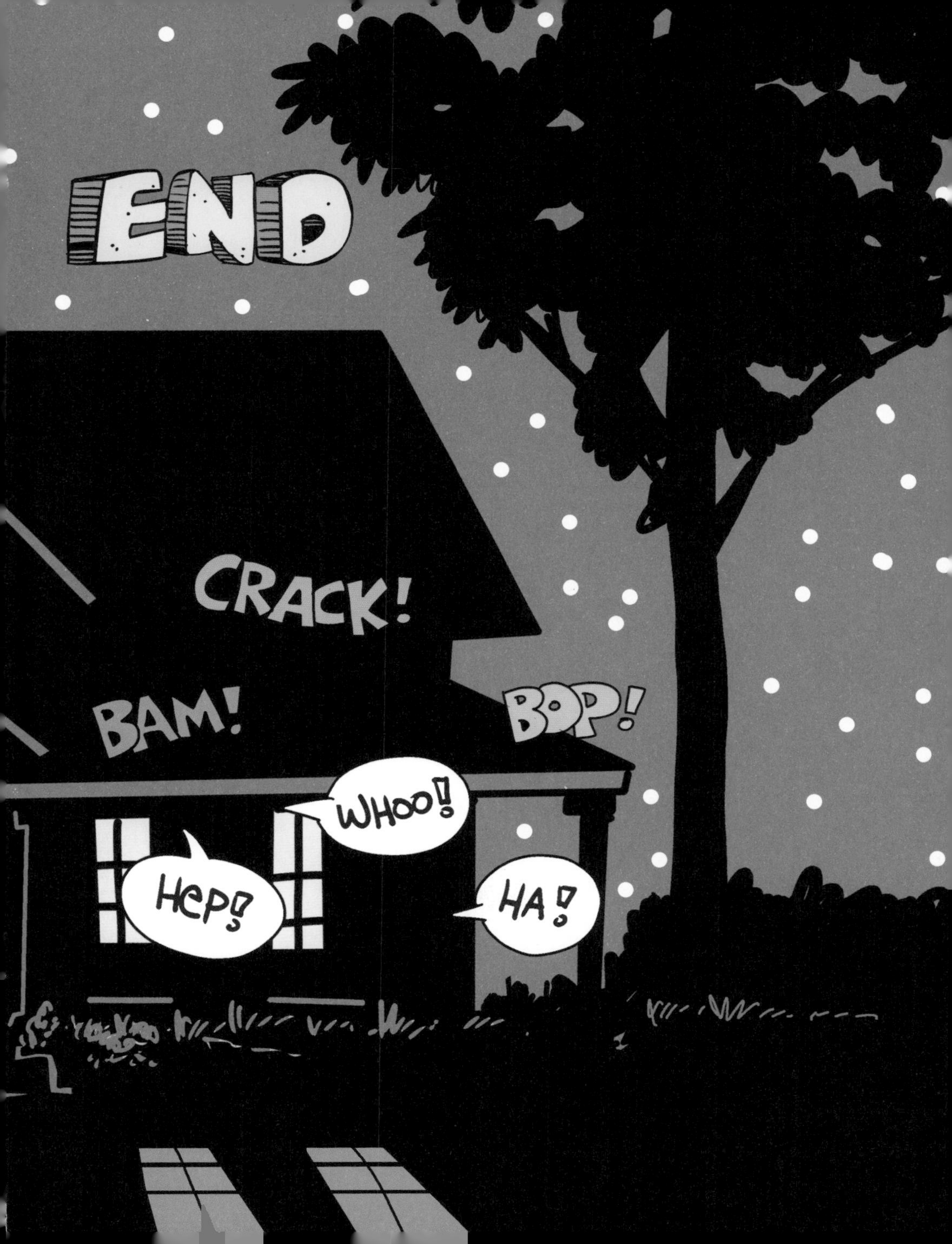
END
CRACK!
BAM!
BOP!
WHOO!
HEP!
HA!

About the Author

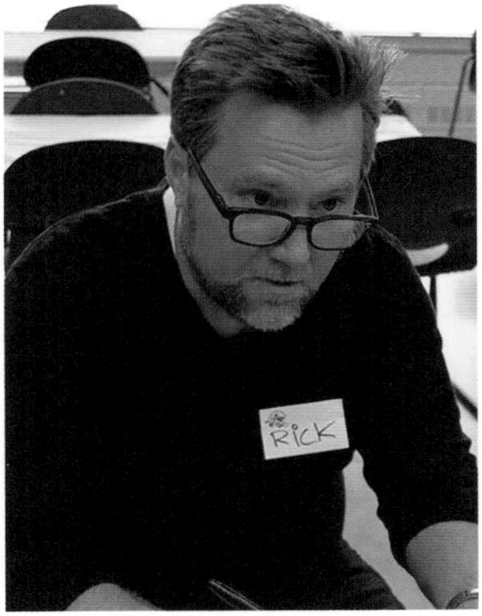

RICK

Photo by Terri Libenson

The seventh in a family of twelve musically and artistically inclined children, Rick Stromoski's illustrations and cartoons have appeared in national magazines, advertising, books, children's publications, licensing, newspaper syndication, and network television. His comic strip *Soup to Nutz* ran from 2000 to 2018, appearing in 150 newspapers. Rick has won a bunch of awards and is a member of the Society of Illustrators, the National Cartoonists Society, and his local Costco. *Schnozzer & Tatertoes: Take a Hike!* is his first graphic novel.

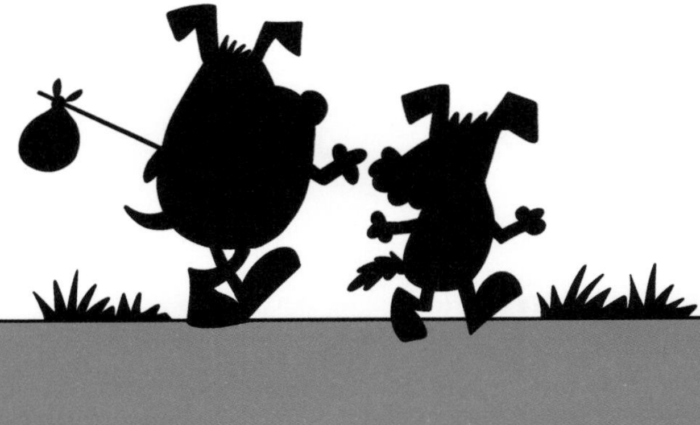

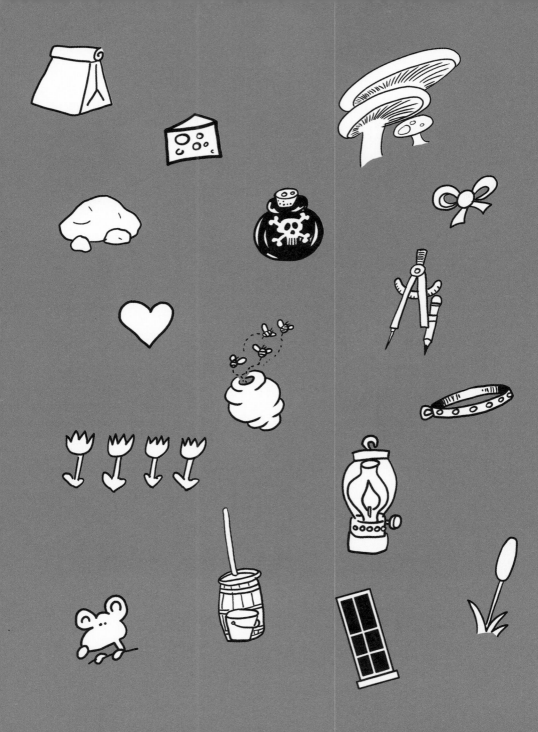